CHECKOUT TIME

JOHN BUKOWSKI

PB
PathBinder
Publishing LLC
COLUMBUS,
INDIANA

Published by PathBinder Publishing LLC
P.O. Box 2611
Columbus, IN 47202
www.PathBinderPublishing.com

Edited by Doug Showalter
Covers designed by Anna Perlich
Cover photo by iStock

First published in 2023
Manufactured in the United States

ISBN: 978-1-955088-60-2
Library of Congress Control Number: 2023900815

To Rhippy, Moxie, and Alfie, three furry children that filled my heart before leaving a huge hole in it. Enjoy the bridge until Mom and Dad get there, guys. Then, what larks we'll have!

Testimonials

Praise for *Checkout Time*

"A well-written, fast-paced thriller!"
— John McManus, author of *Bitter Milk*, and *Fox Tooth Heart Stories*.

"A gripping story with explosive action, high-stakes hookups, and a ticking time bomb of suspense."
— Douglas Boatman, author of the *Ted Danger* mysteries.

Praise for *Project Suicide*

"John Bukowski's debut thriller, *Project Suicide*, keeps you on the edge of your seat. I can't wait to read his next book."
— Larry D. Sweazy, multiple award-winning author of *The Broken Bow*.

"*Project Suicide* is a roller coaster ride filled with unforeseen twists, dips, and dives right up to its stunning climax."
— Matthew Clemens, co-author of the *Reeder and Rogers* thrillers.

Introduction

Checkout Time is a work of fiction made up of fictional characters. Any resemblance to persons living or dead is purely coincidental. Some of the locations are real places, although they may have been fictionalized for purposes of the story. Likewise, liberties have been taken with some of the technical material to enhance the narrative.

— John Bukowski

Chapter 1

Thomas Tomacinski had experienced a bumpy flight before but never in a hotel room. Nor had a roar like a freight train ever awakened him from a dream about silky red hair draped over a trim, athletic frame.

Before his eyes opened, his ears popped, as if the room suddenly lost cabin pressure. Then, turbulence that would make Chuck Yeager lose his lunch launched the king-sized bed a foot to the right. The air filled with debris, bits of plaster and insulation snowing down from a foot-wide rent in the ceiling. Then he smelled an acrid mix of electrical wiring and building materials that had surpassed the activation energy needed to turn them into fuel.

The roof over his head cracked amid a shower of sparks. Tom hit the worn carpet, eyes stinging and lungs hacking, as a section of burning ceiling took his place on the bed.

The air was cleaner near the floor, but the dust still made it difficult to see. Fighting claustrophobia, Tom forced himself to think about the floor plan. The door should be to the left ... somewhere. He winced as his outstretched finger bent back against a chair leg. Keep moving, he thought, shouldering past the chair, knees and palms scraping against the worn carpet. Another piece of ceiling fell behind him, showering his bare legs with hot needles. It was as if fire was racing him to the door. He prayed he'd win.

Tom scurried faster, head low, skin scraped by the cheap carpet. Without warning, his scalp thwacked a wooden surface. Stars flared and the world grayed. Then more cinders hit his leg and full consciousness returned.

The hotel door was flat, smooth, and not yet hot. But the smoke was thicker here, forcing him to snatch a breath in between coughs. He flailed at the metal door handle, which turned but wouldn't unlatch. He jammed up and down a dozen times. Nothing. He rose against the door to get more leverage, but the smoke forced him back down. His throat burned as he fought a coughing jag. I'm going to die like this, he thought, coughing in my underwear against a hotel door. Then a thought burst into his brain—the deadbolt.

Tom thanked whatever god was watching over him and reached for the lock. A spark sent another hot needle into his hand. Cursing, he shook off the insult then attacked the deadbolt. He heard a click as the lock turned. The door unlatched with the next flip.

He banged his head again opening the door but barely felt it, relieved to be in a hallway bathed in emergency lighting. The pale glow changed to a strobe as a claxon sounded. An automated voice announced, "There is a fire. Please evacuate the building."

Ducking his head below the smoke, Tom coughed, "No shit, Sherlock."

The automated voice ignored him, continuing its cold, mechanical drone. "Do not use the elevators."

Tom didn't need to think about the floor plan this time. Stairs would be on either end of the hall. His room was nearest the left exit but that seemed to be the source of the smoke.

Tom shuffled on all fours, body low. Right knee and right hand moved together, followed by left hand and left knee. The smoke got thicker, requiring an even lower crouch. Right then left, right then left. He hung onto the cadence like a prayer. The air ahead was brighter, the flashing strobe bouncing off the gleam of elevator doors. A few more feet and he'd be at the exit.

As he crawled forward, he grabbed something soft and alive.

"Ow," said the person who belonged to the foot.

Tom kept moving as the foot became a shapely calf, the calf a thigh. His face jammed into smooth, taut nylon.

"Get the hell off my ass," said the owner of the panty-covered bottom.

"Move it," Tom shouted.

The exit door opened, and they both tumbled onto cold concrete.

The glow was more constant here, battery-powered lights replacing the strobes. Panting, skivvies providing scant insulation against the floor, Tom looked at his fellow escapee. He recognized the red hair and the face, which looked older without makeup. She was wearing nylon hipsters under a tee that read "FUCK THE WHALES, EVERY MAMMAL FOR HIMSELF."

"Hey, Tom-Tom," she said.

"Hey Agent Sally," he replied. "Would you like that drink now?"

She smiled in the pale light. "I'm buying. Let's go find an open bar."

Tom heard bare feet plopping down the stairs, then a grunted "shit" as those feet found a pebble. Grinning, he sent his feet after hers.

💣 *Chapter 2*

"Just keep breathing, pal."

"Really, I'm fine," Tom said, his voice muffled by the plastic mask. "I got out fairly ..." Further protests were interrupted by a coughing fit.

"Just keep sucking in the oxygen," the EMT said.

Although the spring morning was warm, Tom was glad to have a blanket to huddle in. The cotton cocoon took away the shakes.

The paramedic wasn't looking at Tom. His gaze was directed toward the nearby police cars, their flashing bar lights adding a festival atmosphere to the parking lot. Tom followed the tech's stare to Special Agent Sally Butterworth, who now wore a pair of borrowed sweats over her panties. "Police Athletic League" was written in black letters above her ass, which had lost none of its definition even in the baggy sweats. Hands on hips, she was talking to one of the cops. Another cop was bringing her a blue windbreaker with "Dayton PD" on the back. Tom watched as she turned to shrug her arms into the sleeves, "Fuck the whales" briefly visible. Then the whales were hidden behind the jacket's zipper.

Tom removed the mask. "Really, I'm fine."

"Just breathe the oxygen for another minute," the tech said, patting him on the back but continuing to stare at Sally.

Tom held the mask to his face for the count of ten, then handed it to the EMT. "Thanks."

"No problem," the tech said, still eyeing Sally shaking her red hair over the collar of the windbreaker.

Tom could see why the paramedic stared. The FBI agent looked as good in sweats and windbreaker as she had when he'd offered to buy her a drink in the hotel bar a few hours ago, her dark suit tailored snugly over sculpted curves.

💣

"Can I buy you a drink?" Tom asked.

The knockout at the bar shook her red hair, one hand swirling her half-full glass, eyes glued to her cell phone.

"Here on business?"

The redhead nodded.

"Mind if I sit down?"

She nodded again.

"Is that yes, you mind, or no, go right ahead?"

She held up one finger, still checking emails on the glowing cell.

"Do you ever talk?" he asked.

She nodded again.

"Want to prove it?"

She clacked her cell on the bar as she turned to him, startlingly green eyes flashing. Her features were classically attractive, with high cheek bones, small nose, full lips, and tasteful makeup tying it all together. But the all-business style kept her from being beautiful. Maybe he could get her to smile.

"OK. Let's save us both some time," she said. "I do not *come here often*. In fact, I've never been in this hotel before. In fact, I have never been in Dayton, Ohio, before. I have a meeting in Indiana tomorrow, and this is as far as I got in the drive up from Knoxville before the headlights started to blur. My sign is Aquarius. No, we have not met before. Yes, I know I have nice eyes. No, I was not being rude. I'm just tired and am having my second of two Scotches before I hit the rack. Does that cover it?"

She didn't smile but Tom did. He liked her. Liked her because of the diatribe, not despite it.

"Two drinks a day?" He nodded. "That's a good policy. Lowers your risk of heart attack and early death."

"You a doctor?"

"Second cousin once removed. I'm an epidemiologist."

"A what what what what?"

"Epidemiologist." He pronounced it slowly.

"Skin doctor?"

"That's dermatologist."

"Bug doctor?"

"That's entomologist."

The redhead raised her hands in mock surrender.

"I'm a disease detective. Got my degree from University of Medicine and Dentistry of New Jersey."

"But you're not an M.D.?"

Tom shook his head. "Actually, I'm a veterinarian."

"So, you're a doggy disease detective. Kind of Columbo James Herriott?" She finally smiled at her own joke. He'd been right. She was beautiful. But she must do something that made good looks more an obstacle than an advantage.

"No. I practiced in Jersey before going into public health. Now I'm working for NIOSH. Injury epidemiology. People, not dogs. Mostly computer work, actually."

"Nosh?"

"NIOSH. National Institute of Occupational Safety and Health. We're part of CDC. That's ..."

"Centers for Disease Control." She'd beaten him to it.

He nodded as she turned further, the flare of her jacket revealing the butt of a semiautomatic pistol in a hip holster.

"It's illegal to carry when drinking in a bar. State law."

She sipped her Scotch. Sipped it slowly, he thought, to make it last. To see where this was heading.

"I have papal dispensation," she said.

"You a cop?"

"Better. FBI. Knoxville field office."

"I've never met an FBI agent before."

"We're even. I've never met a doggy disease detective before."

He held forth a hand. "Tom Tomacinski." They shook.

"Butterworth. Sally Butterworth. Funny name, Tom Tomacinski. Sounds like Dr. Seuss."

Tom shrugged. "At least no one's pouring it over pancakes, Agent Butterworth."

"Anybody ever call you Tom-Tom?"

"Only my mother, brother, ex-wife, and all the bullies in grade school."

"Divorced, huh, Tom-Tom?"

He nodded. They were still holding hands. Hers was smooth but firm, with a grip that could probably make him cringe if she tried. "You?"

She paused, as if deciding something. Then she shook her head as ice clinked back into her empty glass. "Been asked, never said yes." Hopping from her stool, she added, "And that's my exit line. I've another hundred miles in the morning, and I'm sure you have pressing business."

"Just an early morning dog-and-pony," Tom said with a shrug, as she started to leave. "I'm on six."

She smiled again, dimples rising below the high cheek bones and patted his shoulder. "Good for you."

He watched her glide toward the elevator, gluteals pumping gracefully in rhythm with her steps. Through the barroom door, he could see her punch the button and head inside the metal box. Looking up, he watched as the elevator stopped at the sixth floor. Smiling again, Tom shook his head and finished his beer. Then he ordered another.

💣

The blare of a loudspeaker brought Tom back to the present. Wrapping his blanket toga fashion, he walked toward Sally, wincing and hopping on the parking-lot gravel. The sun was still a couple of hours from the horizon, but the lot was bright with arc lamps, headlights, news-van kliegs, and a fire department spotlight following the spray of water onto the smoke wisping from the building. A couple dozen frightened guests gawked and murmured, the lucky ones having already escaped to their cars before the hubbub. Tom wiped his nose against the acrid stink of burning plastic and insulation.

"Looks like we got off fairly lucky," said one of the cops talking to Sally. "Only two dead. No other injuries to speak of."

"Who bought it?" Sally asked.

"A man and a woman in 614. Ceiling caved on 'em. That's them." He nodded toward a pair of gurneys being rolled unceremoniously to the ambulance. "White guy in his mid-forties. Black girl in her late teens." The cop shrugged. "We're guessing hooker and John in the wrong no-tell at the wrong time."

"We've contacted your Cincinnati field office," his partner said. "They're gonna send you a change of clothes, credentials, that kind of thing."

Sally saw Tom approach. "Call them back, will you? See if they can also spare some men's clothing." She eyed him in his toga. "I'm guessing thirty-four/thirty-four slacks and a size medium polo."

Tom shook his head and made a he-man pose, muscles rippling along the arms and chest of his six-one frame.

Sally's dimples reappeared. "Make that a large. And maybe a pair of size eleven loafers?"

"Twelve D."

She nodded, still smirking. "Tell them it's for a brother agency. The good Dr. Toma, Toma ..."

"Tomacinski. Thomas Tomacinski."

"Yeah, Dr. Tom-Tom of the CDC. World famous disease detective."

"You got it," the cop said, leaving them alone.

Tom looked at the building. Only one hose was still pumping into the steam, men in black and yellow slickers coiling up the others. "Where did it start?"

"Looks like 616," Sally said. "Fire went through the roof and spread to the overhead insulation and wiring."

"What were they storing up there, ammonium nitrate?"

Sally arched her eyebrows.

"I mean, what exploded?" Tom asked. "Hotel fires usually start in kitchens or with faulty electricals. Then they just burn until the sprinkles kill them. They don't pop like a couple kilograms of C4." He pointed to the building. "And why didn't it blow out the whole corner, rather than just the roof?" Sally followed his finger. "See? The windows are busted, but the walls are still intact. Most of the force went up, like it was sourced *above* the room."

"What did you say you did again?"

"Injury epidemiology," Tom said. "My thesis was on the natural history of commercial fires."

She nodded, then pointed to the Denny's across the street. "Once the cavalry arrives, let's talk some more over breakfast. My treat."

"Well, well," Tom said. "Last night you wouldn't accept my drink. This morning you're buying me breakfast. Just goes to show you."

More dimples as she shook her head and walked off.

💣

The eastern sky was turning pink, but no one noticed in the restaurant, where breakfast traffic was picking up. Two highway patrolmen left with a paper sack, ready for another day of speeding tickets and stranded motorists. Construction workers at the counter pounded down cost-effective calories and hot caffeine. Tom and Sally sat in a corner booth.

The smell of frying bacon and Colombian roast went a long way to removing the stink still clinging inside Tom's nose. A long way, but not enough.

"So, Tom-Tom. How long you been with NIOSH?"

"Five years," Tom said, straightening the collar of his FBI polo shirt.

"Huh. Don't look old enough."

"I'm baby faced. Graduated vet school at twenty-five. Loved the animals but hated practice. Signed up for public health as a way of salvaging my career. Graduated with a master's and spent a year with EPA before transferring to NIOSH, Cincinnati office. Mom and Dad retired to Florida. Older brother's still in Jersey, sells Cadillacs. You now have my life history."

She sipped coffee. "What about the divorce?"

Tom chuckled. "Met Marci in vet school. She thought she was marrying a rich doctor until she saw my starting salary. The student loans killed it for her. Last I heard, she'd hooked a dentist— one of the ten most profitable practices in New Jersey. Written up in the *Star Ledger*, so it must be so." He smiled.

"That's where you're from? Jersey?"

Tom nodded. "Now you."

Sally sipped coffee. "Five years with the Bureau, last March. Baltimore, born and raised. Only child. Dad was a city cop, got killed during a drug bust when I was ten. See my mom when I can."

"I'm going to hazard a guess," Tom said, sipping his own coffee, "that you graduated first in your academy class."

She shook her head. "Third." She paused to sip. "And you?"

"Sorry. I was in the middle of the vet-school pack. I hope you're not disappointed."

Sally smiled. "Tell me more about hotel fires."

Chapter 3

Charles Robinson laid down his electric shaver and picked up his cell. The CEO of the Rest@Home hotel chain never enjoyed calls before 8 a.m. on a Monday. It could be anything from a wildcat union walkout to a tornado. But his was the phone that came with the seven-figure salary. And that's where those bucks stopped. At least he'd managed to avoid an ulcer—so far.

"Morning, Pete. What have you got?"

"Pardon me for calling so early, sir," his assistant, Peter Carvello, said. "But have you seen the news?"

Robinson shook his head. "Just got up. What's the story?"

"Fire at one of our Comfort Rests in Dayton, Ohio."

"Any injuries?"

"Two deaths, some smoke inhalation."

"Are Marc's people on top of it?" Marcus King, his VP of public relations, was as good as they came.

"Yes. We're sticking with 'this was a tragedy, but no comment pending police investigation.'"

"Arson?" Robinson asked.

"Possibly."

Robinson looked at his watch. "Call Andy Hsiu. Get legal on top of things. I'll be in around nine. Have Andy call me then."

He dressed in a classic white shirt, red and blue tie, gray suit. Nothing flashy or casual today; he could be in front of the cameras. In fifteen minutes, he was at the breakfast table.

"There are approximately four hundred thousand home fires each year," Tom said, "which kill about twenty-five hundred people. High-rise buildings, and that's anything over six floors, get hit about fifteen hundred times a year, with just forty deaths. Only about five percent of those high-rise fires are in hotels, and those rarely rise above the sixth story. In fact, only about five percent of hotel fires escape the room of origin."

Tom popped the last of his breakfast sandwich into his mouth.

"Cigarettes have always been a major cause of house fires," he said around a mouthful of bacon, egg, and cheese. "Especially smoking in bed. But with restrictions on public smoking, it's become a minor cause of business fires." He poured more coffee from the silver carafe on the table. "Cooking is now the leading cause in both homes and businesses, the latter usually being restaurants."

"There's a surprise," Sally said.

Tom grinned. "Electrical is another major cause of commercial fires. Overloaded circuits, frayed wiring, and so on." He added sweetener and cream to his cup. "Improper chemical storage can also be a factor, but that's typically industrial settings; hotels don't use them. Maybe a propane tank, but not on the sixth floor." He sipped then replaced the cup. "And that brings us to arson. Either a pyro doing it for kicks, or a business owner looking to collect insurance. Or ...?"

"You think that's what we got here? An insurance claim?"

"I doubt it," Tom said. "Comfort Rest doesn't need the money or the bad publicity. And even the world's worst arsonist knows not to plant a bomb." Sally gave him the skunk eye at the use of the B-word. "Like I said." Tom added. "Hotel fires burn. They don't explode."

"And that last *or*?"

"Either Allahu Akbar," Tom said, "or show me the money."

"Thank you, Matilda," Charles Robinson said, as his cook poured his second cup of coffee.

The story was below the fold of the morning paper. "Fire at Ohio hotel. Two dead." A grainy black-and-white showed the familiar silhouette of a Comfort Rest, smoke steaming from the top, firefighters in their slickers, hotel guests in blankets and pajamas. Charles sipped from his cup and read on. There was little substance to the story yet, "pending results of the official investigation."

His son, Robbie Robinson entered the room. "Morning, Father."

"Where were you last night? You were supposed to meet me at the club. I waited for you."

"I was out with a friend," his son said. "Here's the morning mail."

Charles adjusted his bifocals, then leafed through the pile. "It's good to know you have some. Friends, that is." The junk went into one heap, bills in another. One package—a FedEx mailer with a typed label.

"Scads and scads," his son said with a smirk.

"Why always the attitude?" Charles said, checking out the package that had no return address. "Can't we ever just talk?"

"We just did. Ta-ta, daddy."

Charles shook his head. "Kids."

He pulled the paper tab, unzipping the mailer. Upending the package produced a digital recorder smaller than a pack of cigarettes. "Huh." He held it gently and carefully, like a shard of broken glass. He'd never gotten any death threats, although he'd known other CEOs who had. Could this be one? Before he could ponder further, his fingers touched paper along the back of the device. Turning it over carefully revealed a sticky note with block printing that said, "Play me. I'm not a bomb." Even though that's the kind of thing a bomber might say, Charles placed the recorder on the breakfast table and pressed play.

"Good morning, Mr. Robinson." The voice crackled gratingly but not because of distortion through the small speaker. It was an inhuman, mechanical voice. One that reminded Charles of Stephen Hawking. "I hope you enjoyed your breakfast."

Charles grunted. This is ridiculous. He was getting ready to push stop when the robotic accent read his mind.

"Don't turn me off. I have information on the bombing of your hotel last night."

Charles straightened.

"That's right, I said bombing. That's what the Dayton Fire Department will determine when they send in their investigators. Even those clods are unlikely to miss the residue of plastic explosive: a tad over two kilograms, to be precise."

Charles looked around the room, as if the voice was hiding nearby.

"The police will also identify the room's occupant. Of course, that's not my real name. For now, let's call me Conrad Hilton." The digital message droned its queer singsong. "I'll be sending you instructions soon. Please share them with your friends in the Mid-American Hotel and Lodging Association. It affects all of you. I'm not sure you appreciate just how vulnerable your industry is. Don't make me send along another little reminder. The first charge was placed so to minimize loss of life. The second will not be. Goodbye, and have a pleasant day. Thank you for choosing Comfort Rest."

"Prick," Charles muttered.

Tom yawned into the cabin of the car. "Four hours? Why did it take four hours for the police to take a simple statement?"

"The wheels of justice are rusty," Sally said from the driver's side. "And you weren't the only witness. Besides, it took that long for the Bureau to get me a new car."

"Why couldn't they just bring you new keys?"

"It's simpler to get a new car, then tow the other back to the barn."

"Nice of them to tow mine to the Cincinnati lot. It'll probably be up on blocks with the tires missing by the time I get there." He yawned again. "Why isn't the Bureau involved in the investigation?"

Sally backhanded her own yawn. "Local jurisdiction unless it's found to be terrorism or extortion or something."

"Did you tell them what I said?" Tom asked.

Sally nodded excessively. "Yes, the Columbo James Herriott perspective has been duly noted."

Tom rolled his eyes, then relaxed into the motion of the car. The stress and sleepless twenty-four hours were catching up to him. Each time his lids flickered closed, it was a little harder to open them. He tried sitting straighter, but his body slumped back into the comfortable seat. The Lincoln's smooth ride didn't help. Nor did the hum of the tires. Nor did Sally's thoughtful quiet. His body relaxed. His head bowed. Breathing became regular. His pulse slowed. He was on a boat, bobbing, drifting, gliding. First one way, then another. Consciousness began to leave.

"HONK!"

Tom jerked upright as Sally swerved the car back into the right lane of the freeway. A red Mustang passed on the left, giving her a middle finger.

Tom waited for his heart to slow. "I really don't need to see your evasive driving skills right now, Agent Butterworth."

Sally shook her head and stretched her facial muscles. "Those aren't evasive skills, those are lack-of-sleep skills."

"Did you get *any* sleep last night?"

"It's not the sleep I missed last night," Sally said. "It's the sleep I missed on surveillance detail the night before."

"And you're really going to drive all the way to Knoxville today?"

"They canceled my Indianapolis meeting, but that doesn't mean I'm on vacation. I should be getting back."

"But I'm guessing they at least want the *car* back in one piece."

Sally chuckled. "You work for the government, alright."

"Listen," Tom said. "Why don't you crash at my place, grab a few hours of sleep? You can still make it to Tennessee before dark."

Her red hair shook a negative. "I'll get a motel if it comes to that."

"Come on. You take the bed, I'll take the sofa. We'll meet for dinner in the kitchen before you go." The FBI agent hesitated. "I'm on your way, just a few miles past the bridge."

"So, you live in *Kentucky*. Charming."

"What do you say?"

"What about getting *your* car?"

"Uber." He could tell he was making headway. "Come on. I promise to be a gentleman. No more 'Here on business?' lines."

Sally grinned. "Have you had much luck with that?"

"Now and then," Tom said. "Remember, Babe Ruth led the league in home runs but also in strikeouts."

The FBI agent finally answered. "On one condition."

"Shoot."

"I take the sofa."

💣 *Chapter 4*

"Goodbye and have a pleasant day. Thank you for choosing Comfort Rest."

Charles pressed stop and spoke toward the conference-call microphone. "That's all there is. At least until he or she sends along more instructions."

A voice from the other end of the line said, "What do you make of it, Chuck?"

"Could be a crank," Charles said. "Somebody who saw the news and decided to play with us."

"A crank who managed to overnight the tape *before* the fire?"

Charles nodded to the empty room. "I see your point, Bob."

On the phone were representatives from four of the five other member-companies of the Mid-American Hotel and Lodging Association. Robert R. Rankin was CEO of the Travel-Eze chain. Arthur Chin was president of the Mid-West group. There were also Barbara Gerstel from the Belvedere Group, and George King from Parkway Inns and Suites.

"What does this guy want?" Barbara said. "Money? The Israelis out of Jerusalem? What?"

"Your guess is good as mine," Charles said.

"Do we call the cops?" Arthur asked.

"He didn't say not to," Barbara said. "Either he doesn't care, or he's a rank amateur who doesn't know what he's doing."

"The police told my people that it was plastic explosive," Charles said. "Four or five pounds placed in the suspended ceiling. The blast went mostly up and out the roof. They said it would have been much worse if he'd used a middle room on a lower floor." Charles took off his glasses and rubbed stress from his eyes. "I don't get the impression we're dealing with a rank amateur."

"What about some kind of nut?" George King said. "Just a plain crazy, getting kicks out of killing people."

"Then why send the tape?" Barbara said.

"To mess with us," George replied. "Increases the thrill for this sicko."

"We can speculate all we want," Charles said, "but we're just spinning our wheels."

There was a soft knock at the door. Charles pressed mute and said, "Enter."

His admin, Jan, came in holding a cardboard mailer. "This just arrived by messenger, Mr. Robinson. I thought it might be important."

Charles nodded. Same printed label. No return address.

"Chuck, you still there?" Bob Rankin said.

Charles removed the mute. "We may have the answer to all our questions, folks."

💣

"The three million dollars will be delivered according to my instructions." The robotic voice was unnerving. "Refusal to do so will result in another demonstration of your vulnerability and liability." The last three words were mechanically parceled out, syllable by syllable. "You may contact the police if you like, but any attempt by them to interfere will result in another demonstration." There was a brief pause. "Gentlemen ... and lady. Pay me what I ask, and I assure you that I will never bother you again. Refuse—or attempt to ensnare me—and you will be responsible for many deaths. Your course is clear. Thank you for your attention. Have a pleasant day."

"Well," Charles said, placing aside the second of two identical recorders. "What do we do?"

"Pay him," Barbara said. "He's right about one thing. Three mil is a small price to pay."

"And what about when he asks for the next three mil," George said. "Then the next. Then ten."

Barbara ignored him. "We can divide it up. Share the pain."

"Maybe you have half a million gathering dust. But Parkway doesn't."

"George is right," Bob said. "Once you start paying off, there's no end to it. No matter what this kook says about being satisfied with three."

"I don't think we can afford to take chances," Barbara replied. "This *kook*, as you call him, is right. We *are* vulnerable. And we are liable. What if a hundred guests die next time? I say pay."

"Listen," George said. "I don't pay thugs to not bomb my hotels. My taxes pay police to protect my hotels. I say we turn this over to the cops."

"Could we maybe set up some kind of screening procedure?" Art Chin said. "Like they have at airports. Something to keep out bombs."

"You mean like TSA?" Bob said. "Do you have any idea what that would cost? Not to mention the logistics."

"Let's keep our voices down," Charles said.

Bob paused. "Fine. Look. There's what, one hundred, two hundred international airports in the country. There're more hotels than that in Saint Louis."

"Bob is right," Charles said. "Even if we could do it, it would take years. This guy wants our answer by noon. We're supposed to reply on that chatroom website he mentioned."

"I say, call the cops," George said.

"This is extortion," Bob said. "It's federal."

"Fine. The FBI then."

"What does everyone think?" Charles said. "Does that sound reasonable? Give it to the FBI and follow their lead?"

"What about the reply?" Art asked.

"Post a reply that we'll pay," George said. "Let the bastard think he's got us, then the Feds nail him."

"Is that agreeable to all?" Charles said.

"I don't know," Barbara said, reluctantly.

"Aye," Bob said. "Aye," Art said.

"Barbara?"

"Well ..."

"Barb?"

"Aye."

Conrad Hilton laughed at her sheepish reply. The smartest person in the room, and they bullied her into submission. Women were still their own biggest obstacle to busting the glass ceiling.

The sound quality was quite remarkable, considering the size of the microphone and limited power of the transmitter hidden in the recorder. But the Rest@Home offices had a good network, and, unlike wires and antennas, distance was no problem for the Internet. Thanks to that Internet, Charles Robinson's pompous voice rolled out of Conrad's computer speakers.

"If no one has any objection, my office will notify the FBI and post the reply message. I'll be back in touch once I have more information."

Conrad heard them all agree and hang up.

Soft music hummed in the background. Conrad favored classical and show tunes. Now and then classic rock, back-beat rhythms by the likes of Chuck, Buddy, and Jerry Lee. Or maybe a little John Williams going to a land far, far away. Not the dissonant noise that was so popular with his own generation.

Clad only in a T-shirt and shorts, he wristed sweat from his brow. It was hot and humid in the shed, despite the exhaust fan. But one could hardly cook C4 in the family room.

Equipment and glassware were spread round the table. Plastic jugs held the reagent he'd used: mainly nitric acid, hexamine, di-octyl sebacate, and polyisobutylene. The acid and hexamine were mixed to form a chemical called cyclotrimethylene-trinitramine, also known as RDX. The powdered RDX was blended with water into a slurry, then combined with a hexane-based solution of motor oil and the other ingredients. The entire smelly mess was distilled, filtered, and dried to produce a gray mass with the consistency of modeling clay. A four-pound block lay before him. It was quite stable. You could safely mold it, drop it, or even burn it. But detonation by a blasting cap produced a pressure wave of more than eight thousand meters per second. It went by many names, including C4 and plastique. Most commonly, it was called plastic explosive.

Conrad set aside the gray block and cleared space for the other part of his demonstration. Oh yes, they needed another demonstration. He was naive to think a mere death or two would persuade them. Two deaths were too pedestrian, too clinical. More people died in a highway wreck. Fifty or one hundred deaths would change their tune. Especially if there was more fire. Fire produced a visceral reaction. Fire burned away the doubts, clarified the mind. Fire purified.

Conrad relaxed, letting the music take him. Compared with cooking C4, the next step was ridiculously simple. He filled the plastic containers with gasoline. They'd fit nicely into a roller suitcase, the kind stowed in overhead compartments and trundled through airports and hotels throughout the world.

The next song on the radio was a show tune, one of his favorites. He sang along as he poured ground polystyrene into the containers.

"In olden days a glimpse of stocking, was looked on as something shocking ..."

The liquid thickened as he stirred, forming the jelly known universally as napalm.

"But now God knows, anything goes."

💣 *Chapter 5*

Morning sun was streaming in the window when Tom awoke. Looking at the clock, he panicked at being late for work. Then he remembered yesterday and decided to take the morning off. He might not even have to use personal time, given the circumstances. He thought of his guest and smiled. His smile fled at the sight of the empty sofa, blankets neatly folded. A sticky note awaited him on the fridge. The printing was neat and crisp.

> "Morning, Tom-Tom. Had to scoot with the dawn. The Bureau never sleeps. I left a token to cover inconvenience. Sally."

Tom carried the note to the kitchen table. The wooden surface was as tidy as he'd left it, except now there was a government money card on top. A crisp "$150.00" was printed on the plastic. So, there it was. He'd been paid for his hospitality and reimbursed for the loss of a few toiletries. Thus ended any chance of a relationship, or even a hook-up. He flipped over the note.

"P.S. You're cute sleeping in your undies. Call me if you're in Knoxville. You can buy me that drink."

Her business card was under the money card. Tom smiled again.

💣

"Hi, Scott," Sally said to the empty car.

"Hi, beautiful," the voice on the phone said. "Glad to hear you survived your first, and let's hope only, hotel fire."

"You know, *handsome*, there are workplace sexual harassment laws."

Her boss, Scott Crossfield (like the test pilot) laughed. "Make sure you fill out the complaint in triplicate and I'll endorse it."

"I'm just past Richmond, Kentucky," Sally said. "I should hit Knoxville in a couple of hours."

"That's too bad," her boss said. "Turn around and go back."

"What?"

"You're going to be point person for the Dayton bombing."

"You mean ..."

"That's right," Scott said. "It's officially a bombing. And furthermore, we've officially received an extortion demand."

"From whom?"

"Some guy calling himself Conrad Hilton. Sent digital recordings to the head of the Rest@Home chain. Man named Charles Robinson. I've sent specifics to the Cincinnati office, along with the two digital recorders. Make that your first stop."

"Got it," Sally said, butterflies bouncing in her belly. "So, the ball is in my court?"

"Until I fly in tomorrow afternoon. Then you'll take over in the field while I handle Hilton and Robinson. We'll form a critical incident response group around you. For now, work with the local cops, the Cincy field office, and the resident agencies in Dayton and Columbus. Think about what you need, who you want on your team, and I'll make it happen."

"Okay," Sally said.

"I'm dumping a lot of responsibility on you, young lady, for three reasons. First, you're the best agent under thirty I've ever had. Second, you've already been at the scene, have first-hand knowledge. And third, your preliminary report was spot-on. Not everyone would have pegged this as a bombing right off the bat, especially given the stress of living through it."

"And four, you'll be there to back me up starting tomorrow."

"Why do you have to ruin it?" Scott laughed.

"Just getting all the cards on the table."

"Seriously, Sal. Play these cards right, and it might be Resident Agent in Charge Butterworth."

Sally's gut clenched with a mix of pride and nerves. "Speaking of living through the bombing, can you dig up some info on a Thomas Tomacinski?"

"Who?"

"First name Thomas. Last name Tango, Oscar, Mike, Alpha, Charlie, India, November, Siena, Kilo, India. Works in Cincinnati at the National Institute for Occupational Safety and Health. Expert in hotel fires."

"Roger. It'll be waiting for you in Cincy. Why this guy?"

"He's a major reason my report was spot-on."

"Shit."

Tom listened, key in lock, to the phone ring through the apartment door. He reluctantly decided to answer, given that his landline was currently his sole contact with the world. Rushing inside, he reached the handset on the fifth and final ring.

"Hello?"

"Where have you been?"

His boss, Lynne Faulkner, sounded a little flummoxed, which was typical. Tom had a theory that one of the unenumerated duties of government was providing employment for the socially awkward and logically impaired, those who left private-sector job interviewers shaking their heads. Lynne was exhibit A, and a fine example of how high a seed pod dressed in bargain-basement clothes could rise when merit wasn't a driving force.

"Hi, Lynne. I'm just heading in now."

"Why didn't you answer your cell? I've called three times."

"Because my cell is a puddle of lithium-ion goo on a hotel-room floor. Didn't you get the voice-mail message I left on your office phone?"

"You know I can never figure out how to access those things."

"I've told you, call your own number and at the prompt ..." Tom shook his head. "Never mind. I skipped the Delphi meeting because of the fire. I hadn't slept in twenty-four hours, so I took the morning off. I'm now waiting on a ride from Uber. I should be there in twenty, thirty minutes."

"What's wrong with *your* car?"

"My keys are also a puddle of goo inside a charred pair of jeans in the same hotel room. Please check your voice mail."

"How am I supposed to bill the time you missed?"

"Bill it as an act of God," Tom said.

"I don't have a code for that."

"Fine. It's half a personal day. I'll bite the bullet. I have to run."

"What for?"

"Because I'm waiting for Uber to take me into work." Tom was exhausted, and he wasn't even there yet.

"But you're not supposed to come in today."

"I'm not? Why not?"

"This federal agent phoned me this morning. Susan something or other."

"Sally Butterworth?"

Lynne paused in thought. "Could be. Anyway, she's going to pick you up at your apartment. You've been seconded to the FBI."

"I've been what?"

"Seconded. That means placed on temporary assignment."

"I know what seconded means. How? Why?"

"I don't know. But somebody called Bill upstairs. He confirmed it."

"When is this supposed to happen?" Tom asked.

Honk, honk, traveled through the apartment door.

"Probably now," Lynne said.

"Thanks. Bye."

The horn was Ron from Uber, idling in a red Toyota. Tom apologized and wanted to give him a couple of bucks for his trouble, but all his cash was fire-scene residue.

"That's okay," Ron said. "We'll charge your credit card."

"Great."

As Ron pulled away, a familiar Lincoln SUV pulled in. Tom opened the door.

"Hi Tom-Tom."

"You owe me $10.60 for an Uber ride to Tusculum Ave., Cincinnati."

Sally shrugged. "You know how this works. Submit an invoice."

"Can I ask a question?" Tom said, snugging down his shoulder belt.

"Shoot."

"What am I doing here?"

Sally pulled into traffic and said, "People always envision the FBI as having unlimited access to unlimited expertise. And in a sense, we do." The big car angled toward the freeway. "But said expertise is not always where you want it when you need it. I need expertise in arson and hotel fires. And I need it right now. Fair enough?"

Tom's morning was spent on the ground floor of the Federal Building on Ronald Reagan Drive, undergoing something called Phase I testing. After a urine sample to check for drugs, he sat in a little classroom that reminded him of high school, filling in little ovals (like in high school), answering questions ranging from how promptly he returned library books to how to deal with a disrespectful subordinate. Then, after a polygraph (his first ever) and a psych profile (his first ever), he was run through a cardiac stress test as part of a physical exam. By two p.m., his still sweaty hand clutched shiny new credentials as it knocked timidly on the door of the Division of Digital Evidence, FBI Field Office, Cincinnati, Ohio.

"Enter," a male voice said.

Tom poked his head inside. A series of tables and computer terminals were arranged into a warren of cubes and workspaces. At one of these spaces sat a pudgy, middle-aged man who looked more like a pawnbroker than an FBI technician. He wore a brown sweater over his shirt and tie and a jeweler's loop clipped to his forehead. Sally was standing beside him. On the table in front of them was a digital recorder sitting in the halo of a desktop spotlight.

"Come on in, Tom-Tom," Sally said. "Jerry, this is Dr. Tom-Tom Tomacinski of NIOSH. Tom-Tom, this is Jeremy Shapiro, expert on all things digital."

"Hi, Tom-Tom."

"Hi. Just one Tom is fine."

"Tom-Tom's an expert in hotel fires and arson," Sally said. "He pegged it as a bombing from just eyeing the scene in the glow of parking-lot kliegs."

"Well, I'm not sure that ..."

"Good job, Tom-Tom," Jerry said.

"Just one Tom is fine."

"The device has already been dusted for prints," Sally explained. "Only Robinson's were on it. That's Charles Robinson, CEO of the Rest@Home hotel chain. The recording itself has been digitally stored for analysis at Quantico, which is where this baby is going once Jerry is finished with it."

Sally took off her suit jacket and laid it across a chair back. Tom noticed the black plastic of her pistol snugged against her hip.

"This is the second message, the one with the extortion demand," Sally said. "Jer, please play it for Tom-Tom."

Tom listened to the mechanical tones Doppler in and out. Finally, the cyber voice said, "Have a pleasant day."

"Cheeky little bastard," Tom said.

"Okay, heard enough? Fine. Open her up, Jerry."

Using a series of miniature tools, the cyber tech took the back off the recorder. "Let's see if you hold any proprietary secrets," he said. "Little things that might help us identify Mr. Hilton. You look like a standard digital recording ... Hello, what have we here?"

"Something?" Sally said.

Jerry redirected the lamp and adjusted his magnifier loop. "Looks like a small mic and transmitter embedded below the battery."

"What does that mean?" Sally asked.

"It means Mr. Hilton was listening in while this was being handled. Probably activated once the message was played."

"No shit," Sally said. "Conrad eavesdropped while Robinson and friends were discussing what to do next?"

Jerry placed an ammeter across the leads. "And still is. Current is flowing."

"You mean ..."

Sally interrupted Tom with a silent finger. She nodded to Jerry, who snipped a wire with a small pair of pliers.

The speaker went dead. Conrad Hilton looked up from his labors, smiling at his computer. They'd found his little bug. Oh well, it only took them twenty-four hours. He shook his head. Your standard cast of government bumblers. There was Jerry the tech, who thought himself oh so clever, but probably couldn't qualify for the Geek Squad. Then there was Sally, the lady in charge. She sounded too young for that role, and Conrad thought she was overcompensating. Why were women professionals either door mats or androgynous bitches? Then there was the joker in the deck: Tom-Tom. Tom-Tom Tomacinski. Conrad liked the sound of it. It was lyrical. Sounded like the percussion player in a jazz band. He smiled again.

Zippering up the roller bag, he wiped hands on jeans and moved to his laptop. A few clicks and mouse glides, and he was at the website for the National Institute for Occupational Safety and Health. A few more maneuvers and he was typing a phonetic spelling into the employee directory: TOMASINSKI. No hits. He played with the spelling, humming Benny Goodman's *Sing, Sing, Sing*. Filling in on the skins, he thought, is Tom-Tom Tomacinski. There it was. A photo of a youngish man with brown hair and a round, Polack, baby face. Program specialist in public safety and traumatic injury prevention. After the name were the acronyms DVM, MPH. A vet? This was getting more and more interesting. He could have some fun with this.

Conrad rolled the bag over by the briefcase. The suitcase was lined with odor-absorbing material, so there wasn't any petroleum smell. It probably wouldn't pass up-close muster with a bomb-sniffing dog, but there were none in hotel lobbies. Sitting down at his bureau, he leafed through his makeup kit, noodling disguises. The bump, bump, bump, bump of Tom-Tom's drums pounded through his brain along with Benny's wild clarinet. He felt great.

Chapter 6

"Agent Butterworth. May I have a word?"

"Wait here," Sally said. "I'll be back in a second."

She headed toward a big man in a dark blue suit, steely gray hair cropped in a military cut. Special Agent Daniel Hartsell was fifty years old, all business, all FBI, and all hard-ass. He believed the book was made for a purpose, and any departure from procedure required at least half a dozen good reasons. And even then you made his shit list.

"Good afternoon, Special Agent in Charge Hartsell." Sally knew not to call him Dan and to include his full title.

"I'll get right to the point. I talked to Special Agent in Charge Crossfield this morning, and he explained the situation. Now I don't know why this is being handled out of Knoxville and not my field office."

"That's something you'd need to discuss with Mr. Crossfield, sir."

"I have. So now I am going to discuss it with you." He lowered his voice so that only she could hear. "Listen to me. I've hung my shingle on the top floor for over fifteen years. I was assistant SAinC when we nabbed Iyman Faris and his Al Qaeda co-conspirators plotting to take out the Brooklyn Bridge. I have over fifty special agents under my direction, including assistant SAinCs and supervisory special agents. They handle everything from cyber-crime, to arson, to counterterrorism. And they certainly can handle this. I don't like people skirting my jurisdiction. So as long as you are working out of *my* office, working with *my* people, you will go through *me*. Everything you come up with, every move you make—through me. Do we understand each other?"

"Yes, sir."

"I think it's a mistake to entrust this investigation to someone as junior as you."

"I'm just temporary, sir, until Mr. Crossfield gets here tomorrow."

Hartsell nodded, his face grim death. "I hope you've been around the Bureau long enough to know that you don't screw with Daniel Hartsell. You'll think the building fell on you. Clear?"

"Clear, sir. Thank you."

Hartsell wheeled on his shiny, black Florsheims and stomped away.

"What was that all about?" Tom asked.

"Just a grouchy old bear cuffing the new cub. Guy thinks everyone is after his job. Let's go."

💣

"First stop is the Comfort Rest Inns and Suites," Sally said from behind the wheel of the big Lincoln. She now had three passengers.

"The scene of the crime?" Matt Clemens asked. Matt was the youngest and least experienced agent at the Cincy field office, making him Hartsell's first choice to assist Sally. The old fart thought he was hobbling her investigation, but Sally actually was relieved. The last thing she needed was a hard-ass, ramrod overseer with a direct line to Hartsell's phone. She was also pleased that Clemens was a bit of a computer whiz.

Sally nodded. "The top two floors are closed pending repairs, but the hotel is still open. The manager will meet us."

"I hope he has the surveillance videos queued for inspection," Matt said.

"First order of business," Sally said. "You check it out and we'll get a description from one Ms. Candace Regan, front desk receptionist on the night in question. I'm sure Tom-Tom remembers her. He's our expert on interrogating young ladies in hotels." Sally winked at the younger agent.

"Is that right, Tom-Tom?" Matt said from the shotgun seat.

Sitting with Tom in the back was Detective Stanley Kovack of the Montgomery County Sheriff's office. He grinned and gave the vet a good-natured punch in the shoulder.

Tom shook his head. "Just one Tom is fine. Really."

💣

The hotel manager was a congenial Black man named Alan Woodward. He volunteered to stay while they interviewed Ms. Regan, but Sally politely shooed him and Kovack off to show Matt the video feed.

Sally introduced herself and Tom, then asked Regan to have a seat. "So, Candace. May I call you Candi?"

The young girl nodded stiffly.

"You haven't done anything wrong, Candi, so you can relax."

Tom added a smile to the one Sally was beaming. The desk clerk unwound a little, unclenching her hands and crossing legs that thrust prettily from a green business skirt.

"I didn't know what he had in his luggage," Candi said. "Or I would have called the police."

"Of course," Sally said, holding forth her cell. "Okay if I record this?"

Candi shrugged.

"What can you tell us about him?"

"You mean Mr. Groundhog?"

"Oliver Groenhaage, yes."

"I've already told the police all that."

"Well, tell me too, okay?"

Candi shrugged.

"How tall was he? How old? Any distinguishing characteristics? Whatever you can think of."

"He wasn't that tall," Candi said. "Shorter than agent Tomaci..." She pointed at Tom.

"Ah, I'm not an agent."

"What do you think?" Sally said, giving Tom a sideways glance. "Was he an inch shorter? Two? Stand up, Tom-Tom. You too, Candi."

Candi rose and stared at Tom for a moment. "He was maybe three inches shorter."

"So, five ten, five eleven?"

Candi nodded, still staring at Tom. "You have nice eyes," she said.

"Thanks." He started to sit, but Sally grabbed his arm.

"Please continue, Candi. Was he as broadly built as Dr. Tomacinski?"

The young blonde smiled. "No. He didn't have those broad shoulders and wasn't as muscular through the chest. More slightly built."

"What was he wearing?"

"Oh, I remember that *really* well. He had this tweedy suit coat and those fancy leather driving gloves. The sporty kind."

"Kid gloves?" Tom said.

Candi shrugged. "He touched my hand with them. They were really soft."

"Anything else?" Sally asked.

"One of those European-style hats, like you see in the old movies."

"A homburg?" Tom asked.

Candi raised her shoulders again. "He said he was Dutch. Had like a German accent, only different." She thought for a moment. "His hair was black, but with salt and pepper sideburns. He looked pretty old, maybe sixty or even seventy."

"Any moles or distinguishing characteristics?" Sally asked. "Did he have a beard?"

"No beard. But he had a mustache, which also had flecks of gray. And glasses. Those horn-rimmed glasses. You know, the black kind. Like in that old movie with Gary Busey."

"Would you know him again if you saw him?"

"Oh yeah. I'm sure I would."

"Great," Sally said, still smiling. "Let's go take a look at the surveillance video."

Everyone headed to a back room holding two video display monitors. On the first one, Candi was frozen behind the lobby desk. The second showed only an empty hotel hallway.

"Let's see what you have, Matt."

"This is Mr. Groenhaage's first appearance, 9:47 p.m." Matt punched a button and video Candi began to move on the first monitor. An older gentleman with a continental flair entered the scene.

"That's him," Candi said. They all watched several minutes of exchange between the two, and then Groenhaage exited out of frame.

"Here's the second appearance, on the sixth floor, 9:55." The older gentleman passed beneath the camera, so that only the back of his head was clearly visible as he moved away and stopped at a corner room.

"Why 616?" Sally asked. "Why the top floor?"

"I was going to upgrade him to a suite on two," Candi said. "But he asked for a room on the top floor. So he'd have a view of the city lights."

"Here's appearance number three," Matt said. "11:45." The older gent exited the corner room, without the suitcase. Now he was approaching the camera. "Nothing on the feed from the elevator car, so he must have used the stairs."

"Run that again," Sally said.

Matt tapped keys and the door to 616 opened again. The man placed his hat on his head and headed toward the camera.

"Stop," Sally commanded. "Advance it slowly." The view flipped by, frame by frame. "Stop. This portion." She pointed to below the man's nose. "Can you magnify that?"

"A little," Matt said. "This is not the best equipment." The side of Groenhaage's face grew, so that chin to glasses filled the frame.

"There," Sally said. "Advance frame to frame." The face moved jerkily out of the picture, edge of the mustache waving to and fro like a pennant at the ballpark. "See it, Tom-Tom?"

"Yeah. It looks like Mr. Groenhaage needed a little more spirit gum on that side."

Sally nodded. "I think we can assume the hair and glasses are phony, too."

"You mean," Candi said, "he was in disguise?"

Sally nodded.

"Here's appearance number four. Parking lot. 11:46 a.m." The older gentleman moved swiftly into a grayish rental car, then the vehicle pulled away.

"Make sure that Jerry has this footage back in Cincinnati," Sally said.

Matt nodded.

"Well, that should cover it for now, Candi. You've been a great help. We'll call you if we need more." The desk clerk seemed a little disappointed when she left.

"Did you notice that our seventyish old man made it from the sixth floor to the parking lot in a little over a minute?" Matt said. "Using the stairs?"

Sally nodded. "Looks like his age is phony as well."

The late-afternoon sun was behind them as they headed down I-70. The view ahead was macadam monotonous, so Tom cast sideways glances at Sally. Her face was still pretty, but there were signs of strain. Tom wondered if she was biting off more than she could chew.

"Are you sure you want me there when you talk to Charles Robinson?"

"Sure," she said, eyes glued on the highway. "You're very valuable to me."

Tom smiled proudly.

"It's nice to have someone around with even less experience than me." A hint of a grin dimpled her cheek.

"You've been with the agency ..."

"Bureau," she corrected.

"Right. You've been with the Bureau for five years. You must have *some* experience."

She nodded, eyes still on the road. "About 500 background checks, a few dozen stakeouts, filling out maybe a thousand forms. Glamorous."

"Nothing with more substance?"

"A couple of hostage negotiations, a racially motivated killing, and one almost suicide bombing."

"Almost?"

"We caught Mahmud in a hotel room getting ready. He's cooling his heels at Leavenworth now." She paused. "That last bit, the *more substance* stuff, was all the past year and a half. Since I came under Crossfield."

"So, *he* must think you can handle it. Otherwise, he would have dropped it with what's his name in Cincinnati."

"Hartsell," Sally said.

"Right, Hartsell. Crossfield must have had a good reason to make an enemy of him and take a risk on you."

Sally smiled again. "Hartsell was already an enemy. At least not a friend. And it wasn't really up to Scott. He's a Bureau go-to guy for serial bombers, terrorists, that kind of thing. Broke a big case down in Atlanta a couple of years ago. And he was only a few hundred miles away. And I'd been at the scene. So ..." She shrugged. "Between you and me, I'll be relieved when he helicopters in tomorrow."

They were meeting Robinson at his home in a ritzy suburb north of Columbus. The big car glided down wide, tree-lined boulevards and onto a driveway that curved through lawn the size of a par-five golf hole. The house was a large, white colonial with pillars from *Gone with the Wind*. They parked behind a nondescript van, guys in blue windbreakers unloading equipment. Tom recognized Jerry Shapiro riding herd.

"Hi, Jer," Sally said. "How're we doing?"

"Just got done bugging his corporate offices," the tech said. "Now we're doing the house and cell phone. Shouldn't take too long."

Sally nodded and headed toward a glossy red door that belonged in a medieval castle.

"What if Hilton contacts someone else? You said he was extorting a bunch of companies."

"Six," Sally said.

"Right," Tom said.

Sally shook her head. "So far, our man has contacted only Robinson. Twice. Looks like he's the point man."

Sally knocked on the already opened door, then headed inside. The house was cooler than outside, and the air smelled different. There wasn't a bad smell or a perfumed one. In fact, there was no detectable odor at all, except for a slight scent of cleaning fluids and floor wax. Tom was reminded of a laboratory clean room.

"Hello? Mr. Robinson?"

Her voice echoed through the cavernous foyer of ceramic tile and plaster walls. A crystal chandelier hung from a ceiling high enough for rocket assembly. Tom glanced at a polished-wood stair rail winding up and away to his left. When he looked back, a man in his late fifties was entering from a side hallway.

"Special Agent Butterworth?"

Charles Robinson extended his hand. He was a solid figure with presence. Not tall exactly, but imposing. His frame looked solid, a tribute to golf, tennis, swimming, and proper diet. A broad forehead blended into white-gray hair, shorn short in a respectable business cut. He was dressed in tan slacks and a blue sport shirt with an alligator on the pocket. Underneath his pleasant smile was a face dedicated to business.

"Sally Butterworth. Thank you for seeing us on such short notice. This is Dr. Tomacinski, one of our technical experts." Tom shook his hand.

"I thought we could talk in my study. This way, please."

The study had the feel of a club frequented by Sir Arthur Conan Doyle. Two walls were lined with dark wood shelves, although photos and knickknacks were as plentiful as books. The desk was a mahogany affair, sparsely populated as is often the case for powerful men with others to clear away the clutter. Robinson took the comfy desk chair, pointing opposite to two in matching brown leather.

"I guess we should get right to business." Sally produced her cell to record the conversation. Then she pointed to two mailers in clear plastic bags sitting beside a computer terminal on the nearly empty desk. "He sent the recorders in these?"

"Yes," Robinson said. "Your Mr. Crossfield asked me to save them for you. The FedEx arrived first thing this morning. The other was delivered by messenger to my office." He handed them over.

Sally nodded. "I'll send them to Virginia. Our lab will check for prints and should be able to tell us what kind of printer made the labels." She looked at the FedEx. "We'll also be able to trace this back to the site of origin, although it'll probably be a drop box." Pointing to the second mailer, she added, "And this was delivered by messenger?"

"Yes. Speedy Delivery. I called them, and they said a request came via email, telling them where to pick up the package. Some apartment, I believe."

"We'll check that out, as well," Sally said. "This second package. This held the ransom demand. The one with the noon deadline?"

"That's right," Robinson said. "As I told your Mr. Crossfield, I posted this on the website, as Hilton requested. Agent Crossfield said it was okay."

Sally read from a computer printout. "Dear Conrad. We agree to your price. It will take a few days to raise the money. I'll write again when all is ready."

"That was okay, wasn't it? We only had a couple of hours."

"Fine," Sally said. "Let me ask you something. When you and the other members of the trade group ... is that Mid-American Hotel and Lodgings Association?"

"Yes, that's right. We're the owners of the smaller chains. Hotels and motels mostly, although we have some restaurants. Even a few retirement villages. We're the independents. The guys that haven't been gobbled up by Wyndham and Hyatt." He smiled. "At least not yet."

Sally smiled back. "When you were discussing what to do, was the recorder sitting there? The one with the ransom demand?"

"Yes," Robinson said. "I'd played it during the conference call. Why?"

Sally spread her hands, noncommittally. "What did you talk about during that call? Specifically."

Robinson leaned back in thought. "Well, I played the tape. And we talked about what to do. Barbara—that's Barbara Gerstel from the Belvedere chain—thought that we should pay. But two other members felt that paying was a mistake. That it would lead to further demands."

"And who was that? Who disagreed?"

"That was Bob Rankin, of Travel-Eze, and George King of Parkway. We had a rather heated discussion about what to do. They thought it was a mistake to pay, Barbara wanted to pay, and Arthur and I were more noncommittal."

"Arthur?"

"Arthur Chin of the Midwest group of hotels and restaurants."

"And that's everyone in the MHLA?"

"Five of the six members. Roger couldn't make the call. Personal business, I believe."

"Roger?"

"C. Roger Caldwell, CEO of the Bungalow 5 chain. They're the smallest member. Low-budget lodgings. You may have heard their radio commercials?"

"Excuse me, Father."

Tom and Sally turned toward the doorway, where a twenty-year-old face had poked in. A stubble of new growth was fighting against acne pimpling the chin and cheeks.

"I'm busy," Robinson said. "Excuse me, Agent, I mean, Ms. Butterworth, Dr. Toma ... ah, this is my son, Robbie."

"Robbie Robinson," the boy said, sliding aviator frames up the greasy bridge of a greasy nose. "My name is a bit of a family joke." His smirk said both 'I hate my father' and 'fuck you.'

"What is it, Robbie?"

"I don't mean to interrupt your *company*, but I've come up short of cash this month."

"Again?" Robinson shook his head. "So, use your ATM account."

"There's the rub. The account is short as well."

Robinson gave Tom and Sally a rueful smile, then said, "I'll transfer some money. Now please leave us alone for a while."

The fuck-you grin returned. "Always, Father. Ciao."

"Excuse me for just one moment." Robinson clacked computer keys with an oft-repeated cadence, then twice pressed return. "Now, where were we?"

"You were telling us about the conference call with the MHLA," Sally said.

"Yes. Roger couldn't be there, so it was just the five of us. We finally decided that we should call you people, but pretend we were going to pay. Like I said, we only had a couple of hours to decide."

Tom watched Sally thinking—those lovely wheels turning.

"So, what now, Agent Butterworth?"

"We wait. Not much we can do until Hilton makes the next move. Special Agent Crossfield will be here tomorrow, and he may have more ideas. But for now, we wait."

Sally rose, taking the envelopes with her. Tom followed her lead.

"I'm going to have someone camp out here if that's okay. Sofa will be fine."

"Not at all," Robinson said. "I'm sure we can find him ... or her a bed."

"I'll also ask the police to post a car out front. Just in case."

"Am I or my family in danger?"

"Oh, I don't think so," Sally said. "But you are obviously his chosen point of contact. He'll probably figure we've bugged the phones, so he may try and get in touch some other way." She headed toward the door, Robinson and Tom in tow. "If he tries to contact you again, I need to know." She paused mid step. "And no more conference calls without Bureau input."

"Fine," Robinson said. They said their goodbyes.

Out front, Jerry was packing up.

"All set?" Sally asked.

"Wired tighter than teenage braces. We'll be able to hear an ant sneeze."

"Good. I want someone on headphones twenty-four-seven."

"You got it."

She handed Jerry the envelopes. "See that these get to the lab. ASAP. I want them run for prints, trace, and point of origin."

"Roger."

Tom rushed to match her stride to the SUV. Once inside, he asked, "Why am I here again?"

Sally just raised her hand and spoke into the phone.

"Matt? It's me. I'm gonna send you a recording of my conversation with Robinson. I want you to get me everything you can on the six member companies of the Mid-American Hotel and Lodging Association, and the six corporate heads we discussed.

Run down the personal and corporate finances, medical histories, and any criminal records. Even if it's just overdue parking tickets. I'll need it first thing tomorrow morning." She started the car. "Contact the Columbus resident agent in charge. What's her name, Cartwright? Yeah, Sarah Cartwright. Have her camp people out at Robinson's house. He knows they're coming. Have her also get in touch with the Highway Patrol and request an unmarked car outside the house. Right. We also need to check out the local apartment where the second mailer originated. Instant Delivery or something. It's on the recording."

Tom was amazed she didn't need to pause for breath.

"Likewise, ask Stan for anything Montgomery County has on the Dayton bombing. Get it to the lab. And be polite. Brothers in law enforcement. All that jazz." Bluetooth headset donned, Sally turned the big car out of the drive and back onto tree-lined streets. "The Dayton resident agency. Who runs that?" She listened to the other end of the line. "Who? Gyzinski. Right. Can never trust them Polacks." She gave Tom a wink. "Fill them in with what we've got. We're gonna need their manpower. No, I'll call Hartsell. Check back with me in a couple of hours."

Sally grabbed her phone, clicking and swiping, car navigated toward the freeway by knee pressure. Tom heard the squeech of a text or email being sent. Then the phone landed back in the console, bouncing against a water bottle before settling into place.

"Now," Sally said. "What was your question again?"

"I'm not sure I remember. But I think it was, what am I doing here?"

"I need to pick your brain. Let's get some dinner. Bureau's buying."

Chapter 7

"Lovely place you picked for us. Couldn't you find a Bungalow 5?"

Tom and Sally sat in a booth at the half-empty Starlight Lounge attached to a Fairways Motor Lodge. The place had seen better days, but that was years ago. Now, the low-light ambiance hid its age. But grunge was grunge, in this case the sticky residue from years of spills on multiple layers of decomposing varnish.

"It's called per diem," Sally said. "Millions for defense, but not one penny for fancy restaurants. Make the best of it. Help yourself to any gum under the table." She smiled and was beautiful again. "Plus, I figured this would be right up your alley. Great place for picking up chicks."

"Come on," Tom said. "Is that fair?"

"Well, maybe not."

"Besides. If I hadn't hit on you, you wouldn't have access to my *vast* expertise."

The matronly waitress brought their drinks. Scotch rocks and a Bass ale. They raised glasses and drank.

"So," Tom said. "Back to my question. What just *is* my expertise?"

She sipped her Scotch. "If I wanted to cause a lot of casualties at a hotel," Sally said, "with no more than a couple of suitcases, how would I do it?"

"Publish a list of the license plates outside during noontime maneuvers. I guarantee a dozen husbands with wife-inflicted traumatic injury. Maybe a few secretaries, too."

"Funny, Tom-Tom. How would I do it?"

"Why?"

She gave him a "you should know" look. "You heard Robinson. They had their little powwow with Conrad listening in. Had a 'heated discussion' about how they'd trick him and sic the feds on his ass. Given what you know about our boy, you think he'll sit still for that?" Pretty red hair shook back and forth. "No, he's going to give them another demonstration. Get their minds right." She sipped her Scotch again. "But where?" Sally looked into his eyes. "Where?"

Tom leaned back and gulped his beer. He switched to business mode. "Okay. First, you wouldn't hit someplace like this." His arms took in the surroundings. "You'd stick with multiple stories. A bigger, high-rise place favored by business types or conventioneers. Hit them during the workweek. Late at night or early morning, when most people are in their rooms." Leaning forward, he put down his glass. "I'd hit a lower floor. Probably not the first—easy access for emergency responders. I'd go with second or third."

"Conrad hit a top floor last time."

"And he also said he was trying to make a point, minimize casualties. I believe him."

"Hey honey, put the game on," yelled a middle-aged voice.

Tom and Sally looked over as a balding bar patron with a beer gut dropped his ass on a stool. Lowering his voice, Tom continued.

"You want people trapped on the upper floors. Remember 9/11?"

"I'm not *that* young," she said.

"And you'd need fire," he said grimly. "Lots. Not just an explosion."

"There was a fire at the Dayton hotel, remember."

"Relatively little," Tom said.

"Took out two whole floors."

He swigged some beer. "Most of that was water damage. Listen, hotels are the mecca for fire safety. Especially high-rises. Sprinklers in every room. Sprinklers in the hall. Fire-resistant construction materials. And compartmentalization. To overcome all that, you need to generate a lot of heat. And you need to figure out a way to let it spread."

The waitress returned. She said her name was Melba and that the special was something called "Fisherman's Surprise." They ordered dinner and another round of drinks.

With his second beer in front of him, Tom wet his whistle and resumed the lecture. "I'd use some kind of accelerant: gasoline, kerosene, napalm."

"Napalm?"

"You can make it at home," Tom said. "Link that to some plastic explosive on the second or third floor."

"Where? Precisely."

"I don't know," Tom said. "I analyze fire patterns, not how to start them." He thought for a moment. "Probably somewhere in the middle."

"Why the middle?"

"Like I said, hotels are all about compartmentalization. And they're laid out horizontally, even high-rises. Each room is a unit. Each floor is a unit. Even the ducts and defusers for the air-handling system run horizontally. The only vertical channels for fire to travel are the elevators, stairs, and ductwork running to and from the furnace in the basement and AC on the roof. But those are all steel and concrete. The flammables are in the rooms and lobby." He drank and thought. "Get yourself a room in the middle of the second or third floor. Plant a bomb so that the explosion goes up and out, carrying the accelerant into the horizontal space above the rooms. Fire spreads from room to room. Air handlers distribute the smoke. That's probably how ..." He paused in mid-sentence, a devilish grin on his face.

"What?" Sally said.

"Atrium."

"Atrium?" Sally asked.

Tom nodded. "Hit one of the swanky high-rises where rooms ring a central atrium."

"You mean one of those floor-to-ceiling jobs with plants in the lobby, like Jurassic Park?"

Tom became more animated. "Right. Those spaces are designed with an updraft, to carry smoke and smells away from paying guests and out the roof."

Now Sally nodded. "Fire loves an updraft."

"Get a room on the second floor, facing the atrium. Plant the bomb at the junction of the outside wall and an adjacent room. Explosion sets off everything in two rooms and scatters accelerant into the atrium."

"Plant it high," Sally said, "it might blow into the floor above as well."

"Fire follows the updraft, rising to the higher floors."

"And smoke fills the open walkways," Sally said, "where guests have to go to reach the stairs."

Tom nodded, all smiles.

Sally considered this, staring into space. Then she hit him with those beautiful dimples. "I'm glad you're on our side, Tom-Tom."

Tom lay in his motel bed, scratchy blanket against his neck, stomach fighting the remains of a turkey dinner unlike mom's. He could see a faint light creep from under the door to the adjoining room. And he could hear Sally's faint but familiar voice from behind that door, her words barely audible against the background of street traffic and AC hum.

"Make it a standard warning, reason to believe, yada yada. No, *credible threat* is too strong." The voice paused. "Let's cover as far north as Michigan, south to the gulf, from the Rockies to the Appalachians. Right. Send it to all hotels with more than five floors." Her voice paused again, listening. "Really, that many? Okay, make it ten or more floors. Report any suspicious persons making unusual requests. Like? Like insisting on a room on the second or third floor. Asking for a room in the middle of those floors. Wanting to pay cash. Asking about evacuation procedures in the hotel. Fire procedures. You know, standard arson stuff. Right. Oh, Matt? How many of those hotels have atriums? The big central plazas that run up to the roof." The voice listened again. "Fine. Give those the credible-threat warning." More listening. "Let me worry about Hartsell. Ha, ha. Okay. Bye."

Tom wondered again why he was here. Yes, he had special expertise, applicable expertise. But so did others. Certainly, there must be some in the Bureau. True, he'd been in the wrong place at the right time. But even so. He thought about today, making the rounds with Sally. He'd mostly listened. At least until she wanted to bounce ideas off him. Was that his role, sounding board? Or was he a security blanket? One of those well-worn plush animals that a child needs to fall asleep. Part of him thought Sally wanted a friendly face to look at across the unfamiliar landscape of barking orders she'd never given before to men who might not take her seriously. A face that might look up to her, convincing herself she was up to the task. An admirer, providing courage to her false bravado. Truth be told, he liked the role. And he did admire her. But he, too, would be happy when Crossfield arrived to take on the load. Although Sally fought bravely to maintain an even strain, as the flyboys used to say, cracks were showing. He liked her better when she smiled. Tom fell asleep thinking of her dimples.

It took Tom a moment to figure out where he was and why. The room was dark, shapes around him strange and unfamiliar. The bedside clock glowed 1:35, a little red dot indicating a.m. The fullness in his bladder said it was time to give back the beer. He vaguely recalled that the commode was toward another source of light, the bright line under the exit door.

With a flush, he returned to bed. That's when he saw a bright line under another door. It took him a second to remember where it led. Eyes now accustomed to the dimness, he walked softly to the connecting door and listened. The early morning held few traffic noises, and the AC had clicked off. Ear to wood, he could hear faint sounds coming from Sally's room. The characteristic click, click, clack that could only be computer keys. At 1:40 a.m.

After some hesitation, he carefully opened his side of the door. After more hesitation, he softly knocked. The clacking stopped. He knocked again. "Yes?" came a reply. He pushed. It wasn't latched.

Sally was seated by a laptop at the desk, but she'd swiveled his way, long T-shirt draped over bare legs. Across her chest read "77th Annual FBI 10K Race." The lettering was in two lines, with "77th Annual" sloped over her underlying breasts, the I and K below tented into diamond points of interest. His eyes swept downward, following the curve of her legs to equally bare feet, then traveled back over the slopes and valleys to her face. There were no dimples.

"What is it, Tom-Tom? Did I wake you?"

He shook his head. "Had to pee. What are you doing?"

"Reports. One to Hartsell, one to Scott. I clunked out before I could write them. But paperwork never sleeps. So, I'm playing catch-up. Hartsell will be pissed that he didn't get this by five yesterday instead of after midnight. Scott will understand, which is why he's last. Go back to bed. A lot to do tomorrow."

Swiveling back to the computer, Sally groaned.

"Problem?" Tom asked.

"Muscle cramp." She massaged the base of her neck. "Nothing that more sleep and less stress wouldn't cure."

"Let me help," Tom said, crossing the threshold.

"Don't worry about it. It's nothing but ... ooh, that feels good."

"Marci used to say I had educated fingers."

Tom massaged the knotted muscles running from her arm to the soft skin at her nape. Sally's shoulder was muscular, with a sinewy strength his ex never had. Such shoulders came from swimming, or weightlifting, or both. Kneading to the left, his fingers extended up the neck, gently but firmly bunching flesh and then releasing.

"That feels great, but I need to get back to ... oh, yeah. That's it. Right there."

He felt her stiffness melt, replaced by a rising firmness in his shorts. Pushing down the collar of her tee, he exposed more shoulder, one hand rolling onto bare arm while the other continued massaging the ever-shrinking knot of tissue in her neck. She leaned into him, softly moaning, head tilted, neck extended, shirt collar riding down her bicep. From his vantage point above and behind, Tom caught a glimpse of heaven.

She moaned again. "Yes, oh yes. A little harder. That's it. Mmmm. That's it, Tom-Tom."

Her head swiveled in gentle circles as she rocked forth and back in rhythm with his fingers. Tom added downward pressure as his hands slid apart, riding repeatedly from shoulder to ear, then back together. The area grew warm and fluid with friction. His hands separated, kneading flesh before rejoining. Out and back. Back and out. With each pass, he allowed his fingers to advance ever so slightly down the front, pressing tips into softer tissue that was not muscle. Out, back, down, back, mindful of his own ever-growing stiffness. Knowing this was crazy, but not caring.

Sally spoke in short phrases that were not entirely coherent but communicated a clear message just the same. "Ah, ah, yes, that's ... oh, right there, oh. Don't stop. Oh ... no ... yes."

His right hand was now traveling halfway into the hill country nestled below "77th Annual." She didn't stop him, so he didn't stop. He felt her sway, he heard her coo and moan, his own breath shortened. He edged his hand a little lower, as he bent toward her. Her only response was to lean her head back and to the left, soft sounds coming unbidden in a deeper, dusky tone. He took the plunge, sending his right hand toward a hardened hilltop while he gently kissed her neck. Her head rolled right and sought his lips, a gasp of breath filling his mouth as his hand cupped its target. Then everything blended into a strange and wonderful heat and dampness. Conscious thought was gone. He was left only with snippets of sensation. The texture of her lips. The feel of her tongue. Her nipple as it rolled between his fingers. Her muscular half nelson pulling him down with an irresistible force. Then they were on the floor, the bed a forgotten and unnecessary extravagance.

● Chapter 8

For the second time that morning, Tom woke with a start in a strange bed. This time the impetus was the single word, "shit," muttered by the naked woman beside him. Then he heard the unremitting wail of a cell phone's siren song. Sally's naked form vaulted effortlessly over him. He watched her dash toward the desk, muscles rippling with equine grace, looking even better in morning light than she had in fluorescent. The linger of her musky sweat reminded him of fresh-mowed hay.

Through bleary eyes, he caught the flash of the cell sitting next to a black plastic pistol in a black leather holster. But instead of heading directly to her phone, Sally paused to scoop up her tee and slide it on, as if her handlers would see her nakedness even via satellite. Tom watched as she glanced at the glowing phone number, then uttered, "shit" again, this time more insistently.

"Morning, Scott. Hey, I'm sorry about that report. I haven't gotten much sleep lately, and I guess it caught up to me." Her words came rapidly, in a panic to fill the void of recrimination with the excrement of excuse. Then she stopped abruptly. "What? The news? Why?" She paused to listen, wiping sleep from her eyes, then said, "Alright," and flicked the cell on speaker as she headed to the TV.

With a click and a hum, the TV screen flared to life. The letters "CNN" and "Breaking News" overlay a chaotic outdoor scene viewed from a low-flying helicopter. It was some kind of commercial venue, with a concrete overhang and a large parking lot. There were two ambulances that Tom could see, at least five police cars, and, oddly, a large bus with a sleek racing hound painted on the side. The caption below read, "Terror attack at Chattanooga bus depot. At least nine dead." A network reporter droned softly in the background.

"Shit!" Sally said, muting the set.

"You got that right," the voice on the phone said. "It broke about forty-five minutes ago. A van pulled in just as the 8:05 from

Atlanta was unloading. Five perps armed with AKs and handguns opened up. Allahu Akbar, black face scarves, the whole nine."

"No explosives?" Sally asked.

"No," Scott said. "No suicide bombers. And no suicides. These guys were professional. Did their business and drove off."

"They're still at large?"

"They are. And I'm en route. This is Knoxville's bailiwick, so I'm in command. But we'll be tapping resources from the Nashville and Louisville field offices as well." He paused for this to sink in. "Looks like I won't be choppering up this afternoon as planned."

Sally stared at Tom, jaw dropped, eyes glazed. For a moment, he saw a glimpse of an adolescent tomboy who missed her daddy.

"Sal, are you there?"

"Ah, yes. No. Of course. I understand. Do you want me to come back? I can ..."

"Negative, Special Agent Butterworth. You still have your fish to fry. But you'll be reporting to Hartsell now. Sorry, nothing I can do about that."

"No, of course not. I understand."

"Have you kept Dan in the loop?"

"Affirmative," Sally said, turning away from Tom. "Sent him a report last night."

"I'll give him a call," Scott said. "Just maintain an even strain, do your job, everything will be fine. And Sally?"

"Yes, sir?"

"Don't forget to breathe." The line went dead.

Sally passed a coffee to the right, then sipped her own, eyes glued to the tablet balanced against the steering wheel. The drive-through attendant handed her a bag and credit-card slip. Sally nodded at the girl's "Have a nice day." Driving forward, still looking at the report on her screen, she put the coffee in the cup holder and retrieved a greasy wrapper from the bag, handing it to her passenger.

"This is yours," Tom said.

"Huh?"

"I had the McMuffin, you had the bacon, egg, and cheese biscuit."

"Yeah, right," she said, barely registering what he'd said. She checked parking lot traffic then studied her tablet again.

"No, that's okay," Tom said. "I'll eat the biscuit."

"Okay," she said, finishing Matt's report.

Sally passed the paper sack to her passenger, then turned into highway traffic. Retrieving her cell from the dash, she punched a number then tossed it back among the dust, letting her Bluetooth take over.

"Morning, Matt. I'm just looking at the report now. Good job. We'll discuss it when I get there. I'm en route, ETA thirty minutes. Out."

"You are a delightful breakfast companion," Tom said.

"Huh?" Sally said, eyes on the road, expression blank.

"Shouldn't we talk about last night?" Getting no response, he spoke for her. "Yes, lets, Tom-Tom. You were fantastic, like a wild beast. I've never felt such pleasure." Sally felt her cheeks dimpling. "Ah shucks, ma'am. Twarnt nothin' any red-blooded-American epidermiologist-vet couldn't handle. Although you, little filly, were a buckin' bronco."

The dimples peaked as Sally laughed. "Okay, hotshot. It was good." She turned to him. "It was great. And yes, it was bound to happen sometime." Then she became more serious. "Just don't make too much of it, okay? I'm kind of busy with other things right now."

Tom shrugged. "I still say, don't worry so much. You're doing fine."

"How would you know? You've been with the FBI for less than twenty-four hours."

"Yes, but you've been there five years. And you graduated third in your class. Remember?"

"And you," Sally said, 'finished in the *middle* of the vet-school pack.'"

Tom smiled at her mimicry.

"I don't call ninth out of a hundred and two, the middle. And you failed to mention that you graduated suma in undergrad, with a 4.2 GPA. How the hell does somebody even get a 4.2?"

Tom shrugged. "Get more for an A in honors courses."

"And you finished first in your MPH program."

"After vet school, it was easy."

"And is that where you learned your amorous skills? Vet school?"

"There, undergrad, government. I believe in lifelong learning."

"Does that include hotel bars?"

"It's called continuing education."

Sally burst out laughing, as her cell buzzed and chimed. Smirking, Tom bit into bacon, egg, and cheese, while she punched the phone. "Butterworth," she said, still giggling.

A stern, familiar voice filled her ear. "Good morning, Special Agent."

"Ah, Special Agent in Charge Hartsell," Sally said. "Good morning."

"I'm assuming you heard about the incident in Tennessee."

"Yes, sir."

"Bad business, that. A very bad business. And I understand from Special Agent in Charge Crossfield that you've been informed about the changes in our investigation here in Ohio, administratively speaking."

"Yes, sir."

"Fine."

"I'm on my way to meet with Special Agent Clemens," Sally said. "Then I'll be returning to Columbus to monitor ..."

"That won't be necessary, special agent. I'm en route to a helicopter, ETA to the Columbus resident agency is sixty-five minutes. I'll take over hands-on operations, as was the plan with Special Agent in Charge Crossfield."

"Alright, sir. What are my orders?" She fought to keep her voice calm, but subservience to Hartsell was against her nature.

"You and Special Agent Clemens will work the Dayton bombing. Assist the local authorities and act as liaison with my office. Shuttle evidence, shoe-leather leads, you know the drill. I'm sending Special Agent Levine up there as my representative. You'll work directly under him. Clear?"

"Yes sir. Quite clear."

"Fine. Oh, special agent?"

"Yes, sir?"

"This *technical expert* you've hired." He made the title sound unclean. "This Dr. Toma, ah ..."

"Tomacinski, sir."

Tom paused mid bite at mention of his name.

"I don't think we'll be needing his services any longer. Please thank him for his cooperation and send him back to OSHA."

"NIOSH, Mr. Hartsell."

"Whatever. Hartsell, out."

"Well?" Tom said.

"Well," Sally replied. "I've been demoted to getting coffee. And you've been fired." She paused. "Nice knowing you."

Chapter 9

"Hello. Knoxville Parkway Tower. Can you hold, please? Thank you." The harried desk clerk signaled to a younger employee and then, smiling, turned to the next guest in line. "Hello, sir. Welcome to the Knoxville Parkway Tower. Checking in?"

"I sure am, pretty lady."

Assistant manager Cheryl Wagner smiled at the guest. He looked to be mid-thirtyish, maybe a little older. About her age. She guessed him to be another veterinarian. The Tower had hosted the Upper-South Veterinary Conference for the last eight years, although she'd only worked there for four. The desk would be busy from now through the start of the conference tomorrow morning.

The Tower was an older hotel, part of a late-seventies construction boom. At the time, it had been among the swankiest lodgings in Knoxville. The large, centrally located atrium was a first for the area and still presented a breathtaking view of all nine floors. But like other forty-odd-year-old ladies, the old girl needed new war paint and some cosmetic surgery to update décor that still suggested disco. But it was clean, well maintained, and efficiently run. A place at which Cheryl was proud to work. A good distraction after her divorce.

"Name, please?"

"Tomacinski. Dr. Tom-Tom Tomacinski." The new guest's knuckles pounded her counter with a paradiddle. "I'm checking in, while I'm checking you out."

Oh brother, she thought, smiling. "That's an unusual first name, Dr. Tomacinski." She pronounced it slowly, but correctly.

"Nickname," he said. "Cause I play the skins." His hands bongoed another tune. "You know, percussion, the sticks. Drums, sweetheart. Drums." He smiled.

He had a nice smile, although she couldn't see his eyes behind the dark glasses. The goatee beard made him look like the hippies in her parent's college photos, or maybe a beatnik. The gray suit was older style, almost 1950s, and the driving cap also fit that era. Well, it took all kinds, she thought.

"I see that your credit card has already been verified online, but I'll still need to make a photocopy."

"You got it, kitten."

Cheryl didn't think anything of the fact that he took the card from his breast pocket, not a wallet. Nor did she notice the subtle blur in the VISA trademark. Nor did she think it odd that he asked to keep the pen after signing in.

"I see you requested a room on the second floor?"

"Fear of heights."

"Well, I might be able to get you something on ground level. Let me check."

"No," he said loudly. "Two is fine." His voice returned to normal. "So long as I'm not in the nosebleed seats, I'll be good."

She shrugged. "Very well. We've got you in 236. Will one key be sufficient?"

"Fine. Unless you want to come up and join me?" His smile broadened at Cheryl's eye roll.

She slid over the paper folder with the room key. "Here you are. Can I get someone to help with your bag?"

"No need. It rocks and rolls." He wheeled the heavy suitcase forth and back. "Like me."

"Well then. Elevators are across the atrium." She pointed. "Have a nice meeting, Dr. Tomacinski."

He shot a finger-gun her way. "Tom-Tom. Call me Tom-Tom."

She smiled again. "Enjoy your stay."

The lobby camera watched him stop to put on a pair of leather driving gloves, before pressing the button for the second floor. Then he clutched his briefcase protectively, as he and his large roller-bag disappeared inside the car. The time was 5:22.

💣

Nobody had made coffee yet. Typical, Tom thought, pulling a filter from the pack. He'd spent the rest of Wednesday morning filling out papers separating him from the FBI. Perhaps the shortest stay on record. When Sally dropped him at his car, he'd suggested they keep in touch, maybe have dinner sometime. His mind replayed her reply. "Let's leave it alone, Tom-Tom." That night, he got drunk. Now he was hung over and heading back to the government routine that hadn't seemed boring before.

As he poured water into the carafe, a familiar voice said, "What are *you* doing here?"

"I work here, Lynne. Remember?"

"But you've been seconded."

"You say that like I've lost my virginity." He shook his head. "It didn't work out."

"Nobody called *me*."

"Take my word for it," Tom said, dipping a measuring spoon into a can of Chock full o'Nuts.

"How am I supposed to bill the two days?"

"Say I was seconded by a beautiful FBI agent."

"I don't have a code for that."

"Fine. Call it personal time." Mumbling, he added, "At least it was personal to me."

"That will leave you with only two personal days."

"I'll risk it," Tom said, as he pressed the "On" button. Putting creamer and sweetener in his cup, he added, "That's the least of my problems."

Walking down the hall, he wondered what Sally was doing now. Whatever it was, she'd be in a foul mood. He couldn't blame her. He thought about calling but knew that was the wrong thing to do. So, he thought about the way her kisses felt on his lips and on his neck. He remembered how her body felt, like sprung steel under a layer of smooth sensuality that was unbelievably arousing. Quickening his steps, he hurried to the privacy of his office.

The hot coffee felt good on his stomach as he entered his drab, workplace-home for the past half-decade. The green-metal desk with the black, rubberized surface held a couple of notes, as well as two articles he'd requested from the library. The red light on his phone was blinking, indicating a voice-mail message. He punched the speaker button, filling the room with a dial tone, then dialed his own number, followed by his pass code. A chill rode his spine from the mechanical voice, which reminded him of Conrad.

"You have ... two ... voice-mail messages. To get your messages ..."

He pressed the star key.

"First voice-mail message."

The mechanical tones listed a 937 telephone number, followed by a 1:23 p.m. time stamp from Monday. During the brief pause, he put down his coffee cup and sat in his old desk chair. Maybe the message was from Sally. He shook his head—*unlikely*. Maybe *he* should call *her*. She might appreciate some cheering up. He shook his head again and filed the thought away with other desperately obsessive ideas sure to lose a prospective lover. Especially one who put business first.

A human voice said, "Hi Tom. This is Bob Hughes at Maxwell. Sorry to hear about your bad luck. Nice hotel we put you up in, huh. Geez. Anyway, hope you're okay. We've rescheduled the meeting for one p.m. this Thursday. Give me a call if that's a problem. Bye."

"Why today," he muttered.

Maxwell Diesel Systems was north of Dayton, near the airport. It'd take him well over an hour to drive there, even from work, which was closer than his apartment. He looked at his calendar. He had a staff meeting at ten. He could head out right after, grab some lunch (something bland), and still make the meeting. And he could call it a day after that, thank God.

"Second voice-mail message."

Now an 800 number was followed by, "Today, 8:12 a.m."

"Good morning," said a human voice from the phone. "This is Darcel Washington of Universal VISA and MasterCard. This message is for Thomas Tomacinski."

"Call me Tom-Tom," he said to the empty office.

"Please contact me about possible fraudulent activity on your credit card." The voice gave an 800 number before concluding, "Thank you."

"Huh," he said. "Why didn't she call my house?" Tom wondered if it was some scam artist trying to get his credit card info. He sometimes used his work number on websites, to avoid phone spam at home. But had he done that with his VISA? He wrote the name and number on a sticky note and shoved it in his shirt pocket.

"Morning, Tom." Karen, the department statistician, poked her head in the door. "You going to the staff meeting?"

"Yeah," Tom said, grabbing his coffee. "I'll walk over with you."

💣

"In conclusion, lung cancer is still the greatest risk," Tom said to the attentive audience of diesel engineers and corporate administrators. The lunchtime chicken sandwich had settled his stomach, and Tylenol and coffee, his headache. He was feeling almost human, if a little tired. He'd be glad to see the bridge—and home. He'd hardly thought of Sally all day. Only every few minutes.

"But if you can keep exposure below four hundred micrograms per cubic-meter-months, then risk should be minimal. Any questions?"

Everyone looked at each other and then applauded politely. A portly man in a checked sport coat approached as the meeting broke up.

"Nice presentation, Tom. We really appreciate you helping out with this. A lot of government people, well, you know."

Tom smiled. "My pleasure, Bob. How's that new software working out?"

"Great. Thanks for the recommendation. You know your stuff."

"De nada."

Bob smiled. "Sorry this couldn't have been an early morning meeting, so we could put you up in another hotel." He noticed Tom's grin darken. "Geez. Sorry about that. Not funny, I guess. I'm glad you were okay. Did anybody die?"

"Two," Tom said. "Two people died."

"What caused it? Do they know?"

Tom shuddered slightly, then shrugged.

"I talked to Lynne. She said you'd been lent to the FBI. Is that true?"

"She told you that, huh?"

"Well, actually she said seconded."

"Shortest secondment in history," Tom said.

"What was it like?"

Tom shrugged again. "One-night stand."

Tom placed the laser pointer into his pocket. A piece of paper was in the way, so he removed it. For a moment, he stared at the number in confusion. Then he remembered.

"Hey, Bob?" The departing engineer turned Tom's way. "You got a phone I can use?"

"Sure. Use the one here in the conference room. Stay as long as you like." He closed the door, leaving Tom alone amid the papers and coffee cups.

Picking up the handset, Tom dialed the 800 number. The phone rang twice before a voice said, "Universal VISA and MasterCard."

"Darcel Washington, please."

"This is Darcel. How may I help you?"

"Hi, this is Thomas Tomacinski. You called me this morning about fraudulent activity on my Visa?"

"Yes, thank you for returning my call."

She read off the digits of his card, which sounded familiar enough to be correct. He said it was.

"This card was used on Monday to register for two nights at the Parkway Tower Hotel near Knoxville, Tennessee. Was that an authorized purchase?"

"This past Monday?" Tom asked. "Three days ago?"

"That's right. 7:03 p.m."

"Two nights in Knoxville?"

"Correct. Today and Friday."

"Well, I don't see how that could be me," Tom replied. "In fact, I need to get a replacement for my card."

"Was it lost?"

"Destroyed," he said. "It's a long story." Something struck him odd about the hotel name, but he dismissed it. "So, it definitely wasn't me. Are there any other questionable charges?"

She read off several, all from several days earlier, including some at the Comfort Rest Inns and Suites. He thought of Sally.

"What was that last one?"

"Reasonable Rental Car?" Ms. Washington said.

"I've never even heard of them."

"So, you didn't rent a car from them this morning in Fort Mitchell, Kentucky?"

"That's not far from where I live, but no. I did not."

"So those are the only two fraudulent charges?"

"I guess so," Tom said. Something nagged his brain but couldn't fight its way past hangover fatigue.

"Fine. I'll disallow those charges. They'll show up on your bill, along with a credit refund. I'll also issue you a new card to replace the damaged one. You should receive it in seven to ten business days. Is there anything else I can help you with today?"

"No," Tom said. "I guess not." They said goodbye and hung up.

💣

Something kept nagging at Tom. It nagged its way through rush hour traffic. It was still there when he cursed the Cincinnati stop-

and-go on I-75. It detracted from his sigh of relief as he saw the bridge over the Ohio River. But it didn't reveal itself until he was in Kentucky. He put on his shades against the afternoon sun peeking through the overcast when it came to him. That name, Parkway.

That was one of the chains that Robinson had mentioned. He'd mentioned it two days and a thousand years ago when he and Sally sat in the fancy study of his fancy home. Well, so what. All six companies in the Association were being extorted, so most any hotel could be in one of their chains. Coincidence, nothing more. He was attuned to the name because he'd heard it. Like when you buy a new car, and suddenly notice how many of that model are on the street. Coincidence. But was it?

Was it mere coincidence that his credit card got a fraudulent hotel bill at the same time Conrad Hilton was extorting hotels? And the rental car? Conrad had used a rental car, as well. It showed up in the surveillance video. But there was something more. What was it? What was it about Parkway?

Robinson had mentioned the five other hotel chains on his call. There was Parkway Group, Travel-Eze, and one with a southern name. Was it Magnolia? No, it was Belvedere. Belvedere was associated with the sole woman on the call. Barbara something. She was for paying up. But two other members were decidedly opposed. A Bob ... Bob Rankin? And a George King, or was it Prince? Rankin headed up Travel-Eze. George was the Parkway big shot. He thought it was a mistake to pay. He maybe badmouthed our boy Conrad. And our boy Conrad had been listening. Sally figured this would make Conrad sore. He'd plan another little demonstration. Would he hit Barbara or Robinson? No, they were for paying, or at least weren't against it. He'd hit one of the two chains that pissed him off. Parkway or Travel-Eze.

A tailgater honked in his rearview, so Tom edged right to let him pass. That was his exit up ahead. But his mind wouldn't let it go. There were too many coincidences, and there was something else. What?

Sally had wondered where Conrad would strike. They jawed it over and decided he might hit a hotel with an atrium. Those were tall, with a large open space. And they were usually round. Round, like a tower. Could that be the where? The Parkway Tower.

His foot slipped from the accelerator, car slowing. Another horn honked behind him. An angry motorist passed, flipping Tom the bird.

So, what about the when? He heard Darcel Washington say, "Correct. Today and Friday." A flashbulb popped in Tom's head. "Shit!"

He scanned the car's cabin, looking for his cell. He remembered it was now a molten puddle in Dayton. He edged into the exit lane. Several thousand thoughts wracked his brain in maybe two seconds. Then he made his decision. Turning the wheel left, the car jerked from the off-ramp. Tom ignored a loud horn blast and the screech of brakes as he accelerated. With luck, he'd be in Knoxville by eight. He hoped that wouldn't be too late.

💣 *Chapter 10*

"Good evening. Welcome to the Knoxville Parkway Tower. May I help you?"

"Yes, I'm looking for ..." Who? Who was Tom looking for? He wasn't sure.

"Sir?" The young desk clerk eyed him and smiled.

If Conrad was here, who would he be? Ollie Groenhaage? No. Then it hit Tom like a pole ax.

"Do you have a Thomas Tomacinski registered here?"

"Is he with the veterinary meeting?"

Tom finally noticed the scrolling sign in the lobby welcoming distinguished members of the Mid-South Veterinary Medical Association. "Yes. I believe so."

The clerk, Sarah, checked her computer. "Why, yes. He just registered today. Would you like me to ring his room?"

"No, no. If you could tell me which room he's in, I'll stop by and say hello."

"I'm sorry, sir. I can't give out that information. Would you like me to ring him? He could give it to you."

"Ah, no." Tom struggled for something to say. "I'm, I'm with the FBI." He patted his pocket for his temporary credentials, but he'd surrendered them yesterday. This was not going well.

"Oh, my. If you'll excuse me one moment, I'll get my manager."

Tom headed the line of impatient guests waiting to check in, while Sarah approached an attractive middle-aged woman in a similar red blazer. They parlayed for a moment, then both returned.

"I'm Ms. Wagner, may I help you?" She gave Tom a smile that softened her professional demeanor.

"Yes." Tom cleared his throat and tried to sound impressive. "I'm Special Agent Daniel Hartsell with the FBI. I'm looking for a Dr. Thomas Tomacinski."

"Oh," she said, clearly a touch of respect in her voice. "May I see your identification, Agent Hartsell?"

"Well. Ah, you see..."

Ms. Wagner's smile dimmed as she stepped in front of the puzzled Sarah.

"Well ..." Tom lowered his voice. "I'm not really with the FBI, but I need to find out about someone who checked in today under the name Thomas Tomacinski."

"I see," Cheryl Wagner said, although it was plain she didn't. "Why don't I ring his room and you can speak with him directly."

"No," Tom said. "No, we can't do that."

"And why not?"

Tom lowered his voice further and leaned in. "You see, *I'm* Dr. Thomas Tomacinski."

"You're Tom-Tom Tomacinski?"

"What? No, well, I mean, yes. You see, this man, this other man, the one who checked in today, he's an impostor." This was starting to sound like a Hitchcock movie or a story by Rod Serling. Tom half expected to see himself walk off the elevator.

"May I see *your* identification, *Doctor*?"

Tom patted his trousers, then remembered that his wallet was a piece of used kindling. "Ah, well you see, I don't have any ID. My wallet, my ID, my credit cards, all that was destroyed in a fire."

Ms. Wagner only stared. "I'm going to have to ask you to leave, sir. As you can see, we have many guests to check in."

"You don't understand." He tried not to yell. "This guy, this impostor, is a bad guy." Now he sounded like dialogue from a pre-teen playwright. "What I mean is, he's a criminal. I mean I think he may be a criminal, an extortionist. That is ..."

"Then perhaps I should call security?"

"Well, okay. If you think that's the thing to do."

"Sarah," Ms. Wagner said. "Please call security and tell them there's a disturbance at the front desk. Ask them to please escort this gentleman out."

"Me? No, not me," Tom said, as Sarah picked up the phone. "I'm not the problem. I mean, I'm not the disturbance. I'm Thomas Tomacinski. Dr. Thomas Tomacinski. The real one."

"Of course," Ms. Wagner said, a cold smile on her lips. "I'm sure you are, but as you can see, we are very busy. So, if you would step aside while you wait. I'd appreciate it."

Tom leaned back in and lowered his voice again. "You don't get it. This impostor, he might be, I mean I think he's a, you know a ..."

"A what?"

Tom leaned closer to whisper.

"Is there a problem?" A well-groomed black man in a same-color-red uniform stood next to Tom, one hand on Tom's sleeve.

"Yes," Ms. Wagner said. "Thank you, Lucius. This gentleman needs to be escorted outside."

"Right this way, sir." An iron grip on Tom's arm angled him out of line and toward the exit.

Tom broke free. "He's a bomber!"

"A bomber?" Cheryl Wagner yelped.

"Bomb?" cried the next man in line.

"Yes. A bomb. There may be a bomb in this hotel. On the second or third floor."

"There's a bomb in 236?" Sarah gasped.

"That's his room, isn't it?" Tom yelled. "He requested second floor, didn't he?"

"Sir, I'll have to ask you to keep your voice down."

The lobby was turning into a scene from *Titanic*. Panicked guests were leaving the queue, milling into mob-like groups or rushing for the exits. The part of Tom's mind not in the vise-grip of an ex-Marine was thinking this would be an interesting case study in mob panic. He could see the title, C*ivil Unrest: Part I. Descent into Anarchy*.

"Please, everyone. Quiet please!" Cheryl Wagner's clear diction rose above the hubbub, projecting reassurance. Lucius took his cue from the assistant manager.

"Y'all quiet down. You hear?" boomed the cadence of an ex-drill-instructor with ten years in the Corps.

The mob began to calm. Those crowding the exits paused to look back.

"There is no cause for alarm," Cheryl said. "This gentleman may have some form of mental illness, so we've requested the authorities. Lucius, please take Mr. Toma... ah, this gentleman to the holding area until they arrive."

"This way please, sir."

And just like that, order was restored. Murmurs still rose from the assembled guests, but they left their groups and rejoined the line, jockeying for their original positions. Tom was propelled relentlessly toward a side door in an inconspicuous hall beside the counter area. In moments, he'd be securely out of sight, his presence no more than an interesting anecdote that guests could embellish for spouses and coworkers. Those guests who weren't burnt to a crisp or dead from smoke inhalation.

Tom's anxiety rose with each step. He had no hard evidence that Conrad had placed a bomb in 236, or even if he'd been here. But he had to have been here. The bomb had to be here. That was the only thing that made sense. The question now was when would it go off? Was it set for late at night, when guests were sleeping in their rooms? That's the scenario he'd blue-skied with Sally. But seeing the panic in the crowded lobby at the mere mention of a bomb, he wondered if the greedy little sociopath would plan to hit at check-in rush hour. That peak time after the flights had landed, the taxis and rental cars driven into town for a late lunch before check-in. Late afternoon, early evening. Right about now. Something told Tom they might be running out of time. It could be hours before the cops got it all sorted out. They might not have hours. They might not have minutes.

He and Lucius were level with the check-in counter, the steel door with "Authorized Personnel Only" just steps away. Tom stumbled, almost going to one knee, hand on his ankle. "Ow."

Drill Instructor Lucius reverted to helpful hotel employee. "Are you alright, sir?"

His grip on Tom loosened. "I think I twisted something."

"Let me help." The security guard let go to reposition his arm around Tom's waist. It only took a second, but that was enough.

Tom bolted for the counter. One hand hit the marble desk, while his legs vaulted over. Back counter personnel screamed. Ms. Wagner yelled, "Hey!" Tom ignored them and kept his eyes on the prize on the wall, approximately five feet off the ground, midway between the ends of the back counter workspace. It was red and black, about four inches square. Before Lucius, Cheryl Wagner, or anyone else could intervene, Tom pulled the handle in the middle of the fire alarm.

To Tom's mind, time slowed. Silence reigned for a fraction of a second that seemed like minutes. He saw the black handle in his grasp. He saw the look of shock on Cheryl Wagner's face. He heard nothing, as if he'd suddenly been immersed in water. Then he bobbed back to the surface and breathed.

A loud claxon echoed off the walls, plants, and tile, carrying up all nine floors of the atrium. Lights flashed, strobing out a universal distress signal. Then an authoritative, if mechanical, baritone announced, "This is a fire emergency. Please evacuate the hotel. Do not use the elevators. Evacuate the building. Use the stairs, not the elevators. This is a fire emergency."

Then an odd thing happened. The crowd in the lobby, the ones who moments before had panicked at the mention of a bomb, responded like obedient children lining up for recess. Even those who had seen the events of the last several minutes began their orderly departure. They walked toward the exit doors, gentlemen holding them open for ladies or men with canes, smiling politely. The stairway doors opened and closed in a kaleidoscopic fashion, guests leaving upper floors, one by one, then in little groups of three or four.

"Shit," Cheryl Wagner said.

"Shit," Lucius said, regaining his hold on Tom's arm.

"Thank God," Tom said.

Tom sat in the squad car, hands securely behind his back, courtesy of bracelets provided by Knoxville PD. The car smelled a bit funky, like too much fast food and too much fear had spilled inside. Through the window, he could see the crowd milling in the late-evening light. There was a fire truck, slickered men leaning and watching. There was an EMT vehicle, its squat, blocky outline awaiting possible passengers. There were several dozen cars in the parking lot, including several police cruisers. And there was one large, gray van with the words Knoxville PD Bomb Disposal lettered on the side.

The door on his left opened and a cop got in. He had to be a cop, even in civilian clothes. The sport coat was shabby and didn't quite match the shiny pants. His tie was wide, a holdover from decades past, and the collar of his white shirt was frayed. He definitely wasn't FBI. Tom thought of Sally.

The cop unbuttoned his sport coat, which bunched too tight on his gut. "Hi. I'm Detective Sergeant Doolittle Powell. You can call me Doo." His accent was Tennessee, through and through. "Okay if I call you Tom-Tom? They tell me you like that nickname."

"Who told you that?"

"Assistant Manager. Ms. Wagner." He winked. "She's a cutie, huh?"

"How would she know what I like?"

Doolittle shrugged. "Said that's what *you* said when you checked in. Said you played the drums."

"The drums?"

"Or do you guys call them the skins?" He smiled.

Tom gritted his teeth. "I don't know what you're talking about. I never checked in. She must be talking about the other guy, the impostor."

The detective nodded appreciatively. "She told us about that, too. Also told us you were kind of excitable. Why do you think that is?"

This was getting nowhere. "Listen," Tom said. "I have reason to believe there is a bomb in that hotel. Probably room 236. You have to check it out."

"Oh, we are," Doolittle said. "Have to check out every bomb threat. The bomb-squad boys ought to be in there about now. You wanna watch?"

"Inside?" Tom asked.

"Closed circuit," Doolittle answered.

His new friend Doolittle helped Tom out of the cruiser and led him to the bomb-squad van.

"If I promise to be good, can you remove these?" Tom shook his wrists.

Detective Powell smiled. "Sure." He removed the handcuffs and placed them in his jacket pocket. "But remember your promise." He followed Tom into the van.

Inside smelled of oil, rubber, metal, and sweat. Multi-drawer toolboxes were neatly lined on both sides, with a rack holding axes, sledges, and an impact ram for opening doors. The back-wall shelves were piled with bulletproof vests and ballistic shields stacked in an orderly fashion. In the rear corner, a tech decked out in body armor watched a video monitor. A voice spoke from the speaker beside him.

"Have gained entry to Room 236." The video image was a nondescript, run-of-the-mill hotel room. The camera panned over a bed, carpet, bureau, and writing desk. Overhead lights flicked on.

"Roger that," the tech manning the monitor said.

"Beginning search," the cameraman said.

"Roger," the monitor man answered.

"Sorry there's no place to sit," Doolittle said.

Tom shrugged and watched the video camera search the bathroom. Then he saw images of the bureau drawers, the desk, and under the bed. The man with the camera called off each item as it was searched, saying "Lower bureau drawer, clear. Middle bureau drawer, clear" and so on. Next, the image panned past the bed to the closet situated beside the entry door. The closet door opened slowly, revealing a folding camp table, empty shelves, and empty hangers, one with a plastic laundry bag clipped to metal hasps. A higher view showed something more interesting. On the top shelf, a large roller bag was shoved against the outside wall. Next to it sat a plain leather and nylon briefcase. The soft-sided case was standing upright, the bottom squashed out to keep it vertical.

"Okay, Clyde," the man in the van said. "That could be it. Let's send in the remote."

"Negative, Chip," Clyde said. "Swing arm ain't long enough on the danged thing."

"Okay," Chip said. "Let's send in a canine to make sure we got something and to double-check that the rest is clean."

"How's Duke gonna get on the top shelf to check?" Clyde said. There was a brief pause. "Tell you what. Why don't I pass a DetectaThreat over the briefcase? If it's negative, we can take a look inside. Guy might just be storing his luggage out of the way."

Chip thought for a moment. "Roger that. But watch your six."

"Always, partner."

Tom watched as a black device about the size of a large flashlight rose into view of Clyde's visor cam. A digital readout on the top showed a gray circle. The tip of the detector hung suspended for a moment, then rested against the top of the case, near the zipper. Tom watched Clyde run it gently back and forth, then pause a moment. Clyde said, "Looks negative. I'll..." Tom saw the small gray circle on the detector suddenly darken and glow. He could read "Threat Detected" above the circle.

"Back off," Chip ordered.

"Roger," Clyde said. "Backing off." The briefcase tilted out of vertical as the weight of the DetectaThreat wand was removed. Then the screen went gray and fuzzy. Then Tom heard the explosion.

Chapter 11

"Hello, pater." Per usual, the voice from the phone sounded young and petulant.

"What's with this pater crap? I'm your father. Remember?" George King II, CEO of Parkway Inns and Suites, was not happy with his namesake.

"How could I forget?" Georgie King III asked.

"And you can dump the attitude. I've had about enough of that."

"What do you want, Father?"

"That's better." George Sr. killed the speaker and tucked the handset under his chin. "Where have you been? This is the third time I tried to reach you."

"Oh, here and there."

"What'd I tell you about attitude?" Cold silence radiated from the other end of the line. "I've got better things to do than chase your ass down. I've got pressures, responsibilities. Not that you'd understand about that."

"What do you want, Father?"

"I got a call from Dean Schirmer at State."

"How is dear old Paul? Weren't you and he sorority sisters at I Felta Thigh?"

King white-knuckled the phone. "Listen, you little shit. Just keep it up. I'll come over there and beat the living crap out of you. See if I don't."

"What do you want, Father?"

George Sr. grabbed the bottle of Tums off his desk. "Dean Schirmer tells me that you haven't been to class in a month. A *month*. In fact, he's not even sure which classes you're taking."

"I've been busy."

"With what?"

"Oh, this and ... stuff."

George Sr. turned his eyes to heaven and counted to three. Then, chewing two antacids, he said, "I don't get this. You're smart. Got an IQ up in the stratosphere somewhere." He shook his head. "Must come from my side of the family. God knows your mother is no rocket scientist."

"Let's leave Mother out of it, pater."

"If you're so damn smart, why are you drifting through your college years like crap through a sewer?"

"My, oh my, Father. How you can turn a phrase."

"I figured you'd go into business. Maybe hotel/restaurant management. Follow me. But you said you wanted to go off on your own. Do computers. Did I squawk? What did I say?"

"Whatever it was, I'm sure it was loud."

"I told you to *can* the attitude!" Another pause. "What did I say? Do you remember? I said, okay. *Fine*. At least you can earn a living."

"You were very charitable, pater. As usual," Georgie said.

"Then you dumped that after a year."

"The classes bored me."

George Sr. was screaming now. "For seventy-five grand a year, you can be bored a little. Do you think I *liked* all my college classes?"

Georgie sighed. "What's your point, Father?"

"The point is, you dropped out of computers and into ... what? Theater. *Theater* for Christ sake. Wanted to play dress up with your friend Robbie."

"It's called dramatic arts, Father, not dress up."

"Dramatic arts? Give me a frickin' break. Try reciting Shakespeare sonnets door to door, see how much money you make." George Sr. clenched the handset harder. "And now you drop out of theater? What's next, Black studies?"

"It was too plebeian. And even the teachers had no talent."

George Sr. was barely listening. "And the worst part is, I don't even hear about it from you. I gotta hear it third-hand from Charles Robinson. A business colleague. At least *his* son talks to him."

"Robbie Robinson is your idea of the perfect son?"

"All I know is, he's better than mine."

The barb struck home. "Oh Father, I could tell you stories about darling little Robbie."

"I don't give a shit about Robbie Robinson. I care about you. How do you think it makes me look when I gotta hear things about you third-hand? Or when the dean of students tells me you've skipped out? I'll tell you how I look. I look like crap."

"Well," his son said, after a pause. "We can't have that."

"For your information, smart ass, the semester is about over. Finals are this week. But, in case you're interested, I managed to persuade Paul Schirmer to give you a withdrawal for the semester. For *medical* reasons."

"You've always been very persuasive, Father."

"So, you won't flunk out."

"What do you want me to say, Father?"

"For starters, how about thank you, Dad?"

"Thank you, Dad. Are we done?"

George Sr. rubbed at the headache starting in his temple. "No. I want you to come home for the summer."

"I can't do that."

"Why not?' George Sr. said. "There's nothing holding you in Columbus, is there?" Silence. "No classes, no job. Not even a frickin' girlfriend. My God, sometimes I think you must be a fairy. I was banging coeds two at a time at your age."

"Did they wear raccoon coats and say boola boola?"

George Sr. screamed into the phone. "That's enough of that shit." Now his throat hurt as well as his head. In a softer voice, he said, "I want you home. We'll have a little *chat*, and then I'll put you to work in one of the hotels. Try and build a little backbone. A little work ethic. Respect for a dollar, and what it takes to earn it."

"Money is no problem when one has computer skills, Father."

"Then at the end of the summer, we'll have another little chat."

"About what?"

"About whether you straighten up and fly right, or whether I cut you off without a cent. No allowance, no trust fund, no nothing." The silence from the other end was deafening. "Well? No smart-ass reply to that, hot shot?"

The only reply was a mechanical, "Call ended."

💣 *Chapter 12*

The room reminded Tom of his office in Cincinnati: same cin-der-block walls, painted green instead of yellow. Same linoleum floor, possibly off the same roll. Same metal desk and old, sprung chairs. But instead of his papers and journal articles, the desk held a digital recorder and Styrofoam cups. And instead of his framed photo of Errol Flynn, the wall held a large mirror, which was real-ly one-way glass. And there was a video camera near the ceiling, watching it all.

"You want a cigarette? Cigar? Chew?"

Tom looked up at his new best bud, Doolittle Powell. "I don't smoke."

The detective nodded. "Okay, Tom-Tom." The chubby cop leaned back into his perch atop the desk. "Here's the thing. I want to help you out, but we got a dead police officer." His tone dark-ened. "Clyde Mowbray. Man with a wife and two little ones. We take that very serious. Ya hear?"

Tom nodded. "I understand. And I'm sorry. But I keep telling you. I didn't plant that bomb."

"Uh, huh. Then how'd you know it was there?"

"I told you. I've told you over and over. It was a hunch. A hunch based on the pattern of this, this Conrad Hilton guy."

"Famous hotel owner?"

"Yes. No. I mean, the guy pretending to be a famous hotel ... I mean, an extortionist using the name of a famous ... Just call the FBI. Cincinnati field office. Ask for ..."

"I know," Doolittle interrupted. "Sally Butterworth. We called. She's in the field. Gonna get back. At least that part of your story is true."

"I keep telling you, all my story is true."

Doolittle nodded, thoughtfully. "Thing I don't understand, Tom-Tom. Why'd you check into the Parkway, ask for a room on the second floor? How'd a bomb get in your room?"

Tom massaged his temples. He'd waived Miranda, thinking things would be easy to explain. He'd been wrong. "For the millionth time, that wasn't me. Check at the desk, whoever checked him in. He was using my name."

Doolittle pointed, thoughtfully. "Now why do ya think he'd do that? Use your name. Your credit card. You know this guy? He a friend of yours? Colleague?"

"No," Tom said.

Doolittle hunched his shoulders in reply.

Tom sipped cold, bad coffee. "I don't know why. I only have a hunch."

"Y'all got a lot of hunches, huh? Got a hunch this guy was gonna blow the Parkway. Got another hunch he overheard someone talking about you. Maybe this FBI lady named Butterworth. Hunch he'd think it a good gag to use your name. Blow up a hotel. For kicks?"

Tom started to answer, but the look in Powell's eye said it wasn't any good. Powell was buying time. Trying to wear him down. Looking for chinks in his story. Inconsistencies. Tom sighed. "I want a lawyer."

💣※

Cheryl Wagner stared at the video screen, then rubbed her eyes. She was tired. She was stressed. She wanted a drink—boy howdy did she want a drink. She wanted to go home. All she needed to say was, "Yes. That could be him." And she could go home. But it wasn't him. She was sure of it. At least she thought she was sure. It seemed so long ago now.

"Well?" the lady detective said.

Cheryl shook her head. "I'm sorry. I don't think that's him."

"You sure?"

Cheryl looked again at the grainy image. She listened to the voice say, "I don't know why." She leaned closer. Then she shook her head. "Maybe not a hundred percent. But pretty sure."

"You said he was wearing dark glasses. A hat. Old style suit. Maybe some kind of disguise. How can you be sure?"

"Because this guy's better looking."

"Oh," the detective said. "Ya think so?"

"I mean, he's taller. More muscular. Look at those shoulders. That chest."

"What exactly did you and he chat about?" the cop asked, a subtle smile on her face.

"He sounded crazy, okay?" Cheryl said. "What I meant was, this guy works out. I don't think you can fake that."

"Maybe he slouched," the detective said. "You know, the first time. Held himself scrunched up. You want a look at that video again?"

Cheryl shook her head. "He wasn't slouching. He was, sort of, I don't know, out there." She waved her hands. "Flamboyant. Having a good time. And the voice is different on the second guy. It's deeper, more masculine."

"Maybe he disguised that too."

"And this guy's face is rounder, got kind of a boyish look." Cheryl added, "And why would he try and warn me about the bomb if he planted it?"

The cop shrugged. "Kicks? Lots of fire bugs start fires just so they can put them out. Be a hero."

"But this guy *was* a hero," Cheryl said. "A real one. Saved a lot of lives." She'd finally had enough. "I'm telling you. It's not him."

"But not a hundred percent?"

Cheryl got up. "One hundred percent." She grabbed her purse. "I'd like to go home now."

Tom stared in the mirror, watching his reflection. He lifted one hand; his mirror-self responded. He made a funny face. In the movies, the older ones with Al Pacino or Robert De Niro, there'd be another fat detective behind the glass, watching. Maybe an eyewitness, confirming that 'Yes, officer. That's the one.' But Tom suspected that cameras were the main surveillance tool these days. He looked up at the fish-eye. Thought about giving it the finger. But what would that prove? So, he kept staring at the mirror and waiting for his mouthpiece.

The door opened. But instead of a public defender in blue jeans and threadbare sport coat, there was his old buddy Doolittle.

"Good news, Doc. You're in the clear. Eyewitness says you ain't it." Tom rose, with a sigh. "We also heard from the FBI. Your Agent Butterworth vouches for you."

"Am I free to go?"

Powell gave him a queer look. "Well, yes and no." The detective sat back at the desk, signaling to the chair. Tom hesitated. Doolittle smiled and signaled again. Tom sat.

"You been cleared. So, we can't hold you. But the thing of it is, we need your help." His tone deepened. "This is gonna get turned over to the feds soon. Your story says so. So does your Agent Butterworth." He leaned forward. "But we got a brother officer slain doin' the job. Like I said, we take that serious."

"I don't know what else I can do." Tom said. "I've told you everything I know." He stared at Powell. "At least I tried to."

Doolittle shrugged. "Just doin' my job, Tom-Tom. No hard feelings."

"So," Tom said. "What else can I do?"

"We want in."

"In?"

Doolittle nodded. "FBI takes over, me and mine are reduced to fetch and carry. Surveillance. Do this. Do that. Yes, sir, boss." He smiled again. He had a friendly smile. "Right now, you're our best hope for sidesteppin' that. Becoming equal partners."

"How? I'm not FBI. I was seconded for one day. Period."

"You was what?"

"Second ... never mind. I'm saying, I was involved in the investigation for one day. Technical expert. And then I was fired. That's it."

Doolittle winked. "But the perp used *your* name. *Your* credit card. Pretended to *be* you. You think he did that cause he thought you was boring? You think he's gonna lose interest, now you spoiled his fun a little bit?"

Tom stared, mouth agape. He hadn't considered this.

"My pa was fourth-generation moonshiner." Doolittle touched his nose. "I can still sniff out white dog on the boil a mile away." He pointed at Tom. "You're white lightning, boy."

"Listen, Detective Powell."

"Doo."

"Okay, Doo. I'd like to help you. But right now, I can't even help myself. I've got something like twelve dollars in emergency cash left in my pocket and no credit cards. I drove down here, without even a license, on a wild hunch. I'm tired, sore, and a little hung over. And I'm looking at either a four-hour drive in the dark or sleeping in my car."

Doolittle beamed his biggest cracker grin. "Y'all can crash at my place. I can give you some supper and a sofa to sleep on. Maybe a little hair of the dog for that hangover." He winked at Tom.

"Won't your wife mind you showing up with company at midnight?"

"She probably would," Doolittle said, "if she hadn't divorced me." His grin never dimmed. "I'm guessing you're in the same club?"

"I'm chapter president," Tom said.

"You're alright, Tom-Tom," Doolittle said, laughing.

"Really, just one Tom ... never mind."

"Do you have a moment, Special Agent Hartsell?"

"Special Agent Butterworth. Just the lady I wanted to see."

Dan Hartsell was collecting papers from a file folder. His suit coat was off, but shirt and tie were crisp and clean per Bureau policy—and his own personal one. The coat was hung neatly on a coat rack, hanger blocking the shoulders. Next to it was a blue windbreaker with FBI on the back in white letters. Draped over his blotter was a standard-issue Kevlar vest. It and the folder were the only two items on the meticulously clean wooden desk.

"Excuse me, sir, but I assume you've heard about the bombing in Knoxville."

Hartsell nodded. "Very unfortunate."

"Yes sir. I'd like to ask your permission to follow the Conrad Hilton investigation down there."

"That's Knoxville's bailiwick, special agent."

"Yes sir. I understand that. But I'm guessing they're still busy with the terrorist incident in Chattanooga. And I *am* out of the Knoxville field office."

"But attached to this office for the time being."

"Yes sir, I understand that ..."

"Besides, I think I have something you'll like better." He smiled. A rare event.

"Sir?" Hartsell handed her some papers.

"Know what that is, Special Agent Butterworth?"

"Ah, yes sir. It appears to be a financial summary for the Bungalow 5 chain."

"Do you know what all that red ink means?"

Sally scanned the bottom. "It means the chain is not doing well financially, sir."

"And what about this?" Hartsell said, handing her more papers.

"This would appear to be a 66-1 form pertaining to the personal finances of C. Roger Caldwell, CEO of Bungalow 5."

"And what does that report say?" Hartsell's smile had morphed into a smirk.

She scanned the form. "It says that Mr. Caldwell's finances are in about the same shape as those of his company."

"Worse," Hartsell answered. "The red ink on Mr. Caldwell's financial page comes largely from gambling. Mostly sports betting, if you can believe that."

"I can. It did in Charley Hustle," Sally said.

"And what is the extent of Mr. Caldwell's debt, special agent?"

Sally studied the form. "It would appear to be substantial, sir. One point seven million to be exact."

"One point seven five million, to be exact," Hartsell corrected. "That special agent, is motive for extortion."

"Well ... yes sir, I suppose, but ..."

"Compare those two summaries, special agent. Compare them closely." Sally held them side by side. "You'll see two highlighted corporate debits, one for one hundred and twenty-five thousand, one for one hundred and seventy-five thousand. There and there." Hartsell pointed to the paper in her right hand. "And you will see corresponding credits in the same amounts added to Caldwell's personal finances. Here and here."

Now he pointed to the summary in her left hand. "You will further see that those credits were added shortly after each corporate debit." He paused. "Do you see that, special agent?"

Sally didn't need her nose rubbed in it. "Yes sir."

"That is known as embezzlement, special agent. That is a felony." Hartsell snatched up his vest and held it open. "Given that Bungalow 5 does business across state lines, it is a federal crime as well. Which places it in *our* bailiwick." He slid his arms into the Kevlar webbing, and Velcro-ed it in place. "I'm choppering over to Indianapolis to lead a raid on Mr. Caldwell's residence. We'll be seizing computers, records, digital recordings, bomb-making materials, and anything else that looks interesting." He held up a federal search warrant. "I thought you'd care to join me."

Sally was a little flustered. "But Caldwell doesn't fit the profile of an extortion bomber. He doesn't have a criminal history."

"First time for everything," Hartsell said, checking the magazine of his Glock.

"But he doesn't have the necessary expertise," Sally said. "Bombers are usually ex-military engineers, or chemists, or in the construction trades. Caldwell is an MBA."

"Expertise can be learned," Hartsell said, grabbing the blue windbreaker from the rack. "Or hired out. That's my guess."

"But what about the electronics expertise? Bugging the recorder?"

"You can buy bugs off the Internet," Hartsell said.

"And why ask for three million? He only needed two."

"In for a penny, in for a pound," Hartsell said, his silver flat top adding panache to his dapper appearance.

Sally's ponytail shook like a red flag. "Something doesn't seem right about this, sir. I'd still like permission to head back to Knoxville and follow up on the latest bombing."

Hartsell looked her in the eye. "Special Agent Butterworth, I'm trying to help you here. The bombing in Tennessee was regrettable. But the root cause is here in Indianapolis. Once we have Mr. Caldwell in custody, Tennessee becomes a non-issue."

"That may be so, Mr. Hartsell. But I'd just like to check things out. Make sure. And there's also, well ..."

"Yes."

"Well, it's Dr. Tomacinski, sir. I feel responsible for getting him into this."

"Call Knoxville PD. Get it straightened out." He zippered up his windbreaker.

"I have, sir. But the fact that Conrad used his name. That he knew *who* he was. That puts him at risk."

Placing a fatherly hand on her shoulder, Hartsell said, "Sally. Do yourself a favor and come along on the raid. You'll be helping your career. I guarantee media coverage." He sensed he wasn't getting through. "Tomacinski is fine. Knoxville PD will cut him loose. And they'll be highly motivated to collect all corroborating evidence, given they lost one of their own. Learn when to trust the capable hands of a brother agency."

Sally met his gaze. Breathing deeply, she said, "Special Agent Butterworth requests permission to pursue the Knoxville bombing. Sir."

Hartsell glared back and then snatched away the papers she was holding. "Permission denied." He shoved the reports in his briefcase along with the warrant. "Your place is here, wrapping up the Dayton bombing." He snapped the briefcase closed. "Continue as liaison with local authorities. See to it that all pertinent pieces of evidence get where they belong. Understood?"

"Yes, sir. Understood."

His snappy blue jacket moved toward the door. "By the way, Special Agent Butterworth. What does the C stand for?"

"Sir?"

"The C in C. Roger Caldwell?"

Sally didn't have to be told. "Conrad?"

Hartsell shared another rare smile and left.

Chapter 13

"You've got to be kidding," Tom said.

"Hey, best donuts in all fifty-seven states—and the District of Columbia. Long may she wave. What'll you have, Tom-Tom?"

Tom looked at Doolittle, then at the cases of deep-fried dough, some topped in frosting, some filled with jelly or custard. Each, five hundred empty calories that produced a belly just like his new best bud's. It was bad enough he hadn't worked out in days. He didn't need to add cholesterol cakes. Tom pointed. "I'll have a bagel, no butter. And coffee."

"Bagel?" Doolittle shook his head. "Where you from, New York?" He said the city as if it were both Sodom and Gomorrah, with maybe a touch of the mythic Xanadu tossed in.

"Jersey," Tom said.

"Argh. Worse." Nodding toward Tom, Doolittle said, "Rookie."

The counter lady laughed.

Then Doolittle pointed to the glass case. "Give him a half-dozen, assorted, Ruby. And I'll have the same." He rubbed his mitts. "Make sure I get one of those apple fritters, darlin'."

The bleached-blonde counter woman gave him a girlish grin from cheeks that hadn't been girls since Reagan was president. "You want the usual coffee, Doo?"

The fat cop winked. "Extree large. Double, double."

Tom raised his hand. "Make mine one cream, one Sweet'n Low."

The beefy woman with a smile as big as her bosom winked back. "Sure thing, sweetie."

They took their coffee and white, cardboard box to a table by the window. The place looked straight out of 1955. Red vinyl stools ringed the counter, with matching benches at the booths. Stainless steel napkin holders were placed evenly along the counter and on each table. The floor was checkerboard linoleum, although the black and white squares were faded to almost the same colors.

"Breakfast of champions," Doolittle said, chomping into the apple fritter that would be his sole serving of fruit for the day.

Last night's dinner was a barely touched meatloaf-MRE in Doolittle's bachelor flat. The Powell apartment hadn't been what Tom expected. The threadbare furniture and nicked dinette were par for the course, but Tom was surprised by the books. Well-traveled volumes by Hemingway, Maugham, Houseman, and other literary types jammed a large bookcase, suggesting the country cop was more than met the eye.

Now, they were in Doolittle's other world of dirtbags, diners, and donuts. In this alternative universe, Tom's now-settled stomach was hungry enough to bite into something covered with maple frosting and nuts. The first donut he'd had in five years went down sweet and smooth, with a fresh taste that said it'd been fried with love by someone who made them as a career. After he burned his mouth on the coffee, he was ready for another calorie bomb.

Doolittle's becoming smile was back, as if it had never left. "I told ya. Breakfast of champions." Hands spread to encompass the room, he added, "It ain't New York, but that's a good thing." He'd finished three of the fry cakes and was wiping his fingers on white paper. "Now tell me more about this Conrad Hilton fella. What's your gut tell ya bout him, Tom-Tom?"

"I told you," Tom said from around a bite of chocolate and custard. "I'm not a cop. I'm a disease detective."

"Detective's a detective," Doolittle said. "What's this guy like?"

Tom sipped coffee and thought. "One word? Good."

"How good?" Doolittle said.

Tom shrugged. "He's got the skills. He's got the cool. He enjoys the game as much as the reward."

"And?" Doolittle said.

"And he's got a big advantage."

"Which is?"

"He's a sociopath," Tom said. "The suffering of others doesn't matter. I'm guessing they don't even enter much into his thinking."

Doolittle nodded. "That being said, you figure he's a straight shooter?"

Tom's brows raised into question marks.

"You think he'll keep his word, they give him the money?" Doolittle added. "No tricks, no games. He goes away?"

Tom considered this. He didn't know much about Conrad, only what he'd heard on the recordings. Only what he'd seen on the surveillance feed. Only the results of Hilton's labors. But his gut told him there was something simple there. Something behind the smugness and the disguises, the elaborate character portrayals. Something not quite naive, but sincere. Pride. Almost a code of honor, the kind of code that teens develop when they get to the point that they think they know more than adults. Killing didn't bother Conrad, but that wasn't his motivation. It was a means to an end. That end being money. Tom considered further. Money and something else. Respect maybe. Admiration maybe. Look at me, I'm smarter than you. Love me for it.

Tom nodded. "Yeah, I do."

"And if they don't pay? If we try to stop him, or trick him? What then?"

"I think you'll see a tantrum. And a lot of dead people."

The rest of the morning was spent looking through evidence. First was the lab at the Tennessee Bureau of Investigation. A tech named Lamar told them the explosive was homemade C4. Nothing much could be made of the burnt pieces of plastic and nylon from the luggage.

"Found some traces of mercury," Lamar said. "Probably a rudimentary trembler switch. Sent residue samples to Virginia for full analysis."

"Accelerant?" Doolittle asked.

"Some kind of petroleum-based fuel. FBI lab should be able to tell us more." Lamar shrugged. "Probably homegrown napalm. I've seen it before. Burns hot. Easy to pack without leaking."

Doolittle patted him on the back. "Copy me on the prelim when you're done."

"You got it, partner."

Next up were surveillance videos, those grainy fish-eye recordings from the Tower front desk, elevators, and halls. The Criminal Investigation Division of TBI had the video cued up and ready.

"Same as in Ohio," Tom said. "We've got the character du jour at reception, then he goes into the room and comes out half an hour later."

"No shots of him driving off," Doolittle said. "Did he come by cab?"

Tom shrugged. "What now?"

"Now we do what detectives do. We burn some shoe leather and talk to witnesses. We'll start with the best one we got."

💣

Cheryl Wagner's condo was in a northern Knoxville suburb. After spending time in the smooth comfort of a bureau SUV, the drive up in Doolittle's well-worn Ford was nostalgic of other government vehicles Tom had known. They bounced along on worn shocks, the seat slipping forward and back in its runners. The rearview likewise wouldn't hold adjustment, odd-angling down despite Doolittle's numerous attempts. The old-car smell of body odor and fast food was in keeping with the chip crumbs and grease stains.

"Ever have problems with rats in here?" Tom quipped.

Doolittle smiled. "Only the humankind."

The condo was in a row of similar bungalows. They parked in front of the one-car garage and Doolittle rang the bell.

"Yes?" said a feminine voice muffled by the door.

"Detective Powell, ma'am. I wonder if I could ask you a few more questions."

"I'm just on my way out." The voice grew louder as the door opened. Cheryl Wagner was dressed in running shorts and sweatshirt, the latter holding the Parkway logo. Her sandy-brown hair was in a top-knot bun, and no makeup adorned her pretty face. That face blanched a bit when she saw that Doolittle had brought a guest.

The detective smiled and touched finger to head in a doff-the-cap gesture. "Don't mean to inconvenience ma'am. But this'll only take a few minutes. You remember Dr. Tomacinski?"

Cheryl's embarrassed grin said she did. Her hands rose defensively to her face and hair. "Excuse me. I was on my way for a run before work. I wasn't expecting company."

"My apologies, ma'am," Doolittle said. "Won't keep you but a minute. May we come in?"

"Oh, yes. Excuse me. Please." She picked up a cup and newspaper from the coffee table. "I'm afraid the place is a mess. As I said, I wasn't expecting anyone."

"Don't you worry ma'am. Looks fine. Don't bother on our account."

"Please, have a seat." She hurried the clutter into the kitchen. Popping quickly back in to add, "Can you give me just a second?"

Tom and Doolittle watched her scurry down a hall and out of sight, hands to face like a crime boss hiding from the flashbulbs. Doolittle ogled her departing bottom and gave Tom an appreciative wink.

"Nice place you have here, ma'am," Doolittle said loudly.

"Thank you," her distant voice replied.

Tom surveyed the tastefully appointed room from the gray parachute chairs to the matching sofa to the upright piano along one wall. There was a Monet print that he recognized. There was also a photo of a younger Cheryl Wagner in cap and gown, smiling next to middle-aged people who could only be Mr. and Mrs. Wagner. There were no wedding pictures. Tom turned his head toward the clanks and clicks coming from the hallway, then raised his brows at Doolittle, who shrugged back.

Cheryl Wagner reappeared, slightly out of breath. The sweatshirt was gone, replaced by a spandex runner's top that showed off her trim figure. The top knot was similarly replaced by a just-brushed pony tail. The only addition was lipstick and blush hastily but competently applied.

She smiled. "Can I get you gentlemen something? Coffee, water?"

"Nothing, ma'am. Were fine."

Her smile fell on Tom. The smile didn't quite make her beautiful, as it did Sally. But it softened her years. "May I first offer my apologies, Dr. Tomacinski." She held out her hand. Her grip was soft, but firm. Still holding his hand, she said, "I'm afraid I was not very friendly, when last we met. And you were only trying to save lives."

"No apologies necessary, Ms. Wagner."

"Please, call me Cheryl."

"Actually, Cheryl, considering my end of the conversation, I thought you showed uncommon restraint and understanding."

Doolittle cleared his throat. "Yes, ma'am. Is it alright if I ask a few questions?"

She nodded, still smiling at Tom as she sat in the parachute chair.

"I always like to follow up after a witness has had a night to sleep on things." Doolittle took out a pad and pen. "When things aren't so hectic." He smiled. "What else can you tell me about the man who checked in."

"The impostor?"

"Yes ma'am. The impostor."

"Well." She thought for a moment. "As I said. He looked to be between thirty and forty. Although ..."

"Yes, ma'am?"

"He didn't act that way."

"How so?" Tom asked.

She smiled at Tom again. "He acted younger. Like a kid playing an adult." She uncrossed her legs and leaned forward to talk to Tom. "I'm not married." She stammered, embarrassed. "That is to say, I'm divorced, but don't have any children. But I have two nephews. I saw the older one in a high-school play last year. *Fiddler*, it was. Do you know it?"

Tom nodded.

"My nephew was playing the Russian commissar. You know, pretending to be an adult."

Both men nodded.

"The impostor reminded me of that. Someone pretending to be older. He was much better at it than my nephew. And the flamboyancy of his performance distracted me. But as I think back on it, it was the same kind of thing. A younger guy acting older."

"Anything else about him you noticed?" Doolittle asked.

"Well, we were getting busy with check-ins, so I wasn't paying much attention. But he was so out there. Showy. Flamboyant." She thought some more, hand on chin. "It was like he wanted ..."

"Like he wanted you to notice him?"

She nodded at Tom. "And he asked me to call him Tom-Tom. Said it was a nickname because he played the drums. Do you play the drums, doctor?"

Tom shook his head.

"I play piano," she added, nodding to the upright.

"I like piano music," Tom said. She smiled back.

Doolittle cleared his throat again. "Me, too. Don't want to keep you, ma'am. But is there anything *else* that you can think of?"

Cheryl shrugged. "He was holding the briefcase protectively. I think I mentioned that before. Most people just balance it atop the roller bag. You know?"

Doolittle nodded. "Anything else?"

Her eyes half closed in thought. "His accent."

"Accent?"

"Yes. It was East Coast but exaggerated. Put on." She looked at Tom. "Much stronger than yours, doctor. Are you from New York?"

"New Jersey. And please, call me Tom."

"Okay, Tom." More smiles. "His accent was more exaggerated. Again, like someone from middle America pretending to be a wise guy or something."

"Well," Doolittle said. "We'll let you get back to your run."

"I try to work out every day. Keep in shape."

"Worth every mile," Tom said, noticing her color rise again.

"Well, yes," Doolittle said. "Here's my card. If you think of anything else, give me a call, anytime."

She looked at the business card. "Can I reach either of you at this number?"

"Well," Doolittle said. "That's *my* number."

"I better give you one of *my* cards," she said. "Just in case." Retrieving her purse, she handed Tom a business card. "That's work." She pointed at the card. "And my cell is just below. Call anytime. I mean, if I can be of further assistance."

"We will, ma'am," Doolittle said. "Thanks for your cooperation."

Once they were outside, the detective said, "Well, Tom-Tom. It looks like Conrad is studying you." Then he added, "By the way, I'm not married, either." He batted his eyes playfully.

"Shut up," Tom said, placing Cheryl's card in his shirt pocket.

They ran into Doolittle's partner as she was leaving police headquarters.

"Hey, Dell."

"Hey, Doo." The female cop eyed Tom. "Well, if it ain't Dr. Tomashinski."

"Toma-cin-ski," Tom corrected.

"Just call him Tom-Tom," Doolittle said. Pointing to the short, blocky woman in the brown, polyester suit, he added, "This here's my partner, Adele Portifoy. Just call her Dell."

"So, this is the hotshot got all the ladies talking," Dell said.

"Excuse me?" Tom said.

"Desk clerk had good things to say about you." She winked.

"I noticed that, too," Doolittle said.

"Also got a sharp-lookin' redhead been asking on you. Claims to be with the FBI. Got credentials and everything."

"Sally is here?" Tom asked.

"Talking to the boss about fraternal collaboration and all that good crap," Dell said. "Like the feds always do before they take over."

"That's where you come in," Doolittle said, nudging Tom. "Anything from the other witnesses?"

"Not yet," Dell said. "Blue suits are finishing up with them now. For a hotel full of people, nobody saw nothing."

"We'll split up the prelim reports and go over them tonight. Sound good?"

"Nothin' I'd rather do," Dell said, heading toward the parking lot.

"Don't partners usually work together?" Tom said.

"Only on TV," Doolittle said. "Where they got unlimited manpower and the cases always get solved by the last commercial."

Doolittle's office at Knoxville PD was on the second floor of the squat brown building, but they were distracted by the TV in the reception area. The large banner indicated breaking news, with a caption reading "FBI seizes records of alleged serial bomber."

"Hey, Doo," a burly, Black desk sergeant said.

"What we got here, Irv?"

"Got us a federal raid on some corporate big shot up in Indy. Supposed to be the guy behind your tower bombing. Some hotel up in Dayton, too."

The video feed now included a sidebar photo of a middle-aged man of medium build. This caption read "C. Roger Caldwell. Suspected of arson and extortion."

"That's Conrad?" Tom asked.

Doolittle shook his head. "Nah. This is what you call your man behind the man. This guy most likely hired Conrad. He's the brains, Connie's the high-tech muscle."

"Which means Conrad is still out there."

"But probably headin' to Mexico when he sees the news," Doolittle said.

"I don't know," Tom said. "After Cheryl's description, this doesn't seem to make sense."

"Hey there, Tom-Tom."

Tom turned toward the gaze of familiar green eyes. Below them were cheeks without dimples. This face was back to business. But that didn't stop his stomach flipping a jig. "Sally? Hey. Bureau send you back down here?"

"No. I drove down on my lunch hour." Tom raised his brows. "Extended lunch hour."

"Ma'am," Doolittle said with a smile and a nod.

"This is Detective Doolittle Powell," Tom said. "Doo, this is Special Agent Sally Butterworth of the FBI." They shook hands.

"You taking over my investigation, Agent Butterworth?

"Actually," Sally said. "I'm hoping to join it. Just had a long chat with your boss about it."

"Doesn't *this* change things," Doolittle said, pointing to the TV screen.

"Complicates them," Sally said. "Oh, before I forget. Here's a little present." She handed Tom his wallet. "I'm afraid the cash is a little waterlogged, but I thought you'd like your license and credit cards back." The dimples made a brief appearance.

"Isn't this evidence?"

"Technically," Sally said. "Just following orders. Making sure that all evidence gets where it belongs."

"Agent Butterworth?"

Sally turned toward the voice of a fiftyish man in the doorway to a first-floor office.

"Yes, Captain Loomis?"

"I've got your boss on the line."

Sally headed toward the door. "I'm glad you could reach Mr. Crossfield. I know he's busy."

"Crossfield wasn't there. They referred me to a Special Agent Hartsell. He'd like to talk to you."

Sally paused visibly before heading inside. The door closed.

Tom stared at the black letters reading "Captain Karl Loomis," then looked at Doolittle. "Now what?"

"Well," Doolittle said, rubbing his neck. "Nothing much changes for me. But for you, given recent developments," he thumbed toward the TV.

"You don't need me anymore," Tom said.

"Now I wouldn't put it that way," Doolittle said. "Let's just say you're off the hook." He gave Tom a Doo grin. "Looks like my office will be collecting evidence for the Bureau mop up.

Conrad is likely on the wing. He shouldn't be botherin' with you no more. So, you my friend, can go back to Nigh-Osh and do whatever it is you do. With my thanks." He pumped Tom's hand. "But I want you to know, partner, that you got an open invitation to come visit. Don't forget, best donuts in fifty-seven states."

Tom smiled back. "And the District of Columbia."

"Long may she wave," they said in unison.

The sound of the captain's door broke the general laughter. Both men turned as Sally walked out.

"Doo? See you a minute?" Loomis said.

"Sure thing, captain." The door closed again, leaving Tom and Sally alone with only the desk sergeant reading forms and humming Motown.

"How did it go?" Tom asked.

Sally stared into space, ice-queen expression still there but tempered with something else. Something painful.

"Well?"

Sally walked stiffly toward the door.

"Sally?"

She paused, still facing the entrance, back rigid, ponytail waving at the sudden stop. "I've been suspended." He couldn't see her face, but the tone was lifeless. "Pending a formal inquiry." She paused before repeating, "*Formal* inquiry." Then she left. Tom followed her out the door.

"Hey! Sally." He caught up and grabbed her arm. "I don't get it. Why?"

"Simple, really," she said, still walking. "I disobeyed orders. Headed here instead of staying in Dayton."

"But why?'

She shrugged. "Figured something was screwy. Figured I could get Crossfield to clear my checking into it. Figured you might be ... Figured I knew better than Hartsell."

"Well, the latter's a damn-near certainty." His smile was met with that stony stare.

"How the hell would you know?" She was moving toward the parking lot again.

"Hey, wait a minute." Her arm tensed when he grabbed it, so he let go. "You know, it's not my fault."

"Maybe not," Sally said. "But it sure feels like it."

"Hey. I know you're feeling down."

"Feeling *down*?"

Her sudden turn surprised Tom as much as the ice in her stare.

"I'm facing a *formal* inquiry. I'm facing disciplinary proce-dures. Maybe that doesn't matter in your nine to five, hour for lunch, ten frickin' sick days world. But it matters in mine." She took a step, then turned. "I don't want to spend the rest of my career as the same lousy GS-10. *I* have some ambition. And be-lieve it or not, formal inquiries don't help you move up in the Bureau. They nudge you out the door. Or into a resident agency in Helena, Montana, where the winters are a balmy forty below and the phone rings with wrong numbers." She started walking again, then turned, anger, frustration, and fear releasing onto the nearest target. "I spent three and a half years doing crap work. A glorified administrative assistant. I finally get some decent assignments. Get noticed. And then I run into you, and everything goes to hell."

"Hey. I don't deserve that."

Stopping again, she raised her hands and lowered her eyelids. "Fine."

The tension in her body was painful to watch. Like an over-stretched cable or a boiler in the red, it frightened him and made him want to ease the pressure. But that was unfamiliar territory. He'd always found comfort in women. In their bodies. In the easy way they handled emotions as just another aspect of their being, like height or hair color. Now *he* wanted to provide the comfort and wasn't sure how to do it. And she wasn't your typical woman.

"Sally?" He gently touched her arm. "Why don't you let me buy you a drink?"

"Not today, Tom-Tom." She was walking again. He followed again.

"Hey, come on. We can talk."

Her hand flicked a remote key and the lights on her car blinked, locks clicking. In three quick strides, the door opened.

"Come on, Sally." He was at her side again, touching her arm. "Maybe you should call Hartsell. You can blame me, say I called you in a panic. Cite comradery with a brother agency." He tried to smile. Keep it light. But one leg was already in the car, as if she hadn't heard. "Maybe *I* can call him."

Lightening reflexes had her out of the SUV, grabbing the fin-gers he'd laid on her hand, wrenching them back in a defensive move that made him wince. "Fuck off! Okay?" She released her hold, then glared embarrassedly at his stunned expression. "Just leave me alone. Okay, Tom-Tom?"

Tom stepped back as the door slammed shut, the engine roared, and the car pulled away. Rubbing his injured hand, he softly said, "Goodbye, Sally."

Chapter 14

"How big a hit did we take?"

The voice on the end of the line said, "We were lucky. What with the fire trucks already there and the place evacuated."

"How bad?" George King III asked.

"At least a million," the voice said. "Not counting any lawsuits and lost business."

"Shit," George said.

"That's why we have insurance, boss."

"You're right," George said. "And for once the bean counters know exactly who to blame. That bastard Caldwell. I never did trust that guy."

"Yeah, I saw. It was all over Fox News."

"Anybody injured?" George asked. "Except the cop?"

"No," his district manager said. "Again, we were lucky. If that Tomacinski hadn't tipped them, it would have been much worse."

"You know," George said, "it wouldn't be a bad idea to do some PR with that guy. Congratulate the hero. Present him with lifetime free lodgings at Parkway. How much could it cost? He's a government employee, they'll pay anyway."

"That's something to think about. I'll run it by marketing."

"Thanks," George said. "Keep me posted."

He'd no sooner hung up than his personal line buzzed. "Crap on a cracker. Like I don't have enough problems today." He snatched up the handset and said, "What?"

A mechanical voice answered, like talking to Stephen Hawking. "Hello, George. Did you get my message?"

"Who is this?"

"I think you know."

He did indeed. "What ... I mean ... how?"

"How am I making a phone call when I am in FBI custody? Ha, ha, ha." The robotic laughter was unnerving. "I think you know the answer to that as well. Why would you think the FBI is more competent than the rest of the government?"

"But, I ..." George was having trouble processing this. "What, what do you want?"

"Another answer you already know. Only now the price is four million. Any more foolishness, and it goes to six."

George tried to say something but could only stammer.

"You were very lucky. Only some property damage."

"And a dead police officer," George muttered.

"Inconsequential," the voice said. "Although I am pleased that my little surprise worked. Not too bad for my first trembler switch. Ha, ha, ha."

"You son of a bitch."

"Careful," the voice said. "Tom-Tom might not be there to stop my next demonstration."

"What the ..."

"I will deliver instructions soon. Follow them exactly. Do not contact the authorities or I will know. Just as I knew before. The consequences will be dire. Not just for you. Not just for your customers. But ... for your family."

"Listen you bastard, you touch my family ..." George jerked his head away from the air horn blast bursting from the earpiece.

"Do not interrupt or I will hang up."

"No, I won't. But listen, I need to talk to the other hotel owners. That will take time."

"No more conference calls." The staccato tones droned on. "The FBI will listen in. Meet in person."

"Hey, that's not as easy as it sounds." The line went dead.

💣

Conrad drew his hands from the keys, embossed letters glistening with sweat. Wiping his palms against his jeans, he felt them quiver, matching the beating in his chest and the flutter in his gut. It reminded him of opening night. Wanting to go on but dreading it. He took three cleansing breaths. And smiled. Tom-Tom had made this much more complicated. Much more interesting. Much more fun.

He clicked the muted TV from local coverage of the Tower fire to national news. His smile broadened as he read the "breaking news" banner and saw agents removing file boxes and computers from a stately colonial home. "Geez," he said, wondering that anyone still used tower models in the age of laptops and tablets. The picture changed to a microphone in front of a silver-haired Nazi in a crisp FBI windbreaker. The banner told Conrad they were hunting snipe. Hunting them with full field packs and big-bore rifles.

The glistening pads of his fingers tapped cadence on the desk. Speaking in rhythm with the beat, his voice filled the empty room. "Tom, Tom, the drummer's son. Messed with me, now he can't run."

💣 *Chapter 15*

"Bartender?" Tom waved his hand over his beer glass and stabbed a finger at the shot glass beside it. The bartender smiled and came over.

"Another round?"

Tom winked. "Oh, did I ask if you take Discover Card?"

The bartender, Al or Hal, Tom wasn't sure, winked back. "You asked. We do."

"Good enough."

Tom knew he should eat something but was in no mood for it. Just as he was in no mood for a four-hour car ride. What he was in the mood for was Jim Beam with a Bass Ale chaser. He was in an even better mood after the second one.

The bar at the Parkway Inn was fairly busy, which was surprising given that Middleboro, Tennessee, was not exactly a hot spot. The bartender, Al or Hal, told him that the town got its name from being midway between Knoxville and the Kentucky border. Bartenders were fonts of trivia like that. The town's name reminded Tom of the Marlboros he'd smoked in vet school. For some reason, that similarity had seemed very important when he saw the Middleboro exit sign. Although that was not the reason he'd stopped, just as it hadn't been the reason he was driving. He was driving because he had to get away. Had to do something. He'd stopped because he didn't want to go home. And because he did want a drink. Several in fact.

He called to the bartender again. "Hey. You sell Marlboros?"

Al or Hal brought another pint and shot, then pointed to the sign that said, "The Halfway Lounge is a smoke-free comfort zone."

"What if smoking makes one comfortable?" Tom said. The bartender shrugged. Tom sipped his bourbon.

"You want to see a menu?" the bartender asked.

Tom shook his head, then chased down the fiery whiskey with cold beer.

"Well, hello."

Cheryl Wagner was standing by Tom's side, her sandy-brown hair draped over the shoulders of the red blazer she'd been wearing when they first met. That was twenty-four hours that felt like ten years ago. Her smile was warm and genuine, the one she shared with people not under suspicion of mental illness. The kind of smile she shared with handsome heroes. That smile—and the alcohol—took ten years off her. Tom smiled back.

"Well, hello yourself, Ms. Wagn ... I mean Cheryl. Fancy meeting you here."

"I could say the same thing." She nonchalantly fondled her hair. "Actually, this is where I'm managing now. Or should I say again. At least temporarily, while the Tower gets repaired. I saw you come in and since I just got off my shift, I thought I'd stop in to say hello. Mind if I sit down?"

Tom motioned to the stool beside him. "Can I buy you a drink?"

"Thank you. That would be lovely. Vodka and tonic, please, Al."

Tom thumped the bar. "Yes, Al, vodka and tonic."

"So, do you live around here?" Cheryl asked.

"No, northern Kentucky."

"Stopping off to have one for the road?"

"Well, so far, it's three for the road. Or maybe that's six."

"Maybe you should stay over at the hotel. I'd be more than happy to comp you a room. I mean, after what you did for Parkway, for all of us, it seems only appropriate."

"Let me cogitate that," Tom said. "Meanwhile, set 'em up again, Al."

"No can do, pal" Al said. "Unless I see a room key, or you give me your car keys."

"Tell you what," Cheryl said. "Why don't I buy you dinner?"

"Shouldn't *I* buy *you* dinner?"

"I get a discount," Cheryl said. "Let's grab a booth, have a bite, and chat?"

"What shall we chat about?"

"Oh, this and that. Favorite hotels, relationships, life after divorce. You know, stuff." She called across the bar. "We're moving to table nine, Al. Can we have menus and another round of drinks?" She smiled at Tom, but spoke to Al. "Just a beer for Dr.

Tomacinski, I think." Her smile said she knew what Tom needed, and it wasn't more whiskey. Tom liked her smile.

Al called back, "Check," as they crossed, Tom moving with the gentle sway of the slightly inebriated.

Neither Tom-Tom nor Cheryl seemed to notice him. Why would they? He was just some nameless young man watching from the corner. A stranger with a young (maybe twenty or twenty-one) but wise, impassive face. His black bangs hung over his forehead. Tiny beads of oil oozed up from the light pancake make-up covering the rash he always got from spirit gum. Beard stubble poked through the powder, the twenty-four-hour shadow that had not yet matured at five o'clock.

The boy-man watched them sit at a table twenty feet away. Table nine, manager Cheryl had said. Table nine from outer space, he thought, smiling. Tom-Tom would think he was in outer space by the time he was done with him. But he wasn't done with him yet. Not by a long shot.

Charles Robinson put down his drink and looked at his buzzing cell. He recognized the number but paused to look at his desk clock. What was *he* calling about at 10:45 p.m.? He considered letting it go to voicemail, then shrugged and picked up.

"Hello, there, George. You caught me about to turn in. What's up?"

"Hi Charles," George King II said. "Yeah, sorry to call so late. Have you got a minute?"

"I guess. Oh, by the way, I think congratulations are in order."

"Pardon?"

"Well, you and Bob were the voices of reason about our little ... problem. You advised turning it over to the FBI and you were right. I couldn't be more pleased how things turned out. Unfortunate about your Parkway Tower and, the, um, police officer, but that aside, I couldn't be more pleased."

"Oh, yeah. But that's not what I'm calling about. It has to do with, ah ... Georgie. My boy, Georgie."

"Oh?"

"Yeah. He, ah, he's been skipping classes. His grades are crap. I'm worried."

"Well, I don't know what I can do."

"He and your Robbie are close, at least used to be. Maybe you could find out what's going on. You know, kids will tell friends things that they won't tell parents."

"Well, I can ask. But Robbie and I aren't on especially good terms lately. You know how it is. He's at that age where he knows it all and parents know nothing. What was that old Mark Twain quote about being amazed how much the old man had learned?"

"Yeah, I know it. Anyway, if you could talk to Robbie and then you and I could have a chat. Maybe over lunch tomorrow?"

"Tomorrow? I'm not sure I could swing that. But I'll be in Cleveland toward the end of the month. We could plan something then."

"I can drive down to Columbus tomorrow. I ... I have a meeting at State. Dean of students. We could get together for lunch around one."

"Well, I'd need to check my calendar. I may have something on at one."

"I'm flexible. I'll work around your schedule. It's important. Please?"

"I guess it must be. What aren't you telling me? Is Georgie into something? I mean ..."

"Not on the phone, okay Charles? Tomorrow, over lunch."

Charles sipped his Scotch. "Well, alright. Call my office in the morning and ask Jan to fit you in somehow."

"Thanks, Charles. I really appreciate it."

"That's quite alright. I have to admit, you have my curiosity up."

"Tomorrow, okay?"

"Alright. Goodnight, George. And try not to worry. These things have a way of straightening themselves ..." The line went dead.

💣

"Is that you, Robbie?"

"No, it's a burglar here to steal our monogrammed towels."

"Why always the smart ass?" Charles Robinson asked, walking into the kitchen. "You know you're not supposed to be out late until all this FBI craziness is settled."

"I thought they had old C. Roger locked up?"

"Never mind, that. Where have you been?"

"If you must know, I met with my theater group, then I visited my mother. Surely you remember *her*. You were married for sixteen years. By the way, her birthday is Sunday, in case your secretary forgot to write it in your calendar."

"Divorced people no longer celebrate birthdays. That's one of the rules." Charles watched his son cut a piece of apple cake. "And I can smell you've been drinking. Your mother's still fond of Absolut I see." Charles paused. "Are you wearing makeup?"

Robbie sighed. "What do you want, Father?"

"Have you heard from George King, lately?"

"He's *your* golf buddy," his son said from around a bite of cake. "Not mine."

"Not George King the second," Charles said. "His son, George. Georgie. Have you heard from him?"

Robbie shrugged. "We kind of lost touch."

"I thought you guys were close."

Robbie nodded. "Until he told my theater friends that they were no-talent jerk offs. That led to a little falling out."

"His father is worried about him."

"Probably afraid he'll sully the family name. Won't carry on the dynasty, get married, and pop out a little King George IV."

"Why do you have to do that? Can't a father worry about his son?"

Robbie backhanded cake crumbs from his mouth. "Not without an ulterior motive. Judging from personal experience."

"That's not fair. When have I asked you for anything?"

Robbie took another bite of cake. "No, that's true. You never asked me for anything. Not even permission to leave my mother for a fling with a twenty-three-year-old flight attendant."

"Your mother and I had problems. You know that. Your mother *still* has problems. You know that, too. I just don't want you dealing with the same problems." His son started to cut another piece of cake, but Charles slapped the knife out of his hand. "Pay attention when I'm talking to you."

Robbie's head snapped up, bored indifference replaced by pure hatred. "My mother may have problems." The words hissed between clenched teeth. "And I may have problems. But at least neither of us are stuck-up assholes." A tear glistened in his eye. "And if you ever so much as touch me again, I'm gonna take this knife and shove it in the void where your fucking heart should be."

The food took the edge off his buzz, leaving Tom with a relaxed glow. Cheryl had ordered for him, professing to know what was good.

"The rainbow trout is excellent," she'd said. "A little trouty, but quite nice."

He caught the reference to a favorite movie and smiled. She had a way of making him smile.

"Did you work here a long time? You know, before the Tower."

"Three years," Cheryl said. "Al was here the whole time. Others come and go. Nature of the trade."

"I'm surprised that this place is here in the middle of ... wherever we're in the middle of."

"You wouldn't be if you were in the trade. We're close enough to the city to get convention business, but far enough outside to attract those who want to avoid the Knoxville hubbub. And the restaurant does local business. The Middleboro Parkway does alright."

"How long have you been in *the trade*?"

"You make it sound naughty." They both chuckled. "Since my bachelor's in hotel and restaurant management. Going on ... a while now."

"Doesn't show on you," Tom said.

Her smile broadened and the years slipped away. She patted the back of his hand, letting hers rest there for a moment. "You're sweet." Her expression changed. Became less casual. Less flirty. More thoughtful, with another hint of that "mother-knows-best" quality. "I'm quite serious about comping you a room. And, given the amount of alcohol I've seen you consume, it wouldn't be legally or ethically appropriate to allow you to drive."

He looked into her eyes. They were brown, the same color as his ex-wife's. But softer, more feminine. He thought of that actress, Amy something or other, in the movie *Heat*, staring into De Niro's eyes and saying that she was "real lonely." Saying it with her eyes more than her words. Saying it in the same soft, southern way.

"And I never really had a chance to thank you for the other day. For saving so many lives." Her voice was huskier now.

"You've convinced me," Tom said.

She kept her hand on the back of his, fingertips gently sliding across the outline of the veins. "Should I show you to your room?" Her face took on a playful, knowing expression. "Or are you ready for dessert?"

"Both," Tom said. For the first time in days, he wasn't thinking about Sally.

They'd made it to the door, Tom's swaying steps following Cheryl, his eyes following the sway of her skirt, when a hand touched his shoulder.

"Don't want to forget this?"

A young man of maybe twenty-one was holding out Tom's wallet. He held it with the tips of just two fingers. Probably because it was still a little damp, Tom thought. Which was why he hadn't put it in his pocket and had forgotten it on the table. Tom accepted it gratefully.

"Hey thanks."

"Don't mention it," the young man said. Had Tom not been three sheets, he might have caught the sly grin that said more than "screw her once for me, stud." The young man with the black bangs winked. "Enjoy your evening."

Tom woke to the smell of black coffee.

"Rise and shine, sleepy head. It's 9:05 in the a.m. Time to greet the day."

"Do you have to shout?"

Cheryl smiled down at his one eye squinting against the pain of sensory input. "I thought you might need some coffee this morning. I also included some juice to go with these."

She held out two white caplets. They tasted like chalk coated in burnt cotton. Then she held forth a chilled glass of orange juice. The sweet, cold liquid soothed Tom's throat and throttled down the throbbing in his head.

"I have to get home to exercise and freshen up. My shift starts in a few hours."

Her warm lips gently kissed his forehead. She applied more pressure kissing his mouth.

"I'll leave you with this bit of parting trivia, which should appeal to your analytical mind, Dr. Tomacinski." She said his name formally, like a sexy school principal. "Northern Kentucky is only three hours from Middleboro and only an hour from Lexington." Tom watched her slip into her red, Parkway blazer, sandy hair shaken over the back collar. He recalled the firm, mature body under those clothes.

"For your further information," she said. "The Parkway Inns and Suites have a beautiful hotel in Lexington. Wonderful service. Nice large beds." She kissed his cheek. "You have my card, but I left another by your wallet. Both include my cell number. Check-out time is noon." And then the door opened and closed.

💣 *Chapter 16*

"You want to tell me why I'm spending my Sunday in a hotel suite in Columbus, Ohio?"

"Come in, Barbara," Charles Robinson said, closing the door behind her.

"An airport *Ramada*, no less. You couldn't patronize an association property?"

"Is Arthur with you?"

"No," Barbara Gerstel said. "Mr. Chin couldn't make it."

The two other members of the MHLA greeted her simply with, "Barbara."

"Something to do with his daughter's piano recital. State finals or some such." She put her overnight bag down by the coffee table. "Said he could conference in later, if need be."

"No," George King said. "No conference calls."

"Fine," Barbara said. "No need to take my head off. Just a thought."

"Drink, Barb?" Bob Rankin asked.

"I could use one. Thanks. Vodka rocks." Bob clinked cubes from a stainless bucket into a crystal glass, then poured three fingers of clear liquor over it.

"Now," Barbara said, taking the drink and seating herself in an easy chair. "Will someone please tell me what in the hell is going on?"

"Of course," Charles said. "Sorry for all the cloak and dagger. But my house is still under surveillance. And we were instructed not to con-call."

"What are you talking about? Instructed by whom?"

Charles pointed to George King, seated on the love seat of the spacious empire suite. "You want to field that one?"

The CEO of the Parkway Inns and Suites emptied his own glass. "A couple of days ago, I got an unusual phone call. Shocked the hell out of me. Sounded like Stephen Hawking."

Barbara raised her brows. "But I thought the feds had ..."

"Yeah, so did I," George said. "Then this came via messenger." He produced a minicorder identical to the others they'd received. "Written instructions warned to play it only when we were all together, so I'm as much in the dark as you." Placing the small metal and plastic box on the coffee table, he pressed play.

"Gentlemen," droned the mechanical voice. "And lady. Good of you to indulge me. Although your juvenile attempt at deceit has really left you no choice."

The voice paused, the hum of the recorder and background jet traffic the only sounds in the room.

"Because of that deception, the price is now four million. Delivery will be outlined in written instructions you will soon receive. Follow these to the letter. Any more attempts at deception or police interference will produce a further, more dramatic demonstration of your vulnerability. By now you should fully comprehend just how uniquely vulnerable you are."

They continued staring at the little gadget, hoping there'd be no further creepy mechanical tones, but knowing there would be.

"You must also know that FBI involvement is futile, even comic. But ..."

Another pause, making them wonder if the voice was cut off mid-sentence. Then the awkward Hawking-ese rambled on.

"In case you need further incentive, I have added sweetener to the brew. Mr. King?"

George started and looked around guiltily, before staring back at the recorder.

"Have you seen your son lately?"

Everyone stared at George, Barbara giving him a "have you?" look. King sadly shook his head.

Then the voice continued. "One other thing ..."

💣 *Chapter 17*

Tom sorted through the business version of junk mail on his desk. Instead of garden-supply catalogs, there were fliers from lab-supply companies. Instead of invitations to time-share dinner pitches, there were conference announcements, one in Beijing no less.

"Like I'd ever get authorization to attend that," he said to the empty office.

He felt odd after the hustle and adrenaline of the last few days. Anticlimactic. Like something else was supposed to happen. Something more than government routine. He saw an envelope from Jan Sterling at the University of Kentucky and pulled the letter opener from the mug on his desk.

"Where were you last week?"

His boss, Lynne Faulkner, stood in the doorway. After Cheryl's professional red blazer and Sally's crisp, dark suits, Lynne's threadbare double-knits and baggy sweater looked woefully unprofessional.

"How can you wear a sweater in this weather?"

"You know the AC makes me cold. Where have you been?"

He slit the envelope. "Didn't you see the news about the bombing in Tennessee?"

"What about it?"

"Didn't you see that I was a hero, saving countless lives?" Tom thought of the bomb-squad cop. He couldn't remember the guy's name. It had been on the news, but he couldn't remember it. He did remember the man had a wife and two little kids.

"That was you?"

"How many Thomas Tomacinskis are there?"

Lynne shrugged. "How should I bill the time?"

"Surprise me," Tom said.

"Some reporter called for you. I have a message here somewhere." She patted the pockets of her old blue slacks. "And you missed the staff meeting. And the reviewer comments came back on that ES&T article."

"Let me guess," Tom said. "Accepted with revision."

"How did you know?"

"I'm psychic."

The reporter's message was apparently not in either of her pockets. "Hmm. I must have left it on my desk."

"How about leaving *my* messages on *my* desk?"

"Anyway, he wanted to interview you."

"No comment," Tom said.

"There's a meeting about the traffic-fatality project at ten."

"I'll be there," Tom said.

Lynne left.

Tom made coffee, then settled down to listen to voicemail. A little shiver ran down his back as a mechanical voice not unlike Conrad's announced he had two new voicemail messages. The first was from Jan Sterling. She wanted him to speak at a conference in October and had sent the formal invitation he'd just opened. The second message was a bit of a shock.

"Hello, Dr. Tomacinski? This is George King of the Parkway Inns and Suites. You don't know me, but I'm a member of the MHLA, along with Charles Robinson. I would very much appreciate you returning my call as soon as possible. It is something of an emergency. I can't go into more detail right now, but I need to talk to you. Thank you." He left his number.

"What the hell?" Tom dropped the beige handset into the phone cradle, then jumped when it rang. It rang two more times, Tom staring at it like it was a deadly rattler. Then he picked it up just as gingerly. "Hello?"

"Dr. Tomacinski?" The voice was the same he'd just heard. "This is George King. Thank God you're in. Did you get my message?"

"Yes. Just now. What can I do for you, Mr. King?"

"An emergency has come up, and I need your help immediately."

"I'm a researcher, Mr. King, not a first responder. If there has been an industrial accident, I suggest you dial 911. Then maybe OSHA."

"No, no, you don't understand."

"Well, maybe you can explain it to me."

"Not over the phone. I, that is we, the association, need to see you immediately."

Tom slumped into his office chair. "Listen, Mr. King, I've just finished a *very* long week and I'm not in the mood for more intrigue right now. Not to mention that I missed a lot of work, so as you can imagine I've got things piling up."

"Of course, we would be happy to remunerate you for lost time and wages."

"That's very kind, Mr. King, but I'm a government employee. My time isn't really my own."

"How does ten thousand dollars sound?"

"Ten *thousand*? For how long?"

"I'm not sure yet. But let's call that a retainer against twenty-five hundred per day plus expenses."

"Ah, well, I'm not sure, but, ah ..."

"Please, Dr. Tomacinski. It's a matter of life and death that we see you in Columbus immediately."

"Life and death? Well, when you put it that way. I guess you've bought yourselves an epidemiologist."

"A skin doctor?"

"No, that's a derm ... never mind. I'll drive up after lunch. It'll take a couple of hours, so you can expect me ..."

"It's only half an hour by helicopter. I can have a car outside your building in ten minutes. He'll have you at the airport in another fifteen."

Tom stared at the earpiece, then held it back to his head. "Are you sure you have the *right* Tomacinski?"

"Yes. If this is Dr. Tom-Tom Tomacinski."

"Tom-Tom?"

"A limo will be in front of your building in ten. Thank you, doctor." The line went dead.

Tom shook his head and dialed Lynne. "Hi, it's me. I need to take some vacation. Starting immediately."

"How long?" she asked.

"I'm not sure. A few days anyway. Don't you want to know why?"

"I'm not allowed to ask. It could be considered workplace harassment. You know you only have ten days left. Don't you want to save them for a two-week trip? I'm planning one to the Smokies."

"If this works out," Tom said, "I can afford to go someplace better."

💣 *Chapter 18*

"One other thing," the mechanical voice said. "I want Dr. Tom-Tom Tomacinski to deliver the money. I thought the best way to keep the Polack from interfering was to give him something useful to do. Ha, ha, ha." The disembodied laugh carried a spooky finality. Then the machine clicked off.

The four executives looked at the minicorder, then at their guest.

"Well, Dr. Tomacinski?" Charles Robinson said.

"Well," Tom said. "I'm not sure I like being called a Polack, but otherwise I don't get it. Why me?"

George King shrugged. "Must have seen your picture on the news. So, his sick mind thought he'd include you in his little game."

Bob Rankin pointed a finger. "You *did* upset his plans. Probably wants to jerk you around a little."

"But how did he know the nickname?" Barbara Gerstel asked. "I don't remember seeing that on the news."

"It wasn't," Tom said. "In fact, I haven't gone by that since I was a kid." Tom chuckled. "Although it's become a running gag among certain members of the law enforcement community." Tom remembered back to when Jerry Shapiro dissected the recorder. "Son of a bitch," Tom said, snatching up the little gadget.

Gerstel had time to say, "What?" before Tom hurled the recorder. The group let out a collective gasp as the device exploded against a stone statuette that might have been an abstract version of the pietá.

"Jesus," Bob Rankin said. "What the hell are you doing?"

Tom ignored the million bits of plastic and headed directly for what remained of the case. Reaching around back, he ripped out the same type of mini microphone that Jerry Shapiro had found. Holding it like a trophy, he said, "Little son of a bitch listens in."

"It was bugged?" King said.

Tom nodded. "That's how he knew about Tom-Tom. It wasn't on the news, but it was an FBI joke when they found this little baby on the last recorder he sent you."

"That means he listened in to my conference call," Robinson said.

"And knew all our plans," Gerstel said.

"And heard George insult him," Rankin said. King gave him a look. "Which may explain his special interest in him." Rankin paused. "And his son."

Tom looked at George King. He could see the stress lines in a face that had too much coffee and too little rest.

"I think he's kidnapped my boy," George King said.

"Well, Dr. Tomacinski?" Robinson said. "What do you think?"

"You want to know what I think?" Tom said, setting down his coffee cup. "I think you should call the FBI."

"No," King yelled, springing up. "We did that last time and look what happened. One of my hotels got torched and my son is missing. I know when I'm licked."

There was a knock on the hotel room door. "That'll be fresh coffee," Gerstel said, heading to the entrance.

"We've all agreed to pay," Robinson said. Bob Rankin cleared his throat. "All but one," Robinson continued. "And he's agreed to go along with the majority. Right, Bob?"

Rankin nodded, clearly displeased.

"So, Dr. Tomacinski? Will you be the bag man?"

As Tom thought it over, Gerstel returned with a red, nylon duffel bag. A white envelope was taped to the handle. The writing on the envelope read simply, "Open me first."

"What's this?" Rankin asked.

"The front desk said this arrived by messenger a few minutes ago."

"What do we do?" Robinson asked.

"Open the envelope first," Tom said.

"What if its booby-trapped?" Robinson said.

"It's an envelope, for God's sake," Rankin said. "What's going to happen? Paper cuts?"

"I think he's right," Tom said. "I doubt Conrad will try to kill off those paying his salary." Tom ripped the envelope free. "And speaking of salary, my price for bag-manning is more than ten thousand."

"I'll look like a rodeo clown," Tom said.

"Or grand marshal at a gay pride parade," Bob Rankin said.

"Or the world's largest jockey," Barbara Gerstel said.

The four men and one woman stared at the contents of the bag strewn across the king-sized bed. There were red, nylon running shorts; a bright yellow tee-shirt with lettering that read "I had a blast at Cape Kennedy"; an orange hoodie sweatshirt; a pink, size 13 pair of Converse All Stars; and a fluorescent green ball cap with crossed golf clubs over the bill. The only other items were a pair of sunglasses and a XX package of white pantyhose, the kind nurses wore.

Gerstel glanced at the printed letter. "What can I say? This is what you're supposed to wear when you check into the Parkway Motor Lodge south of Lexington, Kentucky. There is a rental car reserved for you at some place called Big John's Auto World in Covington. From there, you go directly to the Parkway. Check-in no later than 3:30." She looked at the bedside clock. "It's 10:30 now."

"I don't know," Tom said. "Conrad's up to something, and I'm not sure I want to be part of it."

"I'd say he wants you highly visible," Robinson said. "Most likely he'll run you around and wants to be able to see you at a distance."

Tom held up the package. "Pantyhose?"

"Probably his little joke," Rankin said. "Some humiliation payback for you messing with him. Come on, it's one day's embarrassment. What can happen?"

Tom glared at him.

"You said yourself, he's unlikely to harm the guy making the payoff."

"It's not making the payoff, I'm worried about," Tom said, "It's after the payoff that has me more than a little concerned."

"Does twenty-*five* thousand ease your mind?" George King said.

Tom tossed the pantyhose back on the bed. "What good is money if I'm dead? I'll be on my own, no backup. With a nutcase pulling my strings."

"Fifty thousand," King said. "That's as high as I can go. That's out of my own pocket, not the association's."

"I don't know," Tom said.

"Make up your mind," Robinson said. "The clock is ticking."

"A chopper can have him at the Cincy airport in half an hour," Rankin said.

"We don't even have the money yet," Gerstel said.

"I've spoken to my bank," Rankin said. "They're going to float me a personal loan for the four mill."

"Gosh, Bob," George King said. "I don't know what to say."

"You can say you're paying me back. All of you. I may have agreed to go along with this cockeyed scheme, but that doesn't mean I'm fronting all the money. Share and share alike. Mr. Chin included."

"But how do we get Dr. Tom-Tom the cash?" Gerstel said.

"Don't worry about that," Rankin said. "I'll chopper it down to Lexington."

"But there's still his drive *to* Lexington," Gerstel said.

"Another two hours," Rankin said. "No sweat. I'll already be there with the money."

"You personally?"

"You bet. I'm not letting it out of my sight. I'll drop it right in the Parkway lot."

"What if something goes wrong?" Gerstel said.

"Like what?" Rankin said.

"I don't know. Car trouble, traffic, a line at the rental place."

"A limo can take him from the airport to the rental place," Rankin said. "And how bad can traffic be once you're past Cincinnati?"

"I just don't think this is something you should take chances with," Gerstel said.

"Hey, Punch and Judy," Tom said. "I haven't said I'll do it yet."

The entire room quieted until George King broke the silence.

"If the money isn't enough, maybe a personal appeal might help. He's got my boy, doctor."

"We don't know that for sure," Robinson said. "I haven't spoken with Robbie in a while, but that doesn't mean he's kidnapped."

George King spun around like a feral animal. "We're not talking about *your* son, Charles." Then he slowly turned to Tom, tears and an unaccustomed humility in the eyes of the Parkway CEO. "Please?"

"I just don't know," Tom said, turning away. "I'd like to help, but I just don't know. Maybe if I had some backup." Tom stiffened. "Let me make a call."

With practiced ease, Sally pulled down the locks and slid the heavy metal slide from the Glock's frame. Popping off the recoil spring freed the barrel, leaving her with four parts to clean.

The range was a good place to burn off frustration, along with some nine-millimeter cartridges. The snap of the automatic and the holes in the paper usually brought tranquility. Peace and relaxation. Mind-clearing focus on sight picture and trigger control. But when the last round left the chamber today, she was still as tense as when she'd jammed home the first magazine.

With that first pop, her mind's eye had transformed the man-shaped target into the image of Agent in Charge Daniel Hartsell. But after a few rounds, her own smaller frame filled the silhouette. She couldn't blame her current predicament on anyone but a bullheaded woman named Sally Butterworth. *At least no one's pouring it over pancakes*, she thought, remembering when she'd first met Tom-Tom. Regret tugged at the edges of her mind. He wasn't to blame, either. She hoped he was okay.

She'd just swabbed the barrel with Hoppes No. 9 when her cell rang. Wiping her hands on a clean rag, she punched the speaker. "Butterworth."

"Hi, Sally."

She recognized the voice immediately, as if she'd conjured it by thinking about him. A familiar voice saying two simple words. But those words carried a wave of emotions with them. Regret was back, as was anger. But there was also passion, even a little tenderness. Even a little loneliness. Maybe a little humility. "Hi, Tom." She almost added a second Tom. "How are you?"

"I'm in a bit of a jam." Now she noticed the strain in his voice, reminding her of the second time they'd met, his face finding her ass in the strobe lights of the smoky hotel hallway. The voice from behind her then held the same note of panic as the one she'd just heard over the speaker.

"What's wrong, Tom-Tom?"

Bob Rankin kept his voice low, so as not to be heard over the hum of the bathroom fan.

"Should I get started?" the voice on his cell asked.

"I don't know yet," Rankin said.

"It's going to take some time," the voice cautioned.

"How long?" Rankin asked.

"Maybe a couple of hours. I've got half a dozen operatives standing by, and I'll pitch in myself, but even so, that's a lot of money."

"Can't we just do it randomly?" Rankin said. "You know, every tenth one or something."

"We can," the voice said. "But that's riskier."

"And he won't be able to tell?"

"Unlikely," the voice said.

Rankin paused for a moment. He was taking a lot on himself. But then, that was a lot of money. His money. The others would promise to chip in, of course they would. But you had to threaten torture just to get them to pay their association dues. And with Roger out of the picture, it would just be the five of them. And Art was a no-show who might not even agree. And that was an awful lot of money.

"Okay, Arbogast," Rankin said. "Get started."

"Right away, Mr. Rankin."

💣

"You want my advice?" Sally asked the speaker phone.

"Of course. Your advice and your help."

"My advice is that you guys don't know what you're doing. Call the Bureau."

"I thought I had," Tom said.

"I'm not the Bureau right now, Tom-Tom. I'm on suspension, remember?"

"That's why I figured you'd be able to help."

"Help how?" Sally wedged the recoil spring below the now-cleaned barrel. "I'd be on my own. No backup. No authority. I'd be no help to you. I'd be a liability." She strategically placed oil on the frame. "If Conrad picked up my tail, he could run you into an ambush. Or he could just get pissed off and kill the kid. Do you want that on your head? I don't." She slid the slide home and racked it open.

"Listen, Sal. The *kid* is the only reason I'm doing this."

"They're not paying you?" Sally hit the slide release, sending the pistol back to battery.

"Course they are. Paying me well. But that's not the point." She heard him take a deep breath. "Listen. I'm the one who pulled that fire alarm in Knoxville. Once I did that, I started a chain."

"And saved a lot of lives," Sally said.

"Tell that to the widow of the bomb-squad cop."

"He knew the risks."

"Just hear me out."

Sally quieted.

"I took it on myself to go to Knoxville. I didn't think about it, I just did it. Maybe it ended up being the right thing to do, but it was *my* responsibility. I stumbled into this thing like a stadium fan jumping into the bull ring. Now Toro is after me, and he's using some college kid for bait. I don't want two deaths on my head. And that's what we'll have if we call the cops or the FBI. I can feel it. I can feel Conrad out there, watching, listening. I probably shouldn't even have called *you*. But it was a new untraceable cell, and I didn't know what else to do. I'm scared, and I wanted to hear your voice telling me it'll be okay." He paused for a moment, dead silence on the line. "I wanted to hear your voice again." Seconds ticked by. "Will you help me?" There was no reply. "Sally? Are you there?"

The empty pistol clicked as she pulled the trigger. "I'll do what I can."

💣 *Chapter 19*

"Why hello there, partner. Circus in town?"

Big John Cavanaugh looked at the strangest sight he'd seen in fifteen years selling cars. He'd heard some craziness that the government reported fifty-eight distinct genders for the human animal, but looking at the guy in front of him, John figured maybe there were now fifty-nine. He couldn't see the eyes through the dark glasses, but the rest of the clean-cut features didn't go with the outfit, which was a cross between a drag queen and one of the flying Wallendas.

"If you need to use the rest room," Cavanaugh said, "we have both men's and ladies', depending on how you identify."

"There's supposed to be a rental for me. Name of Tom Tomacinski."

"You Tom-Tom? I wondered what somebody with that moniker looked like." He eyed Tom up again and smiled. "Kind of the boy-named-Sue thing, huh?"

"Do you have the car? I'm in a hurry."

"You bet. Paperwork's all filled out. You'll just need to sign." He walked to the desk. "Used to only *sell* cars, but I make as much with these rent-a-wrecks. Wife's idea. She's always looking for ways I can make her money." He winked. "Did your *partner* pick out those duds?"

Tom scribbled his name on the rental sheet. "Keys?"

Cavanaugh handed them over, along with a duplicate of the contract. "It's the yellow PT Cruiser. You'll want to check her over first, look for any dings or dents." Tom was already in the front seat, lights flashing as the engine coughed to life. "You bang her up, you bought her," Cavanaugh yelled as the Chrysler peeled out amid a cloud of blue smoke.

💣

Sally swerved from lane to lane, her Miata averaging eighty. It was nearly two more hours to Lexington, and she wanted to get to the Parkway Motor Lodge before Tom-Tom. He was hesitant to call her from the road; Conrad had instructed him to leave his cell behind. Sally agreed. She wouldn't be surprised if either he or the rental had a bug somewhere. So, she'd need to spot him when he went inside the hotel. From what he'd told her about the contents of the duffel bag, he shouldn't be hard to pick out of the crowd. Then she'd tail him. Without backup, it'd be tricky. She could hang back on the freeway but couldn't hide the fact she was following if they left the confines of I-75. Things could get dicey if Conrad was watching. But she didn't have much choice.

💣 *Chapter 20*

Murphy's Law was alive and well during the drive down from Covington. First, Tom noticed that the fuel gauge that was supposed to be hovering around F, was closer to E, necessitating a pit stop before he even hit the freeway. Then an accident outside Corinth funneled all vehicles to one lane, rubberneckers doing their part to keep traffic trickling. Finally, a Kentucky state trooper pitched in after Tom passed him doing fifteen over the speed limit. Being unable to fully explain either his getup or his need for urgency had been a problem, but eventually worked to Tom's advantage. The trooper seemed more afraid of him than anything, letting Tom off with a warning after a field sobriety test determined that he wasn't drunk so might be crazy. Despite the delays, Tom made it to the Parkway lot with forty-five minutes to spare.

But where was the money? He expected to see Bob Rankin grinning like the Publisher's Clearing House Prize Patrol, complete with armored truck. But there was only the smattering of cars standard for a weekday afternoon.

Conrad's letter had been explicit. The extortionist wanted to see the red duffel bulging with cash when Tom checked in. The last part had been underlined and bolded. But the money wasn't there at 2:45. And it wasn't there at 3:00. Now it was almost quarter after, and Tom was sweating—and not just from the heat of the pantyhose cooking his gonads to medium-well sterility. Worse yet, he had to pee, a matter that could not be ignored indefinitely. But Tom couldn't enter the lobby without the duffel in case Conrad was watching.

Tom pondered this situation with increasing urgency and finally decided that behind the bushes beside the building was the better part of valor. After determining that pantyhose, not anatomy, were the real reason women urinated sitting down, he managed to free himself and initiate a stream, along with a sigh of relief. That's when he heard the CHOP, CHOP, CHOP of rotor blades.

The noise grew louder, as did the breeze, indicating that the helicopter was heading for the field directly behind him. It was too late to stop voiding his bladder, that boat having long sailed on a river of gold. So, he was forced to hunch his shoulders against the assault and submit to the indignity of urinating with an audience like a common vagrant. Although common vagrants were rarely dressed in pantyhose while exposing themselves to overhead observation.

The rotor blades slowed to a steady whoosh as Tom's stream slowed to a drip. Keeping his back to the aircraft, he managed the final indignity of putting everything away, getting a painful pinch in the process. After a last tug and squirm, he turned toward the chopper, noticing several things simultaneously.

There was the pilot smiling at him through the cockpit windscreen, shaking his sun-glassed head. There was the scrape of the cargo door sliding open to reveal Bob Rankin exiting the aircraft with the red duffel, followed immediately by a khaki-clad security guard. Finally, there were cheers. Turning, Tom saw a half-dozen onlookers clapping, smiling, and nodding.

Tom wasn't sure if they were applauding the pilot, the chopper, Tom's outfit, or his urinary display. So, he bowed.

"What took you so long?" Tom said over the drone of the idling aircraft.

"You don't get this kind of money from the ATM," Rankin said. "Transactions like this take time." The Travel-Eze CEO was wearing a gray, nylon jacket over his suit pants and spit-shined brogans. His right shoulder was tugged low against the pull of the bundle he carried.

"So that's what four million cash looks like."

"Yep," Rankin said. "Forty thousand one-hundred-dollar bills. I wasn't sure it would all fit, but it did."

"I'm not surprised," Tom said. "Conrad does his homework."

"You better get a wiggle on," Rankin said, handing over the heavy bag. "Take good care of that." Rankin turned toward the chopper and then turned back. Reaching into his breast pocket, he said, "I almost forgot to give you this." He held out a tan business envelope. "Ten thousand dollars. Down payment from George. You'll get twenty more after the drop is made, and the remainder when he knows his son is safe. Okay?"

Tom nodded, feeling a little dirty.

"Good luck." They shook hands.

Tom couldn't move, frozen in place by the enormity of the fortune he held. A career's worth of salary in a four-foot nylon case. He was surprised at how much it weighed, and surprised it didn't weigh more.

"Go ahead," Rankin said. "We'll watch until you're inside."

Tom looked at the CEO, then at the security guard with his hand on the butt of a large, blue-steel revolver, then at the small crowd of smiling hotel residents. There were more cheers when he turned and headed toward the lobby.

Conrad smiled at his computer screen as the camera picked up the man in the white, green, yellow, pink, orange, and red outfit. Quite an effective display if he did say so himself. The vet looked like some exotic bird. "*Tom-Tomus polackicus*," he giggled.

Conrad toggled the zoom to close up on the face of the young female desk clerk, her saucer eyes nothing but whites at the sight of this strange guest. She seemed to stutter as she greeted him, her smile strained to the limits of professional courtesy. Conrad tried to get a look at Tom-Tom's expression, but the glasses and ridiculous golf cap hid much of it. The Polack wasn't smiling, that's for sure.

Now the vet seemed startled, no doubt having been informed his credit card was already on file. Conrad chuckled. "Time to cancel another card," he said, doubting Tom-Tom had yet received the replacement for the last hacked card. This was fun.

Conrad had planted the camera earlier. None of the hotel staff had paid any attention to the young guy in the thrift-store Armani jacket and fake beard. He'd been invisible, just a face in the crowd. No one noticed him adjust the ugly horse picture in the lobby, leaving behind a tiny brown blob.

The micro-cam was no bigger than a pencil eraser, but it provided a nice view of the desk. There wasn't any sound, but he didn't want sound. Who wanted to listen to the jabber of faux courtesy and the mundane drone of small talk among mundane drones? Besides, facial expressions spoke a language all their own.

Conrad watched as Tom-Tom accepted the room key and was pointed to the elevators. The vet picked up the duffel, arm muscles outlined against the weight.

"You're a strong one, Tom-Tom. That's good."

Now the perky little receptionist was calling Tom-Tom back.

"Just one more thing, sir," Conrad said, mimicking Detective Columbo.

The receptionist held out the envelope. Conrad could tell it was heavy by the way she held it. Tom-Tom could tell, too, when he took it and read the printing. Conrad watched the vet put down the duffel, then think better of it, slipping the red carry sling across his body.

"That's right, Tom-Tom. Mustn't let all that dough sit around."

Then Conrad watched Tom open the envelope and slide out the cell phone and associated cords and earbuds. There was a momentary pause, then man and bag headed to the elevator. As soon as the Polack cleared the camera frame, Conrad dialed.

💣

Tom had no idea he could get tired of carrying money. But the most he'd ever had on him was a couple of hundred, not forty thousand hundreds. Why not a wire transfer to a Swiss bank? Probably not dramatic enough. It's like Conrad was playing out a scene from some old movie.

Tom readjusted the nylon strap digging into his shoulder and entered the elevator as soon as the doors dinged open. He pressed six, then stood alone in the car as the shiny doors slid shut. Then he nearly dropped the phone as it rang against his sweaty palm. The ring tone was familiar, a pounding drum solo from some forgotten big band. Tom answered on the second ring.

"Yes?"

"Hello, Tom-Tom." No mechanical voice this time, a human one. One Tom had heard somewhere but couldn't place. "Stop the elevator. Now!"

Tom pressed the red emergency button and the cubicle shuddered and stilled. A bell buzzed in the machinery behind the stainless-steel panels.

"Won't this notify maintenance that there's a problem?" Tom said.

"In a few minutes," Conrad said. "But we won't be here that long. Aren't you having fun?"

"My idea of fun doesn't include dressing like a clown in drag and having a nylon strap gouge my trapezius. This weighs a ton."

"Actually, it's less than ninety pounds. But I'm glad you're using the carry strap. You'd get awfully tired lugging it by the handle from here to there, there to here. Sound like fun?"

"Is that what we'll be doing?"

"Oh yes," Conrad said. "We're going to cover a lot of territory. Well, *you* are anyway." The voice giggled. "Now, start the elevator and press lobby." Tom obeyed, and the metal box moved up again. The doors opened on six.

"Am I getting off?"

"Just stay put, Tom-Tom. Do you mind if I call you Tom-Tom?"

"It beats 'Polack.'"

"Sorry about that," Conrad said. The doors whooshed shut again. "Now, once we're back in the lobby, you and the bundle head to your rental car. Do you like the car I picked for you? Kind of retro-chic, don't you think?"

"It's okay," Tom said, adjusting the shoulder-gouging nylon.

"Just okay? Oh well. Make sure you've got plenty of gas. There's a BP station on the way to the freeway. Fill up there."

"Which way am I going on the freeway?"

"I'll call you at the gas station." The cell went dead.

Sally's Miata was parked with a good view of the lobby entrance. She'd waited for half an hour watching people go in and out. A few business types dropped off by the shuttle. A young family of overweight parents with an overweight kid. A middle-aged man and a much younger girl, possibly a boss–secretary liaison. Just another stakeout, watching the human comedy play out, one snippet at a time. Then she caught a glimpse of color in her peripheral vision. She'd been right, he wasn't hard to spot.

The figure leaving the PT Cruiser reminded her of the Pied Piper, a story her dad read to her many times. Tom was dressed in a ridiculous clash of brightly colored neons and satins, with white tights painted on muscular legs that flexed and relaxed with each sinewy step. She remembered those legs. She remembered the tight glutes outlined in the running shorts. She remembered the flashing smile of the boyish face now hidden behind sunglasses. She remembered them all from a night that seemed long ago—but wasn't. One of the best nights of her life.

But where was the Pied Piper heading? Instead of the path leading to registration, the pink tennis shoes walked onto the lawn by the side of the building. Walked with a bit of an antsy quickstep. She'd lose visual contact if he went too far around the corner. What was he doing?

Sally reached for the door handle; she'd have to risk going out. But then he stopped, his head and shoulders visible above the bushes. At first, she didn't know what was going on, but then the bowed head and hunched shoulders struck a familiar chord, one she'd heard during hundreds of surveillance hours. She'd observed that pose on the inner-city homeless, construction workers at job sites, and drunks in alleys. The universal stance of the male eliminator. Sally shook her head. "Really, Tom-Tom?"

The whomp of rotor blades stole her attention. She knew instinctively where they were heading, the only logical landing pad. And she laughed. "Only you, Tom-Tom, would get caught in flagrante by Sky King."

After the drop went down and the bag man headed into the hotel, Sally resumed her scrutiny of the lobby entrance and waited. She didn't have to wait long. Not more than ten minutes later, Pied Piper and his bundle exited the double doors.

Her eyes followed him to the Chrysler. It's bright color and retro styling should be easy to mark on the road. The bundle went on the passenger seat and Tom behind the wheel. The old car angled out of the lot and headed to the exit. She held back, patiently watching and waiting, noting where he turned onto the road. Then she followed.

💣 *Chapter 21*

"Hey Bozo, nice outfit." The guy in beat-up jeans and armless sweatshirt grinned grubbily at Tom. He tossed a Miller tallboy to his partner pumping diesel into a dinged F-150 with lawnmowers in the back.

"Rodeo finals are in Vegas this year, Cowboy" yelled his partner, cigarette smoke squinting into his eyes. Both men chuckled.

"Shame when cousins marry," Tom muttered.

He had $10,000 cash on the front seat, a driver's license and his NIOSH-issued credit card tucked into the pocket of his hoodie. This wasn't technically government business, but he'd pocketed the wrong card, and cash would require enduring the stares and comments at the c-store register. Even assuming they would break a hundred. So, for the second time, he fished out the NIOSH card. The government could discipline him if they wanted; it couldn't be worse than this.

The pump clicked off a shade before the four-gallon mark. Stowing the handle, Tom wiped sweaty gasoline onto his red shorts, sat in the car, and waited. He had time to say, "Now what?" before the cell rang.

"All gassed up?" the voice from the earpiece asked. Where had he heard that voice before? The identity hid behind a hazy but not unpleasant memory.

"What now?" Tom asked.

"Now we get back on I-75 and head south, Tom-Tom."

"South to where?"

"To where I tell you to get off, Tom-Tom. Just keep the cell handy. I'll know when." The line went dead.

The engine caught after a moment's hesitation, then Tom shifted into D and headed for the freeway. He didn't pay much attention to the shapely form in the hooded windbreaker topping off her silver Miata at the Marathon station across the street. Nor did he notice her leave a few seconds after he did, keeping pace about five cars back.

Sally slid into the right-hand freeway lane, a half-dozen car lengths behind Tom's Cruiser. If anyone was watching, her following would soon become obvious. In a full-blown Bureau operation, they'd have several cars running a revolving tail. Once on surface streets, they'd do parallels. But there was only so much she could do alone. The yellow car merged onto the Williamsburg exit ramp. Sally merged as well.

The Cruiser turned right at the stop sign atop the ramp. When Sally hit the sign, the rental had already U-turned, coming back toward her Miata, Tom-Tom behind the wheel, sunglasses straight ahead, wires trailing to the plastic buds nesting in his ears. She started to change her right turn into a left one but then saw the Cruiser reentering the freeway going south. Now what? If she followed it immediately, squealing across traffic, her shadow would become painfully obvious—if, that is, Conrad was watching. If she kept turning right, changing direction at the service station, the tail might not be noticed, but then she might lose the Cruiser.

She had a split second to decide between the lesser of two evils. Her mind flipped through options. Tom was safe for now, but if she was seen following, he might not stay that way. Sally could lose him if she waited, even though her sports car had a speed advantage over the Granny-mobile he was driving. But she still had an ace up her sleeve. Taking a deep breath, she decided to chance it. Turning right, she drove to a Farmland Dairy service plaza. Sally stopped driving long enough to count to ten, pulse hammering her temple twice for each Mississippi. Then she took a deep breath and drove back toward the freeway entrance ramp. By the time Sally was speeding down the passing lane on southbound I-75, her hands-free cell was dialing Knoxville information.

"Hey, Doo. Where you off to?" Margie Pitblatto was manning the desk today.

"Hey, Mags. I am on my way to a well-deserved night off in the company of my good friends Jack Daniels and Pat Blue-Ribbon. But I will be back in the morning to fight the good fight, protecting John Q. Public from all manner of evil doers, foreign and domestic."

"And putting up with the whining of said John Q. Publics, foreign and domestic?"

"Bingo." Detective Sergeant Doolittle Powell slung his too-small, out-of-style tweed jacket over his shoulder and smiled. "You gonna miss me?"

"I won't be able to sleep tonight," Margie said, "lusting after your fine male form."

Doolittle grabbed a hefty spare tire in each hand. "Two-pack abs."

Margie laughed and waved him off, just as the phone range. "Detective Division," she answered.

Doolitte headed out into a fine late-spring evening. The air was damp, with a threat of rain, but it smelled good. Especially after eight hours of tobacco smoke, BO, and the thousand residual stinks haunting police vehicles and squad rooms everywhere. Maybe he'd delay hitting the precinct bar, sit in the park watching the birds, squirrels, and young lady joggers. He'd only made it halfway to his Ford when he heard Margie calling from the door.

"Hey, Doo." He stopped and turned. "Phone call."

"I'm gone," he called back. "Unless it's one of my many female admirers."

"Could be," Margie hollered. "Young gal name of Butterworth. Says she's with the FBI."

☀ *Chapter 22*

Conrad watched the dot pulse down the line on his tablet screen. Tom-Tom and his money were back on I-75 heading south. Soon they'd be at the Tennessee border. Time for him to move.

A vinyl airline bag sat amid a pile of odds and ends on his bed. One by one, he examined the items and placed them inside. The cell went into his shirt pocket. Donning his windbreaker, he checked his makeup in the mirror, absently scratched his upper lip. Tapping the car keys in his jacket pocket, he headed back toward his desk.

"What's with the getup?"

Conrad spun about, knocking the electronic tablet to the floor.

"Some kind of early Halloween party?" Robbie Robinson beamed a grin from the doorway. "Or are you back into theater? That would be great."

"Where the hell did *you* come from?"

Robbie shook his head. "My Dad's a dick. You know that?"

"Tell me something I *don't* know. Now what are you doing here?"

"I had to cut out," Robbie said, putting down an overnight bag. "I couldn't put up with him and the whole Ohio scene one more day. Thought I'd take you up on your offer."

"Offer?"

"Yeah," Robbie said. "Remember? You said if I ever wanted to get away some time, grab some space, chill, I could crash down here."

"Ah, well, this really isn't a good time."

"Come on. I know we've had our differences. What friends haven't? But I really need to crash." His smile flashed again. "I scored some dope. Good stuff. We could get high. What do you say?"

"Well, you see, I have someplace I have to go."

"I'll go with you. The way you're dressed, it looks like fun. Do I need a costume, too?" Robbie admired the face and outfit. "Man, that's nice work. You were always great at wardrobe, makeup, that kind of thing."

Robbie touched the glasses on Conrad's face.

"You should go into that. As a career, I mean. If nothing else, it would piss off your old man. His kid making bucks in theater. How is Adolph anyway?"

Robbie turned and picked the tablet off the floor.

"What's this? You tracking something? A package?" Now Robbie admired the tablet. "The new I-pad. Sweet. You got some kind of FedEx app or something? Let's you track deliveries?" His finger traced along the moving dot. "You were always good at computers, too. You could have gone into that. Made a fortune like Bill Gates. Of course, that would have *pleased* your old man, so it was probably out of the question." He spun about, grin dying down the short barrel of a snub-nosed .38. "What the ..."

"Sorry about this, Robbie. But you can't come along." Conrad's somber face brightened. "On a positive note, you *are* going on a trip."

Georgie King III chuckled at his own joke. Then he pulled the trigger. The noise was louder than he thought it'd be, with more of a flash. Ears ringing, he retrieved the tablet from Robbie's lifeless fingers. Georgie (aka Conrad) checked his watch. He'd dispose of the body later in some ravine. Now he needed to get into position for his big payoff.

💣 *Chapter 23*

Sally was stuck again. A Chrysler Reliant of 1980s vintage was doing sixty in the left-hand lane, the crown of its occupant's cap barely visible above the headrest. Sally flashed her lights and honked her horn, but she doubted the ancient driver heard or saw. The center lane held a line of three cars bunched together, the tail on the group being a lady in a Prius with a cell to her ear, eyes veering into space.

Sally reached for the cop gumball flasher in her glove box, when the truck in the right-hand lane signaled for the weigh-station exit, daylight showing beyond the departing semi. Sally stamped the brakes, eased behind the Prius, then farther right. Gunning the accelerator, she moved into the far-right lane, passing the Prius and a Honda, before eyeing an obstruction dead ahead in the form of a green Chevy pickup. If she timed it right, she could wiggle the Miata into the gap between the pickup and the SUV at the head of the center-lane triumvirate.

The FBI agent closed the gap to within a car length of the pickup. Then she punched the gas and turned the wheel sharply, only to hit the brakes again as the SUV in the center lane sealed off her escape route. The SUV backed off again, space opening off her port quarter. She once more shot for the gap, only to be forced back when the SUV sped forward.

Sally glanced left. The SUV's driver was a guy in his thirties wearing a Cincinnati Reds cap and a grin as big as Riverfront Stadium. He met her gaze with a shrug and waved her toward the gap in front as his big car eased back. Sally nodded in reply and gunned for the space, only to have it close again, the guy in the ball cap laughing his head off. She gave him a "come on" look and he nodded apologetically, slowing his car so the gap opened invitingly. But before she could jump ahead of him, he cut her off again, throwing his head back in glee. She'd have a clear path forward if she could get past this ball-capped idiot. But given the vagaries of traffic, any second someone could change lanes and trap her in a box behind the pickup.

Sally ran through the possibilities; even considered sideswiping Mr. Baseball. Then an idea popped into her head. Turning, she gave the Reds cap a toothy, dimpled smile. His own smile softened to a leer. Keeping one hand on the wheel, she used the other to lift her top, flashing him a glimpse of lacy demi bra. Leer changed to stunned as the SUV slowed and Sally cut into the gap and a hundred yards of open highway. Waving, she climbed the sports car back to ninety, the SUV dropping to a speck in her rear-view mirror.

Dodging like a slalom skier on a gold-medal run, she weaved from center to left lane to center lane to right. In two minutes, her little car had eaten three miles. Like a fighter pilot, her head swiveled to three, nine, and six o'clock, eyes straining for a gleam of yellow retro styling. There wasn't any. Edging the car to ninety-five, other drivers backing off, yelling, and flipping her the bird, she gobbled down more miles. Still no Cruiser.

Sally cursed the old man in the K-car and the jerk in the Reds cap. They'd cost her precious minutes. Minutes that the Cruiser could use to gain distance or exit the freeway. Once Tom-Tom left the cattle chute that was I-75, she was lost. He could be on any of a dozen surface streets, leaving her wondering which one, while he headed to whatever fate awaited him.

"Shit."

💣

"Are you still there, Tom-Tom?"

The voice joined the sweat pooling in Tom's ears and dripping down the plastic buds connected to the phone in his lap. There was something familiar about that voice. Where had he heard it before? It'd almost come to him, then fly away again.

"And if I wasn't?"

"Why then I'd be *very* disappointed. It would spoil all the fun we're having."

"Yeah," Tom said. "A regular laugh riot."

"Tut tut, Tom-Tom. Mustn't give way to the sulks. Tell you what, why don't you slow down a little. I'd hate for you to get a ticket."

Tom sighed in relief as he eased the Cruiser down to sixty-five, the old car's front-end wobble changing to a steady hum.

"Why don't you take the exit up ahead? Doesn't that sound like a good idea?"

Tom angled right, glancing up at the green road sign announcing State Route 35 in half a mile. Tom had driven I-75 on NIOSH business and knew a lot of the stops. Go right at the top of the ramp, he'd be headed to Deer Lick, Tennessee. Go left, and he'd travel under the freeway toward a little backwater called Buford. He hoped Sally was watching.

"That's a good boy. Now turn left onto Route 35."

So, it was Buford. Tom looked both ways, but the only cars were in a decrepit parking lot below a sign reading Randy's Gas 'n Go. He considered stopping for fuel; the gauge was below the half-way mark, but he'd have to ask permission. As he navigated into the gloom under the freeway, he asked, "Shouldn't I stop for gas?"

"No, Tom-Tom. I don't think that's a good idea. I think a much better idea is to get on the freeway headed north. Right now!"

Tom jerked the wheel left, squealing onto the entrance ramp he'd almost passed. The smell of burning rubber filled air damp with the threat of rain. His pulse slowed as the car sped into the northbound traffic. He hoped again that Sally was watching, but didn't see how she could be.

"Now, Tom-Tom. Let's open her up and see what this retro baby can do."

Tom accelerated into the left lane and watched the speedometer rise. Conrad hummed a pounding beat into his ears. He knew it was an oldie he had once heard performed by Gene Krupa in a late-show movie.

Tom eased down on the accelerator, the front end wobbling again as the old Chrysler topped eighty-five. Then he noticed the flashing blue light in his rearview. There was no bank of bar lights strobing from a police cruiser, just a single bubble atop a red passenger vehicle. Must be an off-duty cop, maybe Buford PD on his way for donuts.

"Shit," he said. "I got a blue flasher behind me."

"Then pull over," the voice in his head said. "And don't forget to be polite. The police are our friends."

Tom slowed the Cruiser and angled onto the shoulder.

"And Tom-Tom. Don't forget that this is *our* little game. We don't need others playing. Just you, me, and the Mid-American

Hotel and Lodging Association. Oh, I almost forgot little Georgie King III, who hopes to see his daddy again."

Tom placed the cell between his legs and dug the small bill-fold from his sweatshirt pocket. He wiped his sweaty palm on his T-shirt, then backhanded more perspiration from his brow. Glancing in the rearview, he saw only a pair of dark trousers that disappeared in his blind spot. Tom hummed the window down.

"Gee, officer, I'm sorry about that. I know I was ..."

"Going a little fast, weren't you, partner?"

This voice was also familiar, and Tom didn't have to struggle to remember where he'd heard it before.

"I'll need to see your license. By the way, nice outfit."

Doolittle Powell winked at Tom, then held up a restraining finger. One hand took the operator's license while the other found an ample hip.

"I was on my way home," Doolittle said. "Noticed you was kind of eatin' up the passin' lane. Someone chasing you?"

"Ah, no," Tom said. "I was just ..."

"Just in a hurry to see the wife and kiddies, huh? Well, I know how that is. I'm not officially on duty, so I'm gonna let you off with a warning Mr. Tomashinski. But slow down and be safe. Okay?"

"I will, Doo ... I mean, will do, officer. Thank you."

Doolittle winked again before handing back the license and heading to his Ford. Once behind the wheel, he grabbed the cell off the passenger seat.

"He's traveling north on 75, just south of Williamsburg. I'll wag a loose tail on him. You wait on the shoulder to see if he comes back south. Okay?"

"Okay, Doo," Sally's voice said. "I owe you."

💣 *Chapter 24*

They were back in Tennessee, headed south. Sally was having no trouble marking the yellow car, which had been moving at a leisurely pace for half an hour. No more high-speed passing, traffic weaving, or sudden exits. She had the feeling Conrad had relaxed, sure he must have thrown off any tail. The more she thought about it, the more convinced she was that he hadn't been watching. Tracking yes. Listening, maybe. But not watching. She closed to within a few car lengths of Tom's PT Cruiser.

Dusk was falling, along with a misty rain. She hoped Tom-Tom would light somewhere soon, as he'd be difficult to follow in the drizzly dark. More importantly, the long stretches of high-speed driving had her gas gauge bouncing near empty. Inside of thirty minutes, her engine would be burning air instead of fuel. And she couldn't coax more miles out of her sports car by showing it her bra. The little car had muscle and determination but was still a she, just like her owner.

Her one consolation was that the PT Cruiser should be in similar straits, running low on fuel, awaiting landing instruction. At least she hoped so. With that thought, the blinker flashed on her quarry as it drifted onto the Middleboro exit. Something told her this was it.

Grabbing her cell, she punched redial.

"Yeah," twanged from the earpiece.

"I think he's going to roost somewhere around Middleboro, exit number ..."

"Yeah," Doolittle said. "I know it. I'm about ten miles back. I'll be there in fewer minutes."

"Shake a leg," Sally said. "I'm running on fumes and I won't be able to shadow him on my own."

"Roger, Pard. I've got a friend on Middleboro PD. I'll give him a call. See if he can lend a hand."

Sally smiled. They might just pull this off.

Sally exited a couple hundred feet behind the Cruiser. The yellow car turned right, and Sally followed, maintaining a discreet distance. Her gut told her it was safe, no one was watching, at least for now. But your gut could get you killed. Or someone else. Someone with a funny name and a boyish charm that made her smile.

She'd met other guys who thought they were cute, or witty, or oh so desirable. But Tom-Tom was different. He was cute, he was witty, he was desirable. But she felt he didn't know it. Or if he did, tried not to use it, or at least not overuse it. There was an honesty there. Nothing smarmy, no lounge-lizard qualities. That had been her dad's term. Her heart ached despite the years.

Once, shortly before his death, Dad had invited a partner over for dinner. Sally remembered the name: Don Johnson, like the TV star on the reruns she watched with her friend, Rhiana. Her evolving, adolescent brain thought Officer Johnson was hot when he smiled at her over dinner. But she couldn't tell her dad that. So, she said that she thought he was very charming. The word had a nice, grown-up, cocktail-party sound. She remembered her dad's reply. "Yeah, he thinks so, too." She'd inquired further, and her pop had said, "That's not real charm, Sal. He's a lounge lizard. You should learn the difference and stay away from guys like that." It'd taken time, but she thought she'd learned the lesson, maybe a little too well. But she was sure of one thing. Despite the way they'd met, Tom-Tom was no reptile.

Moving through downtown Middleboro, they blended into the light evening traffic. The little sports car and yellow retro wagon looked out of place amid the pickups, SUVs, and muscle cars. Stopping for a light opposite a Valero station, Sally once again noticed her fuel gauge nearing empty. The warning light hadn't come on yet, but once it did, experience taught her she had less than a gallon. She thought about topping off with ten bucks worth, running in to pee while she was at it. But that was wishful thinking. The light would change before she even got her pants down. Then the light did change, and thoughts of filling her car or emptying her bladder were washed away.

She let a couple of vehicles get between her and the Cruiser, keeping her distance, knowing that this was the place, that Conrad might be waiting anywhere along the way. Waiting to take the drop. Waiting and watching.

Then the station wagon in front stopped for an early amber light, trapping Sally behind. Panicked, she resisted the urge to lay on the horn. Where the fuck was Doolittle? The wagon put on its blinker and turned on the red. Line of sight restored, the glare of the rain-haloed streetlamp revealed a yellow blur turning right about two blocks up. She turned on red, cutting off a rusty old Ford with a very workable horn that Sally barely heard.

She punched the Miata up to forty. She should now be paralleling Tom. Blowing through a stop sign, she glanced down the intersection but could spy no Cruiser. Her fuel warning light flared by the time she slowed for the second intersection, a long thoroughfare named Parker Boulevard heading out of town at a forty-five-degree angle. There, in the last of the downtown streetlights was a yellow car, taillights receding into the distance. She turned left and followed.

"Come on," she said through clenched teeth. "Stop somewhere."

An old Chevy passed her going the other way, and a heavily Bondo-ed Camaro crossed in front of the Cruiser at a four-way stop. But these were the only signs of life as the road wound through a couple miles of factories, auto shops, and warehouses. When these were gone, so was the light, leaving only the last few dregs of misty dusk and the red glow of the Cruiser's tail. At least she hoped it was the Cruiser. She'd only really noticed the color earlier, and now it was too murky to see details. Hopefully she wasn't following a yellow Civic or minivan.

Another mile sped by. Then another. Her thirsty gas tank was good for maybe another ten of those. Then she'd be pulling over, whether or not Tom-Tom did. As if by telepathy, the Cruiser slowed, its taillights growing to large, glittering penumbras in her windshield. The red lights veered right and came to a stop, Sally now able to make out the rear end of a parked car. "Finally," she said.

Sally drove past, knowing that the wary Conrad might now be watching. The tired agent breathed a sigh. It was indeed a PT Cruiser. It did indeed have dealer plates. Looking in the rearview, she caught a glimpse of a tall, muscular figure in white tights and garish duds bathed in the dome light of the open door. She killed her lights and parked a couple hundred yards ahead.

Tom was parked next to an ancient sidewalk, weed-filled cracks weaving through the concrete. In the distance, he could see a stone and clapboard building with a single light burning above the door. Behind him were a series of blocky shapes that ran away in rows. Some were low, others rose majestically into the misty air. The overall gloom was making it impossible to distinguish more. Then he remembered the sunglasses he wore as part of the costume Conrad had devised for him. Taking off the shades, he squinted into the misty night. Now he could see a sign above the door of the building. There were three words. He couldn't make them out, but the second one began with a B and the third a C. He wiped moisture from his eyes and squinted harder. "Something Baptist Church," he said slowly. Looking again at the short and tall shapes, he realized they were tombstones marching into the distance.

Replacing the shades, he slammed the driver's door, then worked his way around to the waiting bundle on the passenger side. Tom hefted the nylon strap onto his shoulder.

"Still having fun, Tom-Tom?"

Tom flinched at the sudden voice. "I'm wet, tired, thirsty, and semi-blind. And my balls feel like chestnuts roasting on an open fire. What do you think?"

"I'll take that as a yes," the voice in his ears said.

"What now?"

"Now," the voice said, "we'll pay our respects. Head into the cemetery. There's a path to your right. See it?"

"How can I see anything in this muck. Can I at least take the glasses off?"

"But they look so good on you." The voice laughed. It wasn't a man's laugh, more like the giggle of an adolescent girl. "Tell you what, why don't you just slide them down your nose a tad. You'll be able to see over the top. Better now?"

"Great," Tom said.

"Fine. Look down your nose. See how the path looks different than the grass?"

"Yeah. So?"

"Just follow your nose. I'll tell you when to stop. And Tom-Tom?"

"Yeah?"

"Better put your hood up. I'd hate for you to catch cold."

The nylon strap dug into his shoulder as Tom lugged the bag into the cemetery. He felt like a blinkered beast of burden, the glasses and hood tunneling his vision into a narrow band. Focusing on the gravel path, he moved forward, one bright-pink clown shoe following the next, nylon bag banging against his leg with every stride.

"Pick up the pace, Tom-Tom. Little Georgie King wants to see dada. Tick tock, tick tock."

Tom broke into a jog, the nylon strap gouging his shoulder.

Sally flicked off the dome light before exiting the Miata. A quick check of her Glock told her a nine-millimeter hollow-point was in the pipe, with fourteen more in the magazine. Grabbing her cell and windbreaker from the passenger seat, she shrugged into the jacket and broke into a run.

Sally pressed redial as she ran. Ahead she could see Tom's dome light flick off, then come on again a few moments later.

"Where you at?" Doolittle's southern drawl said in her ear.

"I'm on Parker Boulevard, about a hundred yards north of what looks to be a church. Our boy has gone to roost, and I'm in foot pursuit."

"Church on Parker?" Doolittle repeated. Sally heard another male voice, muffled but still audible. "Parker Baptist," the voice said. "Between Parker and Summerville, down by the railroad tracks."

"Who was that?"

"Roscoe Coltrane," Doolittle said. "Friend of mine from Middleboro PD. We'll head up Summerville Road, get our boy boxed in. You follow on foot. Should be in position in five, ten minutes."

"Better hurry," Sally huffed between breaths. "Unless a revival meeting shows up, I'm gonna stick out like a bruised thumb following him by myself."

"We'll make it five," Doolittle said. "Hang loose."

Gravel crunched underfoot as Tom jogged along, dusk ebbing into primeval darkness. He could still make out the path, which was wide enough for a single car, and feel the texture of the gravel, but otherwise was blind. The dim light from the church and another far in the distance were the only rays of guidance. Reaching up, he took off his glasses. "Fuck you," he mumbled.

"What was that?" the voice in his ears asked.

"Nothing," Tom said.

Sweat pooled in his eyes, just one more annoyance in a sea of them. His shoulder was already raw from the weight of four-million bucks. The load was also needling an ache into the small of his back. Worst of all, the pantyhose were strangling him. Clenching muscles to get feeling back in his legs and feet, he shifted back and forth, tugging the fabric at his crotch. But instead of relieving his discomfort, his testicles merely shifted to new and more painful positions.

Tugging, hopping, and quickstepping to the side, he sought to at least reacquire his former state of sweaty status quo. He received only pinches and stabs to his privates. Tom splayed his legs and shifted the money farther back, just as his feet left the path onto slippery grass. Overcompensating against a fall, he stumbled forward into a small, crotch-high monument. The saint or angel guarding the grave site took no mercy on him, delivering a concrete uppercut directly into balls stretched tight as ripe plums.

"Arghh," he moaned, falling to his knees.

"Anything the matter, Tom-Tom?" the voice in his ears asked.

Dull, nauseating pain rose in waves, sending Tom to all fours, duffel on his back.

"Answer me, Tom-Tom. Time's a wasting."

"Punched by a statue," Tom groaned. "Right ... in the nuts."

"Ooh, that's got to hurt," the voice giggled. "You must be more careful. Wouldn't want to lose the Tomacinski family jewels. Not if you want little Tom-Toms and Thomasina-Toms running around some day."

"Ah," Tom moaned, the waves of nausea slowly changing to a muffled ache.

"Okay, soldier," the voice said. "Walk it off. Must pick up the pace. Little Georgie is waiting. Tick, tock. Tick, tock. Hut hoot hreet hore."

Tom stumbled erect and tried to jog in rhythm with the cadence in his head, waves of ebbing pain radiating from his groin. He'd never considered himself capable of killing anyone but thought he could make an exception for Conrad.

Sally dropped to a tactical creep as the dome light on the PT Cruiser clicked off for a second time. Even at fifty yards, she could pick Tom out of the deepening gloom, his white-nylon legs sweeping ahead of her. Mr. Hoover's FBI had required agents to have twenty-twenty vision, although that requirement had been relaxed in the modern Bureau. Sally's vision was thirty-twenty, meaning that she saw at thirty feet what average people saw at twenty. That vision had led her into sniper training, but she didn't have the patience for it. Now it was paying off, although her patience was wearing thin.

Parker Baptist Church was on her left. Tom disappeared into the cemetery beside it. Keeping low, Sally rushed for the spot she'd last seen the white legs.

Her ears were as acute as her vision, making it easy to catch the crunch of gravel in the stillness of the night. Slowing, gathering her breath and her resolve, she followed the sound.

Avoiding the path, she moved on the grass, her footsteps soft and sure, heel to toe, as per her stealth training. Her darting eyes panned for obstruction and glimpses of movement. She paused if the crunches ahead grew louder, sped up when they receded. Then they stopped all together, and she hid behind a tombstone.

Seconds ticked by, her body tight as a spring, ears straining for sound. She heard Tom groan, then cry out in pain. She crouched farther, ready to leap to his aid. There was another, softer moan. She poked her head above the tombstone but couldn't see him. Then a spectral figure rose ghostlike from a grave marker, its legs trembling. The figure with the white legs and blob on its back started moving again.

Sally traveled this way for five minutes, maybe ten. She couldn't be certain and didn't care. Ignoring the growing pressure in her bladder, she fixed her senses on the enveloping night and the path ahead. Tom made no attempts to hide his footfalls, either through cluelessness or an attempt to ease her task. Probably the former, she thought. He was witty, gentle, and boyishly charming. But he was an unlikely hero. Then she remembered something she'd heard about true heroes being terrified but acting anyway. She didn't want to let this one down.

The path ahead seemed to grow brighter. At first, she hadn't noticed, focused only on stalking her prey. But her keen eyes could now make out more of Tom. The blob on his back was now a nylon case. The white legs now connected to a torso, a hoodie obscuring his head. Beyond him was a lighter gap in the trees and tombstones. Beyond and below that a street, the wet macadam gently bathed in a dim glow. Sally paused, crouching behind a tombstone, until Tom's departing figure descended the gravel toward what must be Summerville Road. When the hooded head dropped out of sight, she hurried forward to catch a glimpse of where he turned.

The slope to the street was gentle, making it easy to partly run, partly slide down the wet grass to a tree fronting Summerville Road. Poking her head from behind an old oak, she saw Tom jog onto the pavement and turn left, heading toward the glow she'd noticed earlier. Panning that way revealed a tunnel bermed into a hillside, its black maw lit by a lamp high up on the concrete of the tunnel face. Based on what she'd heard from Doolittle and Roscoe, this must be an underpass allowing Summerville traffic to avoid the trains that rumbled along the tracks above. Those tracks followed the ridge, bending left and right, returning to ground level about a hundred yards distant.

In a very few moments, Tom was going to be lost within the tunnel. If she followed, she'd be bathed in light and easy to spot, even by a casual observer without Conrad's obvious skill. She needed to get to the other side of the ridge, so she could track him unobserved as he exited the underpass. And she needed to do that right now.

Staying in the shelter of the trees, she dashed along the sloping hillside, keeping parallel to Summerville Road. Her sneakers were soaked through, the slick rubber soles frequently slipping as she went. Twice she stumbled. Ignoring branches and pebbles punching into her palms and knees, she scrambled back up and kept moving. Now out of the trees, but also outside the halo of the single light, she scrambled up the final bit of ridge to the tracks above. Her feet reached the other side of the ties in four long strides, before scrambling down the opposite slope, where there was an identical tunnel exit with an identical light. She slid behind some bushes and punched her cell.

"Where you at?" she whispered.

"We're on Summerville, parked a few hundred feet north of the railroad underpass." Sally stared into the gloom but saw nothing.

"He's just entered the south entrance of the underpass," she said. "Should be coming your way any second."

"Roger that," Doolittle said. "I've got binoculars on the exit. Will observe, lights off, keeping fifty yards ahead. You follow up on foot. Copy?"

"Yeah, I hear ya," Sally whispered. Then she waited.

❦

"Almost there, Tom-Tom. Just through the tunnel and a bit beyond. Don't screw up now. Tick tock, tick tock."

Tom chugged along, huffing in the dampness, happy that it was almost over. His back was sore, the duffel had banged a bruise in his thigh, the nylon strap gouged his shoulder worse with each stride, and he stank of BO. At this point, if he never made it back alive, it wouldn't be the worst thing that ever happened to him.

He held out his tongue to let the mist wash away the burnt-copper taste of stress and fear. What he wouldn't give for a cold beer. Beer and Scotch rocks. He thought of Sally. He hoped she was out there, watching over him. But again, he didn't see how. Even he didn't know where he was.

The overhead light was comforting as he neared the opening, as was the light at the end of the tunnel. Not much more, just ten to fifteen yards through the shadows, then a bit beyond.

The light rain had not penetrated inside the dark shaft, but the air seemed as damp as outside. The country smells were tainted by the odor of something dead. Tom imagined this was probably a local make-out spot, used condoms and Walmart panties hidden in the darkness along with candy wrappers, beer cans, and empty bottles of Thunderbird. Keeping his eyes on the exit, he flinched when his foot sent a bottle skittering into the blackness. Five, six more strides and he'd be out.

"Stop!"

The word wasn't in his head. This voice came from somewhere along the wall abutting the sidewalk. What happened next was a blur.

Someone grabbed the rear of his hoodie, jerking him backward. There was scuttling movement to his right, but he barely noticed. All his focus was on the hard metal jammed into his spine just above the kidneys.

"Do I need to tell you what's pressed against your back?"

"No need," Tom said.

The metal against his spine jabbed harder. "Now, keep looking straight ahead, but toss the bundle behind you."

Tom did as instructed, keeping his eyes on the blackness that lay on the other side of the road. The hand released his sweatshirt, but the gun muzzle continued poking viciously into his back with a steady pressure that would have been painful if he wasn't so scared.

"Don't move."

Tom didn't move. Except for the rapid rise and fall of his chest, he might have been a statue. His ears picked up a snicking sound behind him. Was it a pistol hammer being thumbed back? Life events flashed through his mind, just as they said they did in the movies. There was a second click. Then there was silence.

Tom stood motionless and afraid, seconds creeping by like the drips from a faucet. The hard pressure on his back was constant. He listened for a sound, any sound. But there was only silence. The silence of the grave.

💣 *Chapter 25*

The rain had stopped, but Sally didn't notice. Her attention was fixed on the tunnel entrance, waiting long, protracted seconds before Tom finally paddled out. Exhaustion had changed his confident, runner's stride into a shambling, toed-out gait. He stopped a few feet from the exit, fumbling with the duffel. He no longer seemed sure how to manage the load, tugging on the strap and teetering to one side from the weight. Then he stumbled forward, glancing over his shoulder at the tunnel.

Pangs of concern tightened Sally's chest. Stress and fatigue were taking their toll on him. He seemed diminished, smaller as he stooped under the combined burdens of stress and ninety pounds of money mill-stoned around his neck, darkness and fear his sole companions. Now she understood the Bureau policy against assignments involving friends or relatives. You couldn't separate the personal from the professional. And that could get someone killed. She cursed herself for agreeing to this craziness. She should have gone to the Bureau, Hartsell even. No matter what Tom or the MHLA said, this was a job for professionals, not one suspended agent and two local cops. For the hundredth time, she hoped she hadn't screwed up.

Tom paused again, adjusting the load. Then he rolled up the sleeves of his hoodie and stumbled forward at a walk.

She grabbed her cell. "Are you on him?"

"Roger," Doolittle said. "He's the only one there—and hard to miss in that get up."

Sally had to agree. She wasn't sure if this had been Conrad's way of making the bag man more visible or his little joke on Tom-Tom. Despite the rain, the poor guy had to be sweating like a pig inside those pantyhose and hoodie. But he was stuck with it. He might be able to take off the sweatshirt, but he'd need permission from Conrad before unlimbering the load and removing it. There was no doubt he was still in communication with the extortionist.

Wires to the phone still trailed from his ears. Her eyes snapped wide. Something was different. What was it?

Uneasiness swept her like a winter chill. She'd been examining his outfit, which was just as she'd remembered. Face hidden behind glasses, hood, and ball cap. White hose under red running shorts. Floppy, too-big, bright-pink shoes. And that bulky orange sweatshirt. Then something, some subliminal flash perked her spider senses. She thought how he might remove the bundle to take off the sweatshirt. The bundle. The duffel was on the wrong side. When he'd entered the tunnel, it was slung over his left shoulder, the nylon strap draped left to right across his chest. Now the bag was on the right side, strap angling down from right to left. He must have changed it in the tunnel. But why? Her fighter-pilot eyes frantically searched for a reason while he was still within the halo of light at the tunnel entrance.

His outfit was as she remembered, except now the sleeves of the hoodie were pulled up past his forearms. Nothing seemed out of the ordinary. Yes, it did. The sleeves were bunched at his elbows, revealing a dark blotch on the left forearm. It looked too regular, too defined for a smudge of dirt. She spoke into the phone.

"You have the glasses on him?"

"Roger, that."

"What's on his left forearm."

"What?" Doolittle asked.

"The left forearm, dammit. The splotch on his left forearm."

"Ah, some kind of tattoo. I can make out a heart and some writing."

Sally dropped the cell phone and bolted down the hill.

Sally's one hundred and forty pounds of bone and muscle slammed between orange hoodie and scarlet duffel. Even before the two bodies hit the ground, her Glock was out and pointing at Conrad's head. Her other hand held his left arm behind his back, pulling upward with steady pressure.

"Don't move, shithead," Sally yelled. "Or I'll blow your fucking head off." The Glock's barrel thumped his temple for emphasis.

"Don't shoot," screamed the prostrate form in garish garb. "I don't have any money. Just the bag. Take it."

"Later," Sally shouted. "Right now, I want some answers. Where's Tomacinski?" The gun barrel thumped again. "Where?"

"Ow. You're breaking my arm."

"I'll break more than that if you don't tell me what I want to know. Where's Tom-Tom?"

"Ow. I don't know who you mean." He stopped struggling. "You mean the guy who ran into the tunnel? He's still there, I guess. Or maybe he left. Ask Mr. Groenhaage. He'd know. Ask Mr. Groenhaage. He's in there, too."

The clack of footfalls grew louder as Doolittle Powell ran into view with another man in jeans and boots. Both had guns drawn, pointing them left and right.

"The tunnel," Sally shouted. "Check for Tom-Tom in the tunnel."

Roscoe ran for the underpass.

"So that's Conrad," Doolittle said.

Having patted down her quarry, Sally rose, pistol pointed. "Get up, nice and slow," she said. "And let me see your hands."

The man on the ground shrugged off the duffel strap as if it was contagious, then rose to his knees, hands raised. "Don't shoot."

"Take off the glasses and hood ... now."

The perp did as requested, revealing a handsome face of maybe twenty-one. "Don't shoot. It was just a practical joke. A gag. Mr. Groenhaage wanted to surprise his friend. You see, he'd lost this bet."

"Shut up," Sally said.

Pulling down the zipper, Doolittle checked the contents of the bag. "Towels," he said, pulling one free. "Hotel towels."

Sally could read, 'Parkway Tower' in the faint glow of the underpass lamp. "Who the hell are you?" she asked the kid dressed like Tom-Tom.

"Teasdale. Ryan Teasdale. I'm a theater major at UT. Mr. Groenhaage hired me. Paid me a thousand ..." He stopped and sniffed. Then he wiped moisture off his tights. "Shit. You pissed all over me."

Sally looked down at the large, warm stain along her crotch and pant legs. "Perfect," she said.

💣⁎ *Chapter 26*

An east-bound freight rumbled overhead, drowning out the police chatter. Middleboro PD had cars at either end of Summerville Road, with another car spotlighting the underpass. As the train noise Dopplered away, Tom looked at the piece of pipe wedged into the wall of the subway.

"There's what held you at gun point, Tom-Tom," Doolittle said. "Conrad just backed you into that pipe. Must have rigged it earlier when he was setting up the switch."

Tom shook his head. "I'll be a son of a bitch."

"Don't take it too hard, partner." The big detective patted his shoulder. "You did alright."

"Where's the money?"

"Probably with Conrad," Doolittle said. "Wherever this leads."

Doolittle opened a steel door set into the side of the tunnel. The turning knob produced the snick-click Tom had earlier assumed was a gun's hammer. A light bobbed in the darkness of a long passageway. Tom and Doo watched as the beam of light grew larger, coming toward the open door. Attached to the light was officer Roscoe Coltrane.

"Well?" Doolittle asked.

"Dead-ends at a railroad maintenance shed on a dirt side road." Roscoe pointed. "Where the railroad tracks dogleg back over yonder. I saw fresh tire marks in the dirt over there. I'd say they belong to our boy's car."

"That's that," Tom said.

"Yep," Doolittle said.

"Well," Tom said, "I was hired to make the exchange. The exchange was made."

"Go collect your money," Doolittle said.

"It was supposed to be a joke, see. A practical joke."

Ryan Teasdale stood in the glow of the cop cars, looking like some bizarre superhero in tights and orange cape. Sally was wearing a high-water-pair of Mrs. Coltrane's Levi's, waist belt bunching together loose fabric that went with twenty extra pounds of cop's wife.

"What kind of joke?"

"Like I said, I'm not really sure. Something about losing a bet, so this guy is supposed to dress up funny and run through the graveyard. I'm supposed to be waiting inside the tunnel, underpass, whatever you call it, then run out the other side."

"Why?"

"I'm not sure."

"And you didn't ask?"

"He offered me a thousand bucks. Do you know how long I'd have to work at the bookstore for a thousand bucks?"

"What did this guy look like?"

"He was supposed to look like me. Or me like him. Same size, clothes, everything."

"The other guy, numb nuts. The guy who hired you."

"Mr. Groenhaage?"

"Yeah," Sally said. "Groenhaage. What did *he* look like?"

Sally listened to the same description she'd heard from Candi, the Dayton hotel clerk back when this whole thing started. Was it less than two weeks ago? Conrad was smart, sticking with a character they'd already drawn a zip on.

"How old?"

"Pretty old. Guy had to be fifty, sixty even."

Yeah, she thought, Conrad was really smart. College kids lumped people into two age groups—us and old.

"And he contacted you through the school paper?"

Ryan shook his head. "A local arts paper, *Citi Lights*. One of those throwaways they have at coffee shops. We always get them, us theater students, because they have auditions and rock concerts."

"So, you *auditioned* for Mr. Groenhaage?"

"Not really. He advertised for a specific physical type. Six foot, six one. One-eighty pounds, brown hair, roundish face, no beard or mustache."

"No tattoos?"

Ryan looked sheepish. "I was afraid that was gonna kill the deal, so I wore a long-sleeve shirt to meet him. He didn't ask."

"Where'd you meet him?"

"A bar in Knoxville. The Quarter Horse, kind of a grungy joint on Kingston. Paid me a hundred up front, gave me the rest in the tunnel." He reached into the sweatshirt pocket and removed an envelope. "See?"

Sally looked inside at a wad of Monopoly money. Laughing, she shook her head.

"What's the matter?" Ryan asked, "Isn't it good?"

"Only if you want to put a hotel on Ventnor Avenue."

Tom waited while Sally finished her call. Sweatpants covered his tights, his sweatshirt slung around his waist in knotted preppy fashion. The FBI agent looked up once, eyes catching his, then tilted her head back to clandestine conversation.

"All right. Yes, sir. I will. Thank you."

Tom held out his cell phone. "Thought you might need this. Conrad gave it to me. Maybe it's a clue. Fingerprints or something."

Sally smiled. "I think we can safely assume that it has been professionally laundered, given Conrad's track record. But thanks for the thought."

Tom nodded toward her phone. "What was that about? Did I get you in more trouble?"

"Oddly, no. It would appear I have been reprieved, at least for the time being." She held up her cell. "That was Crossfield. He talked to Hartsell. Charges have been dropped. I'm back on duty effective now."

"Hardass have a change of heart?"

"Doubtful," Sally said. "More likely Scott convinced him it'd be a bad idea to advertise falling for a red herring named C. Roger Caldwell. That would come out in a hearing."

Tom smiled. "So?"

"So, I'm back on the Conrad investigation. Debriefing in Knoxville at 7:30 tomorrow morning. We'll need you as well. But I guess the Bureau can let you sleep in till nine or so."

Tom bowed, appreciatively. "Speaking of sleeping in. I'm heading over to the Parkway. How about a drink to celebrate my survival and your redemption? I'm a relatively rich man these days. I'm buying." He grinned his boyish brightest. "You can help me with my pantyhose. I don't have the experience."

Her dimples vanished as quickly as they'd appeared. "Hey, I'd love that. Really. But I've got work tomorrow. I'll need to get some gas in my Miata, then it's back to Knoxville, clean up, grab a couple hours sleep."

Tom's hands went into his pockets, shoulders slumping. "Well then, how about lunch tomorrow. I mean, I'll have to stay around to ..."

"I'm going to be pretty busy, Tom-Tom. I've got to get Crossfield up to speed, then *I* have to get up to speed with what I've missed. Which means talking to Hartsell, unfortunately. You know the Bureau."

"Never sleeps. Yeah, I know." They stood staring through a pregnant pause. Finally, Tom said, "Glad things worked out for you. Thanks for watching out for me." He kissed her cheek the way Donny kisses Marie. "See you tomorrow."

Sally watched Tom-Tom walk toward Doolittle and Roscoe. She started to say something, then stopped herself. She had a golden opportunity to get back in the game, all fouls forgiven. She couldn't pass it up. But part of her said this was going to be another regret. Maybe the biggest one yet.

💣 *Chapter 27*

"Hi, Al. It is Al, right?"

"That's right. Oh yeah. You're Cheryl's friend. Dr. Toma..."

"Just call me Tom."

"What'll you have?"

"Make it a pint of Bass."

"You got it."

Tom was back at the Middleboro Parkway, having a beer in the Halfway Lounge, and having just been shot down once again by the lady he might be falling in love with, if that was possible after a couple of weeks.

This go-round at the Parkway, he was dressed in Walmart haute couture: jeans, polo shirt, and loafers that appeared to be made of vinyl. He already had a room for the night and had made his obligatory call to the MHLA. So, he thought it past time he celebrated not getting killed or crapping his pantyhose during his one and only bout as Dirty Harry.

"On the house," Al said, plunking a frosty pint on the bar.

"Why, thank you, Al."

"Don't thank me, I just work here." Al nodded toward the doorway.

There was Cheryl Wagner dressed in Parkway red, long legs walking toward him. Tom still liked her smile.

"Hello."

"Hello," Cheryl said. "Al? A shot of ... Jim Beam, wasn't it?" Tom nodded. "I'll allow you one, before dinner."

"Kitchen is closed," Al said with practiced finality.

"Not for Dr. Tomacinski," Cheryl said. "He can have any *sandwich* he wants, also on Parkway."

"I actually have money, this time." Tom patted his pants pocket.

"You won't need it. I have instructions from senior management to make you *comfortable*." Hands on hips, her head cocked a pensive pose. "Can you think of any ways that I might do that?"

Tom smiled and sipped the bourbon Al set before him.

Cheryl's finger tapped Tom's lips. "Just the one. It looks like you've had a hard day. And I want you relaxed, but not passed out, when I get off duty in an hour."

"I'm in 311," Tom said.

"I know," Cheryl said. "I have a pass key."

George King II jerked awake. He'd clunked out after one too many anxiety bourbons, and now people kept waking him up. First it was Tomacinski, reporting in that all was well. He'd sent him on to the Middleboro Parkway with his thanks and a call to the afternoon manager, Charleen Wexler or something, to set him up on the house. Now the hotel phone was buzzing again, little red light flashing.

"What?"

"Is this George King?"

"Yeah. Who's this?"

"This is Sgt. Anthony Vescuzzi of the Maryville, Tennessee, Police Department."

"Who? ... What? ... Why?"

"We have a young man here who claims to be your son."

"Georgie? You have Georgie? Is he all right?"

"Looks to have a couple of bruises, a little shaken up, but otherwise okay. I'll let you talk to him."

George King heard muffled voices. Then a familiar one said, "Dad?"

"Georgie? Is that you? Thank God, you're all right. What happened?"

"I, ah, I don't remember much. Somebody grabbed me, over by the Townsend place. I think I was drugged. Then about an hour ago, they dumped me out behind the Maryville Kroger. I didn't see who."

"Never mind that, just so long as you're safe."

"The police want to know if you want to press charges."

"No. Just so long as you're safe. Where are you? I'll send a car."

"I'll put Sargent Vescuzzi back on, I'm still a little foggy." Then George heard his son's muffled voice say, "He wants to talk to you."

The cop's voice droned in the background as Georgie King III slugged down half his Pepsi. He'd had a hard night's work, but it was worth it. He smiled, which hurt the bruise under his right eye.

The five-pound sledge he'd used had clipped him a good one, clipped him harder than he'd intended. But sometimes, make-up won't do it. You need method acting. The bags under his eyes and dirt above his lip were carefully applied burnt cork. The rest was award-winning Georgie King, gifted beyond the ken of those boobs in the OSU theater program. He smiled again, despite the pain.

The money was safely stashed in his room, and Robbie's body was safely stashed in the ravine behind the Townsend house. Within a month, wildlife critters would make his old friend indistinguishable from a deer carcass. By that time, Georgie would be sipping planter's punch on some tropical beach. Life was good.

Chapter 28

"Well, Momma, what do you think?"

"It's nice."

"Okay, what's wrong with it?" Cheryl Wagner knew her seventy-six-year-old mother well enough to know when "it's nice" meant "I hate it." "Of all the places we've looked at, it seems like the best one to me."

"No, it's nice. But I don't see why I can't keep living where I've lived for the past forty years."

"We talked about that," Cheryl said. "Ever since Dad passed, you've been rambling around that old barn. It's too much for you, especially with your arthritis. Too much to clean, too much to heat, too much yard. We talked about all this, remember?"

They had indeed talked about it. The battle had raged for two years. Two years of arguments that started with the pros and cons of at-home assistance versus assisted living, but always ended with Mary asking why Cheryl didn't love her anymore. Left unsaid was the gas stove, which her mom had left on at least twice. Likewise unsaid was the incontinence rash Mary had developed by forgetting to change her Depends—or forgetting to even buy them. Ditto the rotten food Cheryl threw out weekly because Mom never remembered what was already in the fridge by the time she hit the grocery shelves. And neither of them even alluded to the time Mom walked to said grocery store, only to forget her way home. Cheryl had calmed her tears, then vowed to find a nice place that could deal with dementia.

"Yes, I remember," Mary Wagner said. "I'm not senile, if that's what you think."

Cheryl put an arm around her mom's shoulders. "No one said you were. You're just a little forgetful. Me, too. I'm *your* daughter you know. It happens to all of us as we get older." She kissed her mom's head. "I just worry about you. I know you get lonely."

A tear glistened in Mary's eye.

"That's why this place is great," Cheryl said. "There're people to talk to. And you don't have to worry about cooking."

"I can still cook better than you."

"Doesn't your friend Gladys live here? You two can have dinner together. You can play cards, sit, and chat.

"Gladys is a Democrat," Mary chided.

"Then don't talk politics," Cheryl said, giving Mom's shoulder a squeeze. "Let's go have some lunch in the dining room."

Yes, her mom needed a nice, safe place. A place where she could seamlessly pass from minor assistance with daily living, to major assistance, to Alzheimer care, without the trauma of moving again. A nice, safe place like Parkway Village.

Cheryl watched her mom scrape crumbs of cheesecake from the little blue roses on her plate. The chef at the Village was an old friend from Cheryl's days at the Parkway Plaza Hotel in Louisville. She'd asked him to cook something special for Mom. Her mother would have more than enough time to complain about the reasonably tasty, nutritionally balanced, institutional fare she'd be having three times a day. Now, she needed something special as a coaxer. A teaser to help her make the right decision. The chicken Florentine had done the trick. And Cheryl remembered that the cheesecake got raves at the Plaza.

"Well, was that good, or should we send it back?"

"Ha, ha," her mom said. "I don't know where you get that smart mouth."

"Must have been Dad," Cheryl said. "So, what do you think?"

"Well," Mary said, "the food is okay."

"Uh-huh."

"And the apartment is nice," her mom added.

"With two bedrooms, so I could stay over some visits."

"And the people seem friendly."

"And it's on the way to Middleboro, so I could stop by after work. And it's not too far from Knoxville, so we can go to Lorenzo's for lunch sometimes. And you already have a friend here, Gladys the Democrat."

Mary shot her a look. Cheryl ignored it.

"And because it's associated with my employer, you get a discount." Cheryl had saved the best for last, knowing her mom's Scottish blood couldn't pass up a bargain.

Mary Wagner sipped her decaf in silence. Finally, she said, "Well, I guess it's not too bad. If you have to *stick* me some place."

Cheryl patted her hand. "You know that's not true. And you know you're going to love it here." And I'll know you're safe, Cheryl thought.

Chapter 29

"The last couple days didn't hurt your appetite any."

George King smiled at his son, who smiled back from around a mouthful of pancakes. George Sr. gingerly touched his own face, reacting to the large strawberry bloom below his son's eye.

"Are you sure we shouldn't have you checked by a doctor?" George Sr.'s voice dropped a tone. "They didn't, ah do anything to you, did they? You know, molest you?"

"No, Dad," Georgie said, wiping syrup from his chin. "I think I'd have known if they buggered me, drugged or not."

"Alright, sure."

George Sr. poured coffee from the room-service carafe. He had a meeting with Bob Rankin and Charles Robinson at ten in Bob's suite. George II had never cared too much for Rankin, but the whole Conrad episode had shown the Travel-Eze CEO in a different light. Barbara Gerstel had flown back to Madison last night, and Art Chin was a no-show. But Bob stayed in Columbus until they'd found Georgie. And was still here for a strategy meeting. Though not initially on board about paying up, once the decision was made, Bob had seen it through. That showed class.

"I've got a meeting in twenty minutes," the elder George said. "You stay here and rest up." He finished his coffee. "What are your plans, now that we have you back safe?"

"Do you mean, am I going to straighten up, hang around Cleveland, get a job?"

George cringed. "Listen, about all that stuff I said. You know, I was hot under the collar. That's all. People say things when they get mad. It's just that I worry about you. I hate to see you wasting so much of your life. You may not believe it right now, but life is short. You can't waste it. You get to my age, you'll see I'm right. Can't we just forget all that for the time being?"

Georgie King finished his juice glass and smiled. "For the time being."

The other two association members were drinking coffee when George King entered.

"Georgie doing okay?" Charles Robinson asked.

King nodded and smiled. "I think so. Just a little shaken up." He poured a cup from the carafe, more to have something to do than because he needed it. "So, what do we do now? Now that I got Georgie back?"

"I think we call the feds again," Bob Rankin said.

Robinson put down his cup. "Do you think that's wise, Bob?"

"We're still in the same position we were a week ago," Rankin said. "We only have this guy's word that he'll be satisfied with the four million. The word, I might add, of a crackpot, terrorist murderer."

"But he kept his word about Georgie."

"That's right," King said. "My boy's back, as promised. I'd say that's a good-faith gesture."

"Would you listen to yourselves?" Rankin said. "Kept his word. Good faith. We're dealing with a *psycho*. For all we know, there's another bombing planned and ready to go."

"But why would he do that?" Robinson asked. "He's got his money."

"Right," King said. "Four million is a lot of dough. More than most people make in a lifetime. That should keep him occupied for a while. Besides, what would the FBI be able to do now?"

"Track him," Rankin said.

"How?" Robinson said. "He's sure to be long gone. He's got his money."

"But he'll have trouble spending it," Rankin said.

"Why would he?" King said. "It's all hundred-dollar bills. Not exactly that difficult to pass *these* days."

"They are when they're marked," Rankin said.

George King stiffened. "What are you talking about?"

"They aren't consecutive serial numbers, are they, Bob?" Charles Robinson looked grave. "He'd be able to spot that immediately."

Rankin shook his head. "The upper-left corner of each bill has a small spot."

"You shouldn't have done that, Bob. Not without consulting the rest of us."

"Don't worry so much, Charles. Conrad will never see it. Shows up under ultraviolet light. What they used to call pixie dusting, back in the day. Arbogast told me about it."

"Arbogast?"

"Private eye I hired. He and his men marked the bills. Also had Tomacinski under surveillance for a while." King and Robinson gaped at each other, then back at Rankin. "I told them to back off when they noticed another car on his tail." Rankin shrugged. "I figured, let him drop off the money. Then tell the feds. They'll shout out to the banks. Nab Conrad inside of a week."

Charles Robinson and George King continued to stare at the Travel-Eze CEO.

"Well, you didn't expect me to fork over four million dollars without doing *something*, did you?"

"You shouldn't have done that, Bob."

"Charles is right," King said. "What if Conrad knows about this fairy dusting or whatever you call it? He's pretty smart." A thought struck the Parkway chief. "What if he'd checked the bills before releasing my boy?"

"He didn't," Rankin said. "And it's a new method Arbogast told me about. Need one particular type of UV light to see it. This punk isn't going to know that."

"I hope you're right," Robinson said. "For all our sakes."

"How was the meeting?"

"Hmm. What?"

"Your meeting, Dad? How was it?"

"Oh fine, fine. Lot to think about." George King II poured himself a fifth cup of coffee. "Lot to think about."

"I've been thinking, too," young Georgie said.

"Hmm. About what?"

"Mostly what we've talked about. You and me. My getting my act together. The events of the last couple days, well, they've made me take stock."

George Sr. smiled at his son. "I'm glad to hear it. Maybe something good has come out of this whole thing, after all."

"Yeah, maybe. I don't have it all worked out in my head yet. I still have a lot to think about."

"Take all the time you need," George Sr. said. "The whole summer if you need to."

"I don't think it'll take *that* long. But I thought it might be good if I got away for a bit. Off by myself. Did some soul searching. Thought things through."

"Where would you go?"

"Friend of mine has a place up in Michigan. Cabin on a lake. Said I could use it if I wanted. You know, go off the grid. Forget the computers and stuff for a bit. Get back to nature."

George Sr. smiled. "Why, I think that's fine. Ditch that computer crap." He patted his son's arm. "When would you leave?"

"Figured I'd drive up tomorrow. Pick up some things from home, then get an early start in the morning."

"But, but you just got back—safe I mean. I figured that you and I ..."

"There will be time for that after," Georgie said. "After I get my shit together."

George Sr. sighed. "Okay. You can take the Beamer. Carl drives me to work anyway."

"Thanks, *Dad*."

"You're welcome, *son*." Two sets of eyes met in a father–son moment. The first in many years. Maybe ever. "Just remember what I said about life being short. Believe it or not, it is."

Georgie nodded. His boyish grin made him look a lad of ten. "That's why I figure I better get at it." The two men shook hands. Then big George handed little Georgie the keys to his BMW.

"Thanks, Dad. Thanks for everything." Then Georgie King III left his father's suite.

In the hallway, he put a finger into his mouth to feign gagging.

On a bright and sunny Wednesday afternoon, a black Series-6 convertible pulled into the carport at Townsend, Tennessee. Rather than head north, as he'd told the old man, Georgie had headed south to count his money and make his plans. A raucous, jungle beat blared from the speakers as the car settled to a stop.

"That was an original recording of the Benny Goodman Orchestra," the NPR announcer said. "The immortal *Sing, Sing, Sing*." The door opened and the announcer's voice cut out simultaneously. Drums pounding in his head, Georgie hopped from the car to inside the cozy mountain home.

Tossing the keys in the bowl on the kitchen counter, his shoulder twinged where the heavy strap and four-million bucks had rubbed him raw. He smiled, then bounded up the steps, two at a time.

His young, analytical eyes were drawn to the faded spot on the hardwood floor of his bedroom. Bleach was the best way to remove blood and DNA traces but was rough on lacquered pine. Maybe he should touch it up. But why bother. It could be any spill left unattended. He shrugged and headed to the closet.

The second-floor closets were tucked into the eaves, making for low-headspaced, room-wide storage wedged between two louvered doors. Snaking his arm and shoulder into the left-hand door, he pulled the duffel toward the opening. He smiled at the weight, close to ninety pounds of money. Ninety pounds of freedom. Ninety pounds of in-your-face respect. He slid the red bag to the bed and unzipped it.

His hands tossed piles of green bundles into the air, then back through his fingers like wheat at threshing time. Each packet held one hundred, one-hundred-dollar bills. Tens of thousands of dollars rose and fell at the behest of his giddy fingers. He laughed. Then he started throwing bundles onto the bed, first one at a time, then in twos and threes. He jumped on the bed and rolled, like a dog in something smelly.

Before the happy work of counting the bundles, he needed to make sure they were unmarked. He began by rifling the packets, mentally recording serial numbers. Some began with M, some L, K, or F, indicating issuance years from 2003 to 2013. So far, so good. His eidetic memory didn't pick up any long runs of consecutive numbers. Better and better. Then he retrieved the ultraviolet light from under the socks and dogeared copies of *Bondaged Breasts* in his bureau drawer. The light hummed as he plugged it in. A flick of the switch, and a pale blue light shone across his fingers. Passing the lamp over the bills revealed a kaleidoscope of chinks and specks in the rag paper, but no signs of pixie dust. Good, better, best. As he reached over to unplug the UV, he noticed the carry case held filters that could be fitted over the lamp. His photographic memory retrieved an article from a recent copy of *Coins and Currency*, which discussed methods for marking bills.

Ultraviolet covered the range of invisible light with wavelengths between one hundred and four hundred nanometers. George affixed a filter to his lamp, screening out the UV-A, the weakest radiation near the top of the spectrum. The bills were still clean. Now he affixed a second filter, eliminating the UV-B. That left only the UV-C, the smallest and most dangerous radiation. The radiation used to disinfect surfaces and water systems. A radiation barely even produced by the UV lamps commonly sold to consumers. But Georgie King III was no common consumer.

Upping the gain, he held the filtered lamp above the first stack of bills. A faint dot appeared on the top left corner. When Georgie rifled the stack, the dot hopped about like a kid's flip-book picture, jumping to a slightly different location on each successive bill. Dropping the bundle, he retrieved another random stack. Then another. The flip-book picture was always the same. Georgie gripped a bundle tightly, fingers white against the green fabric. The paper band broke when he hurled the pack against the wall, miniature Ben Franklins cascading down the knotty pine.

"Goddamn, mother-fucking, rat-assed bastards!" Another bundle followed the first. "Fucking, cunt-brained shitheads!" Then another. "Twat-rotted sons of whores!"

Georgie's breath came out in short, ragged gasps between clenched teeth. He might be able to pass a few bills with missing corners if he washed age into the currency to make wear believable. But even the morons at the bank would see the significance in a stack of such bills. He might be able to fence the money, but that would net him at most twenty-five cents on the dollar, probably less. Hardly enough for a lifetime on a Bahamian island, assuming he could even find a fence who wasn't, in fact, an FBI informant.

Another stack of hundreds hit the wall but with half-hearted force. Georgie was fading, along with his dreams of money and the esteem it bought. His young shoulders slumped. His oily face slackened. Gradually, oh so gradually, Georgie King departed. His mind's ear could almost hear the shout of "Elvis has left the building." But in his place was a pretty good backup band. A group consisting of Conrad Hilton, Ollie Groenhaage, and a half-dozen other performers. Maybe *Georgie* couldn't make his father and associated cronies pay for what they'd done. But the Conrad Hilton Octet was all tuned up and ready to rock. Maybe something with a Latin beat. But with a touch of soul. Aretha sang in his head about R-E-S-P-E-C-T. Conrad's spirits rose. "Find out what it means to me."

💣 *Chapter 30*

Sally sat stiffly in one of two visitor chairs opposite Scott Cross-field's cluttered wooden desk. She was back in the Bureau and back in her dark suit and pastel blouse, sensible low-heeled shoes, and pony-tail hair—what she'd come to think of as her G-girl outfit.

CNN played in the background, sound off. Photos of two swarthy men with unpronounceable names flashed on the screen above a caption reading "Killed by Tennessee State Police during high-speed chase after Chattanooga terror attack." These faces were then replaced by three more dark-skinned men, two with unpronounceable names and one named Clarence "Willie" Walker. The caption now read, "Killed by FBI assault team," followed by Monday's date. The daytime anchor then reappeared, sharing a split screen with a ten-year-old Bureau photo of a steely-eyed man with black, close-cropped hair. The caption now read, "Special Agent Scott Crossfield."

"I keep telling them to update that picture."

Crossfield walked to the chair behind the room's desk. He had the deliberate, sure-footed gait of a fighter pilot, which he had in fact been during Desert Storm. Now he was a twenty-year Bureau veteran and Special Agent in Charge of the Knoxville Field Office.

"Congratulations, Mr. Crossfield." It was Mr. Crossfield today, not Scott. There would be no playful mentor–mentee banter. Sally was back aboard the boat but hanging on the gunwale by her fingertips. She had a dressing-down coming and wasn't sure what direction it would take.

Crossfield leaned back in his chair, arms behind his head, tie loose, white shirtsleeves rolled to the elbow. "Yeah, we got lucky."

Sally knew that lucky gun battles in which all three bad guys died and no good guys got even a paper cut were the result of training, planning, and expert execution. Facing the man most directly responsible brought on feelings of awe, jealousy, and a little shame—the latter directed at the Middleboro clusterfuck she'd helped orchestrate around the same time. She wasn't sure how to proceed, so went for a preemptive strike.

"Ah, sir, I want to just say that ..."

"You don't really *believe* that, do you?"

"Sir?"

"That we got *lucky*? That we ran three terrorists to ground, secured the location, and administered swift justice because of luck?"

"No, sir."

"How would you say it was done, Special Agent Butterworth? What would be your objective, professional assessment of the reasons behind the successful operation?"

Sally cleared her throat. "Usually, such things are accomplished through careful planning by a team of professionals who gather and interpret large amounts of intelligence and then plan for possible contingencies before executing the most appropriate plan. Sir."

Crossfield nodded. "Can you think of any recent operation where that wasn't done?"

"Yes, sir. The one I participated in two days ago."

He nodded again. "And what was the outcome?"

"The perpetrator successfully extorted four million dollars and I put myself, Dr. Tomacinski, and George King III in jeopardy."

"Sounds about right," he said. "Of course, it needs to be recognized that your temporary suspension means you were not technically associated with the Bureau at the time. And it must also be recognized that acting in the private capacity of a concerned citizen, you used the limited resources available to safeguard the lives of those involved. Furthermore, it should be noted that you had no part in the planning of the operation and had no way of either informing the Bureau or influencing said plan without placing at risk the lives of Thomas Tomacinski and young George King III." His arms came down and he sat forward. "At least that's how my report will read." He smiled across the table. "Not exactly a gold star on your record, Sally. But not a blackball either."

❧

Embossed in white on the surface of the door was "Special Agent in Charge." Below that was "Daniel P. Hartsell." The latter was printed on a card slid into a metal bracket. The card was impermanent, temporary, designed to be replaced with the name of another Special Agent in Charge, just as there had been others before Hartsell. The thought should have given Sally comfort, but did not. It was irrelevant. Dan Hartsell *was* relevant because he was the *current* special agent in charge.

Crossfield had assigned her to interview the witnesses associated with the money drop, then repeat the ones done a week earlier. "We have limited options," he'd said, "besides tracking any bills that show. So, let's go back to step zero while we're waiting for things to heat up."

Crossfield couldn't assign her many resources, which meant borrowing those of the local resident agencies. That meant talking to Hartsell. Crossfield had also "suggested" she mend fences with the Cincinnati chief. Sally was not looking forward to that.

She'd had the option of interviewing Tom-Tom first. It was just a hop and skip to the NIOSH digs on Columbia Parkway. But that would only put off the inevitable. And something about facing Tom-Tom was even more daunting and uncomfortable than her meal of crow with Hartsell. Odd that this should be so, but so it was. Tom-Tom was a reminder of what she was giving up. She feared seeing recrimination behind his hazel eyes, hearing it in his soft, confident voice. Worse yet, she feared recrimination would be absent, replaced by a cold professionalism that said he was done with her and moving on. That's what she wanted—no, needed to happen. Yet, that was what she most feared. She knocked on Hartsell's door.

"Come in."

Sally cleared her throat and swallowed her pride. "Special Agent in Charge Hartsell? Do you have a moment, sir?"

"Of course, Special Agent Butterworth. Have a seat."

Hartsell was leafing through files in front of a computer screen. His pinstriped shirt and red power tie were currently uncovered by the gray suit jacket hanging neatly on the coat rack in the corner.

"Just finishing up some details on the Caldwell investigation." He tossed a folder down. "Didn't net your bomber but nabbed an embezzler and put Mr. Big out of business."

"Sir?"

"Caldwell was no doubt the brains behind the whole affair. Your Conrad decided to go rogue after we nabbed his boss. Wouldn't be the first time. Must have figured why let four million go to waste."

Hartsell graced Sally with a big grin. She smiled tentatively back. The message was loud and clear. So long as Sally played along with the desired narrative, the fiction that proved Hartsell right all along, they could be the best of buddies. She hated politics and all the charades that went with them. But her choices were limited. She continued smiling. "Yes, sir."

Hartsell's nod was as good as a handshake. "But we'll get him. Just as soon as the money starts showing. It was wise of Rankin to mark it." He handed her a sheet from the pile of papers. "We've alerted the banks and credit unions, airlines, law enforcement agencies, major retailers, so on. Once our man starts spending, he's as good as caught."

"Yes, sir." Sally's grin never dimmed.

"Now, then." He tented his fingers over the pile of papers. "From my conversation with Special Agent in Charge Crossfield, I'm assuming you are going to want manpower from the resident agencies in Dayton and Columbus."

"Yes, sir. And Special Agent Clemens if that's alright."

"Of course, of course. Take all the people you need. Let's keep our noses to the grindstone. Keep the pressure on." He smiled again. "The money will eventually slip him up, but let's not let Conrad get too comfortable. Let's make him nervous. Force him to exchange a few thousand for an escape route and some peace of mind. Then we'll have him."

Sally felt idiotic nodding and smiling along. "Yes, sir."

"You'll be under Mr. Crossfield." His "this time" was left unsaid. "But I'd appreciate it if you'd keep me in the loop as well."

Now it was "I'd appreciate it." No more, "am I making myself clear." No more orders. No more master and slave. Now they were colleagues. How simple it was. Eat a little crow. Agree to a little lie. Sally hated it. But she owed it to her career. She owed it to her dad, and to the vow she'd made that night he died.

She said simply, "Yes, of course." She even favored him with some dimples.

💣 *Chapter 31*

Tom pulled the paper tab, ripping the envelope along its width. Upending the large, cardboard rectangle revealed a smaller, paper one, which slid easily onto his desk. His letter opener found the seam, there was a quick ripping sound, and then a second piece of paper slid to his blotter. Tom held it to his desk lamp. Cleveland Municipal Bank was printed in one corner, complete with an address on Center Street. Along the top read "Cashier's Check" in block letters. Embossed further below, in colorful, raised numerals, was "$40,000.00." Attached by paper clip was a W-2 form reporting fifty thousand in income. "Death and taxes," Tom muttered.

"How was your vacation?"

Lynne Faulkner stood in his doorway clad in blue polyester slacks already out of fashion when she'd pulled them from the bargain bin early in the Obama administration. Which might not have been too bad had they matched her ever-present and equally worn brown and orange cardigan.

"Interesting," Tom said.

"And short," his boss added. "I put you down for one and a half vacation days, since you came in Monday."

"Thanks."

"Where'd you go?"

"Ah, down south."

"What'd you get?" She plucked the FedEx mailer from his desk.

"Kind of a Christmas bonus,' he said.

"We don't get bonuses," Lynne said. "And it isn't Christmas."

"Hmm."

"Misty has another mat."

"Have you been brushing her?" Tom asked. Lynne's cat was an ongoing fur fracas. If it wasn't mats, it was hairballs.

"She scratches me."

"I'll bring the clippers over this weekend." He slid the check back into its envelope. "You should buy some. They're not very expensive."

"I like it better when you do it. She scratches me."

Tom's phone rang. "Hello, Tomacinski speaking." Reception was sending down a visitor. Tom's heart skipped when he heard the name. "Thanks."

"Are you okay? You look a little funny."

"What?"

"I could make us some lunch or dinner, if you come over on Saturday."

"Hmm. What did you say?"

"I said ..."

"Knock, knock. Sorry, I didn't mean to interrupt." Sally stood in the doorway.

Lynne stared at Sally as if *she* were the pod person. The contrast between the two was striking. Both were late twenties, early thirties, but that's where similarities ended. Professionally dressed in blue blazer and tan slacks, the tall, trim, confident Sally could be an ad for "join the FBI." The shorter, stoop-shouldered Lynne most fit a poster for "send this girl to camp."

"No problem," Tom said, pointing. "Sally Butterworth, Lynne Faulkner. Lynne, Sally. Sally is with the FBI."

Lynne's limp fingers tentatively shook the firm hand presented to her.

"Oh, yeah," Lynne stammered. "I think we talked on the phone once. I better go. Staff meeting at ten."

"Admirer?" Sally said, watching Lynne shuffle self-consciously down the hall.

"Manager," Tom said. "Please, come in."

The FBI agent looked down at the stained cloth and metal chair opposite the desk.

"That's just old coffee," Tom said.

Sally smiled and sat. "Nice office."

"If you like a concrete box with no windows," Tom said. He moved a pile of journal articles so that he could see his guest.

"How have you been, Tom?" The playful nickname was noticeable by its absence.

"Fine, Special Agent Butterworth. What can I do for you?"

Sally tensed, then accepted the new dynamic. "I need to debrief you."

Tom almost said, "You know I wear Jockeys," but said instead, "Alright."

"Is this a good time?" She pulled a note pad and a digital recorder from her briefcase.

"Good as any."

"I have most of the background from our phone conversation Monday. Why don't you start from there and tell me everything that happened after that."

The red light on the recorder seemed to reproach him as he recounted the experience.

💣※

"Then Doo Powell called out to me in the darkness. Boy, I could have kissed him."

"And that's it?"

"Pretty much," Tom said. "I was surprised you were able to keep up with me, given all the twists and turns Conrad threw my way. But there was your Miata behind me in Middleboro." Tom doffed an imaginary cap. "I tried to spot you earlier on the freeway, but your little car is impossible to see amid all the semis and SUVs."

"Yeah, not the best choice," Sally said. "But my options were limited, under the circumstances. It was more important that *I* see *you*, and your car stuck out like Dolly Parton's cleavage."

Tom shook his head. "A yellow PT Cruiser."

"But even with that, it was Doolittle who saved both our asses. I'd have lost you without him." She bent forward to pause the recorder. "Not that my tracking you did much good."

"Don't be hard on yourself Special Agent ... Sally. You did the best you could." Some of the distance between them had melted in the telling. No more icy formality, but no intimacy either. "And I want you to know I appreciate you looking out for me." Their eyes met for a moment of understanding. Then she un-paused the recorder.

"Tell me about Conrad. Anything you can remember. What did he look like?"

"Never saw him," Tom said. "It was black as sin inside the tunnel, and he was always behind me."

"What did he sound like?"

"He sounded ... familiar," Tom said. "Like I'd heard his voice before."

"Really? Where?"

Tom shrugged. "I tried but couldn't place it. It's hung at the edge of memory, like maybe I dreamt it or heard it in passing. A couple of times, I thought it was going to come to me, but then it'd be gone. All I could think of was Carl Ziffle."

"Who?"

"A client my first year in vet practice. I only saw him once."

"But you remember his name?"

Tom smiled. "Carl was hard to forget. He was a young guy, maybe twenty-five. And he was a cross-dresser. A very ugly cross-dresser. Had a white shepherd named Queenie."

"Queenie?"

"If I'm lyin' I'm dyin'." Tom crossed his heart. "I can't remember what he brought her in for. Vaccinations, probably. But I remember Carl. He was wearing a satiny kind of cocktail dress, you know, with the little beads on it."

"Did he have nice legs?" Sally asked.

"If you're into big calves with manly hair smooshed under nylons."

"He was wearing pantyhose too?"

"Black ones," Tom said. "You could see the hair bulging beneath the material as he wobbled along in his high heels."

"Well, naturally you'd wear heels with a cocktail dress." The playful banter reminded Sally of when they'd first met, jockeying for position at the hotel bar in Dayton.

"Naturally," Tom said. "And makeup. Heavy, sort of hooker makeup. Big red lips, too much rouge." Tom puffed his lips to Mick Jagger proportions.

"And a wig?" Sally asked, trying not to laugh.

"Oh yeah," Tom said. "Cheap blond wig that didn't hide this shock of greasy black hair curling onto his forehead like Betty Boop." For a second, his eyes drifted, as if he almost remembered something. Tom shrugged. "Anyway, whenever I think I can put a face to the voice, it's always Carl Ziffle's."

"Can you spell that?" Sally asked, pen poised over her pad.

Tom smiled again. "Are you going to check *Carl* out?"

"We check everything out. Everything and everyone."

"Fine. Z-I-F-F-L-E. Or maybe it was E-L at the end. I can't really remember."

"And this was in New Jersey?" Sally scribbled on the pad.

"Yep, Flemington. But you're wasting your time. That was ten years ago. Carl would be mid-thirties now. And Conrad was younger."

"I thought you never saw him?"

"He sounded younger. Carl had a deep voice, which made it even funnier, him dressed in drag. But Conrad had a younger, softer voice. Almost girlish." Sally noticed his expression turn chilly, like someone walked on his grave. "I remember thinking he giggled like a girl. And the way he said Georgie, like a kid in grade school."

"That's George King III?"

"Yeah. He kept reminding me to hurry up because Georgie King wanted to see his dada. Then he'd start in with that tick-tock crap."

"King is fine, by the way," Sally said.

"That's a relief," Tom said. "I was afraid I'd gotten him killed."

"Showed up early Tuesday morning in Maryville, Tennessee. A little bruised and shaken, but otherwise fine. He's my next stop, though I'm not sure how much he'll remember. Father said Conrad drugged him." She clicked the recorder off and stowed it.

"Well, he got his son back," Tom said. "That ought to be worth fifty grand to Mr. King. Plus, his part of the four million, of course."

"Once those millions start showing up, we'll be able to track them back to the source and, hopefully, Conrad."

"Wait a minute," Tom said, stiffening. "How are they going to track them? I know it was all in hundreds, but there are a lot of hundred-dollar bills out there these days."

"Not hundreds with pixie dust on them."

"Pixie what?"

"Pixie dust or fairy dust. A dye that shows up under ultraviolet. Rankin marked the bills."

"He did what?" Tom was no longer smiling.

"We've spread the word to keep an eye out. Once Conrad starts spending, we'll nab him."

"You don't think Conrad is going to *know* the money is marked?"

"It's a new technique," Sally said. "We doubt he's that smart."

"And this is based on all the mistakes he's made so far?" Tom asked.

"Don't worry about it. We'll get our man."

"That sounds like Hartsell talking."

"Maybe," Sally said. "But that's the official word."

Tom sighed. "Well, I hope that you and he are right. I'd hate to have risked my life only to have Conrad torch another hotel for spite."

The sun was well west when Sally's government plates slid into the driveway roundabout at 966 Millside Lane. She was expecting another stately colonial that yelled money, like Robinson's place in Columbus. But the King estate near Cleveland was more a sprawling ranch home. True, it was in the posh community of Westlake, but with less than an acre of property in a neighborhood more suited to insurance salesmen than hotel magnates. George King himself greeted her at the front door.

"You're Butterworth?"

"Special Agent Sally Butterworth." She flashed her credentials.

"George King." They shook. Inside, a middle-aged woman was watching someone buy a vowel on a big-screen TV, knitting in her lap. "That's my wife, Lois," King said. "Let's head to my office."

Sally waved to the woman, who smiled back. Then she followed King.

The Dayton resident agents were reviewing video feed and re-interviewing desk clerk Candi Regan. Those out of the Columbus RA were on Robinson. But Sally wanted to handle King herself. Mostly she wanted to speak with King's son, George III. She was hoping he'd provide clues about his abductors. Right now, he and Tom-Tom were her best leads.

King sat behind a plain wooden desk, neatly arranged and clutter free. Sally sat in a plain wood-back chair. The rest of the furnishings were simple and utilitarian. Not quite IKEA, but not Williams Sonoma either. The only personal touch was a framed image of a smirking teenage boy with acne and dark bangs swirled across his forehead.

"I don't know what I can tell you, Agent Butterfield." Sally did not correct him. "You guys have the tape and things we got from that Conrad creep."

"They're being analyzed at our lab in Virginia."

"And it was actually Rankin who handled the money. Handled it and marked it."

"Agents from our Saint Louis office are interviewing him. Likewise, resident agents in Madison have talked to Ms. Gerstel."

"So?" King said with a shrug.

"Actually, I was hoping to get some information from your son. Maybe we should bring him in now."

"Georgie's had a rough go."

"I understand," Sally said. "Just a few questions."

"I mean, he's not here."

"Is he back at school?"

"No, OSU is done for the year. He took off for a few days. Maybe a few weeks. Wind down, clear his head. Detoxify from his ordeal."

"Can you tell me how to get in touch with him?"

"No, I can't."

"Mr. King, it's important that I speak with him. He is our best chance to identify Conrad."

"I don't know where he is."

"Pardon?"

"Said he was going to a friend's cabin up in Michigan. Didn't say where."

"Do you think that was wise?"

King shrugged. "Didn't figure it could hurt. Said he needed it. I said okay."

"Can you give me his cell number, so I can contact him?"

"Said he was going off the grid. Back to nature. Sounded like a good idea to me. Kids spend too much time on those damned cell phones and computers anyway."

Sally leaned forward and spoke slowly and authoritatively. "Mr. King. We need to talk to him. Plus, he should be under police surveillance. For his own safety."

King leaned forward as well, hands on desk. "Hey, I don't know where he's at, okay? And if I don't know, Conrad won't either." He leaned back. "Besides, we've paid off the scumbag, why would he bother Georgie?"

"But there's no telling what he might do if he discovers the money was marked."

King bored holes with his eyes. "Listen, Agent *Buttercup*. My boy took a few days to himself. I don't know where. Is there anything else I can do for you?"

Sally felt like Perry Mason crossing a hostile witness. She had a few questions for King, but mostly needed to debrief his son, the one who had actually been with Conrad, may have seen him or any accomplices. "Can I at least have a description of his car and license number?"

King reached for his wallet. "He took my Beamer. Here's the registration."

Sally copied down the number. "May I have a recent picture of George?"

"What do you need that for?"

"I can send it to the state police in Michigan and Ohio. They can keep an eye out for his car and contact the Bureau."

He leaned toward her again, the pissing match resumed. "You're going to put a *warrant* out on my son?"

Sally held up a restraining hand. "Not a warrant. Just a BOLO. Wanted for questioning."

"Like my boy is some type of damned criminal or something?"

"He's committed no crime, Mr. King. We just need to ask him questions. Until the money shows up, George is the best hope we have. *If* that is, you want to catch the extortionist and murderer known as Conrad Hilton." Sally paused. "If necessary, I can use his driver's license photo."

King hesitated, then handed her the framed picture from his desk. "This is his high-school graduation photo. I want that back."

💣 *Chapter 32*

"Are you alright?"

Tom straightened, hands to aching back in the traditional moving-day posture. "You'd think an injury epidemiologist would know to lift with his legs."

Cheryl walked past the heavy carton and rubbed his lower back. "Better?"

"Hmm. What's in that anyway?" Tom nudged the box with his foot.

"Mom's bowling-ball collection, of course." Cheryl kissed his cheek. "Actually, I think that one is family albums. Photos of my growing up—and older."

"I'd like to see those."

She pecked his cheek again. "After we've known each other longer." Tom watched her taut legs walk to a little red cooler. "How about a beer?"

"Thanks," he said, "Best muscle relaxant I know." Cut-off shorts riding higher, her bottom briefly assumed the shape of rounded hillocks as she reached down to the cooler. "I thought you were supposed to bend with your legs," he said.

"For some things," she answered, smiling between outspread knees. "Not for others." Standing straight again, ponytail flouncing over the collar of her University of Tennessee tee, she uncapped a Bass ale.

"You remembered," he said, taking the chilly bottle.

"I'm in the guest-comfort business," she smiled.

"What's in that one there?" Mrs. Wagner stood in the bedroom doorway, pointing at the new carton.

Years in the melting pot of the hotel industry had dulled Cheryl's southern accent, but Mary Wagner's twang was pure Tennessee.

"It's family photos, Mama."

"Lawd. You'll give this nice young man a rupture carrying those things."

"It's okay, Mrs. Wagner."

"Would you like a cold drink, Mr. Tamaski?"

"It's Dr. Tomacinski, Mama. And Tom already has one." Tom raised the brown bottle.

"Beer? Before noon?"

"It's 11:57, Mama. Besides, we're celebrating. That was the last carton."

Mary scanned the bare room. "I better not unpack them, so people can sit on the boxes."

"The movers will bring the furniture this afternoon, Mama."

"Will Dr. Tom be joining us for lunch?"

"I'd love to," Tom said. "But I have to run." He turned to Cheryl. "I promised to help Lynne with her cat."

"Is it sick?" Cheryl asked.

"A little minor surgery." Tom mimed running clippers. "Fur mat."

"Well, I hope you'll let me show my appreciation later," Cheryl said. She'd used her nondescript professional voice for the sake of her mother, but the underlying meaning was clear.

Tom grinned. "But this time, I'll buy *you* dinner. Pick a nice place in Lexington." He gave her a one-armed hug. "Someplace other than a Parkway."

"What's in this one here?" Mary Wagner said, pointing to the large carton.

"I think that's family photos, Mama." Cheryl's expression reflected both love and frustration.

❦

"It's our last independent-living unit." Tanya Bellis said. "I'm afraid it's only a one bedroom."

"That will be fine," the distinguished-looking gentleman said. "My needs are few."

"You'll have your choice between cooking for yourself or taking meals in our dining room," Tanya added. "You can pay by the meal or using one of our monthly plans. There's dinner alone, or breakfast and dinner, or all three."

"That will not be necessary. As I said, my needs are few, and I'm able to do for myself. At least for now." He held forth his cane and smiled sadly.

"Well, just tell me if you change your mind. You should also know that guests in our independent-living wing get first crack when *assisted*-living units become available. So, you'd be able to transition fairly easily." She smiled. "If the need arises."

"That is very kind of you."

The gentleman spoke slowly and distinctly, as is typical of those with English as a second language. His Spanish accent also reflected this, as did his name. He looked to be about seventy, with European manners and a graying mustache. His skin had a dull, powdery quality that Tanya chalked up to his psoriasis, which was the proffered reason for his gloved hands.

"So, if everything meets with your approval, we can go to my office and start the paperwork."

"That would be fine." He motioned with his cane." Please, after you."

It was a short walk, but Tanya paced herself to the speed of her companion. "Does your family come from Spain or Latin America?"

"I was born in Mallorca," her guest said. "One of the Islas Baleares."

"How interesting. Where is that?"

"A Mediterranean island off the Spanish coast."

"When did you move to America?"

"My company sent me ten years ago. To manage their American sales force. I decided to stay for retirement." He limped a grin. "America has, ah, how you say, lower cost of living?"

"Really?"

"Es verdad."

She held the door as he hobbled inside. "What did your company sell?" She motioned to the chair opposite her desk.

"Pottery," the gentleman said, before slumping into his seat. "Beautiful porcelain pottery."

"How lovely," Tanya said, but her mind was already on administrative details. "There, now. I have the paperwork all prepared. It just requires your signature and, of course, the two-months' rent we discussed."

He took the pen in his gloved hands, then looking at the paper, he signed the way he spoke, slowly and carefully.

"That's an interesting name, Mr. TresReyes. It means 'three kings,' doesn't it?"

He smiled at her. "Muy bien, Señora. But please, call me Jorge."

She smiled back. "George Three Kings—it has a regal sound."

He slid back the paper, still smiling. Then, reaching inside his tweed jacket, he removed a leather billfold. The gloves made it difficult. "Lastima. Por favor. Un momento."

"Quite all right, take your time. We accept major credit cards as well as personal checks. Although it takes three to four days for checks to clear."

"I always pay cash," Jorge said. "From an early age, my papa taught me the value of money." He managed to extract a stack of currency from inside the wallet. His gloved fingers handed them over.

Tanya wondered how long he'd been hanging onto them. The bills were limp and worn, some with corners missing. She began counting, first the hundreds, then the fifties and twenties. The sum was correct, to the dollar.

"Well, that's all I need for now. You'll be able to move in toward the end of the month, as we discussed. If you like, I can recommend a moving company. There are two that we use."

"You are too kind. But that will not be necessary."

"Well, please let me know if there *is* anything I can do for you."

"Yes, there is something." He returned the billfold to his pocket. "I will be having a container shipped here. Mementos, pottery from my old company. Rather special items. It would be possible for you to store them for me? I think you said I would have access to that?"

"Oh yes," Tanya said. "I can assign you a cubicle in the basement. I'll get you a key before you leave. You'll be sharing space with our old records. All the paper files we've accumulated since going digital. I hope that's okay."

"Bien," Jorge said. "Muy bien."

"I'm something of an admirer of porcelain. Would it be possible to see the contents at some point?"

"Oh yes," George Three Kings said. "You'll see my beauties in time. I think you'll find the experience, how you say, *illuminating*."

Tom bit into ham, cheese, and rye bread.

"Is it good?" Lynne asked.

"Hmm," he nodded.

"I made it with lettuce and tomato, butter instead of mayo. Just like you order in the cafeteria. Is it okay?"

"Yeah, great." Tom glanced at his watch, then took another bite. "You're a lifesaver. I've still got a lot to do today and wasn't sure I'd have a chance to stop for lunch."

Lynne's lips twitched briefly with something trying to become a smile. "Thank you for fixing Misty." At mention of her name, the long-haired cat curled her tail around Tom's leg, showing both affection for the vet and love of smoked meats.

"No problem," Tom said, washing down the bite with a swig of beer. "You need to brush her more."

"Is the beer okay? It's the kind I saw you drink at the Christmas party."

"Great." He took another swig. "Long-hair cats always mat up if you don't brush them."

"I'm not good at it. Could you show me how again?"

Tom glanced at his watch. "I'll brush her a little before I go. She actually likes it if you do it gently. Just firm, gentle strokes, down the back, along the sides, then around the legs and onto the rump."

"Hmmm," Lynne murmured.

"You okay? You look a little flushed."

"No, ah, I'm fine."

Tom took another bite.

"That FBI woman?" Lynne asked.

"Sally?" he said.

"Is she your girlfriend?"

Tom stopped mid chew. "No." The bread suddenly tasted stale. "She's all FBI. Through and through."

The thing that normal people called a smile briefly reappeared on Lynne's face. Tom didn't notice, he was glancing at his watch.

"Speaking of girlfriends, Cheryl's expecting me for dinner. I better get a move on if I want to clean up and get to Lexington by 7:30."

Lynne's smile-like expression morphed into one more universally associated with dismay. Tom didn't notice. He was glancing at his watch.

💣 *Chapter 33*

"Okay, that's thirty-five pounds finely powdered aluminum and sixty-five pounds iron-oxide powder. Anything else?"

"Yeah," Georgie King said. Today he was dressed in blue-jean jacket, horn-rimmed glasses, and Green Peace cap. "A pound of dried potassium permanganate and a half-pint glycerin."

"Haven't had the whiskers too long, huh?"

"Pardon?" Georgie said, nonchalantly scratching his beard.

"After a couple of months, you hardly notice 'em."

Georgie stopped scratching. "Good to know."

"Although with your skin, I might keep clean shaven. I'll go get the rest of your order."

Georgie looked at his reflection in the counter glass. White-heads were oozing around the inflamed edges of his whiskers. Beards and mustaches were among the best disguises. People tended to focus on them, losing sight of everything else. But he'd needed more spirit gum than usual for the full beard. Fortunately, the time for masquerades was almost over.

"Here you go," the clerk said, returning with the chemicals. "That will be $277.30. What high school do I make this out to?"

"Excuse me?"

"Teach high-school chemistry, right?"

"Why, yes." Georgie smiled. "How did you know?"

"I haven't worked in chemical supply for ten years without knowing what you make with aluminum and powdered rust. Usually, you guys show up in August, just want a couple of pounds. You know, for demonstration purposes. Gets a lot of oohs, ahs, and bitchin's. Am I right?"

"Well, I, ah, I've ..." Georgie tried not to panic. "I've been asked to pick up some extra. Yes, that's right. For the supply room. And, ah, a summer program in advanced chemistry."

"Okay," shrugged the clerk. "We have accounts open for most of the schools in the area. Which one are you?" The clerk looked up, waiting for a reply.

"Um, Saint Tomacinski."

"Huh. Never heard of that one."

"We're new. The diocese is trying out a charter program for gifted students. I'm teaching chemistry."

"Oh, well, pleased to meet you Mr. ... ."

"Wagner. Chuck Wagner." They shook hands.

"So, should we start a new account? Usually, schools submit a requisition order, then we bill them."

"No, this will be cash."

The clerk's eyebrows rose. "Cash?"

Georgie cleared his throat. "Yes. I'm going to pay now, then they reimburse me. New program, everything still in flux. You know."

The clerk most certainly did not know. "Well, then ... okay. That'll be ..."

"$277.30," Georgie said, tossing two hundreds, a fifty, and two twenties on the counter glass. The hundreds were old and worn, with corners missing.

"Must have gotten these from under the mattress, huh?"

Georgie smiled, causing the clerk to smile back.

"I'll get your change, then we can load up your car."

"No problem," Georgie said. "I'll take a load out now, then take the rest with my change."

"You sure?"

"Sure."

Georgie kept the idiotic smile plastered to his face. He wanted to grab the goods and run, but it would look suspicious if he left without his change. So, he started gathering bags of gray powder, hands sweating and wanting desperately to scratch.

"Cash or credit card?" the clerk asked.

"Cash," the young man said from behind the shadow of his hoodie. Despite the June warmth, the light sweatshirt was drawn tightly around his face. A swirl of black hair swept across his brow, matching the coloring of the narrow mustache below his nose. His eyes and much of his face hid behind large, teardrop sunglasses. He scratched intermittently at his acned cheeks.

"That will be ninety-nine dollars and seventy-eight cents," the UPS clerk said.

The man in the hood handed over a wrinkled one-hundred-dollar bill with one corner missing. The clerk handed him back twenty-two cents change.

"Mr. TresReyes should get this by end of day Friday," the clerk said. "You or he can track it using this number." He pointed to the long set of numerals on the receipt.

"Thanks," the customer said, then left.

The guy reminded the clerk of someone. Although most of the face was hidden, his whole appearance smacked of some vague memory—a photo or drawing from the past. Put to the question, he'd say the kid looked like Weird Al in a sweatshirt. He couldn't say for sure how old; kids all looked alike. But judging by his voice, he was definitely a kid. Then it came to him.

"Hey, Dorrie," he yelled to the woman coming from the stock room. "Remember that crazy guy who mailed those packages twenty, thirty years ago. What was his name?"

"Lots of crazy people mail packages."

"Yeah, but these blew up. Remember? Some weird guy who lived like a hermit. Hated modern technology."

"You mean The Unabomber?"

"Yeah. That's the guy."

"We learned about him in high-school science and society. Ted, something or other. Bundy, I think."

"Nah, that was the other nut." the clerk said.

"A nut's a nut," Dorrie said.

"Just sign here, please." The UPS driver held out an electronic pad and stylus.

"What is it?" the receptionist asked.

"I just deliver them, ma'am."

The UPS driver took back his electronic receipt book and wheeled the empty handcart toward the Parkway Village exit. "Have a nice day."

As he left, Tanya Bellis came out of the manager's office, walking toward the front desk. Pausing halfway, she rushed to grab the entry door before it closed, holding it open for a walker trailed by a nicely dressed old man dwarfed by his straw sun hat.

"How are you today, Mr. Cohen?"

"Just fine, dear. And you?"

"Couldn't be better. I'm surrounded by handsome men like you."

Cohen laughed. "Don't let Melena hear you. She gets jealous." He favored her with a wink. "I'm off for my morning constitutional." She let the door close behind him.

Tanya smiled and continued walking. Saul Cohen and his wife, Melena, could be ads for graceful aging. She made a mental note of the example, filing it away for her golden years, God willing.

Peggy Lehner was at reception, talking on the phone. "Hi Marcus. This is Peggy. Good, hon. And you? That's terrif. Listen, I've got a heavy UPS box at reception. Could you be a darlin' and take it over to Room 126? Yep. Goes to a new tenant, J. Tres-Reyes." Her southern accent pronounced it "trezrays."

Tanya waved and hurried forward, taking the phone from Peggy's hand. "Marcus? This is Tanya. That package goes into basement storage. That's right. The end enclosure." She smiled. "Thanks a million."

"What was that all about?" Peggy asked.

Tanya hung up the phone. "Mr. TresReyes won't be moving in until just before the holiday. He asked us to put his deliveries in storage."

"But 126 is already vacant. Ever since Emma Watson moved to assisted."

"That's right," Tanya said. "But maintenance won't be cleaning carpets until next week. We wouldn't want Señor TresReyes to notice pee stains, now would we?"

"Señor? What is he, Mexican?"

Tanya shook her head. "He's from someplace called Mallorca, in the Mediterranean."

"What's he like?"

"Nice old guy. Very dapper. Fine European manners. Spanish accent."

"Ooh," Peggy said. "How old?"

Tanya's arched her brows. "You lookin' for a sugar daddy?"

Peggy smiled. "I wouldn't mind. Nice old guy with money. I could go back to being just mommy and housekeeper. Let someone else worry about breadwinner. I wouldn't mind a little Latin lovin' either."

Tanya shook her head. "What's it been? Six months since the divorce?"

"Eight," Tanya said. "Which means I haven't gotten laid for twelve. Not that I'm counting."

"Well, I'm not sure Jorge is for you."

"Jorge?"

"Spanish for George." Tanya leafed through the mail.

"He's an independent, isn't he?"

"For now," Tanya said. "But he moves slowly, even with a cane. I think mobility is going to be an issue soon."

Now Peggy raised her eyebrows. "So, we'll stay in bed."

"You're impossible," Tanya chuckled.

Peggy's foot tapped the UPS carton. "What's in the box? Did he say?"

"Pottery," Tanya said.

"What, like clay pots?"

Tanya shook her head. "No, I got the impression fancy bowls or figurines. That's what his company made. Seemed pretty proud of them. Wanted to show them off."

"Ooh. Can I open it and take a peek? Do you think he'd mind?"

"Un uh," Tanya said. "Private property."

"But if he wanted to show them off anyway?"

"Nope."

"Come on," Peggy said, nudging her. "I could use a nice piece for my living room. Sam got the unicorns in the divorce."

"He wanted *those*?"

Peggy shook her head. "He knew *I* wanted them. Probably still in the box. Maybe in the dump by now. What do you say? Just a peek."

Tanya hesitated, then shook her head again. "Nope, rules are rules. We don't look in people's mail without a court order."

A tall Black man with a mover's dolly approached the desk. "Mornin', Peggy. Ms. Bellis."

"Good morning, Marcus. This goes to the corner unit in the basement. Where we store the old files. It's marked fragile, this end up, so be careful."

"Will do, ma'am." He gently rocked the box onto the toe plate and wheeled away.

"When Jorge moves in," Tanya said, "I'll ask if he can show them to us."

"Well," Peggy said, "if that's the best you can do."

Chapter 34

Scott Fitzgerald Crossfield, special agent in charge of the Knoxville field office, tossed the folder onto his desk. "Very nice report." He leaned back, hands clasped behind his neck in satisfaction. "Very nice indeed."

Sally smiled, both from knowing he was pleased and from knowing he was right.

"All the I's crossed and T's dotted as they say." He rocked forward and placed the folder in his outbox. "Good job, Sal."

"Thank you, sir."

"You've re-interviewed everyone worth interviewing and debriefed Tomacinski."

"But not Georgie King III," she said.

"That is unfortunate," Crossfield said, returning his hands behind his head. "But you've gotten word to the cops in Ohio and Michigan. He'll show up."

"He might have gone someplace other than he told his father. Maybe we should ..."

"If he did that," Crossfield said, "he could be in LA for all we know. The Bureau can't launch a nationwide manhunt to locate a safely returned kidnap victim who probably never even saw his captors. No, Sally, I wouldn't start second-guessing now. You've done all you could. And about all we *can* do until the money starts showing up. Problem?"

"Well," she said, "shouldn't the money have *started* showing up by now?"

"Not necessarily. Not if Conrad is as smart as we think he is and have seen him to be. He may be biding time, waiting out pursuit. He may not even be in the country any longer."

"Airports and bus terminals have been alerted," Sally said.

"The major ones, yes. Not the fly-by-nighters or regional fixed-base operators. And you can drive into Canada or Mexico, catch a flight from there." Crossfield sat straight again. "But foreign banks have been notified, along with Interpol. We'll get him eventually." He reached into his inbox. "For the time being, I'd like you to check out something else." He handed her a folder. "I got a call from Charles Robinson."

"The Rest@Home Robinson?"

"The same. Seems *his* son is missing."

Sally looked at the folder. "Why did he call the Bureau? Isn't this local jurisdiction?"

"Technically, yes," Crossfield said. "But we're in a politically gray area here. The Bureau's initial handling of the extortion was ... Let's just say open to some question. It'd be in everyone's best interests if Robinson didn't belabor the point."

Sally could feel the old double-shuffle starting up again. For a moment, she thought she was talking with Dan Hartsell instead of Scott Crossfield. "More extortion?" she asked.

"I wouldn't say that," her boss said. "Let's say we owe him some leeway and at least a minimal effort." Sally hesitated. "Consider it part of your training: public relations instead of criminology." He smiled. "You need to learn that one is dependent on the other."

Sally took the folder. "What would you like me to do?"

"Drive up and talk to him."

"All the way back to Columbus?"

"See if this is a case of a runaway or something nefarious. If the former, turn it over to local jurisdiction."

"If the latter?"

"Then start a file, Special Agent Butterworth. Kidnapping is a federal offense. Questions?"

"Shouldn't this be handled by resident agents in Columbus?"

"Are you saying we should hand this back to Hartsell's jurisdiction?"

Sally paused. "No, sir."

"Take someone with you. Matt Clemens has requested transfer to me. Let's give him a little experience. Test his PR skills."

Sally could tell it wasn't only Matt who was being tested. She no longer lived in the doghouse, but she still hadn't checked out of purgatory.

"Yes, sir."

Sally sat in Robinson's study, the same chair she'd occupied scant weeks ago. There was an eerie déjà vu to the situation, without even dust accumulation to mark the passage of time. She half-expected to see Tom-Tom at her side. It was a warm, comforting feeling. Then Matt Clemens sat down next to her, and both the moment and feeling passed.

"Thank you for coming to see me, Agent Butterworth, Agent Clemens. I hope you don't mind my going directly to your Agent Crossfield."

"That's quite alright, Mr. Robinson," Sally said. There's nothing I'd rather have than someone going over my head to send me on a wild goose chase, Sally thought. "Your son is missing?"

"Well, you see, the truth of the matter is I'm not sure."

"Pardon?"

"Well, Robbie and I, we had a bit of a ... well, words."

"A falling out?"

"Let's just say, words. I figured he took a little time to cool off. But that was a while ago. Usually he contacts me, even if it's just for money. But I haven't heard a word."

"Did you call his cell phone?"

"Half a dozen times. No answer. Of course, if he's still mad at ... if he's still upset, he wouldn't necessarily answer. You know, if he saw my number."

"Have you contacted his friends?" Matt asked.

"I don't know his friends. I called his mother, but she hasn't seen him since just before he disappeared."

"Does he have a credit card?" Sally asked.

"It's my card, in his name. I checked it. No purchases for a couple of weeks."

"Where was the last purchase?" Matt asked.

"I can't remember."

"Can we check that now?" Sally asked. "May give us an idea where he went."

Robinson clacked on his computer. "A BP gas station in Williamsburg, Kentucky."

"That's dated after your argument?" Sally asked.

Robinson nodded.

"May I have a printout of that page, sir?" Matt said.

Robinson nodded again and clacked more keys. A laser printer hummed to his right. He handed Matt the still-warm printout.

"Can you think of a reason for him to be in southern Kentucky?"

Robinson shook his head. "No." Then his eyes lit with an idea. "George King has a house down south. Near Knoxville, as I recall. I think his son uses it at times." Robinson shook his head again. "No, that can't be it. Robbie said he and Georgie King were on the outs. Some school thing."

"Do you have the address?"

"I have it here somewhere." He clacked some more. "Yes, here it is. It's in Townsend, Tennessee."

"Can I have a printout, sir?"

Robinson handed Matt another warm copy.

"May I ask why you called the Bureau," Sally said. "Rather than Columbus PD or the Highway Patrol?"

Robinson grimaced. "I didn't want to go to the police. Somehow that seemed too much like I was, I don't know, siccing the law on my own son. That's how Robbie might see it, anyway. And since the FBI was already involved, well." He shrugged.

"I see," Sally said. "Can I have a recent picture of Robbie?"

Robinson reached into a drawer and withdrew a wallet-sized photo. Like King's, it appeared to be a graduation shot of a smiling, acned teen in suit and tie. "You can keep that."

Ten minutes later, Sally and Matt sat in their Bureau SUV. Armed with the photo and Robbie's Social Security number, Matt was pulling up information on his laptop.

"Red Prius," he said. "License number Romeo Oscar Bravo 1054."

"Let's put it out to the state police in Kentucky and Tennessee," Sally said.

"Robinson said he didn't want that."

"And email them the photo."

"You starting a file? Given the love lost between father and son, sounds like a runaway to me."

"No, no file yet," Sally said, starting the car. "But I don't like this dead credit card. We're basically dealing with an arrested adolescent." She pulled down the tree-lined street. "There should be gas receipts, hotel rooms, fast food, liquor sales, pizza delivery, porno. Something."

"Well, *we'll* never find the reason. Without a file, there's nothing we can do."

"Not officially," Sally said.

"Unofficially?"

"Get me the number for the Knoxville PD."

"Anybody in particular?" Matt asked.

"Detective Doolittle Powell."

💣 *Chapter 35*

Doolittle turned onto the freeway, heading east.

"I thought you were taking me to breakfast," his partner, Dell, said.

"Sure am. I know a place with the best do ..."

"No donuts," Dell said.

Doolittle smiled. "You're restricting my options but anything to please a lady."

"So where *are* we going?"

"I got a favor to run before we eat."

"We get a little breathing room," Dell said, "and you run errands with it."

"I'll have you know I'm doing my civic duty for Uncle Sam."

"Uncle Sam or Aunt Jemima?" Dell said. "I saw you grinning like Minnie Pearl on the phone. How is Agent Pancakes?"

"Nothin' flat about those flapjacks," Doolittle said.

"Is that any way to speak about a brother in law enforcement?"

"Nothing brotherly either, in or out of bed, I'll wager."

"Like you'll ever know," Dell said.

"What can I tell you, partner. When I see a woman like that, I become the Bellamy brothers."

"David or Howard?"

"Both," Doolittle said, breaking into song. "If I said you had a beautiful body, would you hold it against me?"

"That kind of caterwauling might make suspects confess, but I don't appreciate it before breakfast." She sipped coffee. "Did she and Tom-Tom ever ride the rodeo together? I thought I saw signs there."

He shook his head. "You and your signs."

"Hey, women know things."

"Men know things, too," Doolittle said. "And this man knows that whether they did or didn't, Tom-Tom's been dreamin' about it. I know I have."

The black, unmarked Ford pulled into the driveway of the mountain getaway. The two detectives exited into a country bouquet very unlike the city smells they'd left behind. Wildflowers and evergreens replaced the traffic exhaust, with only a burnt-oil hint of their institutional Ford. Humidity and moldy leaves replaced sun-baked macadam. The Ford's fast food and BO morphed into a Febreze ad. Yet, there was a hint of something else. Something that marred the otherwise stimulating freshness. Something with death in it.

"I grew up in the country," Dell said. "Things die out here all the time. Foxes, deer, possum, coons. Folks don't like to think about it, but it's so."

"Well, I lived in the city most of my life." Doolittle slammed the car door. "Except the two years I served in Af-a-ghanistan."

"We been partners for years. I never knew that."

"Not something I like to talk about," Doolittle said. "Something you can't really forget, though. Some of the things I've seen keep me up at night. And the smells? You *never* forget the smells. That's something that don't come through the six o'clock news or the war movies. Cook fires burning soft coal and kerosene. Animal and human dung. The smell of a mountain shepherd not much cleaner than his goats. And three-day-old death." The big detective sniffed the air. "You go knock on the door. I'll take a walk around."

Doolittle walked twenty feet down the drive. A large deck was to his right, along with its pricey mountain view of trees and summer sunshine. He wasn't sure, but the air seemed a little sweeter here. He remembered a kid's game. "Getting colder," he said.

Turning, he walked back toward the carport. A shadow passed as he squinted into the sun above the tree line. Looking up, he saw what looked like a hawk circling the jungle of undergrowth behind the house. Then he noticed there were two big birds in the Lufbery. No, it was three.

Dell approached from the front door. "Locked," she said. "No answer to the bell or repeated knocks. And no car in the port. My keen detective senses tell me that no one is home."

Doolittle pointed at the birds circling the sky. "What do your country-girl senses tell you about those?"

"Like I said, things die out here."

"Uh-huh," Doolittle said, walking toward the ravine behind the house.

"You mind me. You're gonna find a week-old deer carcass."

"Uh-huh," Doolittle said, still walking.

Gravel behind the carport led to grass fringing the trees and brush of the ravine. The smell grew appreciably as he approached. He tossed his ugly sport jacket to Dell. "Hold this, will ya, darlin'?" Walking toward the trees, Doolittle rolled up his sleeves and looked for a path.

"You mark me," Dell said. "You're gonna ruin your pants and scratch up your face, only to find Bambi's ma with her guts rotted open."

"Uh-huh," Doolittle said, heading to a gap in the trees.

The gap became a deer path maybe two feet wide. Doolittle wished he had a machete or even a pair of hedge clippers. "Shit," he said, as a branch scraped his face.

"Told ya," Dell said from behind.

The light faded and the air grew heavy with the smell of mold and water. The odor of death rose as well, a raw sweetness that threatened to summon a dry heave. He was glad they hadn't eaten yet.

Sweat dripped into his eyes as he staggered down the path, his big bulk leaning back to compensate for the grade. Vision was limited to the few feet ahead. His hands stayed busy protecting his face and grabbing branches for support.

"You okay down there?"

"Uh-huh," Doolittle yelled, and kept going.

He'd started to regret the journey, imagining his two-hundred-thirty pounds pinwheeling down the ravine, when his feet found the bottom, landing with a squish-plop in running water.

"Shit."

"What's up?"

"Nothin. Just ruined my loafers."

"Told ya."

The growing stench made it difficult to judge direction. He turned right, then left, then right again. The smell seemed stronger to his port side. Moving left, he slogged along, cold water squelching its way into his socks and toes. "Shit."

He turned and coughed, the stink tugging at his guts again. Fighting away branches, right foot followed left. Then left foot struck something with the feel of a bloated bag of flour. But instead of a white cloud of dust, the draft from a slaughterhouse filled his nostrils, forcing him to turn and gag. "Oh, sweet Jesus," he coughed, hand over mouth.

"What'd you find?" Dell yelled.

Turning back to answer, his eyes caught a spray of red and white, along with something glittery. It took another moment for his vision to adjust and notice a sneaker with a stylized N in the back. The sneaker led to jeans. Doolittle moved the brush. The jeans led to a T-shirt. The shirt was pulled up in the front, belly skin replaced by a large ulcer and what might be intestines.

"What'd you find?" Dell repeated.

Doolittle staggered back to snatch a breath of air.

"I said, what'd you find?"

"I ..." Doolittle's stomach muscles cramped, released, then cramped again.

"Doo? You okay?"

He cleared his throat. "Yeah."

"What'd you find?"

"I think I found Robbie Robinson."

Doolittle spat, then sipped more water. The smell hung to his nostrils like an old booger, but was tolerable now. His belly rumbled—and not with thoughts of donuts.

The meat wagon was backed into the carport, the white "Blount County Coroner" contrasting nicely with its mortuary black. Angled down the drive to the right, an SUV with Tennessee Bureau of Investigation on it waited for the forensic unit that was turning the house and shed. A couple of county cruisers blocked off the lower drive. No gawkers had gathered yet.

"Maryville PD found the Prius in the back of the Kroger lot at Foothills Plaza," Dell said. "They've dusted it for prints, but chances are they'll just turn up the Robinson kid's.

"Hey, Doo, Dell. You wanna take a look here?" Pat Conway of TBI called from the open doorway. He led them to an upstairs bedroom. Pointing to a bleach stain in the hardwood, he said, "Looks like this is where the deed was done. But check this out."

Pat pointed to a desk with a computer terminal. Next to that was a pile of circuit boards and a clock timer, the kind you'd buy at Radio Shack.

"Our boy's been busy," Pat said. "Looky here." He held up a piece of tape with gray granules embedded on it. "Got this off the desk. Tests positive for explosive. Probably homemade C4. There's a whole lot more residue in the shed. Along with nitric acid, hexamine, all the fixins. He knows his chemistry."

Doolittle nodded. "Sounds like Conrad, don't it?"

"What?" Pat asked.

Doolittle shook his head.

"But that's not all," the CSI tech said. "Also found about ten pounds of this stuff." He gave Doolittle a bag of gray powder. "Know what that is?"

Doolittle shook a negative. "My chemistry labs were spent ogling Minnie Jean Tessmacher's tight sweaters."

"Thermite. Mixture of powdered aluminum and rust. Used to weld metal crevices and in fireworks. Military uses it to burn down buildings. Dropped tons of the stuff on Germany and Japan in WWII. It's a bugger to get going, but once lit it burns hot and long. Three-, four-thousand degrees. Burns through anything— even metal."

"There was ten *pounds* of it?" Doolittle said.

"Yep, that we found. Who knows how much was manufactured. You guess."

"Thanks, Pat. Send me a report, huh?"

"You bet, Doo."

Doolittle stared at the packet of powder, massaging the granules between his meaty fingers.

"We gonna call Agent Flapjacks?"

"Eventually," Doolittle said. The feel of the granules in the bag reminded him of kicking Robinson's body, the soft, gassy give of the lump that used to be a young man with his whole life ahead of him. "After we gather more evidence." He tossed the bag up and down several times. "I don't want the feds hogging this one." Lobbing the bag to Dell, he added, "I want a piece of Conrad."

💣 *Chapter 36*

"I remember. Dr. Tomski the hero," Mary Wagner said.

"Tomacinski, Mother."

"And I wouldn't call myself a hero," Tom said.

"But that's what my daughter tells me. She goes on and on about you."

Tom smiled at Cheryl's blush. "Well, thank you ma'am. But if you include my mother, that makes a total of three people who think so."

"What about your father?" Cheryl asked.

"Dad just wants me to get him discounted hotel rooms."

"Where are you children off to?"

"The gym." Tom held up his tote, running shoes dangling from the handle.

"Then dinner and dessert." Cheryl smiled knowingly at Tom.

"Well, you children be careful," Mary said. "People always drive crazy during the holiday."

"That's not until Wednesday, Mama. Today is Saturday."

"I know what day it is. Just like I know Wednesday is Memorial Day, Miss Smarty-pants."

"Fourth of July, Mama."

"That's what I meant, and you know it."

"I know. Common mistake." Cheryl kissed her mom. "I'm going to stop by for the Fourth. The Village is having a barbecue. And fireworks. Won't that be fun?"

"Bunch of old fogies gumming hot dogs," Mary said. "Some fun."

Cheryl kissed her again. "It'll be fun. You can have a beer."

"Lawd. I'll forget what little I know."

Tom laughed. "Well, goodbye, Mrs. Wagner."

"Goodbye, Tim. Where are you children going?"

💣

"I'm sorry about that," Cheryl said in the hall. "But thanks for stopping by with me. They needed those papers signed today."

Tom gave her a one-armed hug. "No problem. That's what heroes do." Cheryl swatted his behind. "I think your mom is taking things well, considering."

"For now. We'll see how she does when the staff starts checking on her next week. Mama likes visiting, but she likes her privacy, too. I don't know how she'll feel with people popping in every couple of hours during the day. Let's hope she doesn't need help with the bathroom anytime soon. Lawd!"

Tom chuckled. "That's a pretty good impression."

"Who's doing an impression?" Cheryl said. "That was from the heart."

"I'm no expert," Tom said, still laughing. "But it seems to me she's just a little forgetful."

"And a little more every day," Cheryl said. "That's the problem. I'm dreading the day when I come to visit, and she asks who I am." She wiped a tear.

"I'll remind her," Tom said, then took her in his arms and kissed her.

"You two want a room?" Tanya Bellis smiled at them, arms crossed. "They usually go by the month, but I might be able to set you up for just a night. Although you're a little young for us."

Cheryl blushed again. "Hi, Tanya. Thanks for coming in on the weekend to take care of that paperwork."

"No problem. I had to come in anyway. New tenant moving in today. Looks like you two are going for a run or something?"

"On our way to the gym," Cheryl said.

"Then it's dinner and dessert," Tom said. Cheryl jumped as he pinched her bottom.

Tanya laughed. "Well, have fun. Oh, I see Mr. TresReyes now. Gotta run. Take care."

An old man doddered toward Tanya, limping forward with a step, step, cane. He looked oddly familiar. He made eye contact with Tom and smiled. Tom nodded a smile in return and hurried after Cheryl.

💣

Jorge TresReyes watched Tom and Cheryl walking toward the side door as Tanya Bellis met him down the front hall.

"Hello, Jorge. Como estás?"

"Bien, gracias." He pointed to the departing couple. "Amor joven. Muy bonito, no?"

"Pardon?"

"No es importante."

"Here, let me help you." Tanya reached for his briefcase, but he held it defensively to his side."

"Gracias, no. I use it to keep balance." He shook the cane with one hand, then carefully lifted the case with the other.

"Ah, alright. They've moved your things into your room. It seems kind of spartan. Is there more coming?"

"Yes, in time. For now, my needs are simple. Did my package arrive safely?"

"The pottery? Yes. I locked it in your storage unit as you asked. I'm anxious to see the pieces. Peggy Lehner has also expressed an interest. She's fond of figurines."

He smiled. "In time. I'd like to rest now."

"Then let me walk you to your unit."

"Is not necessary. I remember."

"Okay, then. Is there anything else I can do for you?"

"No," he said, lifting the briefcase. "I have all I need."

💣 Chapter 37

Sally stormed into Doolittle's office and slammed the door.

"Well, happy Monday morning, Agent Butterworth," Doolittle said. "Nice to see you. I believe you know Detective Portifoy."

"And nice of you to contact me about the murder of Robbie Robinson. I had to hear about it from his father. That was a pleasant conversation."

"I'm gonna step out for coffee," Dell said.

Doolittle Powell held up his palms, defensively. "Now, as you might recall, special agent, you asked me to check into the disappearance *unofficially*. You said it was not part of an active federal investigation and was most appropriate for local jurisdiction. You remember that?"

"And I also asked you to let me know what you found out."

"And here I am doing that. You were on my list of calls today. I can't help it if you heard before I called you."

Sally pointed a finger at him. "Listen you redneck son of a bitch."

"Is that what you call inter-service-cooperation language?" Doolittle asked.

"You knew that Robinson might be hooked into the Conrad case—which *is* an active federal investigation."

"Now how would I know that, special agent? I'm just a redneck hick."

Sally stabbed an accusing finger. "And you knew that the location of the murder suggests a prime suspect."

"Same answer."

Sally closed her eyes and took a deep breath. Raising her hands in surrender and her eyes toward heaven, she said, "Fine. Then in the spirit of inter-service cooperation, I'm letting you know that a Bureau CSI team will be sweeping the scene today."

"And they're welcome to," Doolittle smiled. "Of course, TBI has already collected most everything worth collecting. Those fellas are pretty thorough." He tapped the fat report folder on his desk.

Sally squinted. "Is this a shakedown, detective?"

"I am shocked, special agent, shocked, that you suggest I'm implying a quid pro quo." He smiled again. "That's fancy legal talk for you wash my back, I'll wash yours. And a lovely back I'm sure it is." His smile widened. "Not bad for a redneck SOB, huh?"

"What do you want?"

"First off," Doolittle said, "I want you to have a seat." He pointed to the visitor's chair. "Then I want to know if *you* would like a cup of coffee?"

Sally sat upon the stained fabric. "No, thank you."

"Then I'll forgo any quaint redneck pleasantries surrounding the health of your family and get right to the point." He tapped the folder. "I would be more than happy to share what is in this here file. If ..." He raised an index finger. "If Knoxville PD and yours truly become equal partners in the Bureau's investigation."

"And if I just put a formal request through channels, then take over your investigation?"

Doolittle frowned. "You know how these redneck bureaucracies are down here. Files have a way of being mislaid."

Sally paused, then smiled, showing those dimples that made men want to please. "Fair enough, Detective Powell. I would be honored to have your assistance in this investigation. And yes, I would love a cup of coffee."

Doolittle picked up the phone. "You can come back in now, Dell. And bring a cup of coffee with ..." he looked at Sally.

"Black," she said.

"And a black cup of joe for our distinguished guest, if'n you please." He slid the folder across the desk.

"Sorry about the redneck thing, Doo."

Sally angled down the slope, sneakers finding roots and rocks for support, coveralled arms beating back the assault of leaves and tree bark. The sun was at its apogee when she started down, but it was dusk in the overgrowth of the ravine. Still, she could see the approaching creek bed, her feet landing dry on either side of the shallow water. The air smelled moist and green, with only residual traces of the sweetened stink that marked a murder scene. Voices spoke only a few feet ahead.

"This is where we found the body," Pat Conway of TBI said. A couple of federal techs were also on the scene, scanning the ground of the ravine with mag lights and metal detectors.

"Did you get an ID from a wallet?" Sally asked.

"No," Conway said. "Dental records. The body was clean, no wallet or ID. The face was pretty badly chewed by nature. But there isn't any doubt. It's Robert J. Robinson."

"Was he the only one?"

"Yeah," Conway said. "Dogs have been through here, didn't find anything but a dead squirrel."

"Thanks," Sally said, before starting her ascent.

Coming out of the brush, she saw Doolittle talking to Pete Aiello, a Bureau forensic tech.

"Hi, Sally."

"Pete. How's it going?"

"I've got people down below searching for residual trace," Pete said. "But TBI is pretty thorough. I doubt we'll find anything."

"Good afternoon, Agent Butterworth," Doolittle said, his cracker smile wider than a certain English cat's. "Them Tennessee boys certainly do a fine job, shore 'nuff."

"That's a pretty good accent, Detective Powell. Can you do Cagney?"

"We've also had people inside," Pete said. "Came up with the same things TBI found, thermite, traces of homemade C4, black powder, bits of circuitry, gadgets for making IDs and credit cards. Pretty much everything the same."

Doolittle nodded and mimed spitting tobacco juice.

"Everything except this." The CSI tech held up an evidence bag containing a small wedge of green paper. "Found it in a corner of the shed. It's rag paper from currency. In fact, one of the extorted C-notes."

"How the hell can you tell that?" Doolittle asked, no longer smiling.

"We ran it under UV-C," Pete said. "Pretty blue dot right in the middle."

"Well," Sally said, "that solves the mystery of why the marked money hasn't turned up."

"Yeah," Doolittle said, swatting at his neck. "But how much can he pass with missing corners. He could maybe break one here or there, have a cashier make change. That's about it. You can buy yourself a pizza that way, but you can't buy a yacht."

"No," Sally said. "But you can buy the fixings to make C4 and thermite and who knows what else. You can buy yourself a little revenge." She handled the paper corner through the plastic.

"Should we pull out?" Pete asked. "Put the place under surveillance? See if he comes back?"

Sally tossed Pete the evidence bag. "If he hasn't already seen the three-ring circus we've got going here."

"Or the media coverage," Doolittle said.

"I'll run it by Crossfield when he takes charge this afternoon," Sally said. "But I think I know what he'll say. Conrad isn't coming back. He's flown the coop. Off to buy himself some payback. The question is ... where?"

"And when," Doolittle added.

💣 *Chapter 38*

Tom leaned back and wanted a cigarette. It'd been ten years since he'd touched a coffin nail, but there were still times when he longed for one. Smoking was a calorie-free dessert after a great dinner, a smoky chaser to the fire of good bourbon, and a capper to good sex. And the sex with Cheryl was good. It didn't have the heat of his night with Sally, his *one* night with Sally. But it was good.

He'd be lying if he said Sally was never in his head while doing the deed, but he did find Cheryl attractive and desirable. What their nights lacked in smoke and hot embers, they made up for with an easy, relaxed rhythm free of performance anxiety. He knew he pleased her, which was half the fun. He pleased her and she pleased him. Their lovemaking was like the rest of their relationship, relaxed and comfortable. But was comfortable enough? And she was older. Maybe only a few years, but it was something new for him. He wasn't sure how he felt about it.

"Penny for your thoughts?" Cheryl snuggled into the crook of his arm, warm muskiness radiating from her.

"Just thinking. Ah, listen, Cheryl."

"Hmm."

The nibbles on his neck distracted him. "Listen, we've only known each other for a few weeks."

"I know what you're going to say, so you don't have to say it."

"What was I going to say?"

"Listen, babe." Her voice took on a husky quality not unlike his own. "We've only known each other a few weeks. Maybe we should slow things down a little. I've met your mom, and she's great, but let's not start picking out silver patterns. We've never said we were exclusive. And you're older than me. And I might want to have kids. So maybe we should slow things down and just take them as they come." Her voice reverted to her own. "Did I leave anything out?"

Tom chuckled despite the underlying seriousness of the discussion.

"Don't worry, Tom. I won't kill myself when you leave. I'll just enter a convent. I'll kneel on bottle caps and devote my life to praying for misguided epidemiologists."

His chuckle turned into a laugh.

She hugged him, adding, "Whatever this turns out to be, I'm glad for it. I feel comfortable with you. More comfortable than I have with any man since my divorce. Heck, before my divorce."

"Is comfortable good enough?" Tom asked.

She kissed his cheek. "Comfortable, my darling Tom, is the *most* important thing. It's the base, the foundation. What's left over after the passion cools. It fills the empty silences. It bridges the chasm between the early fire and the later tedium. It changes that tedium into contentment and shared experience."

Tom smiled in the darkness. "You are wise beyond your years."

"Then I must be *really* smart," she said.

His hand stroked the soft skin of her stomach, tiny hairs rising at his touch. "I really don't think much about your age. When we're together I mean. Well, most of the time."

"Does it bother you?"

"Your age, or my not thinking about it?"

"Either. Both."

"I'm not sure. I guess *that* does bother me a little. Not being sure."

"Are you usually sure about things?"

"Yeah," he said, looking at the ceiling. "Usually. At least I used to always think so."

"I turned forty last March," she said. "In case you were wondering. Or if it helps you be sure. Whichever."

He turned to her. "You didn't have to tell me that."

"I know."

"Forty, huh? A bit more than five years." He thought in silence. "That's not that much."

"Less than half a dozen," she said.

"But probably too old to have kids?"

"Yes," she said more slowly. "*Probably.*"

For the first time, there was seriousness in her voice. A bit of hesitation. A bit of uncertainty. A bit of apprehension. The silence lingered in the air like stale tobacco smoke. Just a simple question and its answer. Less than ten words total. But the import they carried could span a lifetime of happiness or regret.

Finally, Tom spoke. "How do you feel about dogs?"

Cheryl exhaled. "I love dogs. Just not much of a stable home life for them right now."

"Yeah," Tom said. "Me, too. After I settle down, I'd like to have a couple of dogs."

"That sounds fine," Cheryl said, snuggling closer.

"And maybe a cat," Tom said.

Her hand took his and moved it to her breast. He felt the nipple rise to greet his fingers.

"Definitely a cat," she sighed, soft hands turning his head to hers. "And I do think you're a hero." She kissed him long and hard.

💣* Chapter 39

Red, white, and blue bunting hung below the "Happy 4th of July" sign with starburst fireworks on the corners and "Parkway Villages" on the bottom. Tom pulled to the end of the line of cars queued up and down the street. Vendors were positioned on either side of the lawn, handing out popcorn and ice cream from carnival carts. Tables were set up under a large awning with more tricolor bunting. Barbecue grills were further back in the sun, the aroma of roasting burgers and dogs making his mouth water.

"Why do they always call these places villages?" he said. "Is it supposed to evoke some sense of shared tribal responsibility? As in, it takes a village? We're all looking out for each other?"

"Don't ask me," Cheryl said, grabbing her purse. "It's probably just tradition. You know, 'retirement village.' They've used that term since way back when I was a girl. Back when the Vikings were making wine in Greenland. But speaking of being on the lookout, I want to show you something." Reaching into her handbag, she withdrew a flier. "We got these from the FBI on Monday."

"We?" Tom asked, taking the paper.

"Middleboro Parkway. Actually, Parkway management. My manager gave it to me for distribution to the staff. He got it from Parkway Regional, who's responsible for corporate-wide distribution. I thought this Conrad thing was over."

Tom scanned the flier. "That's right. He's been paid off and is now spending his millions, which will ultimately lead to his ruination and capture. At least according to sources within the government. Details at eleven."

"So why are they distributing these?"

He stared at the flier, several grainy images staring back. There was a surveillance still of an oldish gentleman in a homburg hat, another of a smiling beatnik in dark glasses, and a third, clearer image of a smirking teen with pimples and a wisp of black bangs.

The text of the flier advised all employees to be on the lookout for anyone resembling these men, or anyone registering under the names Groenhaage, Hilton, King, or Tomacinski.

"So, I'm famous again," Tom said.

"More like infamous," Cheryl said, pointing to the flier. "Wanted for murder and extortion. May be armed and dangerous. Contact the FBI. Why now?"

Tom shook his head.

"We've already had two Kings this week," she said, grinning, "although no Tomacinskis thank goodness. One of those is plenty."

"Any fit the description? The Kings?"

"Nope. A middle-aged black man and a youngish business-woman. I doubt if either of those was Conrad."

"Don't be too sure," Tom said. "He's good."

"Speaking of disguises, I better put on my party face. I see Mama scowling over there with her friend Gladys the Democrat. Shall we join them?"

Peggy Lehner pushed the silver paddle, gliding open the door to the back patio. "There you are, Mrs. Dwight. Enjoy the party."

"Why is it so hot out?"

"Gee, I don't know, Mrs. D. I'll bring it up at the next staff meeting."

"Why can't we eat in the dining room?"

"Certainly, you can eat in the dining room," Peggy said. "Would you like someone to bring you a tray?"

"I might as well go out," Emma Dwight said, wheeling her chair under the patio awning.

Peggy headed back toward the desk, passing a gray-haired woman in a sundress and walker. "Hi, Ruth. Going to the party, I see. Where is Paul? Is he coming?"

"He's feeling a little poorly today. He's going to stay upstairs."

"Well, I'm sorry to hear that," Peggy said. "I'll try to stop in later and say hello."

Peggy saw the lobby entrance opening to allow Mr. TresReyes to leave. Despite the July heat, he was dressed in trousers, sport jacket, and golf cap. His gloved fingers held a wooden cane in one hand, a leather briefcase in the other.

"Hola, señor," Peggy said in an accent from south of the border, Ohio not Mexico.

"Buenos dias, puta. Cuando vuelves a tu perrera?"

"That sounds lovely," Peggy said. "What does it mean?"

"Means you look beautiful today, señora."

"Why, bless your heart. Are you going to the fiesta?"

"Just a walk."

"Be careful. It's rather warm out. Want me to hold your jacket?"

"No, I leave it on. I am now getting very chilly. Is the way of things, getting older."

"Okay. But not too long."

He smiled and left.

"He's such a sweet old guy," Peggy said.

💣

"Hi, Tanya," Cheryl said. "They have you working today?"

"No," Tanya Bellis said, as she crossed the sidewalk headed toward the parking lot. "I just stopped in to say happy holiday. You two going to the party?"

"For a bit," Cheryl said. "I *do* have to work today, four to midnight."

"Well, it's nice of you to spend the time off with Mary. I know she'll appreciate it."

"How's Mama getting on?" Cheryl asked.

As the two ladies chatted, Tom noticed an elderly gentleman exit the building. Something about him seemed familiar. Then Tom realized it was the same guy he'd seen moving in last weekend. He waved, the old man smiled and waved back, lifting his cane but not the briefcase he carried in his left hand.

"Briefcase? That's strange," Tom muttered. "Is he going to the office?"

"Oh," Tanya said. "No, that's Jorge TresReyes. He usually carries the case, for balance."

The old man moved slowly but steadily in the July heat. His doddering gait improved a little as he followed the sidewalk out of sight around the corner of the building.

"Coat and long pants? And gloves?" Tom said. "In this heat?"

"You get used to it around seniors. They thrive on heat, kind of like premature infants. And Señor TresReyes has psoriasis." The manager looked at her watch. "Got to run. I've my own barbecue to tend to. Enjoy your visit." Tanya gave Cheryl's shoulder a squeeze. "And don't worry. We'll take good care of Mary."

"Thanks," Cheryl said. "Try to steer her away from politics if you can."

Tanya laughed and waved.

"Looks like your mother is in good hands," Tom said.

"Yes, thank goodness," Cheryl said, a hint of sadness in her voice. Then her face lit with a bright grin. "Shall we join the revelers?"

Tom followed her down the path to the back patio. He caught a glimpse of Mr. TresReyes returning and waved again. The old man waved back with his empty left hand.

💣 *Chapter 40*

Tom sat in the now familiar tavern in the now familiar hotel. Hard to believe that just a few weeks earlier, he'd picked Middleboro out of the hat. Just a random stopover to drown a broken heart (or at least a bruised one). Now, The Halfway Lounge was like a second home. He had a room waiting upstairs and a girlfriend awaiting the witching hour.

"You ready to order dinner, Tom?"

Sometimes you want to go where everybody knows your name, Tom thought with a smile. "Yes, Al. In honor of Independence Day, why don't you grill me a burger, well done."

"Lettuce, tomato, onion?"

Tom nodded. "On second thought, make it a cheeseburger."

"Fries?"

"Of course."

"You got it, doc."

"And put some bacon on that cheeseburger.

"Check," Al said. "You want another Bass?"

"Why not. It's a party."

Tom looked around at the nearly empty bar. "Surprised you guys are open today."

"Only till ten," the bartender said. "For business travelers. People mostly drink at home on the Fourth." Al plunked a frosty mug on the oaken surface. "What about you? Not spending today with family?"

Tom sipped his beer. "Next best thing."

"You want a shot of Beam with that?" Al slipped him a wink. "I won't tell Cheryl."

"Actually, she allows me one." Tom tapped the bar. "Put it right there."

Al placed a dram glass on the spot, then poured two fingers of brown liquor into it. "On the house."

Tom sipped slowly from the glass, the whiskey warming his stomach.

"You want to eat at the bar, or a booth?"

Tom gulped some Bass. "Thank you, Al. I think ..."

A wave of déjà vu washed over Tom. It was so much like his first time here. He half expected Cheryl to show up, order a vodka tonic, then escort him to table nine. The memory brought on other memories. They'd chat about this and that. They'd flirt, coyly at first, then more openly. After dinner, they'd leave for his suite. But before he left the bar, something else would happen. Something that had been nagging at the edges of his memory for weeks. Something intimately associated with recent events. A murky picture swam into view. A picture of someone handing him something. It was almost becoming visible, like an image popping out of photo developer. Any second, he'd see the face. Any second.

"Staying out of trouble?" Cheryl asked from beside him.

Tom snorted beer through his nose.

"Sorry," she said, kissing his cheek. "I didn't mean to startle you. Just checking in to see how you're doing."

The image was gone. He was left only with a vague recollection, the remnants of a dream. He was also left with a vague feeling of foreboding, as if he was missing something important.

💣

Tom nursed four drinks until eight o'clock, shooting the breeze with Al. He learned the bartender was divorced with a daughter in high school and had once studied classical piano before pursuing his dream of helping travelers get drunk. When Al said, "You know, you're supposed to be telling me your troubles, not vice versa," Tom took the cue and headed to his suite. A cable station was rerunning one of his favorite TV shows, and he nodded off watching Laura Prepon naked in a prison shower.

Tom snapped awake two hours later. His mouth was dry with the taste of greasy bar food and beer, which a burp allowed him to enjoy a second time. But none of that was important. What was important was the dream he'd just had. At least it seemed like a dream. Or maybe it was just an old, half-forgotten memory drifting up from his subconscious. Tom didn't know which. He was only certain of two things: the imagery was fading fast, and it was important. Somehow, he knew it was very important. It was, in fact, the key to something that had been nagging at the corners of his brain for weeks. Wiping sleep from his eyes, he fought frantically to put memories together before they drifted apart like smoke on a summer breeze.

Closing his eyes, he saw a face. There was no context in which to place it, so he just concentrated on the image, studying it with his mind's eye, willing his foggy brain to remember things, add details. It was a young face, which was correct but also odd. There were pimples on it, despite a photographer's efforts to brush them out. It had a smile that was more an adolescent smirk. And there were black bangs over the shiny forehead. In his mind, it morphed into another face. This one had dark glasses and a goatee below a wild smile, the acne smoothed over with makeup. Same Betty Boop bangs. Then it changed yet again. Now it was a continental-looking gentleman of perhaps sixty, homburg covering the bangs, gloved fingers rubbing at his mustache. This face he knew. It was Ollie Groenhaage, Conrad Hilton's alter ego. The face Conrad had worn in the surveillance video at the Dayton Comfort Rest. That was many weeks ago, now. But Tom had seen that face more recently. He'd seen it on the flier Cheryl had shown him. That's where he'd seen the other images as well. They'd all been on the flier, along with the aliases, Groenhaage, Hilton, King, and Tomacinski. Was that it? Was it just a memory of the flier bobbing into his head? Why would that be important?

The image transformed again. Now it was an older man, seventy or seventy-five. The goatee was gone, but there was a mustache, just like Groenhaage's. The image was rubbing at the mustache, just as Groenhaage had. It wore gloves, just as Groenhaage had. Where had he seen ... at the retirement village! Tom sat up straight. The old man waving to him at the retirement village. The one he'd seen before. The one who always looked familiar.

The kaleidoscopic image changed one more time. The face grew younger, and the shit-eating smirk was back. The acne was there as well, but smoothed over by something, probably makeup. Tom had been drunk and busy watching Cheryl's ass, hadn't paid much attention. The face spoke when it handed him his wallet downstairs in the Halfway Lounge and Restaurant. The voice was young, with a girlish giggle; Betty Boop curl bouncing when he smiled.

"Shit!" Tom said.

Chapter 41

Cheryl signaled to Martha Biggers. "Can you watch the desk for a bit, Marth? I just got an unannounced visit from our mutual friend."

"Really?"

"Yeah, three days early."

"I'm sorry," Martha said.

"Not as sorry as me. Tom and I had plans for tonight."

"I've got some Advil in my purse. Want some?"

"No, thanks," Cheryl said, "I just need the ladies room." She grabbed her handbag.

"Take your time. I'll mind the store."

No sooner had Cheryl left, then the phone rang. It was a guest room.

"Hello, front desk."

"Is Cheryl, ah Ms. Wagner there?"

Martha noticed it was room 311. "Oh, hi. Is this Dr. Tom?"

"Just Tom. May I speak to Cheryl, please?"

"Oh, I'm sorry. She stepped away for a moment. May I help you?"

"When will she be back?"

"Well, ah ..." This would have been delicate even if it wasn't Cheryl's boyfriend. "No, well, not *too* long, I don't think. Maybe I can help you."

"Shit!"

"Beg pardon?"

"Tell her I had to leave. Something came up."

"Alright, I'll pass on ... hello?"

Tom's SUV screeched out of the hotel parking space. Before he even reached the exit, he was reciting the number he'd gotten from Google. Siri said she "did not understand, please repeat the number." She did not understand "shit" either. Nor did she understand the fireworks banging in the distance. Fourth time was the charm. A phone rang over the ether.

"You have reached Parkway Village."

"Yes, this is, I mean, I have reason to believe a bomb has been planted ..."

"For Tanya Bellis, dial one. For ..."

Tom punched zero on the dashboard display.

"One moment ... Thank you for calling the Parkway Village retirement center. Our office hours are seven a.m. to seven p.m., Monday through Friday. Nine to three on Saturday. If this is an emergency, please dial 911. Otherwise, leave ..."

"Shit!"

Tom ended the call and turned onto the freeway. His SUV slowed and skewed left as he dug into his pocket for his wallet, eliciting a honk from a driver behind. Punching the accelerator, he retrieved Sally's card, which was first in line inside a leather pouch. After a few more seconds with Siri, the FBI agent's cell was ringing.

"Hello?" said a disgruntled voice that Tom recognized all too well.

"Sally?"

"Yeah. Who the hell is this?"

"It's Tom Tomacinski."

"Goddamn it, Tom-Tom. You woke me from the best sleep I've had in a month. What's so important?"

"You've found Conrad, haven't you? Identified him, I mean."

"It's an active investigation. I'm not allowed to comment."

"It's some guy named King, isn't it? Some kid named King."

"Well, keep this under your hat, but everything points to George King's son. Did you just wake me up to tell me you guessed that?"

"What's the kid's name?"

"Georgie King. I mean, George King III. Listen, can't this wait until tomorrow?"

"Shut up and listen."

"Excuse me?"

"I know where he is."

Sally's voice was wide awake. "Where?"

Tom swerved left to pass a Camry. "He's moved into a retirement village about ten miles north of Knoxville."

"A retirement village? Are you nuts? His MO is hotels, not senior centers."

"It's run by the Parkway chain—Parkway Village."

"How do you know this?"

"I saw him," Tom said. "He's dressed like an old man, but it's him. The face matches the photos of Groenhaage and Tom-Tom. From the flier."

"What flier? Oh, you mean ..."

"And the voice matches the one I heard in the Middleboro tunnel."

"You talked to this old guy?"

"Not exactly, but he talked to me, a month ago. In the Halfway Lounge."

"You're not making much sense, Tom-Tom."

"I tell you, it's him."

"Okay. I'll send someone out there in the morning. What's this guy's name?"

"You can't wait that long." Outside, the lights on I-75 flew past. But all Tom could see was the old man doddering out of view, cane click-clacking, briefcase bobbing up and down. "He's gonna plant a bomb. Could already have planted one."

"How do you know this?"

"Long story. But it all fits, don't you see? Revenge on daddy and the Parkway chain. Old folks who can't get out of their own way. And it's the Fourth of July. Skeleton staff. Fireworks blasting off everywhere. It fits his flair for the dramatic."

"Hell," Sally said.

"What?"

"We found bomb-making materials at his place in Townsend. Homemade C4. Thermite."

"Thermite?" Tom shouted.

"Yeah, at least ten pounds of it."

"That stuff burns at four thousand degrees. And you can't put it out. It cooks through metal for Christ's sake."

"I'll call Knoxville PD and the fire department. Get a car out there to evacuate the building. Then I'll be en route with a critical-response unit from the field office. ETA maybe thirty minutes. Who are we looking for? What's his name?"

"Something Spanish. Mister Tres something or other." Tom concentrated for a second. "TresReyes, I think. Jorge TresReyes."

"Jorge TresReyes?"

"I think."

"Thats means George three kings."

"As in George King III?"

"I'll see you in thirty. Good job, Tom-Tom."

![bomb icon] *Chapter 42*

The schnapps felt good, the sweet liquor warming and calming his belly. Lying on his resale-store twin bed in rumpled suit and makeup, Georgie had had second thoughts. Each pop and bang in the distance raised a flinch. His intestines clenched, threatening to send him running to the can. But now, fortified by sixty-proof courage, he chalked it up to opening-night jitters. Nothing was irrevocable. He was burning an old-fart home but not any bridges. There was no Rubicon here. Jorge TresReyes would simply disappear. Perhaps they'd blame it on the fire, list his remains as mixed among the ashes. It's too bad, they'd say, he was such a nice old guy. His rouged lips smiled and sipped again from the bottle.

He should touch up his makeup before leaving in case anyone was downstairs. He'd tell them he just needed to get something from his car. Simple responses worked best. Would they notice when the car was missing? Maybe, maybe not. If they did, it wouldn't be for a while, not with tonight going on. He was glad he'd changed his dad's plates for stolen ones. Leave nothing to chance, that was his motto. An easy one to keep when one was "all that." He smiled. He sipped.

Gloved hands rubbed at the new mustache growth. Damn thing itched almost as much as a fake one but was better than the spirit gum. George removed a glove, careful not to touch anything, and scratched again. Sweat coated his fingers and upper lip. Fucking old folks' home was like a hothouse. Even with the AC ramped, it had to be pushing eighty. He looked forward to the cooler night air. His watch said it was time to go.

Donning his glove, Georgie King III rose from the bed, spinning the plastic cap onto the clear-glass bottle and placing it in a breast pocket. Checking to make sure his cell and car keys were in the other inside pocket, he stopped at the mirror long enough to add a little lipstick, deepen age lines, and dust gray powder over his sweating face. The makeup case went into the left-hand outer pocket of his jacket, balancing the weight of the snubby revolver in the right. Tugging his cap over his eyes, he nodded approval to Jorge TresReyes, who smiled in return.

Double checking that his cell was in his coat, he scanned the apartment. Counters were littered with pop bottles, candy wrappers, half a baloney sandwich, and a pizza box. They would all burn as beautifully as his Value Town furniture. He considered quickly rummaging drawers to see if he'd forgotten anything. But impatience and arrogance combined to nix the idea as overkill, nothing more than nervous second-guessing. Everything he needed was in the Beamer. He was ready. It was checkout time. Grabbing his cane, he left the TresReyes' apartment for the last time.

He'd bounced halfway down the hall before he caught himself. It wouldn't do to see feeble old Señor TresReyes pounding along. Georgie slowed his pace and went back to character, left leg limping, right hand shifting weight onto the cane. The change added fifty years to his movements and steadied him into the moment.

The lobby was empty, but Georgie kept his pace old and regular, jerking forward to the front door. There would probably be an electronic warning that an entrance had opened, but he'd be gone by the time one of the skeleton staff arrived. His gloved hand clicked the deadbolt, cane and hand pushing the door open, when he suddenly flinched erect, frozen in the partly opened entryway.

Strobe lights bounced in the driveway turn-around like a blue and white disco ball. Two cops stepped out of a Knox County cruiser, one pointing at him and hurrying over. Georgie dropped the cane as his hand reached for his pistol. But before he could draw it, the cop was on him.

"Are you alright, sir?"

For perhaps the first time since childhood, Georgie King III couldn't think of a smart-ass comeback, or any comeback.

The cop's expression softened as he noted the deer-in-the-lights look of senior befuddlement. "Where you going this time of night, Grampa?"

Georgie continued to stare, mind a blank. "I, ah, I ..."

"Well, keep right on going. We gotta evacuate the building. There's been a bomb threat. Do you understand?" The last was said loudly and distinctly, as if speaking to Helen Keller.

"I ... I, my car ..."

"What's that?" the deputy said, voice rising above the approaching wail of a fire truck.

Georgie cleared his parched throat. "My car."

"That's a good idea. You get to your car and stay there." The cop patted his shoulder and headed toward the door. "Just stay out of the building." Then he and his partner were gone. They missed the sight of a seventy-year-old man sprinting down the street.

Georgie wanted to grab the cell and punch the app, sending signals to the two devices. That had been the plan. He'd watch the first one blow, maybe see the glow of the second through the basement window. Then drive away before alarms were raised. But that got scuttled when the cops showed up. Now he needed to get gone, while he could.

The BMW's engine was barely audible above the growing din. A firetruck rounded the corner, siren wailing, red lights adding their flashes to those from the cop cars. The big, red vehicle pulled opposite the front entrance, followed seconds later by a parade of marked and unmarked vehicles. There was a large van, unmistakably labeled "BOMB SQUAD" in gold letters below "KNOX COUNTY" in blue. Several SUVs jerked to a stop behind it, their dark silhouettes disgorging men in body armor with FBI stenciled on the back. Another van pulled into the parking lot about fifty yards from the Beamer, its black sides proclaiming Tactical Unit in silver. Closely behind the black beast were two cars. The first was the shiny sports car that belonged to the FBI chick. The second was another SUV, one Georgie didn't immediately place until the vet bounced out and ran to the leggy redhead.

"Shittin' mother-fucking asshole-cunting dickwads," Georgie muttered. *Tom-Tom—again.* The injury detective had made the connection between Jorge and Conrad. But did he know about Conrad and Georgie King? No time to worry about that now. Either way, Georgie needed to put distance between himself and the growing crowd of law enforcement. Then he could start the fireworks, giving them something else to worry about. And destroying any evidence that George King III had ever been there.

Leaving the headlights off, Georgie lurched the Beamer out of his space and gunned it toward the far entrance to the lot. Tom-Tom and the tactical boys had entered off Palmer, which was now parked up like a side-street yard sale. Georgie would exit onto

Elm, drive a couple of residential blocks, and pop the cap. He didn't know what he'd do after that, his brain still fogged by shock and schnapps. But he knew one thing. He'd make that drum-banging Polack pay.

"Watch it, Doo," Dell yelled. A black BMW barely missed the Knoxville detective's car. "You almost hit that old fella."

"Shouldn't be driving at night anyway," Doolittle said, as he parked opposite the Elm Street side of the building. A pair of Knoxville PD blue and whites snugged up behind him as he exited.

"Secure that parking lot," he yelled to the uniforms in the first cruiser. "Nobody gets in or out unless they're on the job." Pointing toward the second cruiser, he added, "Ditto that Elm Street intersection. Comprende?" Then he and his partner hurried toward the hubbub on the other side of the lot.

Tom-Tom and Sally Pancakes walked toward Palmer Avenue as the FBI agent shrugged into body armor, her head shaking back and forth in response to something Tom-Tom was saying.

"But Cheryl's mother is in there," Tom said.

"Who?" Sally said.

"Mary Wagner. A friend of mine."

"I don't care *who's* in there," the FBI agent said. "*You* stay out here."

"But she's going to be confused. She knows me. I can get her out quickly."

Sally paused for a moment, then gave up. "Fine. Get this Mary out and then *stay* out. Understood?" Tom nodded and ran off.

"Hey, special agent," Doolittle said. "My folks secured Elm Street."

"Good," Sally said. "We'll bring the residents out the main entrance. I'll lead the assault team once we locate Conrad's room." She drew and checked her Glock. "You want in?"

"Do rednecks eat grits?" Doolittle grinned.

"Fine," Sally said, thumping her vest. "Grab yourselves some hardware and follow me."

Peggy Lehner stumbled out of the resident apartment, stubbing a toe on her slipper. One of the admin staff always had to be present, and she'd gotten stuck with the July 4 sleepover. She'd been dealing with complaints all day, what seemed like the longest day of her life. Why weren't the beans hotter? Why were those fireworks going off? Didn't they know old folks needed rest? She was exhausted and ready for a few hours of blissful oblivion. Now this.

"What the hell is going on? Is that you, Dr. Tom?"

"Listen. Peggy, right?"

Peggy nodded and clutched her robe around her. A wizened face peered out from Apartment 102. "It's alright, Mr. Schwartz. Go back to bed."

"It's after eleven, you know," Schwartz said.

"Yes, I know. I'll take care of it."

Tom smiled at the old man, who ducked back inside. "We have to evacuate the building."

"What?"

"How many staff do you have to help?"

Her robe fell open. "What? Why?"

"Never mind. How many?"

She clutched her robe closed again. "Just a skeleton crew. I'm overnight manager. There's one nurse and an assistant in memory care. Another staffer in assisted. And ..." Peggy pointed at a tall Black man running toward them dressed in sneakers and sweats. "And Marcus."

"What's up?" the orderly asked.

"We're evacuating the building," Tom said.

"We're what?"

"You two get to it. I'll help out, starting with Mary Wagner."

Tom bounded up the steps to the second floor.

"What's up, Peg?" Marcus said.

"Damned if I ..."

The front door burst open, and men armed with shotguns and bulletproof vests burst through. In the lead was a redheaded woman who looked more like a runway model than a cop.

"Get those wheelchairs in here," the lady cop said. Two paramedics entered on cue, chairs in front.

"Special Agent Sally Butterworth," the woman cop said. "Where is the apartment of Jorge TresReyes?"

"Señor TresReyes?" Peggy said.

"Yes. Where?"

"Ah, 126." Peggy pointed down the hall to her left.

"Stay here and evacuate the building," Butterworth said, moving toward the pointed direction. The other cops followed.

"Let's start with memory care," a female paramedic said. "Which way?"

Peggy pointed again.

They burst open the door to Room 126, knob banging against the wall before rebounding back. The cop with the battering ram retreated to the hallway, allowing the tactical team to spread across the living room. In a matter of seconds, all doorways were secured, all rooms scanned.

"Clear!" Sally yelled.

The bomb squad entered, leading a German Shepherd. The dog was walked past closets, cupboards, and the few pieces of cheap furniture. The Shepherd ignored the chip bags and other food items. She was a professional; this was business. Her reward would come later from the love and praise of her master. The dog sniffed continually, but never paused, never sat down. The handler looked at Sally and shook his helmeted head.

"You sure?" Sally asked.

"It's a small place," the bomb disposer said. "Maggie would have found it."

Doolittle walked over from his position by the TV. "I'm just a country cop. But I think it's possible Conrad heard the sirens and skedaddled. Just my redneck opinion."

"Maybe," Sally said, reholstering her weapon. "*If* he was here."

"Maybe Tom-Tom is seeing things?" Doolittle said. "This here's just some old slob spending the Fourth with his daughter?"

"Wouldn't be the first time," Sally said.

💣 Chapter 43

Georgie killed the engine and panted in the darkness. He was on some side street, lit only by porch lights. The sirens had died, replaced by occasional pops of distant fireworks.

It took two tries to peel off his gloves, the leather painted to his skin by sweat and tension. Holding his clammy hands together to quell their shaking, he summoned his relaxation training, one of the more useful tidbits from drama school. Eyes closed, he took deep, cleansing breaths, fighting against the steel cables constricting his hammering heart. Seconds ticked by, but he ignored them, concentrating on inhaling and slowly exhaling. His mind's eye found light behind the lids, starbursts and changing colors that provided focus, a point of attention. He let the light show take him, following where it led, emptying his mind. His breathing slowed. His heart rate slowed. Georgie opened his eyes and could see into the darkness. He was alone.

Wiping sweaty palms onto Goodwill pants, he retrieved the cell from his suit pocket. A single push brought up the number pad, as expected. What wasn't expected was the battery image with just a single red line on a dark rectangle. The panic attack hung on the edges of returning, as his fingers entered one pass code digit, then two, then three. Before he could punch the fourth and final number, the screen went dark. Georgie jabbed the home button. He jabbed it again, index finger blanching with pressure. The touch screen remained dark as the night.

The face reflected off the phone seemed to shrink, as if he was rising out of himself, above and away from it. Then his mind filled with an image of the charger cord lying in the drawer of the cheap bedside bureau in Jorge's apartment. The floating Georgie saw another Georgie sliding the cord inside the drawer, making a mental note to charge the phone before he left, even if just for a bit. Enough charge for a few minutes of life. More than enough to activate the app. The floating Georgie descended, the dark touch screen growing larger. He was back in the car, phone in his hand, cold sweat beading on his brow. Unable to breathe.

His heart rate quickened until individual beats blended into a rapid thrum. Breathing was reduced to brief gulps of air painfully pulled from a chest frozen to immobility. The phone slipped from his grasp as he clawed at his constricted throat, fighting for air. His vision narrowed, as if the edges were slowly closing like curtains on the theater of his mind. What was left of Georgie's rationality knew that if he allowed this particular show to close, the police would find him here, collapsed behind the wheel of his dad's fancy car. Dead cell phone on the floor. Dreams of revenge unfulfilled. The panic shifted, first to anger, then to rage. The curtain opened, just a little, then all the way. His vision cleared. His hands balled into fists.

"Fuck!"

Georgie King vented rage on the expensive appointments of the BMW's interior. The wood-inlaid steering wheel vibrated from repeated blows. The dome light blinked on as punches dented the roof's fabric-covered steel. An elbow assaulted the plushily paneled door. Fists pounded the leather of the dash. The glove box popped open. A car phone charger slid onto the floor. The passenger seat thudded from ... A phone charger lay on the floor? Georgie King III paused, fist held above plush leather. Then he started to laugh.

Tears rolled down his cheeks as he snatched up the cord. The cap was ripped off the Beamer's 12V outlet, severing the plastic connection holding it in place. He ravaged the bulbous male end of the adapter into the opening. Then semi-rational Georgie took control, slowing his movements and gently inserting the other end of the cord into the base of the phone.

With shaking fingers, he gently placed the cell on the car's console and waited. He counted to ten, slowly, then tenderly pressed the home button. The screen remained dark. Georgie started the car, revving the generator to life. Then he punched the home button again. Again darkness. Panic rising, he forced himself to recite Mississippi's until the number thirty. Carefully, prayerfully, he pressed the button a third time. A battery outline appeared, a faint white line filling the bottom. Georgie stared at the phone and waited. Seconds ticked by. Minutes followed. Air-conditioned chill dried his sweaty brow. Yet still, he waited. He waited until the line rose a quarter of the way from the base. Then he tapped the home button. This time, only the keypad appeared. Georgie carefully entered four digits, changing the dark screen to a colorful display of icons. He found the app, the one he called his zap-app. He pressed the icon.

💣 *Chapter 44*

Tom pounded on the door.

"Who's there?" a voice answered.

"It's me, Mrs. Wagner. Dr. Tomacinski. Tom. Let me in."

"Go away. I have a gun."

Pound, pound, pound. "Let me in, Mary. We have to evacuate the building."

"Who's there?"

"It's me, Tom Tomacinski. Cheryl's friend."

"Cheryl's Tim?"

"Yes. Cheryl's Tim. Let me in." Still the door remained closed.

"What are you doing here? It's dark out. Where's Cheryl?"

"I need to take you outside."

"Outside? I'll catch my death. Why?"

Tom spoke again to the locked door. "There, ah, ... there's a problem with the electrical system. They need to check all the rooms to find it."

There was a pause before Mary answered. "You mean like a short? My husband told me about those. They can be hard to track down."

Tom nodded. "Yes, that's right. A short."

"He was an electrician, you know. My husband."

"Yes, Cheryl told me. Please, let me in."

Tom heard the snick of a deadbolt. Then the door creaked open to the end of a brass chain.

"It's stuck," Mary said.

"The chain is on," Tom said, trying to remain calm.

Other residents were peering out of doorways, or wandering into the hall, bathrobes clutched. A chubby man with a big nose walkered his way out of 205, clad only in baggy boxers and a T-shirt, varicose veins lining spindly legs. "What the hell is going on?"

"There's been a problem," Tom said. "The fire department is asking everyone to go outside."

"Outside?" the old man said. "It's after eleven o'clock. What kind of a crazy place is this?"

"Just for a little while," Tom said.

"I'm going back to bed."

The old man turned toward his door. Tom hurried toward him, hands gently stopping his return.

"What the hell are you doing? Take your damned hands off me, or I'll kick your ass."

"Ah, sorry, sir." Tom let go. "But you can't go back inside just yet. I need you to head toward the lobby."

The guy's right hand swatted Tom's, then returned to the walker frame. "You're crazy." Speaking toward the gathering rubberneckers, he shouted, "Go back to bed. This guy's crazy."

Tom heard Mary's door close and reopen, the clink of a taut chain again catching his ear.

"It's stuck," Mary said, peering from below the chain.

"No, Mary. You have to remove ... Step back from the door, please."

"What?"

"Step back," Tom said. Mary stepped back. Tom threw his weight on the door amid a crack of flying brass.

"Who are you?" Mary asked.

"I'm Cheryl's Tim. Let's go down and get some cheesecake."

The lady paramedic rolled a woman in swaddling blankets out the exit, oxygen tank strapped to the back of the wheelchair. One of the county cops was slowly walking a man with a cane out of the independent-living wing. Peggy Lehner pushed another chair holding Lena Cohen, the old lady tucking her robe about her legs in girlish modesty, her husband Saul's walker bringing up the rear.

"Let me help, there," the male paramedic said, grabbing Lena's chair from Peggy. "Why don't you make an announcement over the PA, so we can speed this up?"

"We don't have a PA," Peggy said.

"Looks like my morning constitutional is eight hours early," Saul Cohen said with a wink.

Another walker clumped back in from outside. "No, Mr. Doubleday," Peggy said. "You have to stay outside for a while. Until the police say it's okay to come back."

"Like a fire drill?" Doubleday asked.

"That's right," Peggy said. "Just like a fire drill."

The night manager saw Tom Tomacinski walking Mary Wagner down the hall, a little dot of sanity amid the bedlam. Tom moved slowly to keep pace with Mary's fuzzy, shuffling slippers.

"I'll take her," Peggy said. "Hi, Mary. Quite the excitement, huh?"

"Where's the cheesecake?"

"In a bit. After we go outside." Arm around Mary's slender shoulder, Peggy turned to Tom. "Why don't you help some of the independents?" She pointed to a couple huddled in the hall, unsure which way to go.

"Can't we clear the building any faster?" Tom asked.

"You want to suggest how?" Peggy snapped. Then she and Mary headed outside.

Rushing down the indie wing, Tom spied Sally and Doolittle walking his way. "Well?"

"Looks like a false alarm," Sally said. "Nobody home."

"May have beat feet with all the hubbub," Doolittle said.

"Right this way, folks," Doolittle's partner, Dell, said. The clump of confused residents followed her authoritative command out the front door.

"But the bomb?" Tom said.

"My people are turning the room for evidence," Sally said. "Bomb squad is walking the perimeter to see if there's anything."

Tom suddenly remembered. "The briefcase."

"What briefcase?"

"When I saw TresReyes today, he was walking outside with a briefcase. When he came back, he didn't have one."

"Could have been taking it to his car," Doolittle said.

"No," Tom said. "That was it. That was the bomb. It had to be."

"Why would he plant thermite outside? What's he gonna burn?" Sally asked.

"I don't know. But that must have been it." Tom started toward the door; Sally stopped him.

"You stay put. The squad will find it—*if* it's there. I have to report in."

Tom watched Sally stride out the door, a twinge of regret fluttering up like a moth from the basement of his heart. Peggy Lehner passed her coming toward him.

"So, false alarm?" Peggy asked Tom. "Can we start bringing people back inside?"

Tom shook his head. "How are we doing? Is everyone out?"

"Maybe half," Peggy said. "I knew Señor TresReyes couldn't be a mad bomber. He's too nice and so charming." She smiled. "And that would dash my hopes for an early retirement."

"What?"

Peggy chuckled and shook her head. "Just a joke between me and Tanya. About him being my boyfriend. Showing me his etchings, or in this case porcelain figurines."

"What figurines?"

"No, Marjorie," Peggy said to a woman sitting down in the lobby. "You need to go outside."

"What figurines?" Tom repeated.

Peggy shrugged. "He worked for a company that made beautiful porcelain. Had the best of the lot shipped here. Was going to show them to me."

"Shipped here? When? How?"

"No, Mrs. Connor. Just keep heading outside," Peggy yelled to a woman walking toward the dining room.

"Tell me," Tom said, grabbing her shoulders.

"Ow," Peggy said, shaking free. "Take it easy."

"Sorry. What was shipped here?"

"Big box, UPS'd in a few days ago.

"Where is it?"

Peggy moved aside so firemen could help a man in his pajamas. "Tanya had it put downstairs. In the storage cage."

"In the basement?"

"Yeah, with the old files. Marcus took it down. I didn't know porcelain and packing could weigh so much. Hey, where are you going?"

Tom was already sprinting toward the fire stairs.

Concrete steps led down to a cavernous space with the universal smell of dusty cellar. Guided only by the LED light on his key chain, Tom searched out a bank of switches with gray conduit snaking toward the ceiling beams. Fluorescent lights fluttered into life as he flicked all three.

Two large banks of lights lit the length of the space, which was perhaps thirty feet wide by eighty long. A third, smaller bank of fluorescents hovered over a workbench, tools hanging on a peg-board wall behind it. Metal shelves to the left of the workspace were piled with cleaning and plumbing supplies. Folding chairs and tables were stacked against the left wall. The rest of the space marched away to Tom's right, with less clutter than he'd imagined. There were a few packing crates and cardboard boxes, along with plastic drums sprouting an assortment of quarter moldings, broom handles, and plywood strips, the mixed lengths giving the drums the jagged look of broken bottles. Tom's eyes took it all in but focused on the row of wire-metal enclosures against the wall ahead and to the right.

Several of the wire-enclosed pens held old furniture: sofas, chairs, dinette sets. In the gloomy light, it was hard to distinguish colors below the gray coats of dust. The nearest enclosure held mostly cardboard boxes, stacked side by side. At least half an inch of the omnipresent dust coated these as well, except for one. Its bright tan contrasted against the dull gray of the others, like a living thing among old bones. Its plastic-covered UPS packing slip shone in the fluorescent light, almost shouting "I'm new. Open me." Tom ran over and jerked the enclosure door, the wire mesh coming up short against a stout padlock. He jerked several more times, metal clangs echoing off the dusty walls, before running back to the workbench.

Tom searched in vain for bolt cutters, settling instead for a small pry bar and a five-pound sledge. Turning back toward the cage, he caught a glimpse of a retractable box cutter on the surface of the bench. He thrust the cutter in his pocket and ran back to the cage with his treasure.

Wedging the pry bar to where the hasp seated into the lock, Tom tapped lightly with the sledge. Satisfied that the chisel wouldn't slip, he tapped harder, painful vibration thrumming into his hand holding the bar. Steeling himself for greater pain, he raised his right hand high and brought the hammer down full against the bar. The lock held, but the sledge slipped off his make-shift chisel, chipping the metal and jamming the rusty pry bar back into his left hand.

"Fuck, shit, no good ..."

Hammer and chisel clashed against the concrete floor as Tom danced about, holding his wounded hand, blood dribbling toward his wrist. Snaking a handkerchief from his hip pocket, he wrapped it tightly around his injury, wincing in pain as blood soaked through the white cloth.

Retrieving his tools, Tom began again, wedging the bar against the base of the lock's hasp. Ignoring the pain howling into his gouged hand, he tapped the sledge repeatedly, each successive tap with slightly greater force, seating the chisel against the lock. The clang of metal on metal echoed off the boxes, walls, and Tom's eardrums, raising a ring that stabbed his head like an ice pick. He pounded with increasing force and rapidity, hand rising slightly higher with each backstroke. Finally, before his blood-slicked grip lost hold of the chisel, he raised the hammer over his head, then struck savagely downward. Both the lock and pry bar gave way, the former swinging free, the latter flying from his grasp to skitter across the concrete.

Fire radiated from Tom's injury as he rewrapped the make-shift bandage. Tossing the sledge toward the chisel, he ripped the razor cutter from his pocket and approached the box addressed to Jorge TresReyes. The knife sliced through the name as Tom slit open the packing tape and pried apart the flaps, blood coating the cardboard and glistening plastic. Instead of the figurines of Peggy's imagination, there was more plastic. He sliced through that as well, then tossed the cutter on the floor.

In the dim light of the cubicle, Tom could now see the handiwork of Jorge TresReyes, aka Georgie King III, aka Conrad Hilton. A black-plastic device sat atop a baggy, which in turn sat atop gray powder. As Tom watched, the red light on the device flickered and a loud snap penetrated past the ringing in his ears. The baggie began to smoke, then burst into brilliant purple and yellow flames. Tom stared in fixated fascination as the blinding flames flared into a more intense, white-hot fire that burned down into the underlying granules.

✦ *Chapter 45*

Maggie trotted along, sniffing the night air. She and her handler rounded the rear corner of the independent wing and began walking the parking-lot facade of the building. The big Shepherd moved past a large electrical box, pausing, sniffing, then walking on. Her delicate nose no doubt picked up many scents but not the one she was trained for. The pair moved past basement windows covered in wire mesh, the scent still missing. About midway down the side of the building, a large-diameter pipe jutted from the brick and cinder block. Maggie sniffed around it. She sniffed again. Then she casually sat down.

"Hey, Sarge," her handler yelled. "I think we got something."

Another blue-clad man in body armor and face shield trained a powerful flashlight on the pipe. Brown leather jutted from one side, the edge of a briefcase handle visible. He nodded and the two men and one dog moved off. Then the sergeant spoke into his walkie-talkie.

"Got a suspicious case wedged under a pipe on the eastern facade. Let's bring in a robot to check it out."

"Roger that, Sarge," crackled a voice from the black box. "Will dispatch the Dragon Runner and monitor from here."

"Copy. Will remain on scene ..."

The earth tilted as the night lit with a tremendous flash, dropping the bomb-squad sergeant to one knee, arms protectively over his head. A fist-sized chunk of rust-brown metal zinged by his kneeling form, propelled by the tremendous blast that roared from the pipe. A moment later, a geyser of water shot into the night, as if the Parkway Villages had added a new fountain in an unusual location.

Maggie and her handler rushed over to their sergeant. "You okay, Bob?"

"What?" the sergeant said.

"I said, you hit?"

The dazed sergeant wrenched off his helmet and tapped his ringing ear. "What?"

"Are you okay?" Maggie's handler shouted.

Sergeant Bob nodded. Then, training his flash on the dazzling fountain, he said, "Son of a bitch blew the main water line."

"What for?"

"My guess," Bob said, "to kill the fire sprinklers."

As Sally reentered the building, Peggy was helping her millionth old lady out the door, her cheerful banter flagging amid the exhaustion and bizarre circumstances. The FBI agent paused, scanning the lobby.

"If you're looking for Dr. Tom," Peggy said, "he went down to the basement."

"Basement?"

"Yeah, something about a package."

"What package?"

"The one Señor TresReyes mailed here a few days ago. Big heavy box. We locked it in the storage area. Supposed to contain ... Hey, where are you going?"

💣 *Chapter 46*

Tom turned away from the brightest light he'd ever seen, like staring into a welder's flame or the face of the sun. A light that would burn through his retinas as easily as thermite burned through metal. Somewhere, the building shook with an explosion, but he barely noticed. All his thoughts were consumed with the intense flame—and what that meant.

Right now, at this moment, the fire was confined to a small nidus in the center of the granules. Within seconds, it would spread the width of the opening, then through the depths of the underlying box. Then it would consume everything in sight. The wire mesh would not impede its spread to the dried-out furniture, mattresses, and paper, which were so much kindling. The sprinklers might slow these secondary fires, but the low-hazard systems in institutional settings were never designed for something that burned at four-thousand degrees and carried its own oxygen supply. Once the whole box got cooking, the fire department would be reduced to dousing upper floors to minimize fly-off damage to adjacent buildings. Well before that happened, smoke would have spread throughout the structure, asphyxiating any residents still inside. All this ran through Tom's head in the instant it took the purple ignition flame to change to thermite white.

Mind reeling, Tom acted on instinct. Turning his head away from the glare and acrid stink, Tom's fingers found the inside edges of the box, nails brushing plastic and cardboard, tips brushing fine, gray granules, heat burning his palms. If he was going to do anything, he needed to act now, before his brain caught on to how dangerous this was. He hesitated for just an instant, then shoved his hands deep into the granules. Like a kid digging in the sand, he scooped under the ever-growing lump of burning metal and heaved to his left.

What happened next would be remembered only in a series of awkward still pictures, like a slide show from a bad photographer.

Light popped in his eyes, leaving a blue, flashbulb afterimage. Pain shot through his palms and fingers. Something landed on his head; a hundred needles stinging across his face and ear. He collapsed to the floor. The back of his left hand burned. His eyes stung as they blinked away a dry white powder pouring over his face and body. A familiar voice said, "Hang in there, Tom-Tom." Then the throbbing pain left, and he floated in silent darkness.

Tom snapped awake to the smell of ammonium carbonite snaking into his brain. His right hand swatted at the smelling salts, sending pain stabbing through his fingers. This pain was joined by others radiating from his face, arms, and hands.

"Take it easy, sir," a Tennessee drawl said.

Opening his eyes, Tom saw a guy of about twenty-five staring down at him.

"Now that you're conscious, I can give you something for the pain." The EMS tech withdrew clear liquid from a vial and syringed it into a plastic tube.

Tom's vision followed the IV tube to its end in his left arm. On the trip down, he saw a bandage covering his left hand and forearm. He tried to touch the dressing with his right hand, but that was bandaged as well. Then the pain blew away like a cool breeze.

"Just take it easy," the tech said.

"How's he doing?" another voice said. Tom's numbed brain followed the sound to a pair of beautiful dimples smiling down from below flashing green eyes.

"That's the best *I* can do for him," the tech said. "I've given him a quarter grain morphine and antibiotics, but we should get him to the hospital. A couple of those burns are pretty nasty, might need debridement or a graft." The tech bent the needle before forcing the cap back on the used syringe. "Good thing you hit him with that extinguisher when you did or burning clothes might have finished what the thermite started. As it is, the burns will lay him up for a while, but he should be okay."

The smile never left Sally's face. "Good to see you, Tom-Tom. You wonderful, brave, crazy son of a bitch."

Her face swam before his drug-clouded eyes. "Hi there, Agent Sally," he mumbled. "How's the prettiest G-man in the Bureau?" The dimples deepened. Tom drew a deep breath that smelled like cut grass and nighttime. "No smoke," he croaked. "Everyone okay?"

Sally nodded. "Thanks to you. Fire brigade foamed down the basement, which now has a nice hole burned in one wire cage. And a bunch of senior citizens are missing beauty sleep and water for their morning decaf. But otherwise, Tomacinski two, Conrad zero."

Tom's vision grew hazy around the edges.

"Okay if he sleeps now?" Sally asked. The tech nodded. "Why don't you rest your eyes, Tom-Tom?"

"I don't know," he whispered. "I'm liking the view." The last thing he remembered was smiling dimples and green eyes.

💣 *Chapter 47*

"Just a second," Georgie said, putting on his sunglasses and muting the TV. He'd awoken around four p.m. in the Sleep Tite Inn in New Bethel, Kentucky, according to the room's guest-information binder. His cell phone, which he'd evidently remembered to bring in from the car, said he was in Owsley County, about thirty miles off the freeway. That meant he'd driven one hundred and fifty miles, thirty on country roads, with no recollection of having done so. He also had no recollection of checking in at the Sleep Tite, or of when he'd last eaten. But his rumbling stomach told him it had been awhile, so he combined the phone with the guest-information book to rectify at least that part of the puzzle.

The delivery man from Wonton Palace said the bill was twelve seventy-five. Georgie paid with a twenty, noting he had only one twenty left. He'd need to break another hundred, and soon. The Beamer was almost on empty. Odd that he remembered that, but not getting here.

With a hot container of lo mein in one hand, plastic fork in another, Georgie plopped on the bed to watch the grainy TV. Mute removed, the local newshound, without a trace of southern twang in her accent-less voice, said to stay tuned for national news.

The lead story had something to do with the budget, but essentially concluded that Republicans and Democrats couldn't get along. Georgie was more interested in noodles, meat, and vegetables. The next story dealt with an air strike that may or may not have killed some high-ranking terrorist. His stomach still wasn't interested. Then the news got interesting, and his brain took over.

"In regional news," the anchor said, "A Tennessee retirement village was in the spotlight yesterday as the center of a bomb plot. For more information, we go to Karen Underwood, on the scene near Knoxville."

"Thank you, Jon. Behind me is the Parkway Villages retirement center. This sleepy rest home was popping with fireworks yesterday but not those normally seen on July Fourth. Last night, police discovered not one, but two bombs planted here. The first device blew out the main pipe providing water to the building, rendering it defenseless in the case of fire."

The camera closed in on two municipal employees bolting on a new section of painted pipe.

"The second, an incendiary device, was located in the basement storage area. Had it been successfully detonated, there is little doubt the building would have been engulfed in flames, with much loss of innocent life. But fortunately, that was prevented by one brave man."

The screen switched to a handsome man in a sport jacket and tie.

"Dr. Thomas Tomacinski, a visitor to Parkway Villages, managed to foil the attempt by manually separating the fire from its fuel supply, receiving second-degree burns in the process. He is currently being treated for his injuries and is expected to make a complete recovery."

Rice spilled on the bedspread as the half-empty carton crumpled in Georgie's clenched fist.

"We spoke with Ms. Peggy Lehner, the resident manager on that fateful Independence Day."

The TV image switched to a familiar middle-aged brunette. "Once I grew up, the heroes in my life kind of drifted away," Peggy said. "But I've still got one. Dr. Tom is my hero." Then Peggy's face was replaced by the reporter's.

"Police have yet to release information on the motive for the crime. Special Agent Scott Crossfield of the FBI's Knoxville field office would say only that it is part of an ongoing investigation. However, authorities have asked the public to be on the lookout for *this* man."

Now the screen held a series of photos, most grainy and hard to make out, one bright and smiling. Georgie recognized them all.

"The suspect is George King III, although he goes by many names. He is described as five feet eleven, one hundred and eighty pounds, with dark hair. He is thought to be approximately twenty-one years of age but may disguise himself as older, using make-up, clothing, and false facial hair. He should be considered armed and dangerous and is wanted in connection with at least two murders. Anyone with knowledge of his whereabouts should contact the FBI immediately." A 1-800 number was listed on the screen. "Back to you, Jon."

Georgie heaved the carton—rice, shrimp, and bits of carrot exploded across the television screen.

Sally held up the pizza box.

"I didn't see that," the nurse said, rolling her eyes. "Try not to stay too long, he's still kind of out of it."

Tom lay propped up in bed, eyes closed. Bandages covered his hands, glistening ointment covered angry scabs on his scalp and left ear. For just a moment, Sally was a preteen again, looking down at her father in his coma. The feeling was so strong, she softly said "Daddy?" just as she had more than a dozen years ago.

Tom's eyes opened. "What?"

"Um, I said, how you doing, Tom-Tom?"

"Hey, Sally." Tom winced as he smiled. "I'm okay for a man who's just had his first saline debridement." He held up his freshly bandaged hands.

"Rough?"

"Not too bad, but then again, I'm on enough pain meds to bring down a small rhinoceros. What you got there?"

"I read somewhere that pizza was good for burn patients."

"Was that in the *New England Journal of Medicine?*" Tom smiled.

"No, I think it was *New Jersey Culinary* magazine. Want some?"

Tom held up his bandaged hands.

"Allow me," Sally said, pulling a slice of the almost-warm pie from the box. She held it out while Tom took a bite.

"Mmm. Beats the hell out of cold scrambled eggs and toast."

Sally pulled a can of Bass ale from her pocket. "Something to wash it down?"

He shook his head. "Don't tempt me. I can't afford to get any higher."

Sally slid the can back in her pocket. "Listen, Tom. There's something I want to say." The normally confident agent cleared her throat and fidgeted with her ponytail. "Well, I was a little, you know, hard on you back in Knoxville." She cleared her throat again. "Right after I got suspended, I was, you know ..."

"A bitch?"

Like a charade player, Sally tapped a finger to the tip of her nose. "But I just wanted to say, that ..."

"Forget it, Sal. Water under the bridge."

"Yeah, I know. It's just that. Well, I felt bad about how I treated you. And, more than that ... you see, that wasn't really the way, the way I felt." She shifted feet, hands in pockets. "I mean, the way I *feel*. Because you see, I think I may be ... That is to say, what I mean to say is." She stomped one foot. "What I'm trying to say is that it's not impossible that I've fallen ..."

"Tom! My darling, Tom." Cheryl rushed to the bedside. She reached to hold his face, then noticed the glistening burns. "I don't want to hurt you." She gently pecked his cheek, then found his mouth for a longer kiss. "Pizza? Should you be having that?"

"That was my fault. I brought it."

"Oh, Agent Butterworth. I'm sorry, I didn't notice you. I saw Tom, and, well, that's all I really saw."

"No need to apologize. I should be going. Give you two some privacy."

"No, don't leave on my account."

"Yeah, Sally. Stay awhile. You wanted to tell me something." Tom's eyes had a drug-induced haze. Sally had seen enough junkies to know. And her own eyes were threatening to haze up as well.

Sally waved them off. "No. It wasn't important. You're probably tired. And I'm sure you want some time alone with your girlfr ... your friend.

"Okay. Stop by tomorrow. I'm here all week, or so they tell me." Tom's lips took on a crooked grin. "Most of the time I can't remember much."

Sally's return smile held a hint of sadness. "Just as well. I'll see you later."

Three steps down the hall, the agent almost bumped into the nurse. "Did you have a nice visit?" The nurse's face took on a softer expression. "Here's a tissue."

"Thanks," Sally said, wiping her eyes and nose. "Allergies."

"It's hard, isn't it?" the nurse said. "Seeing a friend in pain, wrapped in bandages?" She touched Sally's arm. "But his burns aren't that serious. No infection, no grafts. He's very lucky. Probably be discharged by the end of the week."

Sally nodded.

"He's in good hands," the nurse said.

Sally's dimples rose to another sad smile. "Yes, I can see that."

💣 *Chapter 48*

Dr. Myer looked at the raw pink tissue. "This is coming along fine. You're a fast healer, Dr. Tomacinski."

"Thanks, but I can't take all the credit. I've had good care."

"Always nice to hear from a satisfied customer." The middle-aged man in the lab coat smiled. "Wait till you see the bill."

"Dr. Tomacinski won't be seeing any bills," Cheryl said from the doorway. "Parkway will be handling all medical expenses."

"Damn things starting to itch a little," Tom said, as Myer released his hand.

"That's a good sign," Myer said. "You're pretty lucky to end up with first- and second-degree burns, considering what you were handling. Thermite, wasn't it?"

"Well, I wasn't exactly handling it as much as I was shoveling it. And the parts I was shoveling weren't lit yet."

"Still, that was a very courageous thing to do."

"He's a very courageous man," Cheryl said.

"That's what they tell me. I don't really remember feeling courageous, just scared."

"And a very modest one," Cheryl said.

Myer switched his inspection to the left hand. "Yes, coming along very nicely indeed. The first-degree burns have basically healed. So has that gouge. We only need to deal with the second-degree lesions on those three fingers and here at the base of the left palm. Second-degree burns are more dangerous because they extend below the surface of the skin, opening underlying tissues to infection."

"I'm a veterinarian, Doc."

Myer chuckled. "Sorry. Most of my patients can't tell a liver from a lung lobe. Anyway, you've got nice beds of granulation tissue here, which should heal fine with little scarring. No grafts will be needed so long as you take it easy, finish up the antibiotics, and change the bandages every day. I don't suppose you need someone to show you how to do that."

Cheryl raised her hand. "I do. I've been appointed resident nurse during his recovery."

"Was that Parkway's idea?" Tom said.

"Mine," Cheryl said. "But senior management agrees. I've been granted three weeks paid leave."

"Well then," Myer said. "I'll send a nurse in with the bandage materials. She'll run through it and leave you written instructions."

When the lab coat left the room, Tom said," Listen, Hon. It's great that you want to help out. But I can change a bandage. I've changed hundreds. You've done enough. Really, above and beyond."

Cheryl grimaced. "You have no idea. Those sores on your hands are ga-ross."

"You mean these," Tom said, waving his fingers like angry red worms."

"Yuck! Makes me want to upchuck."

"Your Tennessee is showing, darlin'. Sounded like 'uhp-chuyk.'"

"Is that a fact," she said, hands on hips, smile on lips.

"Sho' 'nuff."

"Well, I guess you bring out the Southern belle in me."

"Seriously, Scarlett. It's time you tended to your mom, and it's time for me to get home and back to work."

Cheryl pecked him quickly on the mouth. "It's cute that you think you're going to win this argument. Part of your boyish charm. By the way, *you've* also gotten three weeks paid medical leave."

"What? How? I don't need time off."

"The how is Parkway talked to the FBI, the FBI talked to CDC, and CDC talked to NIOSH. And what *you* think you need is irrelevant. The doctors and I know what's best for you." She kissed him again. "So, you will be stuck with a nurse with benefits for the next twenty-one days. I'll make sure you get your bandages changed." She kissed him a little harder. "I'll fix your meals and make sure you take your antibiotics." She kissed him longer. "And I'll provide you with my own, patent-pending pain relievers, guaranteed to make you forget your hands." Her tongue found his.

💣 *Chapter 49*

Georgie King nonchalantly scratched at the natural, if scraggly, growth along his chin and lip. The beard's itch was annoying, but nothing compared to the spirit gum with which he'd had a love-hate relationship. The adhesive irritated and bred zits but also led him down magical roads where make-believe became reality.

The theater kids he'd worked with had various motivations: some wanted an easy A, others to meet girls (always in good supply) or to grab the center of attention. Only a very few loved the work of creating characters that came alive on stage. To lose themselves for a time in a fantasy land with different sets of problems, aspirations, joys, and fears. Georgie surpassed even those rare actors. His characters were more real to him than reality. They molded him, sculpting his personality into unique new shapes, so that it was difficult to tell where he ended and they began.

A horn honk startled him. He flipped a bird to the review mirror and accelerated the Beamer through the green light. That was when he noticed the county cruiser in his driver's side window. Sun-glassed eyes watched him speed away, then abruptly slow to a more legal velocity far slower than the beating of Georgie's heart. The police cruiser was now in the rearview, pulling behind the sleek, late-model BMW so out of keeping with the beaters and pickups common to rural Kentucky. Georgie held his breath in anticipation of the flashing gumball that might flare behind him at any moment. But the cruiser just held its position several car-lengths back.

They were heading out of a sleepy burg called Wyattsville, still a few miles from the freeway. Georgie hit his turn indicator and made a slow and sober right onto a road called Caulfeld. The cruiser followed, still several car-lengths back. Georgie could see the mouth below the sunglasses speak into a microphone, no doubt checking the Tennessee plates on the luxury car. Soon, he would learn that the plates were stolen. Georgie made a hard left onto SR-31, gunning for some distance. The cruiser turned as well and matched his speed. Then the cop's light bar flashed on. A second later, Georgie punched the gas.

The speedometer read eighty when the siren joined the flashing lights. The state road ran straight into the distance like a bridge to infinity. Georgie added foot pressure, raising his speed to ninety. He knew the performance car could gain him distance on this straightaway. He also knew the cruiser had a big engine and a radio. Worst of all, the county cop knew the area, could call in help to cut him off.

Staring down the tunnel of the road opened a tunnel in Georgie's mind. Time slowed and his twenty-one years passed before him like a heads-up display on the windshield. He heard each of his father's harsh words, felt each smack. He saw his mother's cowardly retreat into subservience, hating her for it while still loving her. He saw himself suspended from Beaverbrook Academy, heard the headmaster wonder why such a bright lad with such a promising future would intentionally harm an animal. He slipped deeper into defiance and then isolation, drifting from one college major to another, discarding friends before they could discard him. Then he saw *The Plan,* the scheme that would garner him independence and prove his superiority. How had it gone so wrong? He saw Tom-Tom's face, the last image before the Beamer reached the curve.

Georgie hit the brakes too late, bringing him to the edge of a spinout. He overcorrected his steering, sending the black car sideways, perpendicular to the highway. Before he could straighten the wheel, he'd punched the gas and hurtled the Beamer down a dirt track that entered SR-31 from some farmer's field. Grass snickered against the car's bottom as branches lashed the hood and windshield. Suspended in the surreal clutches of eternity, he sensed the Beamer slow, although he could not feel the brake under his foot. Then he jerked forward against the shoulder harness, the front tires wedged against some obstruction.

He sat dazed, the world slowly spinning back into shapes, colors, and sounds. He saw his hands white-knuckling the wheel, then looked past to the spider crack across the windshield. He heard the ticking of the hot engine. Then the siren grew in volume, piercing into his skull before its wail slowly receded into the distance behind him. Awareness gradually returned, but much of his sanity was gone. Now he was a hunted animal, struggling for survival and revenge. A boyish, Polack face swam across his vision. He smiled and slowly backed the car down the rutted road.

❧

Dealin' Don Coogan stepped out of the old Honda and said, "What'd I tell you. Runs like a champ, don't she?" He hitched the waistband of his Sansabelt slacks over his beer-gutted shirttail. Then he folded his bare arms over his comically short tie, its dark color hiding a grease stain from some long-forgotten hamburger.

His customer kicked a tire. "How much?"

"Well, sir. I know she's old and not much to look at, but every gal has her charms. This particular lady's got only 59,000 on the old odo."

"How much was on it when *you* got it?"

Don crossed his heart. "Would I do that? That engine is cherry. So, I'm gonna have to get thirty-five hundert."

The young kid walked to the rear, kicking another tire. College kid, most likely. Don knew the type. Probably spent a couple of years at Berea Community before transferring to Cumberland or UK. They grew their Fu Manchus on their pimply faces, studied alternative history, and thought they knew everything. But they didn't know jack about dickering over a set of wheels. What was a few hundred more of mommy and daddy's money?

The college kid surprised him. "Not worth a penny over twenty-five."

Dealin' Don gave him an aw-shucks grin and shook his head. "I could *maybe* go three."

"You could maybe go lower than that," the kid said.

Don thought about it, putting hand to chin and closing one eye. "Normally, three would be rock bottom. But I'm trying to move inventory, clear space on the lot for the newer models. And you look like a nice young man. So, I could split the difference with you. Let's say twenty-eight."

"Splitting the difference is twenty-seven-fifty," the kid said.

Don held out his hand and they shook. "Come back to the office and we'll settle up."

The little building was three walls of dirty glass covered in soap writing that declared "Dealin' Don Is Slashin' Prices." The air smelled of dusty paper and the proprietor's BO blended with artificial pine from several tree-shaped deodorizers. The kid took one of the two customer chairs while Don went behind the cluttered desk that backed up to the solid wall with a single door in it. Don reached into a gray file cabinet and removed the Honda's paperwork.

"Seein' as you got no trade, I'm gonna need everything up front, cash or money order. Personal check's okay, but we'll need to wait three days till she clears. Now, if you wanna *finance* her, I can give you my student rate."

"I'll pay cash," the kid said, removing beat-up bills from an envelope.

Don watched him count out the twenty-seven-fifty. "Did you have them under the mattress or buried in a tin can?" he said with a chuckle. The kid handed over the money.

Stacking the bills, founding fathers lined up, Don noticed that the corners were gone from the hundreds. Not just one or two, but all twenty-one of them. He squinted at his customer. "Where you get these?"

"What do you mean?"

Don held up one of the bills. "This here's what I mean." He flicked the edge of a C-note. "See this corner's gone? That mean's marked money. They put the mark there, somebody tried to remove it." He looked closer at the bill. "Beat to shit but only two years old."

The kid hesitated. "So?"

For the first time, the kid sounded nervous. Don noticed sweat dripping from the corners of his Fu Manchu. The face looked familiar. Damn if it didn't. It had been nagging at him all during the test drive. Now, it came to him.

"Nothin' I guess. Listen here. I need to get some papers from the back room. Just relax yourself, I'll be right back. Have a coffee."

The kid glanced at the Mr. Coffee as Don exited through the door behind his desk.

The clutter in the back room made the office look like House Beautiful. Don moved a cardboard box, groaning at a twinge in his back. Behind the box was a corkboard full of fliers. He pulled a red push pin and leafed through the old paper. He'd seen it here; he was sure he had. A cop flier circulated a couple weeks ago along with the hot-car lists. Bingo—fifth from the top. Wanted for extortion, arson, and murder. Several grainy photos and one smiling wallet size. One of them even had the Fu Manchu. "Well, I'll be goddam." Memorizing the 800 number, he folded the flier and put it in his shirt pocket. Hand on doorknob, he said, "I'll need to fill out some papers and make a call, so why don't you step out and check on your new car? Won't be a minute." The office was empty.

"Take me straight to the office, Carl."

"Yes, sir."

George King II sat on limo leather reading a promotional brochure from the new ad agency, when his cell phone rang. "King," he said simply.

"Hi, it's me."

"Who is this?"

"Don't you know your own son, Dad?"

"Listen you little shit! I don't know where you got this number, but I'm sick and tired of these phone calls. They weren't funny when the news story hit, and they're not funny now. So, go back to your mama's basement and pick zits or jack off or whatever. But leave me alone."

"I'm not a little shit, pater. I'm George King III, your son. And I don't live in the basement of your house on Millside Lane. Until recently, I had an apartment in Columbus."

"Georgie?"

"Hi, Dad."

"Just tell me one thing. Did you do it? This heinous bullshit the police and FBI said you did? Just tell me. Did you?"

"Are you kidding, father? How can you even ask that? I'm at my friend's place up in Grayling, and I see my face on a TV screen in a store window. My high-school picture along with a couple of grainy, fish-eye surveillance stills that could be anybody. I hear that I'm wanted for murder? *Me*. Murder? When I'm five hundred miles away. And you want to know if I did it? Jesus Christ, Dad!"

"Okay, okay, sorry. Keep it down." George Sr. slid up the partition separating him from Carl. "Where are you now?"

"I'm at a gas station south of Flint. But I need money."

"Sure, yeah, of course. But shouldn't you give yourself up? I mean, if you can prove you didn't do it."

"Are you crazy? You know how cops are when they pick their scapegoat. They've got me pegged for this, and they're going to crucify me one way or another. Even if they have to make it up."

"But if you can prove you were up in Michigan. Friends saw you. Guy in a bar. Anything. I'll get you a good lawyer. Best money can buy. He'll rip that cop story to shreds."

The voice on the phone paused a moment. "Listen, Dad." Now the voice was more controlled, more constrained. "I was at a cabin, remember? Off the grid. Nobody saw me. At least nobody would remember me. If I go to the cops now, that's what they'll run with."

"But if ..."

"I need time, Dad. Time to think. Work out the best way to proceed. And I need money."

"How? How much?"

"Maybe ten thousand. Wire it to Western Union in Covington, Kentucky."

"Kentucky? I thought you were in Michigan?"

"I am now. But I know a guy near Cincinnati will let me crash there till things die down."

"But shouldn't, I mean can't you ..."

"Is it too much money, Father?"

"No, of course not. It's not that. I just mean, why don't you hit an ATM, take an advance on your credit card?"

"Those transactions leave a paper trail with locations."

"But wouldn't a wire transfer also leave a trail?"

"Wire transfers are not considered cash transactions under the Bank Secrecy Act and, as such, are not reportable. Listen, Dad, I've got to hang up. Cops might be tracing this call."

"No, this is a new cell. The house phone, maybe."

"They set up anything on the phones or in the basement? Florist van parked down the street? Anything?"

"No, nothing like that," George Sr. said. "They've been mostly apologetic. Sorry for the questions. Need to find your boy for his own protection. That kind of thing."

"Even so. Keep your eyes open. And wire the ten grand to Western Union in Covington. Tristate Mall. Send it to Pat Duncan, 1398 ..."

"Let me write this down. Okay."

"Pat Duncan," Georgie said more slowly. "1398 Prescott Avenue, Ryland, Kentucky. Got that?"

"Yeah, got it. As soon as I get in the office."

"Use your cell, not the office phone."

"Yeah, sure, okay."

"Thanks, Dad. I appreciate it." Another pause. "I love you, Dad."

"I love you too, son." The line went dead.

Before he could put it down, the cell rang again, a number he recognized.

"Did you get that?" he said.

"Yes," said a special agent from the Cleveland field office. "The call came from a cell tower near Berea, Kentucky."

"Lying little bastard."

Pardon?"

"Nothing. What do you want me to do?"

"Go ahead and wire the money," the agent said. "Give us half an hour. We'll have people watching Western Union."

"Fine. Thirty minutes."

"Thank you for your cooperation, Mr. King. You're doing the right thing for all concerned, including your son."

"Son? I have no son."

The helicopter touched down at the CVG cargo terminal. This was the third leg of Sally's trip, which started in Crossfield's office and would end at the Tristate Mall. Scott had given her the ball and was letting her run with it. She'd do her best not to fumble—and to keep her personal problems walled off within a dusty niche of her heart. She hoped no clanking chains gave her away.

She exited the dark-blue chopper, heading for the dark-blue SUV waiting on the flight line. The tinted windows of the car mirrored her aviator sunglasses and her mood. The air smelled of kerosene and regret.

Sally recognized the man behind the wheel and another pair of aviator shades.

"Hi, Sam," she said, sliding into the shotgun seat.

"Sally," said Sam Levine of the Cincinnati field office.

"Good morning, Special Agent Butterworth," said a familiar voice from the rear seat.

Sally flinched. "Mr. Hartsell. Ah, good morning. I wasn't expecting you, sir."

"Quite alright, special agent. I've decided to oversee this operation personally. Something of this importance needs a firm hand at the tiller. Don't you agree?"

"Of course, sir. But I understood from Mr. Crossfield that I'd ..."

"Fine." Hartsell paused to look at a folder. "I've been reading your reports on the Conrad Hilton investigation. Very thorough. My compliments."

"Thank you, sir."

"From what I've read, it seems to me that the suspect might know you."

"Sir?"

"That is to say, might have seen you before. Might recognize you on sight. Do you agree?"

"Why, I don't know. I guess it's possible, sir."

"Then let's have you monitor the video feed with mall security. Okay? Special Agent Levine and I will direct operations from the command center here. That will allow me to stay in audio contact with all units and still be ready to move to any critical vantage points."

Any place where there might be TV cameras, Sally thought.

"You give a shout if you see anything on video. Understood?"

Sally understood all too well.

The security tech was a little younger than Sally, with blond hair just as long, tied in a ponytail with a leather thong. Instead of Sally's dark, tailored suit, he wore jeans and a cream-colored polo with a shoulder patch reading CastleKeep Security. His name was on a plaque over his breast pocket: Buck Rodgers. Like the comic-book hero, he was athletic with the looks of a strip-club dancer, complete with a grin that said he knew it. Sally noticed the single earring in his right ear and the absence of a wedding band. She also noticed the way his eyes traveled up and down her body, pausing at her legs and breasts. It was going to be a long surveillance.

"Unit one in position," crackled a soft voice Sally recognized as Matt Clemens. His grainy image in jeans and Top-Siders was on a bench reading a book in front of the Barnes and Noble.

"Roger, unit one. Have you in sight," Sally said.

"So, you're with the FBI," Buck said.

"That's right," Sally said.

"Unit two, in position."

"Roger, unit two," Sally said. "Let me see Western Union on monitor one."

Buck flipped a couple of switches, revealing a man in a short-sleeve white shirt and black tie working behind the counter. He was from the Cincinnati field office and Sally didn't know him. Like Matt, he had an earpiece on his left ear, hidden behind large, horn-rimmed glasses.

"You like working there?" Buck said.

"Unit three, in position." That was Teri Hollander from the Covington resident agency.

"Roger, unit three," Sally said. "Put the Korn Krib on monitor three."

Buck flipped switches, showing Teri in a brown smock selling candy and caramel corn by a popcorn wagon, long, brown hair hiding her earpiece.

"I said, do you like it as a G-man. Or is it G-babe?" Buck's grin became a leer.

"You bet," Sally said. "That's why I'm here."

Buck nodded. "Ever have to go undercover? You know, as a model, hooker, go-go dancer, that kind of thing?"

"No, I've never done that. I've been too busy catching bad guys."

"All units in place?" Sally recognized Hartsell's officious voice.

"Roger, command," she answered. "All units in place and in sight."

On monitor two, Matt sat calmly, slowly turning both his eyes and paperback from side to side, scanning the crowd. Sally used a track ball to do the same.

Late weekday morning was still light foot traffic. The senior mall walkers had mostly departed, and the lunch crowd hadn't arrived in force. A Black man with a cane left the Drug Depot, heading toward the exit. A harried woman juggling a two-year-old dragged a wiggling kid in sneakers toward the Shoe Loft. A fat guy bought a hot pretzel from Teri.

So went the longest hour in Sally's career, trying to concentrate on the video feed while dealing with Buck's not-so-veiled overtures and Hartsell's growing impatience. A steady trickle of new blood entered the mall: nurses in green scrubs heading to the food court, pierced kids in low-riders entering the Game Stop, a tall woman in dumpy slacks and summer jacket checking out a purse at Everything Handbag. No sign of Conrad, Ollie, Tom-Tom, or Georgie.

Finally, a mid-height kid walked into view, aged anywhere from late teens to twenty-three. The acne on his cheeks and upper lip made him look younger, but the conservative black hair made him look older. He was wearing aviator sunglasses not unlike Sally's and had a scraggly Fu Manchu beard and mustache. He paused outside the Western Union, then window-shopped the Game Stop.

"I have a young white male that fits the general description," Sally said. "Currently opposite the Western Union, browsing the gaming store. Do you copy, unit one?"

She saw Matt's head turn slowly. "Copy," he whispered.

Sally watched while the bearded kid checked out a game called Freelander, then turned abruptly toward the Western Union storefront.

"Suspect is approaching the Western Union."

💣 *Chapter 50*

Cheryl slowly pulled off the tape stuck to her finger and awkwardly wrapped it over Tom's left palm. "There, all done."

"That was painful," Tom said from the kitchen table of his apartment.

"Oh, I'm sorry," Cheryl said. "Did I hurt you?"

"No, I meant watching you put on a bandage. I thought you were going to have a stroke."

"I think I did a *fine* job," Cheryl said.

"Not too bad," Tom said, inspecting his hand. "Except you went through three Telfa pads and half a tube of Silvadene. There was more tape on your fingers than the bandage."

"I just need practice."

"My burns will be healed by the time you get the hang of it."

She threw a roll of gauze at him. "Well, maybe you should do it yourself, Dr. Smarty Britches."

"That's *my* line," Tom said. He kissed her cheek. "Sorry, Hon. You did fine. I'm just cranky sitting here with nothing to do. I think I'll run out for medical supplies. At the rate we're going, I should probably open a line of credit at Drug Depot."

"I can do that later," Cheryl said.

Tom looked at his kitchen shelf. "We're low on sterile saline, Telfa, and tape. Anything else you're planning to waste?"

"I don't want you driving around on those hands."

"Actually, I drive on tires. It's safer."

"Ha, ha, Smarty ..."

"Britches. Yeah, I know." He kissed her lips. "I'll be fine." Tom flexed his hands, wincing slightly. "They don't even itch much anymore. And the mall is only a few miles away."

"Well, I don't know."

"I'll be back before you finish making lunch." He gingerly grabbed the keys from the bowl and was out the door.

💣

The tall woman put down the handbag she'd been examining and picked up a small clutch. She held it up to the light, allowing her to focus on the Western Union office in the background. One mall geek in birth-control glasses behind the counter. Everything looked okay. She put the clutch down and reached for another purse, holding it in the opposite direction.

"Can I help you find anything?"

The tall woman smiled at the tattooed girl manning the hand-bag kiosk. "Just browsing," she said.

The clerk smiled back. "Take your time. That black one looks good on you, goes with your hair."

The tall woman smiled again, then picked up a large tan ba-guette purse. Draping it over one arm, she turned as if checking herself in the mirror. The reflection showed that the aisle was clear, except for a guy on a bench reading a book. She put the purse down and thanked the salesgirl. Then she wandered toward the Western Union office. She'd taken only two steps when she saw a young guy walking the same way. She paused to see if he was going in. She wanted to get her money and run, not stand in line. The guy walked up to the WU counter. The tall woman walked back to the handbag kiosk and picked up one of the purses she'd been handling before.

"Changed your mind, huh?" the salesclerk said. "I told you that one looked good on you."

"I'm still not sure," the tall woman said, looking over the clerk's shoulder at the man who had just entered through the far mall en-trance. Boyish features and short, brown hair parted on the left. He walked with a confident gait, bandaged hands swinging at his side. The woman didn't need a photographic memory to recall him.

💣*

Sally watched the subject approach unit two. The special agent at the Western Union counter kept one hand on his comput-er keyboard, but the other moved toward the JIC shotgun in the hideout below the desk. She knew he was ready and that the other two units were ready to move in. So, they waited. They didn't have to wait long.

"Excuse me, mister?" The kid's voice was picked up clearly by the mic.

"Yes, sir? May I help you?" unit two said from behind the WU desk.

"Yeah. Is this a good job, you know, working for Western Onion?"

"Pardon?"

"My Dad says I'm supposed to get a job this summer. Actually, he *got* me a job, the Lumber Barn, but it was real bogus. You know? Long hours, no time off, and splinters. I must have had twenty splinters in a week. You know? So, I figured, maybe you guys are hiring. At least I'd be at the mall. But can you tell me about the job, first? You know, if you're hiring."

"All units standby," Sally said.

"What do we have, Butterworth?" Hartsell's voice said. "Conrad or a prospective employee?"

How the hell do I know, Sally thought. What she said was, "Uncertain, all units stand by."

"Well," unit two said, "You can fill out an application form. Anything else I can do for you?"

"Yeah. I need some money."

"Subject is reaching into his pocket," Sally said. "All units, stand ... what the hell?"

A window into childhood opened along with the double-glass doors. The smell of caramel corn. The rich aroma of leather during Saturday shoe shopping, his mother picking out clunky oxfords while his brother giggled and called him Captain Klutz.

Tom paused by the Korn Krib but decided that sticky caramel didn't go with dental crowns, antibiotics, and bandaged fingers. And Cheryl would kill him if he spoiled his lunch. When had he started to think like an old married man?

"What the hell," he said, intending to ask the trim-figured gal at the Korn Krib the price of a small bag, when he saw a familiar face reading a book in front of Barnes and Noble. "What are the chances?" he muttered.

"Pardon?" said the Korn Krib salesclerk in the brown smock, her tone oddly tense.

"Never mind," Tom said, heading past her to the centrally located bench.

"Matt, right?" Tom said.

"What?"

"Sorry, didn't mean to startle you. Matt Clemens, right? Sally's FBI friend? You live around here?" The FBI agent's face went from startled to concerned, eyes flashing wide. "You okay?"

"Ah, yeah. I, ah ..."

"I live just a few miles from here," Tom said. "Came down to pick up some bandage materials." Tom held out his hands. "I guess you heard."

"Yeah. Listen Tom-Tom, I'm kind of busy."

"What's up? Waiting for your wife to pick up a pair of shoes?" Tom grinned. "Or is this some kind of stake out?"

Matt Clemens froze, hand moving to his right ear. Then he bolted from the bench, knocking Tom down as he dashed across the aisle.

*

"Repeat," Hartsell's voice said.

"Dr. Tomacinski just entered the mall," Sally said.

"What?" Hartsell screamed.

"He's speaking with unit one. Subject at Western Union is removing something from his pocket."

"Shit," Hartsell shouted. "All units move in!"

As with all highly trained teams, things happened quickly. Clemens bolted from the bookstore bench, sending Tom-Tom on his back, clutching his injured hands. Clemens reappeared in the counter monitor, pistol drawn. Likewise, Teri Hollander shot away from the Korn Krib, sprinting across the intervening distance. Both units yelled "Down, down, down!"

Staring down the maw of two Glocks and a Remington pump-gun, the white-faced kid at Western Union dropped to his knees. In seconds, Clemens had him cuffed and on his stomach.

"If you don't have a job, that's okay," the frightened boy gasped. "I only, I only wanted change for a ten. But I can get it at the Shoe Barn. Really." Then he threw up.

No one noticed the tall woman hurry from the mall.

💣 *Chapter 51*

"You want to tell me what the hell you thought you were doing?" Hartsell yelled.

Tom clutched his hands, tears of pain in his eyes. "I thought I was going to the Drug Depot," he said through clenched teeth. "What the hell were *you* doing?"

"I ought to arrest your ass."

"For what?" Tom snapped. "Intent to buy Telfa pads?"

"For obstruction, interference with a criminal investigation, and assault on a federal agent."

"He ran into *me,* you dumb son of a bitch!"

Sally stepped between the two men, Tom cringing on the bench, Hartsell's hot breath puffing from the reddest face she'd ever seen. "Take it easy, Tom-Tom. How are the hands?"

"Feels like I'm shoveling thermite again."

"Listen, you NIOSH flunky," Hartsell said. "Maybe you can get away with that shit in ..."

"It wasn't his fault, Mr. Hartsell. It's a public mall."

"Which means open to the public," Tom muttered, hands held protectively, body rocking in rhythm with the pain.

"You going to pass out?" Sally asked. "Put your head between your knees."

"I'll deal with you later, Butterworth," Hartsell said, stalking off.

"I'm sure you will," she muttered. But for now, she had an injured civilian to tend to. An injured civilian she just happened to be in love with. Sally noticed red fluid seeping through the bandages on Tom's fingers. "Let's get you to a hospital."

"No," Tom said, still rocking . "I've got some pain meds in the car. Cheryl can change the bandages once the embers cool."

Cheryl, Sally thought, shrugging off a cold shiver. "Can you drive?"

"I don't know." Tom's teeth clenched. "Son of a ... I can try."

"I'll drive you," she said.

A small crowd was gathering as she helped Tom to his feet. Hollander was uncuffing the stunned kid. A mall custodian was shaking his head as he tossed sawdust on the puke. Clemens was talking to Hartsell in secret conclave, shoulders hunched together. Sally noticed the young agent glance over at her and Tom-Tom every few seconds. Clemens smiled shyly as she caught his eye, more from embarrassment than friendship.

※

Tom-Tom again. That explained a lot. That explained everything.

The Polack pain in the ass had started as a joke but had become the bane of Conrad's existence, the focus for all his anger and frustration. He'd spoiled Conrad's revenge and reduced him to begging for a measly ten grand instead of relaxing on a tropical island with millions of dollars. Yes, Conrad Hilton, aka Patricia Duncan, aka Georgie King, knew Tom-Tom. Knew him and hated him.

Georgie King was still there, oh yes. But he was no longer the only one, never that. Now his was just another voice in the chorus, another part to play. Another instrument in the band led by Conrad Hilton, master criminal. An instrument for revenge. And revenge was all that mattered now. That thought lightened Conrad's heart and gave him pleasure. Things were much simpler when reduced to that single, simple, solitary fact. That obsession.

He thought of *Star Trek*'s Khan Singh. "He tasks me. He tasks me and I must have him." Yes, they would have him. Conrad, and Patty and Georgie and Ollie and even Tom-Tom would have him. Nothing else mattered before that. Nothing mattered after it.

Conrad no longer cared that he was dressed as a woman in a stolen car that had bomb-making materials and a marked four million in the back seat. He was no longer worried that he sat in a public lot, in plain view of nearby law enforcement agents. They were searching for Georgie King, not innocent Patty Duncan, smile on her face, watching the world roll by the Chevy's windows. Cars drove past one way and then the other. Conrad imagined them bursting into flame, their driver's faces drawn out in agony like Munch's *The Scream*. He brushed the wig's long hairs from his face and smiled again. The smile froze as another image appeared.

The redheaded FBI agent was helping the injured Tom-Tom, hands held protectively against his chest, hints of red coating his bandages. The pair approached a Ford Escape, one Conrad knew well. One he'd once followed in a different guise, watching through different eyes.

The redhead said something. Tom-Tom smiled briefly. Conrad noticed how tenderly she placed her hand on Tom-Tom's shoulder as she fished car keys from his shirt pocket. Opening the passenger door, she reached inside to retrieve a small pill bottle, then slammed the door. The pair walked off, her gently guiding him, angling to a dark SUV that virtually shouted government vehicle. An FBI man in jacket and tie exited the SUV as the two entered it. The FBI man walked toward the mall as the silhouette of the SUV disappeared behind the rows of parked cars and pickups.

Conrad's smile widened. He'd vowed revenge and, just like that, providence provided the vehicle for it. The poetic justice was almost orgasmic.

He thought again of *Star Trek*. "And he piled upon the whale's white hump the sum of all the rage and hate felt by his whole race. If his chest had been a cannon, he would have shot his heart upon it." Not correctly quoted by Captain Picard but every bit the exquisite sentiment Ahab spoke so well. Conrad spoke aloud, his accent changing, moving among the many voices singing in his head.

"To the last, I grapple with thee. From hell's heart, I stab at thee. For hate's sake, I spit my last breath at thee." Then, still dressed as Patty Duncan, Conrad left the Chevy's cozy interior and got to work.

He didn't know when Tom-Tom would come back. But come back he would. Good government boys and girls didn't leave their cars at the mall overnight. Yes, he'd be back. A thought struck. Or would it be the lovely FBI agent? The music in Conrad's head switched from big-band drums to cartoon kitsch. The voice of *Spider-Man*'s Green Goblin filled his brain. "The heart, Osborne. We attack the heart."

💣

Cheryl rushed to Tom before he'd even cleared the doorway. "My God! What happened?"

Time had killed the pain as much as the Tylenol-3 tablets, so Tom could smile. "I fell at the mall."

"Fell? How?"

"Well, I kind of caromed off an FBI agent, then ... It's a long story."

Cheryl guided him toward the sink. "Let's get those bandages off and flush that down with saline."

"Well, I should go," Sally said, standing awkwardly at the door.

"Agent Butterworth. I'm sorry, I didn't see you. Please come in. This will only take a few minutes."

Cheryl's fingers worked with the sureness of a surgical nurse. The tape was removed and the bandages carefully unwrapped. The fresh, pink tissue was now an angry red, bloody exudate oozing from cracks in the surface. Without a bit of queasiness, she rinsed them in saline, raising a wince from Tom. "Sorry, darling." Dabbing the wounds with gauze, she deftly applied the Telfa and ointment, then wrapped gauze mesh around the bleeding fingers. Tape was snipped and skillfully applied. The entire process took less than five minutes.

"You do that like a pro," Sally said.

Cheryl smiled. So did Tom.

"I guess you're getting the hang of it," he said.

Cheryl kissed his cheek, then said to Sally, "I was just making lunch. Won't you join us?"

"No, I ... I should be getting back."

"Come on," Tom said. "Tell hardass you had to take me to the ER. If he gives you any shit, say you talked me out of suing. *Maybe.*"

"Hardass?" Cheryl said. "Suing?"

"He took some pain pills in the car, as you can probably tell," Sally said.

"I mean, it's got to be his nickname," Tom said, slumping into his recliner. "I mean it's got to be." He yawned. "Man, I feel sleepy. I think I'll take a nap before lunch." He closed his eyes and began softly snoring.

"My hero," Cheryl said with a smile. She turned to Sally. "Well, why don't you and I have a sandwich?"

"No thanks." Sally pointed toward the door. "I need to get the car back to hardass, I mean Agent in Charge Hartsell."

"Alright then, can you drive me to the mall? You can tell me what happened on the way. I can pick up a few things at the drug store and come back in Tom's car. I'm assuming it's at the mall?"

Sally nodded toward sleeping Tom. "Okay to leave him?"

"I don't think he's going anywhere," Cheryl said. "And I'd kind of like to chat with you alone, girl to girl."

Sally's eyebrows rose, but she said only, "After you."

💣

Sally completed the story as she pulled the government SUV into the mall lot. "Coincidence, bad luck, that's all it really was. Of course, Hartsell might not see it that way. But I guess there isn't much he can do about it, at least officially."

"Unofficially?"

"Make my life hell," Sally said. "But don't worry, wouldn't be the first time."

Sally pulled the car into a spot near the drug store. But instead of saying her goodbyes, Cheryl said, "I'd hate to see that happen, Sally. Tom speaks so highly of you, it's almost as if I know you." She paused and the two ladies made eye contact, a silent message being sent and received. "I'd like us to be friends." Another pause. "If you think that's possible."

Sally cleared her throat. "How long have you two been dating?"

"Over a month."

"Sounds like things have moved a little fast."

"Perhaps," Cheryl said. "But when I know what I want, I go after it."

"And what Tom-Tom wants?"

"He's a big boy," Cheryl said. "He can make up his own mind."

"Has he?"

Cheryl's subtle smile answered the question. "I'll be good for him, Sally. Next to my mom, he's my highest priority." Cheryl paused again. "Can you say that?"

Two sets of eyes, one flashing green, the other determined brown, locked horns across the front console. They held for a second, maybe three, until Sally looked away. "Well, we're here. I'll walk you inside."

"That's alright. I can manage." Cheryl's voice took on a winner's tone. She held out her hand. "Goodbye, Agent Butterworth."

"Goodbye, Ms. Wagner." As Cheryl opened the door, Sally added, "Take good care of him."

"Don't worry, you're leaving him in good hands."

Sally watched the older woman disappear into the mall. So, that was that. Or was it? She could still fight for Tom-Tom. She could win. He wanted her. She'd known it since they'd met at the hotel bar. And their night together had only heightened the desire.

She had never used her looks to get ahead, not in school or in the Bureau. But she knew what she had. Had known it since the ninth grade. She knew she *could* use them, and it might be enough to land Tom-Tom.

Sally thought about her father, what she'd given up since her promise to him. Her promise to herself, really. The promise that had changed her life, directed it down a new path. In retrospect, it was almost childish, like something from a preteen adventure comic about a girl crime fighter avenging her father's death. She briefly saw a spandex version of herself, cape and all. It was comical but still she couldn't laugh. To do so would somehow betray her father's memory. Betray the road she'd chosen. Had chosen her? No, the choice was hers. But what had she given up in the choosing?

She'd said that Tom-Tom wanted her, had from the first. That was only part of the truth. The whole truth was she wanted him, as well. Maybe it wasn't too late. Sally's mind considered the possibilities, skidding as a mind does along streets bright with future sunshine or dark with cobwebs of the past. She saw a large colonial home in some suburb where she ran the resident agency. Tom-Tom putting soccer equipment and a uniformed son or daughter into an SUV. She saw her father in his coffin, police officers in crisp blue and spit-shined leather paying their respects. Her mind spun further back, skipping like a stone to an odd, unexpected spot, a long-forgotten memory:

> Sally had been holding her father's big hand in her eight-year-old one. Her other hand was on the dark fur lying on the steel table, the rapidly rising chest expressing canine pain and fear. Her dad had defined it simply as "Sparky's not feeling well. He's got a tumor." She'd asked what a tumor was. "A growth," her dad said. "A bad growth, like an animal inside him." Couldn't the vet kill the bad animal? "Not without killing Sparks." Couldn't they leave it alone? "It's eating up his insides, Sally. Eating them slowly. It makes him feel sick. A little sicker each day."

Aren't there pills to make him feel better? "Not anymore. He's suffering, Sal. More each day." Can't the vet make him feel any better? "He can only end the suffering now. Give Sparky peace in heaven." Sally didn't want to hear it. Sparky was her dog. She'd take him home and care for him. "That's not fair to Sparky, Sal. He's suffering." What about her suffering? She loved Sparky. "If you really love someone," her dad said. "You have to do what's best for them. Not what's best for you."

Once again, Sally was looking at the world through adult eyes. Eyes that saw Cheryl Wagner leave the mall, plastic sack in her arms. Cheryl was walking quickly, purposely, toward Tom's car, Florence Nightingale in shorts and polo. In her mind, Sally heard the older woman's voice say "I'm good for Tom. He's my top priority. Can you say that?" No, she couldn't. Even now, Sally's top priority was reporting in to Hartsell, assessing the damage to her career. Damage that part of her, a selfish part, still blamed on Tom-Tom, the man she was supposed to love, the hero who had saved dozens of lives, maybe hundreds.

She watched Cheryl open the door to the red SUV. Watched the woman who made Tom-Tom her top priority slide behind the wheel. Mind made up, Special Agent Sally Butterworth exited into the summer sunshine. Before Sally could slam her door, a flashbulb pop lit up the interior of Tom-Tom's Ford. As Sally watched, the cabin of the red SUV darkened briefly before a second flash blew the windows out with a thunderclap that knocked Sally to her knees.

Chapter 52

The parking lot had taken on the trappings of a traveling carnival; all that was missing was a Tilt-A-Whirl and a cotton-candy machine. Barriers held back the crowds as police and federal agents hustled back and forth amid flashing lights. Firemen packed up their brightly colored gear, preparing to depart. Hartsell spoke officiously into a TV camera.

The bomb-squad tech placed a fragment of black wire into a plastic bag already containing a thicker red wire. She shook her head.

"What?" Sally asked.

"What did you see again?" the female tech asked. "Exactly?"

"Small flash," Sally said. "Then the whole cabin went dark. Then the big explosion that ripped the car apart."

The tech held up the plastic bag with the wires. "I'd just be making a guess, mind you. We won't know for sure till the lab checks it all out."

"Go ahead and guess," Sally said.

"Okay. Thermobaric bomb. If you can believe that shit."

"Thermobaric?"

"Yeah. They used them in Afghanistan, bigger ones of course, to blow Taliban out of caves. The first charge is small, spreads out a cloud of inflammable dust. Finely ground metals like aluminum or magnesium. The second charge ignites the cloud. Whoosh. Pressure wave blows everything to hell and gone."

"Sounds kind of complicated."

"It is," the tech said. "Look here." She held up the plastic bag again. "First charge was probably set off with this black one wired to the ignition. The main charge was triggered by the red wire. See how much thicker it is?"

Sally nodded.

"Thicker means more resistance, so it took a fraction of a second longer for the signal to get there. Time enough for the dust cloud to fill the cabin. Quite an elegant little solution. This guy knows his shit."

"Why not just use dynamite?"

The tech shrugged. "Maybe showing off. Look what I can do. Or maybe the perp didn't have enough high explosive to do the job right. Used what was available as a force-multiplier. Wanted to be sure of killing the driver." The tech paused. "You know anyone who'd hate that lady enough to blow her to hell?"

"No," Sally said. "But I don't think she was the target."

Tom woke with a start and a smile. The dream was already fading, as they invariably did. All he could remember was the pleasant sensation as Cheryl softly called his name. He was sure it was Cheryl, not Sally. First dream in a month where Ms. Pancakes didn't put in an appearance. At least he was making progress, he thought.

Thanks to the pain pills, his mouth was dry as cotton batting. Twin sensations struck as he rose to get a drink: a twinge in his back from sleeping in the chair, and a hot pain where he leveraged his hands against the arms of the recliner. Old habits die hard, he thought. Bandages held protectively like a scrubbed surgeon, he shifted weight to his elbow and awkwardly rose out of the sprung cushion with a groan. He looked at the clean, white bandages. As good a job as he could have done himself. He smiled again. Then the knocking distracted him. He scanned the room quickly before his foggy brain localized the sound and sent him shuffling toward the door.

"Excuse me, ma'am," he said with a grin. "I don't have the use of my hands. Perhaps you could let yourself in and then assist me in the bathroom?"

"Tom? It's Sally."

"Oops." Tom gingerly opened the knob. "Sorry about that, Sal. You weren't the lovely lady I was expecting." He stood back to let her in. "Whew. How long was I out? Judging from the throbbing in my hands, I'm guessing more than 'repeat every four to six hours, as needed for pain.'"

Sally's long face did not share his grin.

"You look like the one in pain," he added. "What's going on? Did Cheryl get called into work or something? Left you here to babysit the invalid?"

"Tom, I ah ..." Sally brushed back a tear.

"What is it? Oh my God. Did someone get shot, Matt or some-one? I know you wouldn't be this broken up about Hartsell." Sally looked him in the eye, tears tracking her cheeks in a steady drip. "*Was* it Hartsell?"

She shook her head. "No ... um, I ... I don't know how to say this."

"Well, just say it."

Sally hesitated, her eyes speaking volumes.

Tom frantically scanned the room. "Where's Cheryl?" Sally didn't answer. "Is she hurt?" He grabbed her shoulders despite the pain beneath his bandages. "Tell me. Is she in the hospital?"

Sally looked into his eyes and softly said. "Cheryl Wagner is dead."

💣 *Chapter 53*

"I've known Cheryl since she was quite young," the minister said. "I knew her to be a good, kind, and caring child who grew into a good, kind, and caring woman. I'm often asked at moments like these why a loving God takes a good, kind, and caring person, one still in the prime of life. I never have a very good answer, except to say ..."

Tom was numb. No, that wasn't quite right. Numbness suggested lack of feeling. The feelings were there, but on hold, paused like a DVD. It was more like that moment immediately after ripping off a Band-Aid. You knew the pain was coming, was in fact already there, but for a split second your skin didn't recognize it. Like when your fingers flinched away from a hot handle, knowing there would be intense pain, but first that pause. That split second before its arrival. Tom was living the longest split second of his life.

He'd never fully realized how much he was pinning on a future with Cheryl, had never even admitted it to himself. Now that she was gone, the realization came down like a heavy rain. He knew that once that split second had passed, once time resumed, he'd be drenched in tears and chilled to the soul.

"Let us pray."

Tom stood and said the Lord's prayer in unison with the assembled mourners. He mouthed words dredged from childhood, words never really forgotten but not really believed. The kingdom, power, and glory were no longer in Tom's spiritual vocabulary. Not with a loving father who watched while a petulant, sociopathic prick killed a kind and gentle woman. But the prayer helped. It helped to prolong that split second, to fill it with ritual.

Tom's mind would need to find other things to fill that time, to prolong the second, defer the pain. He'd subconsciously considered several, mulling them over beneath the mundanities of making the arrangements, picking out the box, contacting the minister.

It was a closed casket, so no need to select clothes from Cheryl's closet, thank God. But with no close relatives but her mom, Tom was left to attend to most other details. Tanya at the Village helped break the news to Mary Wagner, who was rapidly slipping from mild dementia to full-blown memory care. She'd been told only that there was a car accident and had already forgotten that. Helping her to the church this morning, she'd asked Tom if Cheryl was coming?

"She'll be there," he'd said.

It was at that moment when his subconscious mind decided to take the path of least resistance. It had settled on the obvious choice, the easy choice, the choice most likely to fill the time with satisfaction.

Revenge may be a dish best served cold, but Tom was in the mood for a hot meal. A long, hot supper that would consume his waking minutes from split second to split second. Whether you called him Georgie King, George III, Conrad, Ollie, or Señor TresReyes, Tom would make the son of a bitch pay. Nothing else mattered.

The minister was now passing among the mourners. He started with Mary, who smiled and introduced Tom as her son-in-law. Then the Reverend gently took Tom's hand and shook it, whispering only, "I'm sorry." Tom was helping Mary down the aisle when he spied a familiar if unexpected face.

"Would you see Mary to the car?" he asked Tanya.

"Of course, Tom."

He walked toward the back corner of the church. "Nice of you to come. Very nice."

His NIOSH supervisor, Lynne Faulkner, looked down at her shoes, as if to check that they matched. "I ... people were talking about it at work. I knew she was your friend."

Tom leaned in and hugged Lynne, who stiffened then softened in his arms. He kissed her cheek. "I appreciate it. There's a lunch afterward. I hope you'll come."

"No, I, I have to get back."

He took her hand. "Thanks again."

As Lynne scurried off, Tom saw Sally approach. There was only one awkward pause before she embraced him.

"I'm so sorry about this, Tom-Tom. I'd switch places with her if I could."

"Don't talk nonsense." He held her at arm's length. "What did the lab find out?"

"Confirmed the preliminary findings. Thermobaric device. Cardboard box in the back seat, wired to the ignition."

"She wasn't the intended target, was she?"

"Unlikely," Sally said. "It wasn't *her* car."

"I want back in, Sal."

The FBI agent shook her head definitively. "Uh, uh. No way."

"You seconded me before." The phrase elicited no smiles this time. "I probably still have clearance."

"Well, that was a mistake. My mistake. Sorry that Cheryl had to pay for it. More sorry than you can know." She reminded him of Lynne, eyes averted to her shoes. "The Bureau is fully committed to it now. We've got agents, evidence techs, and violent-crime experts on the case. Not to mention local PD. Everybody on the planet is looking for Conrad." She gently took Tom's hand. "Don't worry, we'll get him."

He stared determinedly into Sally's eyes. "I want in, Sal."

Sally's look was just as determined. "No. That's final."

"Either put me in, or I go after him on my own."

"*Don't.*" She clutched his hands, then noticed his grimace and eased up. "You don't have any jurisdiction or credentials. And you might screw up the investigation, like with the stakeout earlier."

"That wasn't my fault."

"No, it wasn't," Sally said. "But it didn't work out too well, did it?" She bullied through his pregnant pause. "Besides, you're disabled."

He held up his hands, burns now only lightly dressed under cotton gloves. Flexing the fingers, he said, "Almost good as new."

"*Maybe.* But you don't have the skills. You'll end up getting someone hurt, probably yourself." She gazed into his hazel eyes. "I'm not sure I could live with that."

"The only way you're going to stop me is to put me back in. I've got to be involved. Either that or arrest me.

"Don't tempt me." She lowered her voice. "Listen, Tom-Tom. This isn't a game. He's tried to kill you once already."

Tom held out his wrists, ready to be cuffed.

Sally sighed. "Let me see what I can do."

❋

"Special Agent Butterworth, you are getting to be known as the sand around which forms the pearl of a clusterfuck."

Sally's last visit to the fourth floor had not been pleasant, but Crossfield at least let her know there'd been no permanent damage. Now she was back in a leather chair behind the plexiglass office of the Knoxville special agent in charge, and his mood was even darker. But this time, her mood matched her boss's.

"You mean from my vantage point behind a bank of monitors fending off a handsy rent-a-cop?"

"I don't need attitude right now, Sally."

"And I don't need to keep getting blamed for dumb luck and Hartsell screw-ups."

Crossfield held up his palms. "Hartsell was the agent in charge closest to the stake out. He wants to step in, nothing I can do. And dumb luck is part of any investigation. It all depends on what you *do* with it."

"What was I supposed to do? Tomacinski wandered in and made Matt."

"You could have had Clemens hustle him out of there. Quietly. Was your mic broken?"

Sally wasn't sure how to answer. But her face warmed.

"Are you sleeping with this guy, Sal?"

"No," she blurted. "Of course not." But the heat in her cheeks intensified.

"*Did* you sleep with him?" He stared at her. "I guess I don't need a polygraph to answer that." He pointed to paperwork on his large mahogany desk. "Now you ask me to *again* make him a part of the investigation. Why didn't I know that he'd already *been* a part of the investigation? I thought you were just going to talk to him."

"It was a special need at the start. Hartsell killed it after twenty-four hours."

"Beat me to it," Crossfield said.

Sally looked him in the eye, not in confrontation, but to reestablish that bond they'd shared when he'd been her mentor.

"Listen, Scott. This guy almost got killed and lost the woman he loved because of government screw-ups. You want to blame me, fine. But don't take it out on him." Her father's words came back to her. You do what's best for them, not yourself. "Think of it as a form of protective custody. Conrad tried to kill him once, he could try again." She could see her boss weakening, but he wasn't there yet. "Besides, Tomacinski is a true hero. If he *were* a special agent, the director would be writing him up for a Star and a Medal of Valor right now."

"Then tell him how much we appreciate it. I'll write him up for a Medal of Freedom."

Sally's clenched fist nearly pounded the desk before she caught herself. She took a deep breath. "He says he'll go after King on his own if we don't put him back in the game."

"Threaten to arrest him," Scott said.

"I have," Sally said.

Crossfield picked up the folder on his desk. Leaning back in his chair, he turned away and stared thoughtfully at the gray partition separating his inner office from the outer reception area. After a few moments, he said, "Can this guy handle computers?"

She smiled. "He's an epidemiologist, which as far as I can tell is someone who crunches numbers like a statistician and has the smarts to interpret what he gets back."

"Fine. We can always use help in the Operations Center, what with summer vacations and Ruth's maternity leave. Tell him to report to the first floor for clearance."

"He's already passed phase 1 testing, polygraph, and drugs. He's had a federal background check at NIOSH."

"Oh really?" The "what else don't I know" was left unsaid. "Then have him report to the OC Monday afternoon. He can help Elsie out on the four to midnight shift."

"And the Medal of Freedom?"

Scott shook his head and threw the folder in his outbox. "Next you'll want to give him *my* job."

💣 *Chapter 54*

"Let me give you a hand with that."

Sally took Tom's briefcase and opened the back door of her latest federal SUV. The case went in the passenger-side foot well and Tom placed the cardboard box on the back seat.

"What's in the box?" she asked.

"Just a few things I might need."

"Such as?"

"Well, a couple of computer books. My copy of *Arson and Extreme Fire Risks*. You know, stuff."

"Anything else?" She saw him hesitate. "You're going to have to show it all to security anyway," Sally said. "Give."

"Okay. Some bandage materials and Silvadene. Just in case."

Sally shook her head as she pulled the big car out of the lot of the Parkway Hotel. "I thought you said your hands were 'almost good as new.'"

"They are. Just a precaution."

"Listen, Tom-Tom. Why don't you go back to your hotel room and rest up? Maybe in a few days, you'll be up to snuff."

"Let's not go through this again. I'm fine." Sally shut up. "Thanks for picking me up. But I could have driven."

"No problem," she said. "I'll stop by and introduce you to Elsie Montoya in Operations. Let her know how things are and, you know, what you'll be doing."

"Ask her to keep me out of trouble, you mean."

Sally smiled. "You said it, not me." Looking straight ahead, she added, "How are you holding up?"

Tom's grin faded. "I'm okay. As long as I keep busy."

Sally saw the cold set to his boyish features. A kid on a mission. The determined look she must have had when her dad was killed.

"I know this isn't your idea of 'back in' the investigation, but I'll see if I can call in some favors and get you out in the field somehow," she said.

"Just so long as I'm involved," Tom said.

Tom sat in the fourth-floor Operations Center behind an FBI computer. The name plate at his station read "Ruth Quonset." Next to that was a pink coffee mug with "Baby On Board" emblazoned on the side.

Elsie leaned over his shoulder, smiling. She was a mid-thirties Latina with a little meat on her but a friendly personality and a killer smile. If the old Tom had spied her in a bar, laughing with friends, he might have bought her a drink and took things from there. Now, the only thing he wanted from her was orientation on the Bureau computers.

She'd already run through several federal databases; some, Tom had used at NIOSH, others were basic software. None of it was rocket science. Now she pointed to a glowing icon. "That's where we back-trace license plates and VIN numbers."

Tom clicked E-Dentify, and a standard set of drop-down menus appeared. He moused the tab labeled "License ID" and entered his plate.

"Looks like I won't have to teach you much," Elsie said.

There was a brief flicker on the screen, then Tom's name and address appeared, along with information on his last three residences, his current occupation, even organ-donor status. The line for *Political Affiliation* said that he was registered as independent. There was even a link to his college records and alumni memberships.

"As you can see," Elsie chuckled, "it's pretty thorough. This data retrieval is tied into other federal databases."

Tom pointed to an icon of a video camera.

"That brings up surveillance footage for ongoing investigations. We can ID specific dates and times and send pertinent stills or video feed to our agents in the field or to other law-enforcement agencies." Elsie's phone rang and she said, "Excuse me." Her voice took on an official timbre as she settled into her spot at the head workstation. "Federal Bureau of Investigation, Knoxville Field Office. May I help you?"

As his trainer chatted with someone reporting a drug party at the house next door, Tom clicked the video icon. They had their idea of "back in the investigation," and he had his. The search engine requested case numbers or key words. He entered "George

King III." There were several hits, with "Conrad Hilton Investigation" at the top of the list.

Elsie's phone rang again, and Tom heard her put someone on hold. He rubbed his gloved hands, momentarily satisfying the itch that still plagued the healing tissue, then tapped the Hilton investigation. A second search engine asked for dates and times. He entered the date of his run-in at the mall. A date that burned in his memory, along with the image of Cheryl's beautiful face seared to horrible disfigurement by a crazed maniac named Georgie King.

The search produced grainy but recognizable mall footage. He toggled among feeds labeled (1), (2), and (3). The first was focused on the Western Union desk. Number three on a popcorn stand. Number two was wider angled, with the best overall view. He recognized Matt Clemens reading his paperback, but no one else was visible.

Tom fast-forwarded at three times normal speed. People entered and left with the comical haste of a silent movie; he half expected to see Chaplin twirling his cane. Instead, there were a few mall walkers with canes. Some nurses in green scrubs. A mother cradling a toddler while hauling a rug rat into the shoe store. A largish woman checking out purses at the handbag kiosk.

Something about the big woman looked familiar. Tom slowed the speed to normal, then one half. The woman slo-moed a bag into the light, looking toward the Western Union. Then she held the bag toward the popcorn stand. Why did she seem familiar? She wasn't much of a looker, too tall and a little dumpy in her bargain-basement clothes. Had to run five-ten or five-eleven (in Tom's experience, no woman ever admitted to being six feet). Not his type, so why did she look familiar?

He heard Elsie say, "Just a moment, Paul," and click the hold button. Tom exited from the video as the OC manager stood up.

"Okay, Tom. Or should I call you Dr. Tomacinski?"

"I wish you wouldn't."

She smiled. "Okay, Tom. Here's your first assignment. I need an ID check on Tennessee license number 9-9-9-Quebec-Lima-Mike."

She looked over his shoulder as he typed the info into E-Dentify. His cell phone rang, and he clicked it to vibrate. "Sorry about that," he said. The search brought up an ID on Charles Messinger of Maryville, Tennessee.

Elsie tossed a sticky note on his desk. "Email it to this iPhone, please." She smiled as Tom hit the send-to tab. "Looks like you're ready to solo."

"If it isn't Special Agent Buttermilk. How are you, darlin'?"

"When are you going to change the oil in that tie, detective?"

"It ain't oil," Doolittle Powell said. "That there is donut grease. Nectar of the gods. Have a seat."

Sally dropped into a sprung desk chair that overbalanced backward with little resistance.

"Don't mind the office décor," Doolittle said. "It's used to folks my size, not pretty young things like yourself. What can I do for you?"

"Wanted to update you on Conrad Hilton, per our agreement to work with mutual respect and cooperation as brother agencies under the law."

"You mean when I blackmailed you into including us?"

"Right." She handed a folder to him. "Marked bills have started showing up."

"Old Georgie throwing caution to the wind, huh?"

"Looks that way. We've gotten positive hits from banks in Fort Mitchell, Cynthiana, and London, Kentucky."

"So, he's headin' Knoxville way," Doolittle said. "Papers are gonna call him the damn I-75 bomber."

"He's sticking to smaller towns," Sally said. "Staying clear of population centers."

"Must be skittish after his run in at Dealin' Don's Used Cars. Any luck in that department?"

Sally shook her head. "A few dealerships reported likely suspects making cash transactions, but none checked out." She crossed her legs, trying to keep from ejecting backward out of the old chair. "The Beamer showed up in a Walmart lot in Cincinnati. We think he must be stealing new rides, since he isn't buying them."

"You want us to check stolen-car reports?" Doolittle asked.

"Just watch the hot sheet carefully. Make sure every unit knows our man."

"The watch commanders have passed out fliers," Doolittle said. "I promised a bottle of Jack to the cop that makes him."

"That should be incentive enough for any cop," Sally smiled.

Doolittle slumped back; his chair groaned. "Any more contact with papa or the other members of the MHLA?"

Sally shook her head. "We're asking everyone to canvas local motels. The smaller, mom-and-pop places that might not get the word."

"Or might be swayed by easy cash," Doolittle said. "Already being done."

"My compliments." Sally doffed an imaginary hat.

Doolittle smiled. "But I'm guessing a big-time G-woman wouldn't come down here to tell me things we're already doing." He winked at her. "How's Tom-Tom doing?"

"Funny you should ask." Sally leaned forward, hands on knees. "I've got him riding a computer at the field office, afternoon shift. I'll pick him up and drive him in."

"Give him something to do in protective custody?" Doolittle asked.

She flashed her dimples.

"I'll ask Middleboro PD to patrol the Parkway hotel," Doolittle said. "Keep an eye on him when he's off duty. How's that?"

"Great, but ..."

"Just ask me, darlin'."

She scanned both ways looking for eavesdroppers. "Do you think you could take him on a ride-along or two? You know, make him feel he's pitching in, making a difference?" Her tone softened, the official FBI morphing into a concerned friend. Concerned former lover? "He's hurting ever since ..." The words caught in her throat. "Ever since Cheryl ..."

Doolittle gave her hand a gentle squeeze. "Will the Bureau give him the time?"

Sally squeezed back, then let go. "Are you kidding? Crossfield didn't want him there in the first place."

Doolittle winked again. "Consider it done. Now that the business is out of the way, what say I buy you coffee and a donut?"

"Tempting," Sally said, "but I've got to get back. I'll have Tom-Tom give you a call. Set things up."

"Kind of sweet on that old boy, ain't ya?"

She smiled and left.

Sally considered the question during the walk to her car. She was never one to wear emotions on her sleeve. But Crossfield had seen it. Now Doo. Had she admitted it to herself yet? She wasn't sure. Then she felt a pang of guilt. The same guilt she felt when talking about Cheryl's death.

A part of her, a small, vindictive part felt good when the hotel manager died. Not happy but relieved; rival eliminated. Now that small, guilty part was making her keep her distance from the very goal she sought. She told herself that it was too soon for Tom, that she needed to play things cool until time healed his heart. But was that the reason? Or was it the guilt of going for a man after wishing his lover dead? Or was it still her promise to her father? Or was it only her, not excuses and rationalizations? Was there something about her that kept her from committing? She still hadn't decided when she reached her SUV.

The locks clicked open when she grabbed the door handle. Tossing her blazer into the passenger seat, she noticed Tom's cardboard box still sitting in the back. She'd been on the phone when he left for security and hadn't noticed him forgetting it. She shook her head and made a mental note. Then she got behind the wheel. Before she could fire up the engine, she heard someone call out.

"Yo, Agent Pancakes. Sally!" It was Doo Powell huffing across the municipal macadam. "Captain wants to see you for a bit, if you don't mind."

She flashed a thumbs up, then exited the big car. Grabbing her cell, Sally dialed Tom-Tom's number. She'd let him know she had his bandage materials and would drop them off later.

💣 Chapter 55

In ninety minutes, Tom had run two criminal background checks, three license plates, and a manpower survey. He'd also retrieved information on amatol-based explosives using more prosaic on-line search engines. Elsie said things would die down around suppertime, which they did.

"I'm gonna hit the ladies room," she said. "If anyone calls, just put them on hold. I won't be ten minutes."

Tom gave her a smile and a nonchalant wave. As soon as she left, he was back into the video feed from the mall.

He thought it must have been déjà vu. When he looked this time, the handbag woman would only be another large, dumpy woman, no different than the hundreds he'd seen during his life-time. Yet, her video image still looked maddeningly familiar, very familiar. He watched her check out the small clutch, holding it one way and then the other. Then she said something to the kiosk proprietor, before checking out a purse with a strap. She looked in the mirror to see how the purse hung on her, holding one leg to the side as women will. And then she put ... She looked in the mirror to see how the purse looked on her? Tom couldn't see her face clearly, but he could see that her head wasn't angled to focus on the purse. It was level with the floor, as if she were looking only at the strap—or at what was behind her.

Keeping speed at half normal, he forwarded the video until her face was visible. Then he froze the image and searched for the zoom. Right clicking the cursor pulled down another menu. Tapping "Crop" produced a box that he adjusted to cover only her head and shoulders. The picture quality would suffer, but he'd get magnification.

Sweat beaded his brow as he blew up the image. It was grainier than before, but he could still make out detail. The woman wore heavy makeup, layered over orange-peel skin. Adjusting the contrast helped him see the individual pits and valleys of adult acne.

The sweat on his face turned cold. The eyes had a familiar set to them. Another click, and the woman moved away toward Western Union. He followed her, still at half speed. Then she stopped and retrieved one of the purses she'd been looking at. Her face filled the frame. The kiosk attendant must have said something funny because the large woman smiled. It was more a smirk, with a familiar, shit-eating quality he'd seen before. Then he noticed the wisp of black hair laying across the forehead.

"Jesus Christ," he whispered. "He was there. The son of a bitch was there all along—in drag."

Leaving the enlarged image frozen on the screen, he called Sally. After half a dozen rings, he got her voicemail.

"Hey, Sal? Give me a call as soon as you can. It's important."

Before putting away the phone, he noticed he had a voicemail from Sally. He put it on speaker.

"Hey, Tom-Tom. I just wanted to let you know you left your goodie box on my back seat. Either you're an absent-minded professor or you were nervous about your first day of school. Have no fear, I'll drop it by after I tend to some business at the Knoxville PD. Shouldn't be more than thirty minutes. Ciao."

Tom looked at the phone, holding it at arm's length. Then his eyes traveled slowly to the floor next to his workstation. His vision seemed to float in slow motion, like the video on his computer. His gaze settled on cardboard that had once shipped Amazon books but now contained medical supplies and texts. It was right where he'd set it down when he came up from security. Then he looked back at the phone. Then he thought of Cheryl and the package in her back seat.

"No!"

Both he and Elsie hit the doorway at the same time, almost knocking each other down.

She yelled "Hey" as Tom's feet pounded down the hall toward the stairwell.

"I've got to go," he shouted back, one hand on the exit handle.

"But the men's room is the other direction."

💣

Sally looked at her watch, only half listening to the Tennessee twang of Captain Karl Loomis of the KPD Detective Division. Not as heavy as Doolittle, and a few years older judging by the gray at the temples of his receding hairline. A man closer to his thirty-year anniversary than to his graduation from the academy.

"This is the kind of cooperative spirit that we should all be striving for. The Bureau and PD working hand in hand. A partnership."

"I couldn't agree more, Captain Loomis. But now I have to go."

"Please call me Karl."

"Very well, Karl. But I really must ..."

"May I call you Sally?"

"Ah, sure, alright. Now if you'll excuse me."

"This hasn't always been the case, I'm sorry to say. Our interactions with the Bureau have been, well, rather one-sided at times. But now I believe we're really part of a team. Equal partners in law enforcement. And I feel I have you to thank for that."

Sally smiled. "I'm just a cog, captain, I mean Karl. Mr. Crossfield believes that mutual respect and cooperation are the best ways to ..."

"Yes, we have you to thank. And I'd like to do that a little more formally."

"Letters of commendation are always welcome." Sally smiled.

"Perhaps you'd allow me to buy you dinner?"

"Even an email to Mr. Crossfield ... beg pardon?"

"I know a place on Kingston Pike, best Italian in Knoxville."

It came out eye-talian and Knoxvul, but it was still the same old pitch. One she'd heard from college profs, academy instructors, and businessmen in airports. They all knew the best Italian, or Chinese, or Mexican in places like Cleveland, Arlington, Chicago, and Dallas. And they were all hungry for the same thing.

"That's very kind of you, Karl. But I'll just grab some drive-through. I've still got reports to file. You know what they say, the Bureau never sleeps."

"Then how about just a quick drink? We could discuss the case over a couple of Scotches. I've got some ideas for closer interactions between KPD and the Bureau."

I'll bet you do, Sally thought, noticing the band of pale flesh on the empty finger of his left hand. Recently divorced or separated. Or just a randy goat with a wife visiting her mother. She wondered briefly about the effect of a ring on *her* fourth finger. Nothing fancy, just a single diamond, even a zircon. She could pick one up cheap at a pawnshop. Or maybe it would be a present, one attached to an important question. She thought of Tom-Tom.

"Thank you. And as attractive as that offer is, I'll have to pass." She looked at her watch again. "As a matter of fact, I'm late for something now. So, if you'll excuse me."

"Maybe another time?"

Sally smiled and shook his hand.

Doolittle was coming into the building as she was going out.

"Have a nice chat with the captain?" he asked with a smirk.

"I'm guessing he's separated from his wife?"

"Way past that," Doolittle said. "Got divorce papers coming in a week or two."

"Well," Sally said. "He must be lonely. Why don't you join him for some eye-talian tonight? I think he'd like the company."

Doolittle laughed, sending waves through his waterbed gut. "Don't think it's *my* company he wants."

"Well, that's the *only* company he's gonna get. See ya, detective."

"See ya, Agent Pancakes."

She left amid more laughter. All she wanted was to drop off the box, have a salad, and get a few hours' sleep before she drove Tom home. Maybe he could stay at her place; it was closer. No, that was a bad idea all around. She yawned and headed to her SUV.

Tom heard his own footsteps echo down the stairwell, his mind flying faster than his feet. Both moved past the third floor, vacant now with room for growth. Then he was at the second floor, where the worker bees hung out: the special agents, electronic techs, and computer analysts that handled violent crimes, civil rights, and cybersecurity. He wasn't sure where he was going because he didn't have a car. He just knew he needed to get to Sally.

Pausing at the bottom of the steps, he pulled out his cell and brought up a familiar app. It told him that help was only four minutes away, in the form of a guy named Michael with a brown Buick Regal. He accepted Michael's Uber invitation, then bounded onto the first floor.

His previous visit to the field office provided some directional bearings, but he still made a wrong turn and ended up at prisoner interrogation. Running back, a tall, athletic guy coming out of the gun vault asked, "May I help you?" Tom waved a gloved hand and ran on, the guy's yell of "Hey" fading into the distance. A quick left at applicant testing, and he was opposite the door he thought led out.

Tom's hands yelled in pain as he punched through the doorway into the lobby. He almost lost his footing on the polished marble, nearly tumbling onto the large FBI seal inlaid ostentatiously on the floor. Then he was past the Wall of Honor on his left and the rich, brown, leather seats on his right, again punching the glass exit door, again ignoring yelps of pain from his injured hands.

The early evening air was warm and fresh, with the sharp smell of newly mowed grass. More steps and a concrete walk led past a row of privacy shrubs to the exit gate outside the security booth. He remembered thinking how picturesque the long walk was when he'd first arrived. Now he only cursed the distance he had to cover. Finally, he was at the gate, banging his injured hands against the metal.

"Whoa," a voice said from the window speaker. "Take it easy, I've got to buzz you out."

"Then buzz!"

"You need to drop off that visitor badge. It's just a one-day ID."

Tom ripped the laminated card from his lapel and threw it into the drawer extended from the plexiglass. The drawer disappeared and the gate clicked. He barely heard the "Have a nice evening" from the man behind the glass.

Doolittle sat behind the gray metal of his desk, his ancient swivel chair creaking against the weight as he sank in. He and Dell still had a half hour of paperwork before they clocked off, then they'd be at it bright and early tomorrow. They were getting close to Conrad, Georgie, whatever you wanted to call him. According to Sally Pancakes, he was back in Tennessee, maybe Knoxville. Doolittle wondered why a smart guy like Conrad would keep hanging around the two-hundred miles from Cincy to K-ville, when there was a whole wide country to hide in. All Doolittle could figure was that Conrad must have some unfinished business. The more he thought about it, the more that business pointed to a guy named Tomacinski. Doolittle made a note to call Tom-Tom tomorrow to set up the ride-alongs. He'd feel better when he could keep an eye on him. Sally Pancakes wasn't the only one with a fondness for that boy.

"Coffee, Doo?" Dell asked, rising from her desk.

"Thanks, darlin.' Double cream, two ..."

"Sugars," Dell finished. "Like I don't know that by now."

Doolittle started to say something to his departing partner, but his ringing phone cut him short.

"Powell, Criminal Investigations."

"Doo, ... Tom Tomac..."

"Hey, that you Tom-Tom? Speak of the devil."

"I'm ... traffic ... Uber ... Reception ... shit ... attention. This ... important."

"What? You keep breaking up."

"... know! Shut ... listen!"

"Try calling back on the other ..."

"Shut ... attention!"

"Okay. Calm down. What's up?"

"... Sally ... there?"

"Sally Pancakes. No, she just left a few minutes ago after a nice chat with the captain."

"Stop ... Don't ... start ... *car*... box ... back. I think ..."

"I'm only picking up every few words, Pard. What about a car?"

"... start ... her car. Box ... I think ..."

"What box? Glove box? Gear box?"

"Car ...! Car ...! Car ...!" Then the line went dead.

"Here's your coffee, partner." Dell said. "Hey, where are you going?"

"I'll be back in a few. I think Agent Sally is having car trouble."

💣

Sally settled in behind the steering wheel, tenting out the second button of her blouse against the summer heat. The car's AC would feel good after the tepid air of police headquarters. She thought of the old joke that municipal HVAC stood for Hardly Very Air Conditioned. Snapping on her shoulder harness, she shifted forward to punch the ignition. The car keys jabbed her leg painfully, so she undid her seat belt to fish them from the pocket of her slacks, tossing them on the console. Rebuckling the shoulder harness snared the lanyard holding her badge, tugging it against her already chafed neck. She undid the belt again and pulled the cord and badge over her head, yanking upward on her ponytail.

"Ow. Shit." She threw the badge onto her jacket resting in the shotgun seat. "One of those days," she muttered, rebuckling and then reaching to press start.

A horn honked behind her. Looking over, she saw a beat-to-crap Mustang rumble up to the municipal building to pick up a sleazy-looking woman in tube top and hot pants.

"Hookers are out early," she said.

Reaching forward while still watching one of Knoxville's finest get into the Mustang, she jammed her finger on the dash a quarter inch from the starter button, splitting a nail. "Son of a fuckin' bitch," she shouted, sucking the throbbing finger. "What else can go wrong?" She reached forward yet again, saying, "I'll probably have a blowout before I reach the field office."

💣

Still dressed as Patty Duncan, Conrad Hilton, aka Georgie King, smiled from behind the wheel of a Dodge Challenger. The FBI agent was approaching the big blue car, long legs striding confidently in the westering sun. "We'll wipe the swagger off you, bitch," Conrad muttered. "We'll see how Tom-Tom likes them apples."

The Dodge was backed into a corner of the partially full lot, sitting in the shade of an ornamental pear, powerful engine idling. Conrad smiled, fingers tapping on the steering wheel. He felt good, enervated, elated. He didn't worry that his stolen Dodge was in a police parking lot with only two driveways for escape. The muscle car could leap a curb and reach the freeway in less than thirty seconds. Nor did it worry him to be the focus of a nationwide manhunt by federal, state, county, and municipal authorities. They were looking for Georgie King, or Ollie Groenhaage, or Jorge TresReyes, or maybe even Ted Kaczynski the Unabomber—not Patty Duncan.

But more than that, Conrad didn't worry because he was past worrying. He'd evolved beyond it. He'd learned the secret: life was much easier distilled into moments in time, each one to be lived before the next swam into place. This moment was about savoring the sight of the redheaded FBI agent exploding out the top of her government SUV. The next moment would take care of itself. Most of all, he didn't worry because part of him, a secret part he barely recognized let alone acknowledged, knew he was insane. Lunatics were not burdened with worry.

Georgie King III was gone, had left the building with Elvis. Conrad Hilton had taken the stage. Many voices sang in Conrad's head: Ollie Groenhaage, Khan Singh, Patty Duncan, Jorge TresReyes, Norman Osborne, Georgie King's father. Many tunes accompanied them: the jungle beat of Gene Krupa's drums, Richard Rodgers' *Shall We Dance*, the cartoon jingle of your friendly neighborhood Spider-Man, the orchestral swell of the Starship Enterprise going where no one had gone before. The sounds were not a jumble, they blended smoothly into beautiful music—poetry from doggerel, symphony from dissonance.

The redhead was sliding into her car. She looked good, and she knew it. She wouldn't look so good in a moment. Just a moment. The length of time it took to fasten seat belts, shake out her pretty red hair, maybe don mirrored sunglasses, place a stylish foot against the brake pedal, and push a button—the starter button. Oh, yes, it would get things started. Conrad smiled and hummed along with the music in his head. Any second now. Any second now.

💣

"Yo! Sally Pancakes!"

Sally thumbed down the passenger window as Doolittle Powell huffed over.

"Sorry, Doo. I don't want to have eye-talian with you, either. I just want to drop off this shit for Tom-Tom and get to bed."

"Well, not that dinner with you isn't on the top of my wish list, but that's not why I'm here. I just got a crazy call from our boy. Something about your car and a box?"

"Yes, I've got his box. I already told him I'd drop it off. He needs to listen to his voicemail."

"I don't think that's it. Phone kept cutting in and out, but he sounded kind of strung out. Something about a box and starting your car. You been having car trouble, maybe gear-box problems?"

"Gear box? You mean the transmission?"

Doolittle shrugged. "Or something he left in the glove box?"

Sally popped the glove box as the sweaty-faced detective peered inside.

"Nothing in there," he said.

"The only box I have at the moment is right back here." She leaned over the front seat and pointed. "According to Tom-Tom, it contains some bandage materials, and ..." Her eyes picked up the bundle of wires leading from the cardboard into the footwell. Pausing for just a second, she gasped, "Jesus Christ." Then she was out of the car, yelling, "Get back!"

Michael, the Uber driver, looked at Tom like he was crazy. Tom supposed he sounded crazy yelling, "Car bomb!" over and over into his phone.

"Hey, calm down man," Michael said. "We're almost there. That's the PD up ahead."

"The parking lot," Tom yelled from his position in the shotgun seat. Shaking Michael's arm, he added, "Pull into the lot."

"Hey, man, be cool. I'll take you right to the door."

"No, not the door, the lot," Tom said. "It's in the lot. In a car."

"Take it easy, man. There's lots of cars parked in that lot. All you want. It's a *parking* lot." Michael's voice said he'd obviously picked up a nut and would gladly be rid of him. Tom couldn't blame him.

Michael's brown Buick pulled onto Honor our Troops drive, then into the municipal parking lot.

"Cruise the lanes," Tom said. "It's a big, blue SUV."

"Listen, man. You hired my rig to get you here, not for a scavenger hunt."

"Drive down the fucking lanes," Tom shouted, fingers still digging into Michael's arm.

"Alright, alright. I'm driving down the fucking lanes."

Michael's Buick cruised down the first of the five lanes and was starting up the next when Tom saw it. Sally's car sat in the middle of the row—door open. She had a cell phone to her lips, her other hand on her service automatic, eyes swiveling from side to side. Doolittle likewise had hand on hip, head searching. The two cops were backing away from the SUV.

"Thank God!"

Tom's exclamation was drowned out by the throaty growl of an eight-cylinder engine with plenty of blasting powder. Looking around to place the growing noise, Tom spotted the hood of a black muscle car turning in from the end of the row, heading directly toward him. The car picked up speed, back wheels screaming, oily blue smoke billowing from the tires.

"Jesus," Michael yelled, hitting the brakes.

The muscle car continued accelerating, veering toward Sally and Doolittle now standing behind a pickup truck parked four spaces from the SUV. Images jerked by like the clicks of a camera shutter.

Grill work growing large as the muscle car accelerated.

Click.

Doolittle pushing Sally out of the way.

Click.

Michael's hands turning the Buick's wheel left.

Click.

The muscle car's hood heading at Doolittle.

Click.

Doolittle's fat body flying comically under the impact of 4,000 pounds traveling at forty per. That image froze in Tom's brain: ugly sport jacket billowing, Doolittle's body bouncing grotesquely over the pickup and into the empty space beyond. Then the muscle car was barreling toward the Buick.

Michael the Uber driver continued to veer the Buick left and apply brakes, making room for the muscle car to escape.

"No, you don't," Tom yelled. "Not this time, you son of a bitch."

Tom reached over and jerked the wheel right, the startled Uber driver offering little resistance. Then Tom jammed his left foot on the accelerator. The Buick squealed against Michael's brake pressure but managed to edge its way into the muscle car's path. The airbags deployed as the two cars met.

Chapter 56

Tom tingled as if his face and body had gone asleep and were now awaking. His vision momentarily winked out, then blurred before it cleared again. His mind was back, fully conscious, and he almost wished it wasn't.

Pain radiated from Tom's face, chest, and hands. Something warm dribbled past his lips. One taste, and he recognized blood. Gloved fingers dreamily followed it to his nose, where a rivulet ran freely. Touching the area brought fresh pain, along with a wave of nausea that departed as quickly as it came. Red florets blossomed atop the tips of his white gloves.

Looking left, he saw Michael the Uber driver slumped forward against his harness, deflated airbag on his lap. Tom pushed him backward, causing the lenses of the driver's glasses to tumble independently to each side of his face. Both Michael's eyes were already blackening, but Tom saw no bleeding.

"You okay?" Tom asked.

"Huh? What? Ah, that'll be $7.60," Michael mumbled through a fattened lip. "And tips are good."

"You're okay," Tom said, sliding out the passenger door.

The first thing he saw was the Buick's hood, half open and crumpled into a vee. Then he saw the smashed grill of a Dodge Challenger, spider cracks webbed across the windscreen, powerful engine idling uselessly. The Challenger's door was open, and a man had stumbled out. The man's face was heavily bruised, right eye swollen shut and blood dribbling into the left eye from a cut along the brow. A black wig lay beside him. Tom immediately recognized Georgie King, young features clearly recognizable despite the injuries, makeup, and women's clothing. King brushed blood from his left eye, squinting into the face staring back at him. Then his hand pulled a short-barreled revolver from the waistband of his Walmart slacks and fired.

Conrad fired blindly, then ran like a frightened animal between parked cars. Pain lanced his knee as it clipped someone's bumper. Cursing, he brushed blood from his eye and ran on.

His eidetic memory brought up a map of the area. He was running toward Howard Baker Avenue. If he could get across that, he'd be in the trees. But then what? He already heard the chatter of cops leaving the building, checking things out. On foot, he would be easy prey, banging into tree trunks, trapped between Summit Hill and the freeway. He needed a car. If he had wheels, he could reach the freeway and might be able to outdistance pursuit while the cops and medics were still sorting things out.

"Over there," someone shouted.

Conrad sank down between two cars, dropping his gun. He groped forward, fingers scraping hot pavement. Using the sleeve of Patty's blouse for a rag, he wiped sweat and blood from his one good eye. There was the glint of blued steel only inches from his outstretched fingers. Snatching up the weapon, he was running again.

Sally heard the shot and dropped to the macadam, palms singed by the hot tar, her cell clattering away. Then she was up, snaking past the back of the wrecked Buick. Tom-Tom was down behind the car's open door, but she couldn't tell if he was hit or only shaken up.

"Are you shot?" she asked.

Tom patted along his chest and arms, wincing. "Nuh uh. But I felt its wind."

"We're here," Michael muttered drunkenly from inside the wreck. "Yeah, $7.60. What say we make it an even ten bucks?"

Sally popped her head above the open car door, swiveled it back and forth, then ducked back down. Whoever fired the shot was gone. She hadn't seen him, but it didn't take a genius to know he probably went by a name like Jorge TresReyes, Conrad Hilton, or Ollie Groenhaage. A rose by any other name still smelled like a crazy scumbag.

"See what you can do for him," Sally nodded toward the Uber driver. Then her face went dark and cold. "And check on Doo. I'm gonna call an ambulance and get some cops out here. Crazy bastard picked the wrong place this time." Edging around the door, she added, "Be careful, Tom-Tom." Then she was darting down the lane toward the municipal buildings.

Tom looked back at Michael propped against the side of his ruined Buick, lips mumbling something, fingers mechanically counting out nonexistent change. Ahead of him, Doolittle lay against the pavement, jacket and shirt flipped up to expose an enormous red-black bruise, legs twisted in the incongruous juxtaposition seen only in contortionists and the severely injured. Blood dripped from Doolittle's left ear. His eyes stared off in different directions, one pupil wide despite the glinting sun.

"Hey, Doo," Tom said. "Hang in there. Help is on the way."

Tom squatted low to hear the muted reply.

"That you, Tom-Tom?"

"Hang in there. You're gonna be okay."

"Sally okay?" Doolittle whispered, his face taking on an odd, slack pallor.

"Yeah, she's fine. You saved her ass."

The big cop's eyes still stared unchanging, but his lips curled into a smile. "That ass is worth saving."

Tom could hear sirens growing louder. "Just hang in, buddy. Cavalry is almost here. You'll be eating donuts again in no time."

One side of Doolittle's mouth kept grinning. The other side bent downward into a rictal S. His color was almost gone, blanched skin starkly contrasted against black pavement. "Best in fifty-seven states." Doolittle's eyes continued their thousand-yard stare, but any life in them was gone.

"And the District of Columbia," Tom said, wiping tears from his cheeks.

Tom knelt there crying, staring at the face of death. Then the tears disappeared behind a cool resolve. He glanced down to the butt of Doolittle's service automatic belted to his lifeless waist. Tom had never shot anyone or even fired a gun. But he didn't think that would be a problem. He'd have no trouble shooting Georgie King. No trouble at all.

His trembling fingers found and unsnapped the holster's retention strap. Then those fingers steadied at the reassuring feel of cold steel that soothed his burns and strengthened his will. Withdrawing the pistol with two hands, Tom pointed it straight ahead. That was the direction Georgie King had headed. That was the direction of justice. The direction of revenge.

Conrad ducked from car to car, heading north by east. He no longer cared about the money tucked away in his stolen Dodge. It had always been but a means to an end, a way to gain respect, leisure, and finally escape. Now his thoughts were focused on survival.

His vast intellect struggled to resist the animal urge driving it toward the imagined safety of the trees. It was a new experience, intellect versus panic, each fighting for supremacy. Brain versus hormones. Reason versus fight or flight.

He had always been in control, picking his targets, pulling the strings. Now he was the puppet, the target in the crosshairs, the beast driven by the beaters. Except for one thing, the ace up his sleeve—the moderating influence of insanity. Madness, Conrad's kind of madness, calmed and reassured. It juggled intellect and instinct, the conductor producing a symphony from independent instruments, beautiful music from discordant notes.

Conrad stumbled against another car, fender skirt jamming back a finger. Ignoring the pain, he sleeved blood away from his one good eye, momentarily restoring vision but restarting the bleeding. This is how he saw the world now, a series of bleary images. The current one showed flashing police lights in the street beyond the next line of cars. Cops were on Howard Baker Avenue. Even the trees were closed to him now. Well, said Reason, so much the better. Flight on foot was always a losing game.

Moving the gun to his left hand, he tried the door of the green car next to him. Locked. Rubbing more blood from his eye, he poked his head back into the lane, looking forth and back. Then he dashed down the row of cars, heading west. He'd circle back toward Honor our Troops Drive, the way he'd entered the municipal lot earlier.

Conrad's blurry vision made out a pickup, a four-by-four perfect for barreling over curbs past stunned police wagons. Even if it was locked, he'd bust the glass and hot-wire it. He'd gotten good at hot-wiring.

He'd only taken one step toward the pickup's fuzzy, gray shape when the truck's rear window exploded with a boom. Another round thunked wildly into the truck bed. Someone yelled something somewhere. The conductor in his head pointed to "panic," which cued him to dive between parked cars.

Conrad regained his feet, managing to hold onto the revolver, then dashed from between the cars through the lane beyond. He was exposed in the center of the lane for just a moment, then was safely back between parked cars. "Panic" sat down as the conductor raised a hand toward "reason." Conrad faced back the way he had come, pistol pointing in the direction of pursuit.

Conrad paused to take his bearings. A dozen parking spaces past his left shoulder was Honor our Troops Drive. A few more lanes ahead and he was at Howard Baker Avenue. What of it? The situation hadn't changed.

He was still in a police parking lot.

He still heard the blare of sirens and the yells of disoriented cops.

He still saw a growing number of flashing police lights.

He still needed a car, which meant he needed time to steal one. To gain that time, he'd have to eliminate any pursuing threat. Sleeving away more blood, he squinted down the short barrel toward the direction he'd just come.

"Reason" waited, ignoring "panic" saying "run, run, run." No, my friend, the conductor said. Not flight. Now we fight.

Conrad wiped away more blood, clearing his vision, picking up the sight picture. Something moved between a Honda and a Ford. Still, he waited. Vision dimmed again, and he wiped it clear. Still, he waited, arms raised, good eye focused down the short barrel. More movement. Then a head was visible. Then shoulders. Conrad smiled. It was Tom-Tom. The pesky son of a bitch was holding a large semiautomatic pistol the way a monkey held a violin.

Conrad thumbed back the hammer and steadied the sight on the emerging image. Still, he waited. He waited long enough for Georgie King to take over, savoring the long-anticipated moment. The long-expected party, Georgie thought. The one where Bilbo the hobbit disappeared. Just one more moment and Tom-Tom would disappear. Another wish fulfilled. More proof of Georgie's superiority. Another "fuck you" spat in his father's face. He squeezed the trigger.

Tom ran in a crouch, pistol low, its two-pound weight alien to his virgin fingers. Pain throbbed in his hands as the knurling on the wide pistol grip needled the still healing tissue. He ran on through a row of cars, then through a lane beyond into another row. Each step brought a throb of pain to the bridge of his broken nose. At least the bleeding had stopped.

Things were taking on a surreal quality. His own breath thundered in his ears along with the beating of his heart. The air smelled of sweat and sunbaked tar. The long shadows of the cars took on menacing, eerie shapes, each hiding a potential threat.

Part of Tom's mind said wait, you don't know what you're doing. Probably can't hit a barn door, or the barn. But another part, a more primal part, said it didn't matter. When the time came, he'd kill Conrad/Georgie with this gun. Or with his bare hands. He was hoping for the bare hands. The feel of Georgie's larynx breaking under his injured fingers.

Tom stepped into the next lane, then dove back to safety at the boom of a shotgun and the sound of shattering glass. Somewhere a voiced yelled, "Cease fire. You'll hit Tom-Tom." He smiled. At least Sally was okay.

Poking his head out from between the cars, Tom caught a glimpse of movement to his left. Someone had dashed across the lane to the parked cars in his row. He started edging in that direction, but a voice in his head sent him running straight ahead to the other side of the lane; from there he could look across to where the figure had entered among the cars. Tom needed to see who he was pursuing, or possibly shooting at. Maybe he couldn't hit a barn, but he didn't want to hit one of the blue suits roaming the area.

Tom ended up between a Toyota and a Ford. He recognized the Ford as a titanium Escape, red like his. *Funny what your brain noticed while it was plotting to kill someone.* He poked his head above the cars, straining to see between the vehicles across the lane. He rose further, gun shakily before him, his shoulders clearing the car hoods. Then he saw a flash, followed simultaneously by a loud bang and the impact of a sledgehammer. Then he was falling.

Chapter 57

Georgie smiled. He'd hit meat, he was sure of it. He'd seen the Polack drop and the blood spatter across the Honda's hood. "Fuckin' A!" he yelled. Then a bullhorn blared to his right.

"King. George King III. Give yourself up."

It was the redheaded FBI agent.

"There's no way out, Georgie. The parking lot is surrounded. SWAT is on the way. Give yourself up and you won't be harmed."

"Panic" threatened to return, but Georgie kept his cool. The plan hadn't changed. He needed a car. His eyes darted side to side. One side held a beat-up old Chevy that would break an axle on the first curb. To his right was a beetle bug, not a likely chariot for outrunning John Law. He pawed more blood from his eye. And there it was.

Immediately across the lane behind him was a monster SUV. It looked like it could take curbs two at a time without spilling your coffee. And it had power. Power meant speed. Speed equaled distance. And best yet, the door was open. He could sneak in and hot-wire the ignition without the telltale noise of breaking glass. And the car was only one lane removed from the access road next to the freeway. All he had to do was cross one more parking-lot lane and he was there. One more naked, exposed lane. He needed a diversion.

"Georgie! This is your last chance. Give yourself up and you won't be harmed."

A siren screamed as the flashing lights of an ambulance entered the drive at the end of the row. Georgie rubbed away more sweat and blood. This was his chance. Edging to the rear of the Chevy, he raised the gun onto the trunk, steadying his aim. Four shots left. That should be enough.

He could see the redhead behind a blue and white, bullhorn to her lips.

"Give yourself up, Georgie. There is no way out."

He swiped more blood from his eye and squinted down the short barrel. He couldn't hit anything at this distance, but that didn't matter. He fired once. The head and bullhorn disappeared behind a car. Then he wheeled, firing twice at the ambulance approaching from the opposite direction. He could see the ambulance driver bolt from the cab. A hole spider-cracked the ambulance windshield and steam hissed from the perforated radiator. Then Georgie King ran for the safety of the jumbo SUV.

The dash to the open door seemed to take forever instead of two seconds. No gunfire greeted him. Then he was inside the big car, tossing his nearly empty gun to the floor and reaching under the dash. He pawed away more blood, and he saw the key sitting obligingly on the console. All he had to do was start it up.

A new song entered Georgie's head. He hummed along. "We're in the money." His left foot found the brake pedal. "We're in the money." His hand poised above the ignition button. Turning right to sleeve away more blood, his clearing vision noted a federal ID lying atop the blue blazer on the passenger seat. "We've got a lot of what it takes ..." He pushed the button as his lunatic mind recognized the redhead on the badge.

"Shit."

That was the last word ever spoken by Georgie King III. A fitting coda to his life. From that moment forward, his voice, and those of Conrad Hilton, Ollie Groenhaage, Patty Duncan, and Jorge TresReyes, were forever silenced by the two-stage blast that blew the windows out of the big, dark-blue SUV signed out to Special Agent Sally Butterworth.

💣 *Chapter 58*

The air was cool and smelled of furniture polish, flowers, and aftershave. The first ten rows of the Hilltop Presbyterian Church were filled with ladies in dark dresses, men in black or gray suits, and cops in crisp, dress-blue uniforms. Sally and Tom stood side by side in the eleventh row. She in a black sleeveless dress, Tom in black suit, left sleeve hanging limply, left arm in a sling to protect where Conrad's bullet had entered his shoulder. A clergyman in a black suit faced them from the podium. To his left was a kilted man holding bagpipes atop his tartan. The guest of honor rested in the center aisle, draped in an American flag.

"I didn't know Detective Sergeant Doolittle Powell as well as I would have liked," the police chaplain said. "But I've heard so many colorful stories lately that I feel I could talk about him all day long. But he deserves more than second-hand praise for the fine life he lived. And he deserves the true emotion of a person who knew him well. So, I am going to turn the pulpit over to someone who fits that description. His partner, Detective Adell Portifoy."

Garbed in dress blues, Dell rose and approached the microphone.

"Thank you, Reverend Fortner." She adjusted her notes, then paused and tossed them on the podium. "I'm not much of a public speaker," she said. "But Doo never went in much for speeches."

A few people chuckled as she cleared her throat and sipped some water from a clear bottle.

"Doo Powell was my partner. And he was my friend. He was a good cop and a hell of a damned nice guy." She turned left and said, "Forgive the profanity, Reverend, but it's the only way to describe him."

More folks chuckled, including the chaplain.

"He always saw the good in people and the humor in any situation. And he squeezed every ounce of joy from living. Even simple things. I've never known another human being who enjoyed a jelly donut like it was a T-bone steak."

"Best in fifty-seven states," someone said from the crowd.

"And the District of Columbia," someone else muttered, raising another chuckle from the gathered mourners.

"But there was a serious side to him as well, one most people never saw, one that I was privileged to glimpse only briefly. I went through his books, there were a lot of them, and found a few lines from a poem that fit his life and untimely passing."

Dell dabbed her eyes with a tissue, then pulled a pair of reading glasses from the pocket of her uniform. Donning the specs, she retrieved the last page from the discarded notes. Her voice assumed a solemn, sing-song cadence as she read:

> Smart lad, to slip betimes away
> From fields where glory does not stay,
> And early though the laurel grows
> It withers quicker than the rose.
>
> Now you will not swell the rout
> Of lads that wore their honors out,
> Runners whom renown outran
> And the name died before the man.

Dell's voice caught in her throat as she concluded, "Rest in peace, partner."

As she bowed her head to retrieve a tissue, the piper sounded the traditional song of fallen heroes. Reverend Fortner held up his hands, and the crowd began to sing.

"Amazing grace, how sweet the sound, that saved a wretch like me.

I once was lost, but now am found,

Was blind, but now I see."

Still singing and looking forward, Sally casually placed her left hand into Tom's right one. She gently squeezed his gloved fingers. He squeezed back. Holding hands, they finished the song amid the mournful notes of the piper.

THE END

About the Author

John Bukowski is an accomplished writer in both fiction and nonfiction. His short stories have been published in numerous notable venues such as *Dark Secrets, Makarelle*, and *Land Beyond the World*. In a previous life, he wrote hundreds of medical publications, including handbooks, websites, and radio scripts, translating technical topics for the general public. As with his debut novel, *Project Suicide*, he has lent his scientific expertise to *Checkout Time*, blending technical authenticity with fiction for an exciting ride.

When he isn't tapping his computer keyboard, he's tapping his feet to music, singing pop, Broadway, and opera–in multiple languages. Originally from Detroit, he and his wife now reside in Eastern Tennessee.

Printed in the USA
CPSIA information can be obtained
at www.ICGtesting.com
CBHW021132081024
15560CB00001B/1